The Heresy of Time

Clifton Wilcox

Fredericksburg, Virginia

Print ISBN: 978-1-969770-53-1

EBook ISBN: 978-1-969770-52-4

Published by Windward Publishing LLC., Fredericksburg, Virginia.

Wilcox, Clifton

The Heresy of Time

Windward Publishing, LLC

2026

Dedication

For Ferretti—

May God forgive the truths you uncovered before the darkness convinced you they were yours to carry alone.

I still pray that somewhere beyond the machinery, beyond the lies, beyond the terrible silence that followed you through the years... there remains enough light to guide you home.

If not to this world, then to His mercy.

— Monsignor Orsini

Table of Contents

Books by Clifton Wilcox

Fiction

Cool's Last Stand

Where Despair Comes to Play

The Monuments Must Bleed

Keeper of the Fallen Ages

I, Monster

Harvest of Eyes

The Case Against Jasper

Crimson Plume: The Song of Corvus

Framed in Love

Echoes of the Forgotten

Blacktop Harvest

The Plagiarist Game

The Black Forest Protocol

Outcome without Appeal

Deliberation

The Lore Hunter: Brown Mountain

Pact of Shadows: The Black Orchard

The Black Ledger of Salem

The Four That Bind

The Last Star

The Lore Hunter: Devils Highway

Every Cough Was a Crime

The North Doesn't Speak

Chapter 1

The Black Forest Discovery

The rain had stopped an hour before dawn, but the Black Forest did not release its wetness easily. Mist clung to the spruce like gauze, turning every branch into a dripping needle. The narrow road that wound upward from the village was little more than crushed stone and mud, and the tires of the lead truck cut grooves that immediately filled with dark water.

The convoy moved without headlights.

Only a slit of hooded light, pinched downward by metal shutters, skimmed the road's edge. It was enough to keep them from sliding into the trees. Not enough for anyone watching to count vehicles, read markings, or see faces.

Hans Kammler rode in the second car, a staff Mercedes with its windows fogged from the breath of the men inside. He did not wipe the glass. He did not need to see the forest. The forest was irrelevant. What mattered was the cordon that had been thrown around a radius of trees in the night and the report waiting for him at the end of the climb.

The driver's hands were stiff on the wheel. Beside him, an SS-Untersturmführer held a folder like a shield. Kammler ignored both. He sat straight-backed, hat on his knees, gloved fingers resting on the brim as if it were a measurement tool. He had the look of a man who never admitted to curiosity, even to himself. A man who treated awe as a weakness that could be disciplined out of the body.

"Two forestry workers," the officer said, clearing his throat. "They heard it. Saw the light. One is in custody. The other fled."

Kammler's gaze remained forward. "Fled where?"

"The village, Herr Doktor. He spoke to a priest. Then the priest spoke to someone else. We intercepted the call at the exchange."

Kammler's eyes shifted at last, cold and precise. "And the priest?"

"Held for questioning."

Kammler nodded once. The officer hurried on, as if momentum could redeem his anxiety.

“The crash site is secured by men from Karlsruhe. No one is permitted beyond the outer perimeter without your authorization. The local police were told it was an aviation accident. A weather balloon, if pressed.”

Kammler’s mouth tightened at the phrase weather balloon, but he did not correct it. Lies were scaffolding. Useful until the building stood on its own.

“And the object?” he asked.

The officer opened the folder. Pages of typed German, smudged with damp, photographs still glossy with fresh developer. A jagged clearing, trees snapped like matchsticks. Something half-buried in the earth, slick and dark as a river stone. No wings. No propeller. No rivets. Not an aircraft. Not anything built by human hands.

“Unidentified,” the officer said. “No markings. No heat, no smoke. It is… intact, mostly. The men who first approached said it was warm to the touch. Like a living animal.”

“Warm,” Kammler repeated, tasting the word as if it were data.

The car rocked over a rut. The mist thickened, and the trees pressed in close enough that the convoy might have been traveling through a tunnel made of branches. It was quiet except for the engines. Even the birds were absent, as if the forest had decided that sound was a risk.

Kammler had been sent because the report had not gone to the Air Ministry, nor to the Army, nor to the police. It had come through channels that were not written down. A rumor delivered to a man who understood the value of rumors. A message whose real content was not the words but the urgency.

At the top of the climb, the road ended in a rough, churned space where trucks had been turned and turned again. Beyond it, canvas tents crouched between the trees like pale growths. A radio mast rose from the mud. Men in black uniforms stood at intervals, motionless, rifles held as if the forest itself might attempt escape.

The Mercedes rolled to a stop. The driver exhaled as though he had been holding his breath the entire way. The officer stepped out first, boots sinking, and opened Kammler's door with stiff ceremony.

Cold air struck Kammler's face. The smell of wet earth and pine resin was overlaid by something else, metallic and faintly sweet, like ozone after lightning. He paused long enough to register it.

Then he stepped onto the mud with the controlled precision of a man used to walking through ruins.

A senior SS man approached, insignia gleaming dully in the gray morning. His cap dripped. He clicked his heels, saluted.

“Herr Doktor Kammler. Sturmbannführer Dietrich. We have been waiting.”

Kammler did not return the salute with the same theatricality. He offered a brief motion of his hand, an acknowledgment rather than a gesture of camaraderie.

“Show me,” Kammler said.

Dietrich led him past the tents. The path was lined with men who looked as though they had been awake all night. Their eyes were too wide. Their expressions tried to be blank and failed. When Kammler passed, they straightened, but their attention did not follow him. It kept drifting toward the trees ahead, to the place where the forest opened in a scar.

They reached the inner cordon. Here the rifles were no longer pointed outward. They were angled down, as if aimed at the ground itself. A sign had been hammered into a post with the blunt authority of bureaucracy: SPERRGEBIET. ZUTRITT

VERBOTEN. The letters were already bleeding from the rain.

Dietrich hesitated. “Herr Doktor, before you see it, you should know… two of my men refused to go closer. They said they felt sick. One vomited. One… prayed.”

Kammler’s eyes flicked to him. “Prayed to whom?”

Dietrich swallowed. “He did not say.”

Kammler stepped past him without further comment. Fear was not an obstacle, only a variable. A weakness to be accounted for in the men selected for the next step.

Beyond the cordon, the forest changed. The trees were still standing, but the ground beneath them looked bruised. Moss had been peeled back as if by enormous fingers. In places, the soil had melted into glassy ridges, black and smooth, reflecting the dim light. Kammler knelt, touched one ridge with his glove. The surface was colder than it should have been. Not simply cooled by the night. Cold as if it had never known warmth.

Dietrich watched his hand. “We did not build any fires,” he said quickly. “No torches. Nothing that could do that.”

“I know,” Kammler replied.

They walked into the clearing.

The object lay at its center, half-sunk into the earth, not so much crashed as placed. Trees around it were snapped and bent, but there was no pattern of impact, no furrow that described a trajectory. It was a shape that defied the instinct to name it. Not a cylinder, not a sphere, not truly bell-shaped either, though the curve of its hull suggested a kind of symmetry that the mind tried to simplify into familiar forms.

The surface was seamless. No bolts. No visible panels. It drank in the gray light, making the morning seem dimmer for its presence. Rainwater did not bead and run; it spread thinly and vanished, as though absorbed.

Kammler stopped at the edge of the crater. For the first time, the mask of pure calculation slipped a fraction, replaced by a small, involuntary tightening around his eyes. Not wonder. Recognition of magnitude.

"How long since it arrived?" he asked.

"Just after midnight," Dietrich said. "We talked to Sturmbannführer Ernst Falk who witnessed it. Falk stated that the sound was… like thunder, but without echo. The men on watch thought it was an air raid siren at first. Then the forest lit up. Green, like an electric arc."

Kammler scanned the hull. "Any markings? Symbols?"

"None."

"Any attempts to open it?"

Dietrich's voice lowered. "There is a breach. It was there when we arrived. A section… peeled back, as though by force from inside. We have not widened it."

Kammler's gaze snapped to him. "Inside?"

Dietrich nodded, and the word came out reluctantly, like something pulled from his throat. "There was movement. Not like an animal. More like a shadow. One man swears he heard a voice."

Kammler looked past him at the hull again. Warm, the report had said. Like a living animal.

He turned, and in doing so he took in the men stationed around the clearing. Their boots were sunk, but none had stepped too near the object. A wide ring of disturbed earth marked the distance they kept, as if the craft radiated something that stopped them. Kammler noted it without asking. Men were often honest with their bodies when they lied with their mouths.

He extended his hand toward the hull. Dietrich tensed.

"Herr Doktor, we have orders to keep everyone—"

"I am the order," Kammler said softly.

He placed his palm against the surface.

For an instant it felt like metal, smooth and cool. Then something shifted beneath his glove, a subtle yielding, like skin over muscle. Not imagined. Not metaphor. The hull gave, barely, as though acknowledging touch. A faint vibration traveled up his arm, stopping at his shoulder like a pulse.

Kammler withdrew his hand and stared at his glove as if it might show evidence. It showed nothing. But the smell in the air sharpened, metallic and sweet, and somewhere at the edge of the clearing a man made a sound that was half cough, half sob.

Kammler did not look at him. He looked at the object and spoke with measured calm.

"Bring my scientists."

Dietrich blinked. "They are here, Herr Doktor. We summoned the men you requested from Berlin and Freiburg. Physics, metallurgy, medicine. They arrived before dawn. They are waiting at the tents."

Kammler nodded, already moving. "No one enters until I say. No samples are taken. No photographs beyond what has been done. Anyone who speaks of this outside this perimeter disappears."

Dietrich's face tightened with relief at being given clear cruelty. "Yes, Herr Doktor."

Kammler paused once more at the rim of the crater and looked down at the craft, as if it were an equation with too many unknowns.

In 1936, the Reich was hungry for weapons, for miracles, for anything that could turn the world's future into something controllable. Kammler had built his career on concrete and terror, on structures that did not bend. He understood how to force men into shapes that served him.

But this thing had arrived already shaped by a mind that did not care about human intention. It had fallen into the Black Forest like a seed into soil.

And seeds, Kammler knew, did not fall by accident.

By the time Kammler returned to the tents, the scientists were assembled in a damp semicircle, collars up, hands stained with ink and cigarette ash. They looked out of place among the SS men, as if someone had dragged a lecture hall into the mud and expected the forest to behave like a blackboard.

They fell silent when he approached. Their faces tightened with the reflex of men who had learned, in the Reich, to read rank the way one read weather. A wrong expression could invite lightning.

Kammler stopped before them and did not waste words on introductions. Names were secondary; obedience was not.

"You will observe," he said. "You will document. You will not improvise heroism. No one touches it unless I allow it. If you find something you do not understand, you will speak to me before you speak to each other."

A man in wire-rimmed glasses cleared his throat. He was small, with the careful posture of someone used to being ignored until he became useful. "Herr Doktor, what are we permitted to bring near it? Instruments? Geiger counters? Magnetometers?"

Kammler regarded him. "Everything that does not require you to open it further."

Dietrich stepped forward with two soldiers carrying long wooden crates. Inside were the instruments Kammler had demanded be driven up from Berlin: calipers, micrometers, glass syringes in cotton, sealed sample vials, a portable X-ray camera with a hand-crank generator, coils of insulated wire. Objects of human certainty. Tools that made the world behave.

They followed Kammler back through the inner cordon, the rifles and warning sign and the uneasy silence of men assigned to guard something that felt, to them, like a sin with mass.

The clearing seemed darker now. The mist had lowered, folding the craft into a muted outline. Rain continued, but it fell in thin, reluctant needles. When the scientists saw the hull at full proximity, several of them stopped as if struck by the same invisible barrier the soldiers had felt.

It was not only the shape. It was the way the object occupied space, as though the air around it had been slightly rewritten. It should have reflected the trees. It should have shown highlights of wetness. Instead, it absorbed the world and returned it dulled, like an eye that refused to blink.

The man with wire-rimmed glasses stepped forward despite himself, drawn by a hunger that had kept him alive through the last years of purges and funding cuts and petty academic wars. He raised a Geiger counter and held it close.

The needle twitched and then settled. A soft clicking began, steady but not alarming.

"Low," he murmured, and then, after a pause, "But strange. Not like ore. Not like any laboratory source I know."

A second scientist, older, with a surgeon's hands and the faint tremor of fatigue in his fingertips, crouched beside one of the glassy ridges in the soil. He touched it with the tip of a scalpel and hissed, jerking back. Not pain. Shock.

"It is cold," he said. "Herr Doktor, it is cold in a way that does not match the environment."

Kammler nodded once. He watched their movements as he watched soldiers: not for diligence, but for fracture points. A man who froze at the wrong moment. A man who leaned too far.

Dietrich led them around the craft to the breach he had mentioned. Up close, it looked less like damage and more like an opening that had been forced by something that understood the hull's structure better than any human could. The edge of the peeled section was not jagged metal. It was smooth and curved, like bone that had been separated along a natural seam.

Inside was blackness, but not the honest blackness of an unlit compartment. It was thick, as though depth had been poured into it.

The air there smelled sharper. Ozone, wet stone, something faintly organic, like the underside of mushrooms.

Kammler did not step in. He did not need to. His authority was not measured by proximity.

“Light,” he said.

A soldier raised a shuttered lamp and angled it into the breach.

The beam struck the interior and seemed to lose strength, as if the darkness drank it. But it revealed enough to make the scientists inhale as one.

Struts, arcs, lattices that were not bolted together but grown into place. The interior was made of metallic structures that resembled ribs and tendons more than engineering. They rose and braided, meeting at nodes that looked like joints. There were no straight lines. Everything curved with a kind of anatomical inevitability.

One of the metallurgists, a broad man with thick fingers and a scar under his chin, whispered, “It is not welded.”

He reached toward the edge, stopped himself, and looked at Kammler for permission.

Kammler’s eyes remained on the interior. “Take a shaving,” he said. “From the edge only.”

The metallurgist took a small chisel and a hammer from a crate. He set the chisel at the peeled seam and struck once, gently, as though afraid the craft might feel insult.

A thin sliver came away, light as foil but darker than steel. He held it up in forceps. It did not reflect the lamp; it seemed to swallow it.

Before he could place it in a vial, the edge of the seam moved.

Not much. Not a dramatic closing. Just a subtle ripple along the cut line, like skin reacting to a scratch. The peeled metal flexed inward, and the place the shaving had been taken from smoothed over, the surface knitting itself with slow, deliberate patience.

The metallurgist went pale. His forceps trembled. "Herr Doktor," he said hoarsely. "It is… it is repairing."

Kammler took the forceps from him without asking and held the sliver between gloved fingers. It felt heavier than it should have. When he turned it, it made no sound, as though friction itself had been altered.

The surgeon leaned closer. "Self-healing material," he whispered, reverent despite himself. "Like tissue."

"It is not tissue," the physicist with glasses said, and then corrected, almost arguing with his own certainty. "Or it is tissue that behaves like metal."

Kammler placed the shaving in a vial and sealed it. "It is whatever it needs to be," he said. "Proceed."

They moved deeper, inch by inch, lamp beams probing. The interior revealed platforms that might have been floors, though they were uneven and sloped like the inside of a shell. At the center was something that made the men hesitate again: a structure that rose from the lower deck like a pedestal, branching into filaments that hung in the air without support.

It was not a control panel, not in any human sense. It looked like a nest of translucent tendrils, each one ending in a flattened pad, like the underside of a hand. The pads pulsed faintly, their color shifting from gray to a sickly green and back.

The surgeon breathed, "Alive."

"No," the physicist said automatically, and then stopped, watching as one pad lifted slightly, as if sensing their heat.

One of the younger assistants, eager and foolish, stepped forward. His name was Schreiber, Kammler remembered from a file. Too many publications for a man his age. Too much ambition, too little fear. Kammler had approved him because men like that could be used, and if they broke, they were replaceable.

Schreiber reached out before anyone could stop him and brushed the tip of a finger against one of the pads.

The reaction was immediate.

The pad tightened around his fingertip with a gentle clasp, almost tender. A thin filament slid up his finger and touched his skin as delicately as a hair. Schreiber's eyes widened. His mouth opened, but no sound came out.

The lamp flickered.

For a moment, the interior geometry seemed to change, not physically but perceptually, as if the walls had shifted closer without moving. The air thickened. Several soldiers at the breach raised their rifles instinctively, then froze, unsure what they would even be shooting at.

Schreiber's face went slack. His pupils dilated. His lips moved.

"What do you see?" Kammler asked.

Schreiber swallowed. "Light," he whispered. "A corridor. A… map."

"Can you understand it?"

Schreiber's throat bobbed. "It wants… it wants…"

The pad released him. Schreiber staggered back, nearly falling. The surgeon caught his elbow.

"What does it want?" Kammler asked again, his voice low.

Schreiber stared at his own hand as if it no longer belonged to him. "Touch," he said. "It wants to be used. It is waiting."

Waiting. The word lodged in the clearing like a hook.

Kammler stepped closer to the breach. Not into the craft, but close enough that the darkness could look back at him. He felt, again, that faint vibration, the sense of an answering presence. It did not feel like menace. It felt like attention, cold and measuring.

"Show me the occupants," he said.

Dietrich hesitated. "Herr Doktor, there is… something further in. We saw it when we first shone a lamp. We did not approach."

Kammler's gaze sharpened. "Why?"

Dietrich's jaw tightened. "Because it looked like a man."

They brought the lamp beam deeper, and the interior yielded its next secret.

In a recess along the side, cradled by the curved supports, lay a body.

It was humanoid, but wrong in proportion, too long in the limbs, too narrow across the shoulders. Its head was slightly oversized, the face smooth in the way of something unfinished, features subdued as if the sculptor had stopped before adding identity. Its skin had the pallor of wax, but it was not wax. It caught the light with a faint sheen, like something that had never been under a sun.

It wore no uniform, no fabric. If there had been clothing, it had been part of the body itself, a thin membrane fused to the skin in patterns that suggested function rather than decoration.

The surgeon stepped forward, his professional instincts overcoming his fear. "Is it dead?"

Kammler watched the chest. There was no movement. No breath.

The physicist's voice came thin. "Where is the blood? Where is any sign of trauma?"

The body was unmarked, except at the side of the head where the skin had opened in a clean line, not a wound but an access point, like a seam. From it protruded a short length of something metallic and fibrous, like the root of a nerve.

Schreiber, still shaken, stared at the corpse with a horrified fascination. “It is not alone,” he said.

Kammler turned his head slightly. “Explain.”

Schreiber pointed with trembling fingers, not at the body, but at the space beside it. A depression in the organic metal, shaped as if something had lain there. Restraints, perhaps, or a cradle. The impression was fresh, the surface still slightly deformed, as if the craft had not yet finished healing around the absence.

“There was another,” Schreiber whispered. “It is missing.”

Dietrich’s face had gone gray. “We counted only one,” he said quickly, as if insisting could undo the implication. “No tracks. Nothing leaving the crater. No disturbance in the perimeter.”

Kammler’s eyes remained on the empty impression. In his mind, variables lined up like soldiers. A craft that healed. An interface that responded to touch. A body that was more like a component than a pilot. And a second presence that had been here and was now gone without passing through the forest.

Taken, the report had said of the vanished man earlier, but that had been speculation. Now the word gained weight.

Kammler straightened. The lamp hissed softly in the damp air, its light struggling against the thickness inside.

"Seal the breach when you are done with measurements," he ordered. "No one remains inside longer than necessary. Two men at a time, always tethered. If anyone hears voices, if anyone sees something that is not there, you report it immediately."

The soldiers shifted uneasily, but Dietrich nodded, grateful for orders that sounded like control.

Kammler looked one last time at the corpse and the empty cradle beside it. His gloved hand tightened around the sealed vial containing the self-healing sliver, as if he could feel the future pressing against glass.

In the distance, beyond the cordon, the forest stood unmoving. No birds. No wind. Only the steady drip of rain.

It was as if the Black Forest itself understood that something had landed in its heart that did not belong to any earthborn chronology.

And that the forest was holding its breath, waiting to see what would step out next.

Kammler left the clearing with the scientists still murmuring behind him, their voices clipped into technical fragments that did nothing to mask the tremor underneath. Dietrich followed at his shoulder, boots sucking at the mud.

"Post two men at the breach," Kammler said. "Not recruits. Men who have killed before."

"Yes, Herr Doktor."

"And I want a log kept. Every person who enters. Time in. Time out. Names. Physical condition. Any… deviations."

Dietrich nodded too quickly. "We will keep it."

Kammler stopped at the nearest tent and ducked inside. The canvas smelled of wet wool and cigarettes. A field desk had been set up with a lamp, maps pinned beneath a sheet of glass, and a telephone that connected to the radio mast outside. On the desk lay a thin black notebook, the kind used for inventories and executions alike. Kammler opened it and wrote, his pen strokes neat, controlled.

He did not write what he felt, because he did not allow feelings into documents. He wrote facts that could become levers.

Self-repairing hull material. Responsive interface. Humanoid cadaver. Second cradle empty.

The absence was the most important fact of all.

Outside, the sound of voices rose and fell. Kammler listened long enough to identify Schreiber's tone among them, quick and slightly breathless, the voice of a man trying to prove he was not frightened by talking faster than his fear could catch him.

Kammler closed the notebook, stepped back into the rain, and walked toward the breach again.

They had set up a winch line anchored to a pine, crude but sturdy. A rope ran from the winch to a climbing harness. Dietrich stood near it with two soldiers; their helmets beaded with rain. The scientists were gathered in a half circle a few paces back, sheltering their instruments from the damp as though their calipers could keep them safe.

Schreiber was already in the harness.

The younger assistant looked pale, but his eyes had the same shine they had when he touched the interface. Hunger and terror braided into one expression. A man who had seen a door and could not stop himself from reaching for the handle again.

"Herr Doktor," Dietrich began, "I told them no one goes in until you authorize it."

Kammler's gaze moved over Schreiber's harness, the rope, the winch, the soldiers assigned to it. "I am authorizing it," he said.

The surgeon took a step forward. "He should not go alone."

"I am not alone," Schreiber said too quickly. "There are two soldiers."

Kammler's eyes cut to him. "You will not call them soldiers inside. You will call them anchors. You will not touch anything you are not told to touch. You will not speak to it."

Schreiber swallowed. "Speak to it, Herr Doktor?"

"If it speaks to you, you do not answer."

The physicist with wire-rimmed glasses tried to force his voice into neutrality. "We still do not know if there are gases inside. Or radiation pockets."

Kammler held up a hand, not impatient but final. "Then you will measure. And if you find poison, you will die having found it. This is not a university."

The man flinched, but he nodded.

Kammler stepped closer to the breach. The lamp light still seemed reluctant to enter. The craft's interior swallowed brightness as if darkness were a material it could manufacture.

He looked at Schreiber for a long moment, not as a human being but as a function.

"Ten minutes," Kammler said. "You will tether yourself to the rope and you will not unclip for any reason. If you feel disoriented, you say so. If you see something… you say so."

Schreiber's Adam's apple jumped. "Yes, Herr Doktor."

Dietrich gave a short, sharp gesture. The two anchors moved first, each clipped to the line. Their rifles were slung uselessly, a comfort object more than a weapon. They climbed into the breach, boots finding purchase on the curved, organic struts.

Schreiber followed, careful at first, then faster, compelled.

Kammler watched the rope. It was his measure of reality. As long as it remained taut and connected, the world behaved.

Minutes passed. Rain pattered on helmets. A crow called once from somewhere beyond the cordon and then went silent again, as if the sound had been a mistake.

From the breach came muffled voices.

"Temperature dropping," one of the anchors called. His tone was strained. "It's colder inside than out."

"Any odor?" the surgeon asked, leaning forward.

"Mushrooms," the man answered, and then, after a pause, "And metal."

Schreiber's voice followed, thin with forced excitement. "The interface is here. It's moving again. It's like it recognizes… the light."

Kammler's jaw tightened. "Do not touch it."

"I'm not," Schreiber said quickly. "I'm only looking."

A metallic scrape echoed faintly, not like a tool against metal but like something shifting in a joint.

Then Schreiber spoke again, quieter. "There's a corridor. Past the body. Deeper than before. I didn't see it from the breach."

Dietrich frowned. "A corridor? It wasn't there."

Schreiber sounded oddly certain. "It's there now."

Kammler stepped closer until he could see the edges of the peeled hull. The seam had already begun to smooth itself again, the craft knitting around the opening with slow patience. It was not closing fast enough to trap them, but the movement was unmistakable. The object behaved like a wound that did not want to stay open.

Kammler called into the breach, his voice hard enough to cut through damp air. "You will not proceed beyond the corpse."

One of the anchors answered, but his voice had changed slightly, as if he were speaking through clenched teeth. "Understood."

Schreiber did not answer at all.

The rope twitched.

Not the gentle give of a man shifting his weight. A sharp tug, as if something had pulled it from inside.

Dietrich stiffened. "Hold tension," he ordered the winch operator.

The operator braced and cranked. The rope tightened. For a moment it held steady.

Then, from within, there was a sound like a breath drawn too close to a microphone. A wet intake, intimate and wrong. The anchors both shouted at once, their words colliding.

"Something moved!"

"Behind us!"

Schreiber's voice rose into a single syllable, cut off at the end, as if a hand had closed over his mouth.

Kammler's body did not react the way the others did. He did not step back. He did not draw a weapon. He leaned in, eyes narrowed, listening.

"Pull," he said.

The winch operator cranked harder. The rope slid an inch, two, then snagged as if caught.

Dietrich barked, "Pull them out now!"

The rope jerked again, this time toward the interior, so violently that the operator stumbled forward, boots skidding in the mud. The line went taut enough to sing.

For one second, Kammler saw movement inside the breach.

A lamp beam swung wildly and caught a glimpse of something that was not one of the men. Not the corpse either. A shape that seemed to peel itself out of the darkness, taller than a man, thin as a shadow cast by a wrong sun. It was there only long enough for the mind to register it, and then it slipped aside, not retreating but folding into angles the human eye could not follow.

The lamp went out.

The darkness became complete.

The anchors screamed. One voice ended abruptly with a choking sound. The other continued, high and animal, until it too was cut off, as though the craft had simply decided it was done listening.

The rope slackened.

Dietrich stared at it, unable to interpret slack as anything but salvation. "They got loose," he said, voice cracking. "They unclipped."

Kammler reached down, seized the rope with both gloved hands, and yanked. It came toward him easily, far too easily, sliding through mud-streaked gloves in smooth, empty length.

The end emerged from the breach.

The metal carabiner was still attached.

The harness was still attached.

But it was empty, the straps limp and hanging, the buckles clicking softly against the hull as if someone had placed it there with care.

A few paces behind Kammler, someone retched. The surgeon made a sound like a prayer strangled before it could become words.

Dietrich stepped forward, his face blotched with shock. "That's impossible," he whispered. "They can't have come out. They can't have—"

Kammler held the empty harness up at eye level. Rainwater ran off it in threads. The straps were cut in one place, not torn. Cut cleanly, as if by a blade that understood exactly how much force the material could take.

On the inside of one strap, something clung like residue: a fine dust, dark and faintly green, shimmering when it caught the gray light. It did not look like soil. It looked like the film left on a tongue after tasting electricity.

Kammler did not allow himself to look at the men's faces. He looked at the breach.

The peeled edge of the craft flexed again, smoothing, knitting. The opening narrowed by a fraction, not dramatic, not fast, but deliberate. As if the object were swallowing evidence.

Kammler's voice dropped until only Dietrich could hear. "Double the perimeter. No one leaves. No radios beyond this site. If anyone asks why the line went slack, you tell them it snapped. Do you understand?"

Dietrich's throat worked. "Yes, Herr Doktor."

Kammler stared into the darkness of the breach and felt, without any mysticism, that he was being observed. Not by eyes. By attention. A pressure in the air that made the skin under his collar prickle.

Schreiber had touched the interface. The interface had responded. It had shown him a corridor that had not been there. And then it had taken him, not by dragging his body through the forest, not by leaving tracks or blood, but by removing him from the world in a way that made the rope meaningless.

Taken, Kammler thought again, and now it was not a word from a frightened report. It was a mechanism.

He turned to the assembled scientists. Their faces were pale blots beneath wet hats. Their instruments hung uselessly in their hands.

"You have seen what happens when you forget that you are livestock in a slaughterhouse you do not own," Kammler said, his tone calm enough to be a cruelty. "You will not panic. Panic is noise, and noise invites attention."

One of them, the physicist with glasses, managed, "Herr Doktor… what do we do?"

Kammler looked at the empty harness one last time, then handed it to Dietrich as if it were a document.

"We learn," Kammler said. "We learn what it wants. And we learn how to make it want what we want."

As he spoke, the craft's seam tightened another fraction, the darkness inside retreating behind a narrowing curve of self-healing metal. It did not close completely. Not yet. It left a wound just large enough to suggest invitation, or bait.

Somewhere in the trees beyond the cordon, a soldier shifted his rifle and whispered something to himself. Kammler did not ask what. He did not need to.

The Black Forest remained too still, too quiet, as if the entire landscape had been instructed to pretend nothing had happened.

But Kammler could not pretend. The variables had changed.

There were now men missing who had not walked away. Missing in a way that made the world feel less solid, as if the craft had punctured not only earth but the rules that held bodies to it.

Kammler turned back toward the tents, already planning which men would be next to enter, and what pressures would be applied to produce the right kind of bravery.

Behind him, the breach continued to heal.

And in the thickening rain, the empty harness dripped steadily, like a clock that had begun counting down.

Chapter 2

Die Glocke Awakens

The Black Forest site did not become quieter after the vanishing. It became disciplined.

Kammler did not allow grief to form, because grief implied ownership, and he did not own those men. He owned the perimeter, the tents, the instruments, and the silence. Within hours, the clearing was no longer a place where soldiers whispered prayers. It was a place where soldiers learned to keep their mouths shut because the wrong sound might be heard by something that did not need ears.

They sealed the breach as well as they could. Not with welds, not with rivets, but with a lattice of timber braced against the craft's curve and a tarpaulin stretched tight, more to deny the eyes than to deny entry. The hull's seam continued to knit at its own pace, indifferent to human urgency. Every few minutes the edge shifted, smoothing itself as if the craft were deciding what evidence it wished to keep and what it wished to erase.

Kammler watched it once more at dusk, rain turning the tarpaulin into a slick black skin. The smell of ozone still hung in the air, fainter now, like a memory that refused to fade.

"Sturmbannführer," he said to Dietrich, "how many men have been at this site who are not on my list?"

Dietrich blinked. "No one, Herr Doktor. Only those assigned."

Kammler's gaze did not change. "How many have spoken to anyone beyond the perimeter?"

Dietrich stiffened, hearing the trap. "No one. The priest is still held. The forestry worker is still held. The village is being watched."

Kammler nodded once, accepting the answer because it was the one he required. "Good. You will dismantle the tents by morning. You will leave nothing here that suggests we were ever present. The forest will be returned to itself."

Dietrich hesitated. "And the object?"

Kammler looked toward the tarpaulin-covered shape, a darkness among darker trees. "The object is not staying in Germany."

Dietrich's mouth opened, then closed. He was an SS man, not a logistician of the impossible. "How will we move it?"

"With difficulty," Kammler said. "With losses, if necessary. And with men who know that survival is not the point."

That night, Kammler sent messages along channels that did not exist on paper. He did not request permission; he informed. He was not asking the Reich for resources. He was notifying it that resources were already required. Trains would be diverted without explanation. Factories would be instructed to produce components with no blueprint attached, only tolerances and deadlines. A new site would be expanded in the mountains where borders could be blurred and screams could be swallowed.

By dawn, the scientists were gathered again, eyes red from sleeplessness. The physicist with wire-rimmed glasses had ink on his cuffs and the exhausted look of a man forced to translate awe into equations. The surgeon's hands trembled when he lit a cigarette, his body trying to shake loose a memory it could not place. The metallurgist had not slept at all; he sat hunched over the sealed vial with the black shaving inside, staring at it as though it might crawl.

Kammler did not ask them whether they were afraid. He gave them a new word to be afraid of.

"Die Glocke," he said.

The term hung in the air, ordinary and almost stupid. The Bell. Something a child could ring. Something a church could swing above a village.

"The shape is incidental," Kammler continued, as if reading their thoughts. "The function is not. The materials we have recovered are not merely rare. They are not on any table of elements we use. They do not behave like matter that obeys our rules. That is precisely why we will build around them."

The physicist swallowed. "Build what, Herr Doktor?"

Kammler's eyes lifted. "A chamber. A resonator. A machine that can sustain what this object does in brief moments, accidentally. We will force it to do so intentionally."

Dietrich shifted behind him, uncomfortable with the language. Force it. Kammler's vocabulary, always architectural, made even physics sound like punishment.

The surgeon cleared his throat. "And the missing men?"

Kammler looked at him with mild irritation, as if the question were sentimental. "They are data.

Their disappearance tells us the craft is capable of removal without transit. No tracks, no blood, no trajectory. They were here, and then they were not. If we wish to move through time, through space, through whatever boundary this thing punctured when it fell into the forest, then we begin by accepting that bodies are optional."

No one argued. In the Reich, ethics was a luxury that had been executed early.

Within forty-eight hours the Black Forest site was stripped. Trees that had been snapped were cut down and hauled away. Soil that had vitrified into black glass was dug up in blocks and crated like art stolen from a museum. The craft itself, still warm in a way that made men uneasy, was moved at night under tarpaulins and false manifests. The convoy ran without headlights again, like something ashamed of its own existence.

Kammler rode with it part of the way, then peeled off, leaving Dietrich to oversee the remainder. He trusted Dietrich not because Dietrich was brilliant, but because Dietrich was obedient and unimaginative. Imagination was dangerous around objects that answered it.

The new site was in the Owl Mountains, far from the scrutiny of Berlin salons and close to the invisible machinery of occupied industry.

Officially, it was an expansion of a weapons testing facility. Unofficially, it was a buried cathedral built for a science that did not have prayers, only procedures.

When Kammler arrived, the main cavern was already being carved deeper into the rock. Pneumatic drills shrieked. Dust made the air taste like crushed bone. Floodlights threw hard shadows along the walls where miners and forced laborers moved like insects, hauling rubble, laying rebar, pouring concrete that steamed faintly in the cold underground draft.

He walked the site with a blueprint rolled under his arm, though the blueprint was more concept than plan. Men snapped to attention when he passed, not because they recognized his face but because they felt the gravity of his presence. Kammler did not stride like a general. He moved like a man inspecting a tomb he had commissioned for someone else.

At the center of the cavern, he stopped where the foundation ring had been marked with chalk. The circle was enormous, big enough to swallow a house. Steel anchor points protruded from the newly poured concrete, waiting like teeth.

“This is wrong,” said a voice at his shoulder.

Kammler turned. The physicist with wire-rimmed glasses had arrived with the first wave of equipment, crates stenciled with fake department names. His boots were coated with pale dust; his coat collar up against the chill. He was staring at the chalk circle as if it offended him.

"What is wrong?" Kammler asked.

"We cannot simply… build a machine around an unknown material and expect it to behave," the physicist said. He caught himself, then added quickly, "Herr Doktor."

Kammler regarded him. "We can build a machine around anything. That is the only thing human beings are consistently good at."

The physicist's lips tightened. "This is not a turbine. Not a reactor. We do not know what it is."

Kammler's voice remained level. "Then we will make it into something. We will define it by the way it serves us."

He unrolled the blueprint on a makeshift table, weighting the corners with a wrench and a soldier's helmet. The drawing showed a bell-shaped chamber suspended within a framework of coils and counterweights, nested like a heart inside ribs. Around it were annotations in Kammler's precise handwriting: rotational tolerances, insulation requirements, magnetic field containment, access ports sealed by redundant locks.

The physicist's eyes moved over the lines. Despite himself, his mind began to solve problems. "This requires a stable power source far beyond what we have here."

Kammler pointed to a side note. "Not if the material is the source."

The physicist's face pinched. "You intend to place the recovered fragments inside the chamber."

"Not fragments," Kammler corrected. "A core. Whatever the craft uses to do what it does. We will remove it or replicate its environment until it produces the effect again."

Dietrich arrived later that day, his uniform stained with travel, his expression tight with the strain of moving an object that did not behave like cargo. He handed Kammler a folder without being asked.

"The hull remains under cover in the lower hangar," Dietrich said quietly. "It continues to… change. Small movements along the seam. Like breathing."

Kammler flipped through the report without reading it. "And the interior?"

Dietrich hesitated. “We did not reopen it, Herr Doktor. As ordered.”

Kammler nodded. “Good.”

He looked back at the cavern, at the chalk circle that would become a foundation, at the laborers who would never be told what they were building. He heard the drills, the shouted Polish curses, the crack of a guard’s baton. He smelled wet rock and fresh concrete and, faint beneath it, the metallic sweetness that followed the alien object like a trace.

“This will not be a laboratory,” Kammler said, as much to himself as to the men around him. “It will be a bell tower buried underground. When it rings, it will ring through the world.”

The physicist’s voice was brittle. “And who will hear it?”

Kammler rolled the blueprint back up with a snap that sounded like a verdict. “The future,” he said. “And whatever else is listening.”

He stepped toward the marked circle and planted his boot on the edge of it, smearing chalk into the concrete dust. The gesture was small, but it was the kind of smallness that began catastrophes: a man claiming a boundary, believing that because he had drawn it, the universe would respect it.

“Begin,” Kammler ordered.

And the mountain, obedient to violence, began to hollow itself into the shape of a bell.

The lower hangar had once been a limestone cavity where water collected and bats nested. Now it was a sealed chamber with concrete lips poured thick around the rock and steel doors that met in the middle like jaws. Floodlights hung from newly bolted rails. Their light made the air look dusty even when it was still.

Kammler descended the metal stairs without pausing, boots ringing against the grated steps. Behind him came Dietrich, and behind Dietrich the scientists in a tight cluster that tried to look like purpose. They carried clipboards and instrument cases the way men carried talismans.

The smell reached them halfway down. Not the honest stink of wet stone and machine oil. Something else, faint and sweet, with a metallic sharpness that made saliva gather under the tongue as if the body were preparing to vomit.

The physicist with wire-rimmed glasses pressed a handkerchief to his nose. He had ink on his fingers again, as if he could scribble the odor into a formula and neutralize it.

"This is not from the drills," he murmured.

Kammler did not slow. “Nothing here is from the drills.”

At the bottom of the stairs the chamber opened, and the men saw the object.

The hull had been dragged and lowered onto a cradle of steel beams and rubber pads. Chains the thickness of a wrist crossed its curve, anchored to bolts sunk into concrete. Tarpaulins had been thrown over most of it, but the shape beneath them was unmistakable, a dark mass that refused the light. Where the tarpaulin had slid back at one edge, the surface showed: seamless, dull, too smooth. It looked less like a machine than like a black stone that had been shaped by a river in a place where rivers ran through time instead of earth.

Dietrich’s men stood along the walls, rifles slung but hands never far from them. The soldiers’ faces had the blank tension of men ordered to guard something they could not define. A few of them had small white marks at the corners of their mouths, the residue of cigarettes smoked too quickly.

Kammler walked straight to the exposed edge and placed his gloved hand near it without touching.

The hull responded the way it had in the forest, a subtle shift just under perception. Not movement, exactly. More like the air reconsidering its density.

The hair at the base of Dietrich's neck rose under his collar. He did not like to admit to bodily betrayal, but his skin did not consult ideology.

"It is warmer," the surgeon said. He had followed and was staring with the concentrated dread of a man looking at a patient he could not anesthetize. "Or it feels warmer."

"Measure," Kammler said.

A technician set a thermometer against the surface, then pulled it back quickly as if the instrument might be eaten. The mercury climbed and settled at a temperature that made no sense in a cold underground cavity.

"It is holding heat," the technician said, voice too high. "Like an animal."

Kammler's gaze moved along the hull toward the place where the breach had been. Timber and tarpaulin had been replaced by a scaffold of metal clamps and a gasketed plate, but it looked absurd against the craft. Human hardware nailed to a thing that healed itself. The plate did not seal anything. It was a statement, a demand that the object recognize a boundary.

The physicist cleared his throat. "Herr Doktor, the sample vial. The shaving from the seam. It is… changing."

Kammler turned. The metallurgist held out the vial with both hands, as if presenting a relic. Inside, the black sliver no longer lay flat. It had curled slightly, its edge bending inward like a leaf responding to light.

“It was straight yesterday,” the metallurgist said. “I checked. Under magnification. It should not move on its own.”

Kammler took the vial and held it up to the floodlight. The sliver did not reflect. It made a small darkness within the glass.

“Temperature?” Kammler asked.

“Stable,” the physicist said. “No external vibration. No magnet near it. We kept it isolated.”

“You kept it isolated,” Kammler repeated, tasting the word with quiet contempt. “From what? From the world?”

The physicist swallowed. “From fields. From currents. From interference.”

Kammler watched the sliver curl another fraction, slow and patient. It did not behave like spring steel. It behaved like a living thing, adjusting posture.

Dietrich shifted his weight. “It is trying to return,” he said before he could stop himself.

The sentence fell into the chamber. Several soldiers glanced toward him, startled that he had voiced what they had refused to name.

The surgeon made a sound in his throat. "Return to what?"

No one answered, because the answer was too simple. Return to the whole.

Kammler lowered the vial. "Then we will give it a home," he said. "One we control."

They crossed the chamber to a workbench area set up behind a line painted on the concrete floor. The line was a concession to fear. As if paint could restrain a phenomenon.

On the bench lay objects taken from the Black Forest site: blocks of vitrified soil wrapped in cloth, a coil of cable that had been left too near the hull and now carried a faint green tarnish, and three sealed containers stamped with false inventory numbers. Kammler's notebook was open beside them, its black pages filled with tidy script.

A young assistant, new to the site, stood at attention near the bench. His face was too smooth, his eyes too eager. He had not seen the empty harness dripping in the rain. He had not heard the sound of a scream that stopped mid-breath. He still believed danger had the decency to announce itself.

Kammler pointed to one of the sealed containers. “Open it.”

The assistant hesitated only long enough to make it clear he had heard fear described. Then he broke the seal and lifted the lid.

Inside was a chunk of material larger than a fist, wrapped in waxed paper. When he unfolded it, the chamber’s air changed. Not a gust, not a breeze. A pressure shift that made ears pop, subtle but universal.

The soldiers along the wall straightened reflexively. One of them took a half-step back. Another lifted his hand to his throat as if checking whether his skin was still his.

The assistant held the object up. It was not the hull shaving. This was denser, a core fragment recovered from within the craft, one of the pieces the scientists had pried loose at the edge of the breach before the object began swallowing itself. Its surface was matte and uneven, like volcanic rock, but it was too perfect in its imperfection, too deliberate. Faint striations crossed it in patterns that looked accidental until the mind noticed they repeated.

The physicist’s voice dropped. “It is emitting something. Not radiation. Not magnetism as we measure it.”

"Then what?" the surgeon asked.

The physicist's jaw worked as if he were chewing on the limits of his own education. "A field. A distortion. It affects time-dependent processes. Our clocks drift near it. Chemical reactions slow or accelerate. It is… not heat, but it behaves like heat does to probability."

Kammler watched the assistant's hand. The skin at his knuckles had gone pale around the fragment, as if blood had decided to retreat.

"How does it feel?" Kammler asked him.

The assistant's mouth opened. For a moment nothing came out. Then, in a voice that sounded younger than it had a second ago, he said, "It is heavy. And… it feels like it is watching."

Dietrich's eyes narrowed. "Everything here is watching," he muttered.

Kammler did not correct him.

The assistant's fingers twitched. The fragment did not move, but the assistant's hand did, as if responding to a vibration only he could feel. He blinked too fast.

"Put it down," Kammler ordered.

The assistant lowered it toward the bench. Halfway down he stopped. His wrist locked. His arm trembled.

"I can't," he whispered.

Kammler stepped closer. "You can," he said, voice calm. "You will."

The assistant's eyes widened. Sweat beaded at his hairline despite the cold. "It doesn't want to."

The surgeon took a step forward. "Herr Doktor, perhaps he should release it onto cloth. Don't make him grip it."

Kammler's gaze snapped to him. "Do you think it cares about cloth?"

The assistant's breathing turned shallow. His pupils dilated, and his mouth moved again.

"Corridor," he said, and the word made the physicist flinch. "There's a corridor. It's… it's inside my head."

Dietrich's hand went to his sidearm without drawing it. A weapon against a thought.

Kammler's voice hardened. "Name."

The assistant blinked at him as if forgetting it. Then it returned, and he said it like a confession. "Keller. Hans Keller."

Kammler took the assistant's wrist in his gloved hand and forced the arm downward, slowly, steadily. The assistant cried out, not in pain but in panic, as if Kammler were pushing him toward a ledge.

The fragment touched the bench.

For an instant it stuck, not adhering but resisting release. Keller's fingers refused to open. His hand looked like a claw.

Kammler leaned in until his face was inches from Keller's and spoke quietly enough that only the assistant could hear.

"You will open your hand," he said. "Or I will open it for you."

Keller's eyes filled with tears he did not understand. Then his fingers loosened. The fragment lay still on the bench, innocent as a stone.

Keller staggered back as if he had been slapped. He clutched his wrist and stared at his palm. The skin was unmarked, but the fine hairs on it stood upright.

The surgeon caught Keller before he fell. "Sit him down," he said to a technician.

Kammler did not look at Keller again. He looked at the fragment.

"Do you see now?" he asked the physicist.

The physicist swallowed. "Yes."

"This is human fear," Kammler said, and his tone made the phrase sound like a component to be measured. "Not cowardice. Not sentiment. A physiological response to proximity. Your bodies are reacting because they understand something your minds cannot yet describe."

Dietrich stared at the fragment with a soldier's hatred for anything that made him feel small. "Then why keep it near us at all?"

Kammler turned his head slightly. His eyes were cold and awake, the eyes of a man who had built camps and called them necessary. "Because fear is an instrument," he said. "If it can be induced, it can be directed. If it can be directed, it can be used."

The physicist's voice was rough. "Used to do what? We are not even certain it is safe to keep in the same chamber as men."

Kammler moved closer to the bench and placed his palm flat on the concrete beside the fragment. Not touching it, not yet, but close enough that the air between them felt tense.

"It is not safe," he said. "That is why it is valuable. The Reich does not need safe. It needs advantage."

He looked toward the hull on its cradle, the tarpaulins rising and falling by fractions with the illusion of breathing. Not because the fabric moved, but because the men's eyes insisted on seeing motion where something alive might be.

"Schreiber is gone," Kammler continued, and the name struck the scientists like a sudden slap. "So are the two anchors. If this material can remove men from the world, if it can open corridors that do not exist until it wants them to exist, then it can also open corridors we can step through on purpose."

Dietrich's jaw tightened. "And if it takes more men?"

Kammler's gaze did not soften. "Then it takes more men."

Silence spread, heavy and obedient. In that silence, Keller began to sob quietly where he had been made to sit, his shoulders shaking with a humiliation too large for a single body.

The surgeon watched him with something like pity and then looked away, as if pity itself were dangerous here.

The physicist leaned closer to the fragment, forcing himself to stay near it. His hand hovered over his instruments, searching for numbers that would make the sensation go away. "It is altering our perception," he said. "Or our perception is finally accurate and reality is the thing that is unstable."

Kammler's mouth tightened in the nearest thing to a smile he ever allowed. "Then we will build a machine that stabilizes it," he said. "A chamber. A bell. A way to ring this field until it becomes a tone we can reproduce."

Dietrich stared at the hull and spoke with reluctant honesty. "And what if it rings back?"

Kammler did not answer immediately. His eyes moved from the fragment to the sealed breach plate to the shadowed curve of the craft, as if tracking the line of a thought that connected them all. For a moment the air seemed to press in, and several men shifted as if the chamber had become smaller.

Then Kammler said, very quietly, "Then we learn who has been listening since the forest."

He straightened, the decision settling into him like poured concrete. "Increase isolation protocols," he ordered. "No one handles fragments without restraints and a second observer. Logs for every exposure. If anyone reports corridors, voices, maps, you write it down before you pray about it."

Dietrich nodded, grateful again for procedure.

Kammler turned away from the bench and began walking back toward the stairs. The floodlights threw his shadow across the painted line on the floor, stretching it toward the hull until it looked, for a moment, like the shadow belonged to something else.

Behind him, the alien fragment lay on the workbench without movement.

But the men in the chamber moved as if it might follow them.

That was the first lesson the Owl Mountains taught them: the material did not need to chase you to make you run. It only had to exist near you, quietly, patiently, and let your own mind supply the rest.

And fear, Kammler knew, was the easiest force in the world to harness.

It was already doing half the work for him.

The cavern grew louder as the days accumulated.

Concrete cured in slow heat. Steel ribs were bolted into place. Coils arrived in sections, wrapped in oiled paper, their copper windings darkened by the damp. They were lowered by crane into the central ring Kammler had marked in chalk, and the forced laborers below, faces gray with dust, guided the pieces into position with the care of men handling something that could crush them without noticing.

The bell chamber itself took shape as an absence first. A void in the center of the framework, a space reserved for something that did not yet have a name that satisfied the engineers. They called it Die Glocke because Kammler had said the word and the word had become law. But in their notes, when they were honest and alone, they wrote around it: resonator, containment, field cage, interference engine.

The fragment on the workbench remained where Kammler had left it, sealed now under glass and additional locks. It did not move when watched. It moved when ignored. On the third night after Keller's episode, the metallurgist returned to find the fist-sized core fragment rotated on its own by a few degrees, as if it had settled into a more comfortable position. There was no mark on the bench, no scrape. The glass dome over it was undisturbed.

He wrote it down anyway, because Kammler had taught them that denial was not safety. Denial was only delay.

In the makeshift laboratory rooms carved into the side tunnels, they began with the simplest truths. Time was supposed to be measurable. Time was supposed to be shared.

They placed three identical mechanical clocks on a table and synchronized them. They placed a fourth clock ten meters away, behind a thick wall of rock, in a corridor whose air smelled only of limestone and oil. Every hour, a technician compared them and recorded the results.

For the first six hours, there was nothing. The clocks stayed obedient, their hands moving together like soldiers marching.

Then, shortly after midnight, the clock nearest the sealed fragment began to lose time.

Not seconds at first. Fractions. A hesitation in the tick that the ear could not hear but the eye could catch in the delicate tremor of the second hand. The technician thought it was a defect and reached for his tools.

When his fingers touched the clock's casing, he jerked back as if stung.

"It's cold," he said, confused. "Colder than the room."

The surgeon, summoned reluctantly from his quarters, pressed his palm against the casing and felt his skin tighten. It was not merely cool metal. It was the kind of cold that made the body believe it had touched something that did not belong in a living world.

He compared the clocks again. The far clock, behind the wall, was accurate. The other three were drifting, each at a different rate, as if proximity itself had become a variable with weight.

The physicist with wire-rimmed glasses stared at the logbook until his eyes reddened. “This is not a clock problem,” he said finally.

Dietrich, standing in the doorway with two men behind him, said what he always said when he did not like the direction of a conversation. “Then stop bringing clocks near it.”

Kammler had been called down from the main cavern. He listened without interrupting, eyes moving between the instruments and the men’s faces. When the physicist finished, Kammler’s only question was not about the clocks, but about the wall.

“How thick is the rock?” he asked.

“Three meters,” the physicist said. “Solid limestone.”

“And yet it reaches through,” Kammler said.

“It may not be reaching through,” the physicist replied, voice careful. “It may be that the space here is no longer consistent. That distance is… altered.”

Kammler looked toward the deeper tunnel where the bell chamber was being assembled, where coils waited like ribs for a heart. “Good,” he said. “Then we are building the correct machine.”

They expanded the test.

Geiger counters clicked with their steady, unhelpful rhythm. Thermometers behaved normally unless placed too close to the fragment, where they swung a few degrees with no explanation. A pendulum suspended from a beam did not change its period, but on the fifth day its shadow did. A technician noticed it first, because the man had nothing else to do but stare at the moving line of darkness on the wall.

The pendulum swung. Its shadow lagged behind, then caught up, then moved ahead by a hair’s breadth, like an object trying to anticipate itself. The technician blinked hard, certain it was fatigue.

When he looked again, the shadow was still wrong.

The surgeon stood beside him and watched without speaking. He knew hallucination. He had watched men under gas claim to see their mothers in trenches, watched fever make soldiers insist that lice were speaking in Latin. But this was not the mind producing an image. This was light misbehaving.

He made himself say it out loud. "The shadow is out of phase."

The physicist's face tightened at the phrase, as if naming it made it more real. "It shouldn't be possible."

"Not by our rules," Kammler said from behind them.

They turned. Kammler had arrived without announcing himself, coat collar up, hat in hand. He stepped into the room and stood beneath the bare bulb, his own shadow sharp and obedient on the wall.

He watched the pendulum for a full minute, timing the swing with his breath.

Then he reached out and stopped it with two fingers.

The shadow continued moving for a fraction of a second after the pendulum halted, as if it had momentum of its own. Then it snapped into stillness.

No one spoke. Even Dietrich, who had followed Kammler, remained silent, his soldier's instincts confused by a phenomenon that offered nothing to shoot.

Kammler looked at the physicist. "What does that tell you?"

The physicist swallowed. "That cause and effect are no longer locked together."

"And if they are not locked," Kammler said, voice even, "then they can be rearranged."

The first living test was not proposed as a moral decision. It was proposed as a logistical one.

They brought in rabbits from a local farm, delivered in crates by a man who did not ask questions because his paperwork told him not to. The animals were placed in wire cages at measured distances: one cage in the control corridor behind the thick wall, one cage in the lab room ten meters from the fragment, one cage five meters away, and one cage in a small auxiliary chamber where the fragment's sealed dome had been temporarily moved for calibration.

The surgeon protested out of reflex more than conviction. "If it affects time-dependent processes, then living tissue will be—"

"Data," Kammler said, and the word ended the protest the way a slap ended a sentence.

The rabbits were calm at first. Their noses twitched. Their eyes shone in the harsh light. One thumped a hind leg softly, irritated by the noise of drilling in the distant cavern.

After twenty minutes, the rabbit in the auxiliary chamber began to convulse.

Not a seizure. Something slower and stranger. Its body stiffened and relaxed in a rhythm that did not match breath. Its fur rose along its spine as if electricity traveled beneath the skin. Its eyes went glassy, then sharp, then glassy again.

The technician watching it shouted for the surgeon.

By the time the surgeon arrived, the rabbit's fur had changed.

It was subtle at first, a thinning around the muzzle, a blanching. Then it accelerated, as if the animal had fallen down a slope.

Whiskers broke and fell away. The skin around its eyes tightened into delicate folds that did not belong on a young animal. Its breathing became shallow. Its paws curled.

The surgeon's hands hovered over the cage, trained to intervene, but there was nothing to intervene against. No wound. No poison. No infection. Only time behaving like a force applied too quickly.

The physicist arrived, breathless, and stared as if the rabbit were an equation written in blood.

"It's aging," he whispered.

The rabbit's convulsions stopped. It lay still for a moment, chest barely moving. Then, with a small, almost gentle motion, its body slackened. The eyes remained open.

A rabbit in a cage, dead of old age in less than half an hour.

In the adjacent room, five meters from the fragment, the rabbit did something different. It did not convulse. It simply became smaller.

The technician noticed when the animal shifted and the cage seemed suddenly too large. Its ears shortened. Its limbs lost length as if the bones were being re-measured. Its eyes grew proportionally larger, giving it a startled, infant look.

When the surgeon reached the cage, the rabbit was not a rabbit any longer in the sense that its body did not fit any normal stage of development. It was a compressed version of itself, a reversal, youth forced backward through a body that did not understand the command.

It squealed, high and thin, and pressed itself into the corner as if trying to hide from its own skin.

Dietrich watched from the doorway, face pale beneath his cap. "This is witchcraft," one of his men muttered.

Dietrich snapped at him, not because he disagreed but because the word was dangerous. "Silence."

Kammler stepped into the auxiliary chamber and looked down at the dead rabbit. He did not flinch. His expression did not change. Only his eyes sharpened, as if the world had just offered him a tool with a sharper edge than he had dared imagine.

The surgeon forced himself to speak. "Herr Doktor, this cannot be controlled. It is not selective. It is arbitrary."

Kammler looked at him. "No," he said softly. "It is selective. It chose distance as a parameter. That is not arbitrary. That is a rule we can learn."

The physicist's voice shook despite his effort to keep it steady. "Or it chose the animal. Or it chose the moment. The results aren't consistent."

Kammler's gaze moved to the living rabbit in the other cage, the one that had become impossibly young. Its chest fluttered too quickly. Its eyes were wide with pure animal terror.

"Then we build consistency," Kammler said.

That night, the laborers drilling in the main cavern began reporting headaches. Not the normal ache of exertion. A pressure behind the eyes, a sense of standing too close to a great engine. A guard struck one man for slowing down, and the man looked up with a dazed expression and said, in Polish, that he had already been struck and it would happen again.

The guard hit him a second time out of spite.

The man did not react, as if the pain arrived late.

In the lab, one of the technicians stumbled into the corridor and vomited. Between retches he kept repeating the same phrase in German, simple and terrified: "It already happened."

The surgeon tried to question him. "What already happened?"

The technician looked up, eyes unfocused. "You asked me that," he said, and then his face tightened in confusion. "You will ask me that."

The physicist wrote it down with a hand that would not stop trembling. He did not call it prophecy. He did not call it insanity. He wrote what he could measure: repeated statements anticipating immediate events. Temporal displacement of perception.

Kammler read the note, then looked toward the sealed doors of the lower hangar where the larger hull sat under tarpaulin, warm and silent like an animal that had learned patience. He remembered the empty harness dripping in the rain, the cut strap, the shimmering green dust.

He did not say Schreiber's name. He did not say the anchors' names. He did not offer the men comfort, because comfort would have implied this was a disaster to survive rather than a frontier to exploit.

Instead, he issued another order.

"Move the fragment into the bell framework tomorrow," he said. "Not the hull. The core. We begin ringing the field."

Dietrich's face tightened. "And the men? The laborers?"

"They will remain," Kammler said. "If they see the future before it arrives, then they are useful witnesses. If they break, then they are replaceable."

The surgeon stared at him, a look that might once have been accusation in another world. Here it was only fatigue. "And if the distortion spreads?"

Kammler's eyes held his. "Then the mountain becomes our containment," he said. "And if the mountain is not enough, then we will learn that too."

As Kammler turned and walked out, the bare bulb above the pendulum flickered once, dimming for a fraction of a second.

The pendulum's shadow on the wall did not flicker with it.

It remained steady, as if it belonged to a different moment entirely.

Chapter 3

Chronicles From the Future

They moved the core fragment at dawn, when the night shift's fear was raw and the day shift had not yet learned what to be afraid of.

The lower hangar doors opened with a hydraulic groan that sounded too much like something alive waking unwillingly. Cold air rolled out of the passageways, carrying the limestone damp and the sharper, sweeter metallic scent that never fully left the alien material. Floodlights made the dust glitter as men in gray work uniforms and black SS coats formed a corridor, ordered into place by shouted commands and the simple logic of rifles.

The fragment traveled in a box that had been designed like a bomb casing: layered steel, ceramic insulation, rubberized handles to cut vibration. It should have looked reassuring. Instead, it looked like an admission that everyone in the chamber knew they were improvising around a phenomenon with no regard for their precautions.

Kammler walked beside it without touching, hands clasped behind his back, coat buttoned to the throat. Dietrich paced at his other side, jaw clenched, eyes flicking to the men carrying the box as if expecting them to vanish mid-step the way Schreiber had, the way the anchors had, leaving only an empty harness and a rope that meant nothing.

The physicist with wire-rimmed glasses waited inside the main cavern, near the bell framework. His face had the drawn look of a man who had not slept since the rabbits died and were reborn wrong. He held a clipboard, but his fingers gripped it too hard, whitening the knuckles. Beside him stood the surgeon, cigarette unlit between his lips, hands tucked into his coat pockets to hide the tremor.

Die Glocke itself was no longer chalk and concept. It hung within the steel ribs like a suspended organ: a heavy bell-shaped chamber of polished alloy plates bolted into a seamless curve, wrapped by coils and counterweights. Cables as thick as a wrist ran to generators that thrummed quietly in adjacent tunnels. The whole assembly looked like a cathedral's heart ripped out and rebuilt by engineers who believed faith was an inefficiency.

The laborers had been ordered to leave the central ring. Only SS personnel and selected technicians remained. Kammler wanted witnesses who could keep their mouths shut. He wanted men who would obey when the air turned wrong.

The carriers set the box on a rolling gantry aligned with the bell chamber's lower access port. The port was ringed with clamps and redundant locks. The physicist had insisted on them. The locks made him feel like he was doing something other than standing at the edge of a hole.

"Field monitors?" Kammler asked.

The physicist glanced toward a bank of instruments. "As ready as they can be, Herr Doktor. Mechanical clocks, electrical oscillators, chemical rate markers. None of them agree with each other near the chamber."

"Then record their disagreement," Kammler said. "That is still data."

Dietrich leaned in slightly, voice lower. "And the subject?"

Kammler looked past him to the side corridor where a single figure waited between two-armed guards.

The man was in a plain prison uniform. His hair had been shaved close. His hands were cuffed in front of him, and his posture had the resigned tension of someone who had been told enough to understand his choices were not real. He was not a laborer from the mountain. Kammler did not waste experiments on men who might later be missed by an accountant. This one had come in a sealed truck from a camp whose paperwork was designed to swallow names.

"What is he?" the surgeon asked, unable to keep the disgust out of his voice.

"A thief," Dietrich said. It was a lie of category if not detail. "Convicted. Transferred for special work."

Kammler did not correct him. The man could have been a murderer or a dissident or simply inconvenient to someone with authority. In Kammler's mind the only relevant fact was that he was disposable and alive.

The physicist cleared his throat. "Herr Doktor, we still don't know if a living body can survive proximity when the chamber is powered. The rabbits—"

"The rabbits were not in a containment field built to shape the effect," Kammler said. "They were placed near an artifact that behaved as it wished. This is different."

The physicist's eyes flicked to Die Glocke, then away again as if eye contact might tempt it. "We are assuming it can be shaped."

Kammler stepped closer to the bell chamber and placed his gloved hand on the outer framework, feeling the vibration of the generators through steel. "Everything can be shaped," he said. "The question is what breaks while you do it."

He nodded toward the gantry. "Insert the core."

The technicians moved with a careful haste. They opened the box. Even with the fragment's dull surface half-hidden by padded grips, the air in the cavern changed. A few men swallowed hard. One of the guards blinked rapidly, as though trying to clear grit from his eyes.

The surgeon murmured, almost to himself, "It does that without power."

"Then imagine what it does with power," Kammler replied.

The fragment was guided into the chamber's lower cradle, secured within a bracket of insulating arms designed to keep it suspended, not touching the chamber walls. The physicist had argued for that too, insisting that contact might create feedback. He had drawn equations and then crossed them out, his calculations chasing a field that refused to be described.

When the access port sealed and the locks clamped, the cavern felt momentarily smaller. Not physically. Perceptually. The way a room feels smaller when you realize something in it has been listening.

The prisoner was brought forward.

He stopped at the painted line on the floor, the old boundary from the lab translated into a new ritual. His eyes fixed on the bell chamber with animal certainty. Kammler watched the change in him: the stiffening shoulders, the shallow breath. Fear arriving before explanation.

"I won't," the prisoner said in German with a regional accent. "I won't go near it."

Dietrich raised a hand, and one guard shoved the man hard enough that he stumbled across the line. The prisoner caught himself, looked down as though the paint had done it, then looked up again with a sound that was halfway to a sob.

"I didn't do anything," he said quickly, bargaining with whoever might be listening. "I didn't do anything to you."

Kammler stepped close enough that the prisoner could see the reflectionless curve of his boots in the chamber's polished metal. "You will stand where you are told," Kammler said. His voice was calm, almost clinical. "You will be quiet. If you survive, you will have served a purpose. If you do not, you will still have served a purpose."

The prisoner's eyes darted to the surgeon, as if searching for a human face. The surgeon looked away.

The physicist moved to the control bank. His hand hovered above a switch. He looked at Kammler as though asking permission and absolution at the same time.

Kammler nodded once.

The physicist threw the switch.

The generators deepened their hum. The coils around Die Glocke began to draw current, and the sound changed from machinery to something closer to resonance, a vibration that sat behind the teeth. The floodlights did not flicker, but the shadows did. A guard's shadow on the cavern wall slid a fraction to the left, then corrected itself. The painted line on the floor seemed to ripple as if seen through heat haze, though the air was cold enough to sting the lungs.

The prisoner clutched his cuffs and cried out. Not from pain. From disorientation. He looked down at his hands, then up again as if the cavern had rearranged itself while he blinked.

The surgeon watched his pupils. “His eyes,” he said hoarsely. “They’re not tracking properly.”

The physicist called out readings, voice strained. “Clock drift increasing. Electrical phase shift across the coil array. Temperature stable. No, not stable. Temperature is… contradicting itself.”

Kammler did not move. He watched the bell chamber.

A low tone began to build. It was not coming from speakers. It was the chamber itself, the coils, the air, the rock. A pressure wave you felt in the sinuses more than heard in the ears. Men shifted uncomfortably, hands going to collars, jaws clenching as if resisting nausea.

The prisoner swayed. His mouth opened and closed. Words came out, but not German.

The guards flinched. One muttered, “What is he saying?”

The prisoner’s voice rose into a string of syllables that sounded like neither prayer nor any language the cavern had ever heard. His head snapped toward Kammler as if he recognized him, and for a moment his face held an expression of pure, stunned certainty, like a man seeing his own death already written.

Then he was gone.

Not dropped. Not pulled away. Not consumed in light. One instant his cuffed hands were in front of his chest; the next instant there was only empty air, and the guards' momentum carried them a step forward as if they had been holding a weight that suddenly ceased to exist.

Silence hit like a slap. The generators still hummed, the low tone still pressed against the skull, but the human noise stopped completely. No one breathed for a second too long.

Dietrich recovered first. He grabbed one guard by the collar. "Where did he go?"

The guard's eyes were wide, wet. "He was here," he whispered. "He was here."

The physicist stared at his instruments as if they had betrayed him personally. "No displacement signature," he said. "No heat spike. No radiation. He didn't move through space. He simply… stopped being in this coordinate."

Kammler's gaze remained fixed on Die Glocke. His expression did not change, but something in his eyes sharpened, as if a lock had clicked open.

"How long," he asked.

The physicist blinked. "Herr Doktor?"

"How long until return," Kammler said, as if return were the natural completion of a mechanism, not a hope.

The surgeon found his voice. "Return? You think—"

The answer came without words.

Air snapped.

A crack like distant thunder sounded inside the chamber, muffled and intimate. A gust of cold moved outward from the bell framework, strong enough to lift dust from the floor and swirl it in slow spirals. Several men staggered back, hands raised instinctively to protect their faces.

The prisoner reappeared.

He did not materialize gently. He slammed onto the concrete on his side, sliding a short distance as if thrown. The sound of his body hitting the floor made the guards flinch harder than his disappearance had. He curled, coughing violently, and when he lifted his head his face was slick with sweat and streaked with something darker.

Blood.

Not from a wound. From his nose and mouth, as if pressure had ruptured vessels behind the eyes.

He tried to speak. The first sound was a garbled choke. The second was a word that did not belong to the cavern.

Then, with a desperate heave, he got his cuffed hands under him and pushed himself up enough to look at Kammler.

His eyes locked onto Kammler's face with terrifying focus, as if everything else in the world had become irrelevant.

"Heil," the prisoner rasped, and then the rest came out in a whisper that was not reverent, only stunned. "It worked."

Kammler stepped closer and crouched, ignoring the way the air still felt electrically alive around the bell chamber.

The prisoner swallowed, his throat working painfully, and his gaze flicked wildly over the cavern as if trying to match it to a memory that did not fit. He began to laugh once, a short, broken sound that turned into a cough and then into something like sobbing.

"I saw," he managed. "I saw… trains that weren't yours. Men with radios smaller than cigarettes. Voices everywhere, like ghosts. And paper. Paper with dates."

The physicist's head snapped up. "Dates?"

The prisoner's laugh turned into another cough. He spit blood onto the concrete and stared at it as though surprised it was red.

He blinked hard, and his voice dropped. "They were speaking about a war that hasn't happened yet," he whispered. "And they said it like it was already over."

Dietrich took a half-step forward, hand hovering near his sidearm again, as if the prisoner had brought back a weapon made of words.

The surgeon stared at the blood, at the prisoner's bruised face, at the way the man's body shook with delayed shock. "How long were you gone?" he asked softly, unable to stop himself from sounding human.

The prisoner's eyes rolled slightly, searching for a number in the wreckage of his mind. "Minutes," he said, then shook his head violently. "No. Years. I don't know. It didn't feel like minutes."

Kammler straightened and looked at the bell chamber, at the sealed core inside, at the coils still singing around it.

The successful leap was not the prisoner's disappearance. It was his return with information he should not have been able to have, with terror shaped into description, with a glimpse of a world that did not yet exist pressing against the present like a hand against glass.

Kammler's voice was quiet when he spoke, and in the hush of the cavern it carried with absolute clarity.

"Power down," he ordered. Then, after a beat, as if speaking to the future itself, "And bring me the paper."

They dragged the prisoner away on a stretcher because his legs would not hold him. The cuffs stayed on. Dietrich insisted. The man's blood had stopped pouring, but it still filmed his lips, and every few breaths he made a wet sound in the back of his throat that made the guards look away.

Kammler did not follow.

He stood in the central ring while the generators wound down, listening as the deep resonance thinned and vanished. The cavern returned to its ordinary noises: distant drilling, the hiss of cables cooling, boots shifting on concrete. Ordinary was a costume the mountain wore reluctantly.

The physicist with wire-rimmed glasses did not speak until the needles on his instruments settled into a new kind of disagreement. When he finally turned, his face looked older than it had that morning.

"Herr Doktor," he said, voice hoarse, "we did not bring back any paper. We brought back a man babbling."

Kammler's gaze moved over the control bank, the coils, the bell chamber. "The paper exists," he said. "He saw it."

"Seeing is not retrieving," the physicist replied. Then, remembering where he was, he softened the words into caution. "We don't know what exactly happened. He may have hallucinated. Or his mind may have been… expanded, and then damaged."

The surgeon, standing slightly behind, still had the unlit cigarette between his lips. His eyes were fixed on the place on the floor where the prisoner had landed. There was blood there, dark against gray concrete, and dust had already begun to settle into it.

"It was not a hallucination," the surgeon said quietly. "His nose and mouth bled like he went from deep pressure to surface too fast. His body experienced something physical."

The physicist's jaw tightened. "You cannot infer that he was in the future from a nosebleed."

Kammler interrupted with a question that made them both turn.

"How long can we sustain the field without frying the coils?" he asked.

The physicist blinked. "That's what you took from this?"

Kammler's expression remained level. "Answer."

The physicist looked back at his notes, at the heat readings that did not match their own thermometers. "At full power, perhaps three minutes before insulation begins to fail. If we pulse it, longer. If we lower amplitude, longer still, but then we may not achieve displacement."

Kammler nodded as if discussing an artillery schedule. "We will not lower amplitude," he said. "We will shorten exposure."

Dietrich had been quiet, his soldier's mind still trying to reconcile an empty space with an event. Now he stepped closer, lowering his voice.

"Herr Doktor, what exactly do you want? You said bring you the paper. Do you mean… documents from whatever he saw?"

Kammler turned slightly, and Dietrich saw something in his eyes that was not excitement, not fear, but focus sharpened to a point.

"Not documents," Kammler said. "Newspapers."

The physicist frowned. “Newspapers.”

“Yes,” Kammler said. “Printed, dated, mundane. The kind of thing a civilian holds in his hands while thinking the world is stable.”

Dietrich’s mouth tightened. “Why?”

“Because a newspaper is proof,” Kammler replied. “Not of a vision. Of a place. Of a time. And if it contains information we can verify later, then the future becomes an instrument.”

The physicist’s hands flexed on his clipboard. “If you bring back newspapers, you contaminate causality.”

Kammler looked at him with mild impatience. “We already did. You watched a man vanish and return speaking syllables that are not German, not Polish, not Latin. The line is crossed. Now we decide whether we step forward or crawl backward.”

The surgeon finally lit his cigarette, hands cupped around the flame. The smoke looked too white in the floodlights. “The man said he saw paper with dates,” he murmured. “We should question him while he can still speak.”

Kammler nodded once. “Take me to him.”

They found the prisoner in a side room that had once been a storage tunnel. Now it held a cot, a table, a bucket, and two guards who stood as if guarding a contagious idea. The air smelled of disinfectant and damp stone. The prisoner lay on his back, eyes half-open, staring at nothing. His cuffs had been reattached to a metal ring on the cot frame.

When Kammler entered, the man's gaze dragged toward him as if pulled by weight. He attempted to sit up and failed, choking on his own breath.

The surgeon stepped forward, a professional mask over his fatigue. "Do not move," he told the prisoner. "You'll bleed again."

The prisoner's lips cracked into something like a smile, but it collapsed immediately into a grimace. "Bleeding is nothing," he rasped. "I thought my teeth were going to fall out."

Kammler pulled a chair close to the cot and sat with deliberate calm. He did not lean in like a sympathetic interrogator. He sat like a judge reviewing evidence.

"You said you saw paper," Kammler said. "Describe it."

The prisoner swallowed. His throat clicked. "Newspaper," he whispered. "Dirty hands holding it. Black ink. German words, but… not our

German. Some words were the same. Some were twisted."

The physicist stepped into the room behind Kammler, unable to keep away. "Dates," he said, voice tight. "What dates?"

The prisoner's eyes rolled as if the numbers were written on the inside of his skull. "Nineteen forty-one," he said. Then, after a pause, as if another image pushed through, "June. It said June."

The physicist's face tightened. It was too close, too soon, too plausible to dismiss. June 1941 was not a fantasy date; it was a future that could happen.

"What did it say?" Kammler asked.

The prisoner's breathing hitched. "Russia," he said, and the word made one guard shift his stance. "Big letters. Operation… something. Not our words. Like… like a code name."

"Barbarossa," Kammler said, not because he knew it, but because the syllables arrived in him with the same cold certainty as concrete settling into a mold. It sounded like the sort of grand historical vanity a regime would choose.

The prisoner's eyes widened a fraction. "Yes," he whispered, relief and terror mixing. "That. Barbarossa."

The surgeon watched Kammler sharply. "You guessed."

Kammler did not acknowledge it. "What did the article say?"

The prisoner's face tightened as if the memory hurt. "It said we attacked," he whispered. "It said we crossed borders like it was the most natural thing. It listed places. Smolensk. Kiev. Names I've heard in school like they were far away and dead. The paper made them close."

The physicist leaned closer, forgetting caution. "Outcomes?"

The prisoner's eyes flicked. "Victory," he said quickly. "It said victory like a promise. It said the Red Army was collapsing. It said our soldiers were heroes." Then his mouth trembled and his voice dropped. "But there were other parts. Smaller. Not on the front page. Short lines like they didn't want you to look. It said… winter. It said supply problems. It said partisans."

Dietrich muttered, "Partisans," like it tasted bad.

Kammler's face remained neutral. "You saw only one newspaper?"

The prisoner shook his head and regretted it immediately, wincing. "Stacks," he whispered. "On a table. Someone sorting them like they were nothing. Dates different. Some were the same day but looked different. Like… like the paper couldn't decide what happened."

The physicist's throat tightened. "Contradictory editions?"

The surgeon shot him a look. "Do not lead him."

Kammler's voice cut through both. "Can you bring one back?"

The prisoner stared at Kammler as if he had asked him to reach into the sun. "Bring it back?"

"Yes," Kammler said. "Not in your head. In your hands."

The prisoner's eyes watered. "I didn't choose where I went," he whispered. "It threw me. I landed on concrete that wasn't this concrete. I heard engines that didn't sound right. I saw a man with a cap I didn't recognize. Then it took me again."

Kammler sat back slightly, calculating. The prisoner had been a blunt instrument: a body tossed through an opening and returned by whatever mechanism governed the bell. To retrieve an object, he needed a different kind of exposure, a controlled excursion short enough to survive and specific enough to allow action.

He looked at the physicist. "Can you target?" he asked. "Can you narrow the corridor?"

The physicist hesitated, then answered with reluctant honesty. “We can try to bias the field. Adjust coil phasing. Introduce a timing signal. But we do not understand the medium. We are ringing something we cannot see.”

“Try,” Kammler said.

The surgeon’s cigarette trembled slightly between his fingers. “And who goes?”

Kammler’s gaze returned to the prisoner. The man looked suddenly young again despite his crimes, despite his shaved head and cuffed hands. He looked like a body realizing it had become a door.

“The next subject,” Kammler said, “will not be a prisoner.”

Dietrich stared. “You mean an SS man.”

“I mean a man who can follow instructions,” Kammler replied. “A man who can hold onto paper even while he is terrified.”

The prisoner’s breath hitched, hope flickering despite himself. “Then I’m done,” he rasped. It was not a question. It was a plea disguised as certainty.

Kammler looked at him for a long moment. “You are data,” he said. “When the machine is stable, we may have use for you again.”

The prisoner's face collapsed. He began to sob quietly, the sound thin and humiliating. One guard looked away. The other stared harder, as if refusing empathy could erase it.

Kammler stood. "Prepare a retrieval team," he told Dietrich. "Two men. Tethered. No improvisation. They are to locate newspapers, take as many as possible, and return immediately. If they encounter people, they do not speak. If they are challenged, they do not resist. The paper is more valuable than their pride."

Dietrich nodded, swallowing. "And if they don't return?"

Kammler paused at the door and glanced back once, not at the prisoner, but at the room itself, at the way the air seemed a fraction colder near the cot as if the future had left a draft.

"Then we adjust," Kammler said. "And we send more."

In the central cavern, the bell chamber hung silent again, innocent in its stillness. The coils were dark. The instruments waited with their needles poised. Men moved around it with the cautious ritual of those who had seen reality slip and snap back.

By evening, Dietrich had chosen the two men: veterans, faces carved by obedience and war games, not yet by war itself. They stood in the ring with their harnesses and their tether line, holding empty canvas sacks that would soon be filled with something impossible: tomorrow's ink.

Kammler watched them from the control bank. He did not offer speeches. He did not promise glory. He only looked at the bell as if it were a vault door and he had finally found the key.

"Power," he said.

The generators answered. The cavern deepened its hum. Shadows began to misbehave again, slipping a fraction out of loyalty. One of the SS men swallowed hard, then set his jaw as if locking his fear behind his teeth.

The air thickened. The low tone built. The painted line on the floor rippled like a surface under pressure.

The two men stepped forward together, tether tight between them, sacks clenched in their fists. Their faces held the blank determination Kammler preferred: no questions, no wonder, only the grim acceptance that the world could be forced to open.

As the resonance reached its peak, Kammler's eyes did not leave the bell chamber.

He was not watching for their disappearance.

He was already imagining the moment they returned, and the sound of paper hitting a table in the Owl Mountains like a verdict delivered by the future itself.

The two men vanished without drama.

One moment they were stepping into the central ring, tether line drawn tight between their harnesses, canvas sacks hanging empty and stiff at their sides. The next, the air where their bodies had been was simply air again, and the line that had connected them snapped into slack, dropping to the concrete with a soft, humiliating sound. No flash. No smoke. Only absence, as if the mountain itself had blinked and found them gone.

Dietrich swore under his breath. One of the technicians made a small sound that might have been a laugh if fear hadn't strangled it.

Kammler did not react. He watched the bell chamber as if it might confess. The coils continued to sing, the low tone behind the teeth and sinuses building toward a pressure that made men swallow hard. Shadows on the cavern wall slipped fractionally out of alignment with their owners and then drifted back, reluctant.

"Maintain," Kammler said.

The physicist with wire-rimmed glasses hesitated at the control bank. Sweat had gathered at his hairline despite the cold. "Herr Doktor, the insulation—"

"Maintain," Kammler repeated, and the word carried the weight of all the things Kammler had maintained in his life: schedules, secrecy, terror, structures that held only because men were forced to believe they would.

The physicist adjusted the phasing, hands moving like someone defusing a bomb he was no longer sure he wanted to survive. Needles on the instruments jittered in arguments they could not resolve. A mechanical clock on the table skipped forward three seconds, then stopped ticking entirely for half a heartbeat, then resumed as though offended.

Minutes passed the wrong way. Men shifted their weight and checked their watches and then stopped checking, because the act of looking at time felt like an insult to the room.

Then the air snapped again.

It was the same sound as before, the crack of distance collapsing into a point. Dust lifted from the concrete in a sudden spiral. Several floodlights flared brighter for a fraction of a second, not flickering, but intensifying as if the power had been pulled from somewhere else.

The two men reappeared.

They came in low, half-falling, knees slamming hard enough that one of them gasped. Their tether line was still clipped. Their sacks were no longer empty. They bulged and sagged, and paper edges stuck out at odd angles, bent and torn as if clutched in a panic.

One man vomited immediately, head dropping, shoulders heaving. The other stayed upright by pure will, eyes wide and glassy. His mouth opened, and for a moment Kammler thought he would speak in the same unknown syllables the prisoner had used.

Instead, he said, in German so flat it sounded borrowed, "It is real."

Kammler stepped forward, boots precise on the concrete, ignoring the way the air still vibrated. "Give them to me," he said.

Dietrich moved with him, half-reaching as if to help, then stopping himself as if the newspapers might be contagious. He barked at the guards. "Hold them. Don't let them fall."

The men clutched their sacks like lifelines. One tried to stand and nearly collapsed. The surgeon, summoned again from wherever he had been trying to pretend he was a physician and not a witness, hurried in and caught the man under the arm.

"Sit," the surgeon ordered. His voice was sharp, professional, almost angry with the universe. "Breathe. Slowly. You're here."

The upright man stared at Kammler as if trying to remember which world he belonged to. "They looked at us," he said hoarsely.

Kammler's eyes narrowed. "Who did?"

"People," the man whispered. "But not like people here. Their clothes. Their faces. They were… calm. Like the war was a story. Like it had already happened to someone else."

Dietrich's hand hovered near his sidearm, then fell away, useless. "You spoke?"

The man shook his head too quickly and winced. "No. We didn't speak. We took the papers and ran. The sacks—" He looked down at them with bewilderment. "They are heavy. I thought paper was light."

Kammler took the first sack and upended it onto the nearest table.

Newspapers spilled out in a flurry of gray and black, folded and crumpled, some damp as if they had been snatched from a place that smelled of rain and coal smoke. Headlines flashed past in bold type. Dates. Places. Words that made the cavern feel suddenly too small to hold them.

The physicist leaned close without permission, his fear overridden by the reflex that had made him a scientist before it made him a servant. "The ink," he murmured. "Modern printing. The registration is too precise. The paper stock—"

Kammler ignored him and began sorting.

He did not read like an ordinary man. He read like a man looking for leverage points. He flattened one front page with his palm, feeling the roughness, the cheapness, the absolute normality of it. It was a civilian object, meant to be thrown away, and that triviality was part of its power. No prophecy scroll. No mystical tablet. Something bought for coins at a kiosk.

June 30,1941.

The date sat at the top like an accusation.

Below it, in block letters that seemed to shout even under the cavern's floodlights, a headline announced the launch of an eastern campaign with the confidence of an empire narrating itself into history. The word Barbarossa appeared exactly as the prisoner had gasped it, now anchored in ink.

Kammler's gaze moved down the column. There were names of cities and rivers, lists of units, references to advances measured in kilometers, and statements of inevitability. He saw mention of Minsk, of encirclements, of divisions broken. He saw the smug tone of early victory and the careful omissions that suggested what could not be admitted yet.

Dietrich leaned in, unable to stop himself. "This… this is official language."

"It is propaganda," the physicist said automatically, as if identifying it would make it less dangerous.

"It is more than propaganda," Kammler replied. He tapped a paragraph with a gloved finger. "This includes details. Dates. Movements."

The surgeon, still steadying one of the returned men, watched Kammler with the expression of a man watching someone open a door that should remain sealed. "Details can be fabricated."

Kammler picked up a second paper, then a third.

The dates were close, but not identical. Different publications, different cities. Some were clearly German. Others were in languages Kammler did not immediately recognize, but he could read the bones of them: the same names, the same campaign, the same war described from different angles.

One paper had a photograph on the front page, grainy but unmistakable: German soldiers standing beside a sign with Cyrillic letters, smiling for the camera as if they were tourists. Another showed a map with arrows thrust eastward, the Reich rendered as a shape that could extend forever.

And then Kammler found something else.

He paused, the smallest hesitation, the kind that made men who knew him hold their breath.

It was a small column on the lower half of a front page. Not the main story. Not victory. Logistics. Weather. The mundane misery that always lived beneath grand plans.

A sentence about delayed supplies. Another about unexpected resistance. A brief mention of partisan activity disrupting rail lines.

The word winter appeared again, as the prisoner had whispered it, but here it was printed as a warning wrapped in reassurance.

Kammler felt, in the pit of his stomach, a cold clarity. The newspapers were not merely describing a future war. They were describing the shape of a trap the Reich did not yet know it was building for itself.

He turned to the returned men.

"How long were you gone?" he asked.

The man who had vomited wiped his mouth with the back of his hand, then stared at it as if surprised to see the gesture happen. "Minutes," he said weakly. "No. It felt like minutes. But my head…" He pressed his palm against his temple. "The air there was different. It smelled like gasoline and bread. Like… too many people."

The upright man swallowed hard. "We ran through a station," he whispered. "A train station. Loudspeakers. Lights. But the lights were white and harsh, not like ours. There were posters, but not with our symbols. Different symbols."

Dietrich's face tightened. "You're saying it wasn't German territory."

The man shook his head. "I don't know. I saw German words. I saw people who looked German. But there were also uniforms I didn't recognize. And cars without running boards. And a man holding a small black box to his ear, speaking into it like it was a radio, but there was no wire."

The physicist's breath caught. "Portable telephone," he murmured before he could stop himself, as if naming the impossibility would keep it from eating his mind.

Kammler did not look at him. He kept his eyes on the newspapers. On the dates.

"If this is 1941," the surgeon said slowly, "then why are they describing technology that doesn't belong to 1941?"

Silence settled, and in it the bell chamber's earlier hum seemed to echo faintly, like a memory in metal.

Kammler's fingers tightened on the paper.

He understood, suddenly, that they had not simply reached a point in the future along the same line. They had reached a future that had continued to change, accumulating inventions and outcomes and revisions. A future that looked back at 1941 like a museum exhibit.

He spread out more papers, building a mosaic across the table. His eyes moved fast now, searching for anchors.

And there, like nails hammered into a board, were names and dates that had not happened yet, but were written as though they had already become history.

Operation Barbarossa. June 22, 1941. Troop movements described with a specificity that made the present feel amateurish. Predictions disguised as reporting.

And beneath those, in smaller columns and half-buried lines, hints of things that did not fit the narrative: contradictions in casualty numbers, in the tone of later dispatches, in references to allies and enemies that shifted like a mirage when viewed from a different angle.

He lifted one paper and compared it to another from the same date.

The headlines were similar. The triumph was the same.

But the details diverged. A city taken in one was contested in the other. A unit praised in one was not mentioned in the other at all. A date in one article was off by a day, and that single day made the entire sequence of movements impossible.

The physicist saw it too and went pale. "That's not printing error," he whispered. "That's… two different outcomes."

Dietrich's voice was tight. "How can that be?"

Kammler looked up slowly, his gaze moving from the scattered newspapers to the bell chamber hanging silent in its steel ribs, to the men standing around it who suddenly looked like witnesses at an execution.

"Because we are not reading tomorrow," Kammler said. His voice was quiet, but the words carried like a blade sliding free of its sheath. "We are reading possibilities."

The surgeon stared at him. "Herr Doktor—"

Kammler cut him off with a small, decisive motion of his hand, as if closing a file. "Collect every edition," he ordered. "Photograph them. Translate what you cannot read. Cross-reference names, dates, places. I want a timetable built from this ink."

The physicist swallowed, eyes wide. "And if the ink changes? If these are not stable?"

Kammler's gaze returned to the papers. The future lay on the table in cheap pulp and black type, and for the first time he looked, not triumphant, but intent in a way that was almost wary.

"Then we will find what makes it move," he said. "And we will make it stop."

Behind him, one of the returned men began to mutter, not in an unknown language, but in German, repeating a phrase as if it were stuck in his throat.

"It already happened," he said. "It already happened."

Kammler did not turn around. He did not need to.

He had the newspapers. He had the dates. He had the impossible knowledge of a war not yet fought, written as though it had already been won and already begun to slip.

In the Owl Mountains, beneath rock and concrete, the bell had rung, and the future had answered not with a single clear voice, but with overlapping echoes.

And Kammler, holding those echoes in his hands, began to understand that prophecy was not a line.

It was a field.

Chapter 4

Futures in Flux

The table in the central cavern became an altar of cheap paper.

They cleared an entire workbench for it, pushing aside instruments that no longer felt like instruments so much as toys. Under the hard floodlights the newspapers looked brittle and gray, their edges frayed from rough handling and whatever transit had done to them. Some were folded into sharp quarters as if pocketed in haste. Others were crumpled, stained with sweat or rain, the ink slightly blurred where a thumb had smeared it.

Kammler stood over them without removing his gloves. Around him men moved with an obedience that tried to pretend it was confidence. Dietrich posted guards at the cavern entrances as if the future might attempt to walk out on its own. The physicist with wire-rimmed glasses brought in drafting paper, rulers, and a stack of logbooks. The surgeon lingered at the edge, cigarette smoke curling up to the lights and disappearing, his eyes never quite leaving the bell chamber hanging silent in its steel ribs.

"Separate by date first," Kammler ordered. "Then by publication. Then by content."

The physicist hesitated. "Content will take time."

"Then you will work quickly," Kammler said.

A technician began sorting. The dates clustered around June 1941 at first, like a swarm around a single promise. Different mastheads. Different fonts. Some papers clearly produced in German cities, others from occupied territories, some foreign. The ones not in German were passed to translators who looked as if they were being asked to decode curses.

When the first set was arranged in neat stacks, Kammler picked up two newspapers with the same date and set them side by side.

June 23, 1941.

The headlines were nearly identical in tone, both declaring the opening of the eastern campaign with triumph and righteousness. Both used the same grand phrasing, the same language of destiny. Both framed the invasion as inevitable, as if history itself had demanded it.

But the map inset was different.

On the left paper, the arrow thrust eastward from East Prussia split neatly, one branch aimed toward Minsk, the other toward the Baltic. On the right paper, the arrow was thicker, angled slightly south, and the first target city name was not Minsk at all. It was Vilnius, emphasized in bold.

The physicist leaned in, his breath fogging the air just above the paper. “That could be editorial. Different mapmaker.”

Kammler did not answer. He ran a gloved finger down the left column, then the right, stopping at a paragraph halfway down where both papers listed early objectives.

In one, a unit designation appeared: Fourth Panzer Group. In the other, it was Third.

A technician shifted uneasily. “Herr Doktor… are you certain these dates are real? Maybe they printed the date wrong.”

Kammler looked at him as if the man had asked whether gravity was negotiable. “Ink does not misprint itself into consistency,” he said.

The physicist’s voice tightened. “Different papers do make errors. Propaganda offices—”

"Propaganda offices do not change unit designations by accident," the surgeon murmured from behind them. He sounded tired rather than certain, as if the sentence cost him something.

Dietrich reached for a third paper from the same date, his fingers surprisingly careful. He held it up and squinted at the lower half, where small columns ran like afterthoughts.

"This one says the border crossings began at dawn," Dietrich said. "This one says before sunrise. Not the same thing, but close."

"Close is not stable," Kammler replied.

He took the third paper and laid it down. Then he selected a fourth and placed it beside the others. The date matched again. The headline matched again.

The casualty numbers did not.

One paper spoke of "light losses" and provided an exact figure that was low enough to reassure. Another gave a higher number and framed it as noble sacrifice. The third paper offered no number at all, only a vague reference to "expected resistance."

Kammler's gaze moved from number to number, not reading them as statistics but as the fingerprint of a reality. A lie, he understood, could be consistent if it was centrally controlled. Inconsistent lies were either incompetence or multiplicity.

He had built his career inside centrally controlled systems. He knew the texture of official deception. These contradictions did not feel like political manipulation. They felt like a scene being re-shot.

"Spread them all out," he ordered.

They did, until the table and the adjacent bench were covered. The papers overlapped, an ugly quilt of pulp and ink. Dates repeated, mastheads repeated, headlines repeated. The same events declared again and again, as if the future had to keep insisting it was real.

And then, as if the pile itself had become heavy enough to bend certainty, the contradictions multiplied.

A paper dated June 24 described Minsk as "encircled and near collapse." Another, also dated June 24, referred to fighting "west of Minsk," implying the city had already fallen. A third paper from the same day reported a fierce defense "near Brest-Litovsk," as if the initial border fortifications were still holding.

The physicist began marking with pencil on a sheet of drafting paper, building columns. Date. Location. Claim. Source.

He stopped after only a few entries. His pencil hovered in midair like a needle searching for a groove.

"This cannot all be true," he said.

Kammler's eyes did not leave the table. "Not at once."

Dietrich's face had gone slightly gray. "Could it be different regions printing the same story at different times? News delays."

The surgeon exhaled smoke through his nose. "News delays don't make a city fall twice."

A translator approached, holding one of the foreign papers with the cautious reverence of someone carrying a diseased specimen.

"This one is Polish," he said. His voice had the tightness of a man reading a text he did not want to exist. "It reports German advances, yes. But it also mentions… sabotage. Railroad lines damaged. It says partisans already active."

Dietrich's jaw clenched. "Already?"

The translator nodded. "As if it began immediately. It names a village, then it names another. It calls it a pattern."

Kammler took the paper and scanned it, understanding enough of the borrowed place names to feel the shape of it. Partisans were not merely fighters. They were a sign that a war had become something else, something that continued even when armies claimed victory.

He found another brief column in a German paper, tucked low as if ashamed: "Supply disruptions reported in rear areas."

Then another: "Unexpected resistance from irregulars."

Then, in yet another publication, a single line that made the cavern seem colder: "Rumors of mass executions denied."

The surgeon's hand tightened on his cigarette. "That line," he said quietly. "That doesn't belong in an early victory paper."

Kammler looked up, his gaze sharp. "Everything belongs if it is true in one version."

The physicist swallowed. His eyes moved over the spread like a man staring at a floor that had begun to crack. "Herr Doktor, you said earlier we were reading possibilities. That implies divergence. That implies… multiple futures."

"It implies instability," Kammler corrected.

Dietrich's voice was rough. "Instability caused by what? By us? By the bell?"

Kammler did not answer immediately. He reached for one paper, then another, comparing the small details the way a forger compared strokes.

Advertisements were different.

In one issue, there was an ad for soap with a smiling woman drawn in a style that felt familiar. In another issue from the same date and same city, the ad space was filled by a call for scrap metal donations. In a third, the entire lower quarter was blank, as if the paper had been printed in haste or under shortage.

Shortage, Kammler thought. That was not a poetic concept. It was a measurable state.

He felt something shift behind his eyes, a recognition that was not emotional but strategic: the newspapers were not simply telling him what would happen. They were telling him how fragile the told version was.

A technician who had been photographing the papers approached with a tray of developed prints, still damp at the corners. "Herr Doktor, we took images of every front page and the relevant columns. For record."

Kammler glanced at the prints. Then he looked back at the original papers.

The originals looked different from the photographs.

Not dramatically. Not enough for a casual eye. But the spacing on one headline seemed tighter. A word in a lower paragraph appeared slightly bolder than it had a moment ago, as if re-inked.

He leaned down, eyes narrowing.

The word was Kiev.

On the photograph, the paragraph read: "Advance continues toward Kiev." On the paper itself, the phrase had changed to: "Advance halted near Kiev."

Kammler did not speak. He simply held the photograph beside the paper until the technician, the physicist, and then the surgeon saw it too.

The technician's face drained of color. "That's not possible. We just developed it."

The physicist took the photo with trembling fingers and compared it again, his breath catching. "It's not a smear. It's not a printing artifact. The sentence is different."

Dietrich leaned in, his voice almost a whisper. “Did someone swap the paper?”

“No one has left the room,” the surgeon said. He sounded disgusted, as if the universe had broken etiquette.

Kammler’s gloved hand pressed flat on the newspaper, pinning it as though it might crawl away. He stared at the altered line with a kind of calm that frightened the men around him more than anger would have.

“The ink is not fixed,” he said.

The physicist looked at him, eyes wide behind wire-rims. “You mean the paper is changing now, in our hands?”

Kammler did not look away from the table. “I mean the future is not a destination we visited. It is a surface. And we have touched it.”

The bell chamber hung in the background, silent and patient. Its coils were dark, but the men had begun to treat it as if it were still humming. As if the machine had learned to resonate without power, simply because it had been taught that it could.

A guard at the entrance shifted his rifle and muttered something under his breath, then stopped when Dietrich snapped his head toward him.

“What did you say?” Dietrich demanded.

The guard's mouth worked. "Nothing, Sturmbannführer."

Dietrich stepped closer, his voice low and threatening. "Say it."

The guard swallowed. "I said… it already happened."

The phrase moved through the cavern like a draft. The returned soldier who had earlier whispered it lifted his head where he sat on a bench, staring at the papers with the same haunted recognition, as if the words belonged to him but had escaped.

Kammler straightened, finally lifting his hand from the shifting paper. He looked at the table as if it were a map of enemy territory.

"Contradictions are not errors," he said. "They are signals."

The physicist's voice cracked slightly. "Signals of what?"

Kammler's gaze moved from the altered Kiev line to the photographs, to the stacks of June issues that no longer felt like documents from a single timeline but like layers of thin skin peeled from different versions of the same body.

"Of movement," Kammler said. "Of revision. The future is adjusting to our observation."

The surgeon stared at him with something like dread. "Then every time we look, we change it."

Kammler's expression remained controlled, but his eyes held an intensity that made the words sound less like fear and more like opportunity.

"Then we stop looking like amateurs," he said. "We measure how it shifts. We find the rules. And we choose which version becomes real."

He turned to the physicist, his tone sharpening into command. "I want a catalog of contradictions. Every divergence, no matter how small. If a comma moves, you write it down. If a casualty number changes by one, you write it down. If an advertisement disappears, you write it down. The pattern is the only honest thing here."

The physicist nodded, swallowing panic. "Yes, Herr Doktor."

Dietrich opened his mouth as if to protest, then closed it again. His world was made of orders and borders. This was a war against a moving line.

Kammler looked once more at the Kiev sentence, then at the photograph that preserved its earlier form like a fossil.

The future had begun to slip under their fingers.

And in that slipping, Kammler sensed not defeat but a deeper truth: the bell was not showing them what would happen. It was showing them what could be made to happen, and what resisted being made.

In the cavern's cold light, with the bell chamber looming like a silent judge, the contradictory headlines did not read like news.

They read like warnings written by a reality that could no longer keep its story straight.

Kammler's order turned the cavern into a counting house for impossibilities.

By nightfall the workbench had been cleared again and covered not with newspapers but with grids. Drafting paper was taped down in long sheets. Rulers, compasses, and sharpened pencils lay beside stacks of photographs drying on lines strung between steel supports. The originals were placed under glass panels scavenged from instrument crates, weighted at the corners with wrenches to keep the mountain's damp from curling the pages.

The physicist with wire-rimmed glasses worked at the center of it all, his collar unbuttoned despite the cold, as if the air had become too tight. He had stopped trying to explain the contradictions aloud. Now he only recorded them.

Date. Publication. Headline wording. Map arrow thickness. Unit designation. Casualty figure. Weather mention. Advertisements. Even typography. A comma that drifted. A hyphen that appeared and then did not.

Kammler stood behind him for long stretches without speaking. His presence made men careful with their breathing. Dietrich paced the perimeter like a guard dog that could smell something through a wall but could not decide where to bite. The surgeon remained near the edge of the light, cigarette smoke rising straight up until the floodlights bleached it away.

At first, it seemed manageable. The contradictions were obvious. Minsk fell twice. Kiev advanced and halted in the same day. A line about partisan sabotage appeared in one paper and vanished in another. They could catalogue those.

Then the papers began to do something more insulting.

They began to change while being watched.

Not dramatically, not with a flare of light or a tearing sound. The shift was almost polite, as if reality were trying to revise itself without drawing attention. A phrase softened. A number adjusted by a digit. A name gained an extra letter as though the typesetter had corrected a mistake.

The first time the physicist caught it directly, he did not speak. He simply froze with his pencil above the page; his eyes locked on a small paragraph near the bottom of a June issue. His hand trembled once, the way Keller's had when the fragment refused to be set down.

The surgeon noticed and stepped closer. "What is it?"

The physicist swallowed. "It moved," he said.

"Your hand moved," Dietrich snapped, impatient with anything that sounded like weakness.

"No," the physicist said, and for the first time the word carried anger. "The line moved."

He pointed with the eraser end of his pencil. A sentence about "rail disruption in rear areas" had been underlined in red grease pencil earlier. Now the word rail was gone, replaced by communications, and the sentence ended differently, as if the paper had decided the disruption belonged to a different artery of war.

Dietrich leaned in, then looked up sharply as if expecting to find a man standing over them with a fresh edition. There was no one. Only guards at the entrances and the bell chamber hanging silent in its ribs.

Kammler did not react like a man witnessing a miracle. He reacted like a man seeing a machine behave consistently for the first time.

"Again," he said quietly.

The physicist blinked. "Herr Doktor?"

"Make it happen again."

The physicist stared at him, baffled by the demand. "I did not—"

Kammler's gaze remained on the paper. "You were looking at it. You were recording it. The moment you attempted to fix it on your grid, it revised itself."

The surgeon's cigarette paused halfway to his lips. "You think observation is causing it."

"I think the future is aware of scrutiny," Kammler said. "And I think it dislikes being pinned."

Dietrich made a sound of disgust. "It's paper."

"It is evidence," Kammler corrected. "And evidence changes behavior."

That night they designed a test that felt, in its own way, more obscene than the rabbits.

They took one newspaper that had already shown a tendency to shift and placed it under glass. They photographed it at three-minute intervals with the portable camera, using fresh plates each time. They made a stenographic copy of the same paragraphs by hand, word for word, in ink that could not be blamed on a fading pencil. They logged the time on three synchronized clocks, including the one that had once stopped for a fraction of a heartbeat near the fragment.

Then Kammler ordered everyone to look away.

For ten minutes, the men stood with their backs to the table. Guards watched the cavern entrances. Dietrich watched the guards. The surgeon watched the bell chamber as if it might speak. The physicist stared at the concrete wall until his eyes watered, as though his own will could keep reality from moving by refusing to see it.

When the ten minutes ended, Kammler said, "Now."

They turned.

The paper looked the same at a glance. The headline still shouted. The date still sat at the top like a stamped claim. The underlined paragraph still sat in the lower half.

The physicist leaned in and exhaled sharply. "It's different," he whispered.

It was a single word. The kind of change that would have meant nothing in any other context. A sentence describing an advance used the phrase "steady progress" instead of "rapid progress." A different adjective. A different pace. A different implication, like a hairline crack in concrete that told an engineer where the collapse would begin.

The physicist pulled the most recent photograph and compared it. Then he compared the earlier photograph. Then the handwritten transcript.

They did not agree anymore.

The surgeon's face tightened with something like nausea. "So it rewrites itself when we stop watching."

"No," Kammler said. "It rewrites itself when we begin watching again. The act of re-engagement triggers a correction."

Dietrich shook his head as if he could fling the idea away. "Correction to what?"

Kammler's eyes did not leave the table. "To accommodate us."

The phrase settled into the cavern like dust. Even the guards seemed to hold their breath.

The physicist looked up, his wire rims catching the floodlight. "Accommodate us how?"

Kammler finally lifted his gaze. It moved from the paper to the photographs, to the transcripts, to the men gathered around the workbench as if around a body.

"In the same way a witness alters a crime scene by entering it," Kammler said. "You cannot step into a room and pretend you have not disturbed the air."

The physicist's voice cracked. "Then we can never know what is true."

Kammler's expression remained controlled, but his eyes held a hard clarity. "We can know what is stable. Stability is what remains when we interfere with it."

He leaned forward and tapped the edge of a grid the physicist had drawn. "Mark every change. Not just what changes, but when it changes. What triggers it. Touch. Proximity. Light. Attention."

The surgeon watched him. "And if the trigger is thought?"

Kammler did not dismiss the question. He measured it, then answered with a calm that felt like cruelty.

"Then we will learn to think correctly."

They expanded the tests until the cavern felt like a laboratory devoted to the mechanics of doubt.

They placed a newspaper under bright floodlight and another in shadow. They let one be handled by gloved hands and kept another untouched. They read one aloud in German, the heavy official phrases echoing off rock, while leaving another in silence. They sealed one in a metal drawer and left another exposed beneath glass.

Each variation produced a different kind of shifting.

The paper read aloud changed faster, as if language itself were a lever. A phrase would harden into certainty while being spoken and then soften again when silence returned. The paper kept in shadow held its form longer than the one in bright light, as if illumination was not merely visibility but pressure. The paper sealed in the drawer did not change at all until the drawer opened, at which point the first line the physicist saw was no longer the one he remembered.

The clocks misbehaved too. A timepiece near the table gained six seconds over an hour while the far clock behind rock remained faithful. The physicist tried to treat it as a field effect, but it did not correlate cleanly with distance. It correlated with activity. When men argued over a contradiction, the near clock drifted harder, as if agitation fed the distortion.

Once, in the middle of a heated exchange about casualty numbers, the clock's ticking went quiet for a full second.

In that silence, the surgeon heard a sound that did not belong to the cavern.

A faint rustle, like paper being turned by a careful hand.

He looked up sharply. So did Dietrich. So did the guards at the entrance, hands tightening around rifles that had never felt so useless.

The table was still. No pages moved under glass. No draft crossed the cavern. The floodlights did not flicker.

The surgeon exhaled slowly. "Did you hear that?"

Dietrich's jaw worked. "No."

One of the returned soldiers, sitting on a bench near the wall with a blanket around his shoulders, looked up with the same haunted recognition as before. His mouth moved.

"It already happened," he whispered, not as a warning this time, but as if repeating it might anchor him.

The physicist wiped sweat from his upper lip. "This is not a library," he said. "This is a… a live system."

Kammler looked toward Die Glocke in the background, its polished curve catching the light without reflecting it properly. The bell chamber had been silent since the retrieval. Kammler had insisted it remain unpowered while they studied the papers. Yet the air around it never felt entirely dead. The mountain itself seemed to remember the resonance.

"A live system," Kammler repeated, and there was something almost satisfied in the way he said it. "Good. Then it responds. And if it responds, it can be trained."

The physicist stared at him, horrified. "Trained?"

Kammler's gaze returned to the table. "The future is shifting because it is not fixed. It is resisting fixation. Like an animal that refuses a harness until it learns there is no escape."

The surgeon's cigarette trembled slightly, ash elongating and refusing to fall. "You speak as if it has intent."

Kammler did not answer immediately. His eyes moved over the newspapers spread like skins, each one a thin slice of a world that might exist. He thought of Schreiber vanishing into a corridor that had not been there before. Of the prisoner returning with blood and syllables. Of the craft healing itself as if injury were a minor inconvenience.

Of the way the bell's resonance had made shadows detach from their owners.

"Intent is irrelevant," Kammler said at last. "Behavior is enough."

Dietrich stepped closer, voice low. "Herr Doktor, even if we map the shifts, what then? We can't fight a moving line."

Kammler looked up, and Dietrich saw something in his eyes that made him feel, for a moment, like the subordinate he was. Not because Kammler was louder or stronger, but because Kammler's certainty had found a new foundation.

"We do not fight it," Kammler said. "We select from it."

He reached down, lifted a newspaper whose headline declared victory with clean confidence, and set it beside another whose smaller print hinted at delays, shortages, winter.

Two futures on a table.

"We find the version that serves us," Kammler continued, voice quiet and absolute. "And then we make it the one that holds."

The physicist swallowed, eyes darting between the papers as if they were mines. "And if holding one version collapses another?"

Kammler's gloved fingers smoothed the edge of the paper, flattening it as if flattening the world beneath it. "Then that is simply the cost of building," he said.

As he spoke, a line of print on the second paper tightened, the ink darkening by a fraction, as though the sentence had decided it needed to be more definitive. The physicist saw it and flinched. The surgeon saw it and went still.

Kammler did not flinch.

He watched the shifting like a man watching wet concrete settle into a mold. Not fearing the movement, but learning its timing, its limits, the way it could be forced into shape.

Above them, unseen beyond rock and war and weather, the world marched toward the dates stamped on the papers. But down here, in the Owl Mountains, the future had become something that could slide under a fingertip.

And as the timelines shifted, Kammler began to understand the deeper danger.

Not that the future was unstable.

But that it was listening for whoever learned how to speak to it first.

Kammler sent the others away in shifts, not out of mercy but out of need. Exhaustion made men careless. Carelessness made noise. And noise, he had said, invited attention.

By midnight only the essential remained in the central cavern: the physicist with wire-rimmed glasses bent over his grids until his handwriting began to crawl, the surgeon sitting on a crate with his cigarette forgotten and burning down to a long ash, and Dietrich pacing in a slow square that never brought him too close to the table of newspapers.

The floodlights stayed on. The mountain did not sleep.

Kammler stood alone at the workbench for a long time without touching anything. He watched the papers under glass as if waiting for them to betray themselves again. He listened to the cavern's ordinary sounds and the not-ordinary ones beneath them: the faint settling creaks of steel ribs, the distant drills, the occasional pop of cooling cable insulation. And, threaded through it all, the memory of resonance. Even unpowered, Die Glocke seemed to mark the air with a pressure the body could not fully forget.

"Read this," Kammler said at last.

The physicist looked up too quickly. His eyes were red-rimmed, but the reflex to obey was still intact. "Which one, Herr Doktor?"

Kammler slid a photograph across the bench. It showed a front page they had retrieved earlier, the version in which the advance toward Kiev was described as continuing. He did not hand him the original under glass. He handed him the fossil, the preserved earlier truth.

The physicist scanned it, then reached for the corresponding original and compared it through the glass panel. The sentence no longer matched. His mouth tightened.

"It's still different," the physicist said. "It hasn't reverted."

Kammler nodded, as if confirming a measurement. "Now read the second paragraph aloud."

The physicist hesitated. "Herr Doktor, reading aloud accelerates shifts. We observed—"

"Read it," Kammler said.

The physicist lowered his gaze and began, voice rough in the cavern. The German was official and inflated, built from certainty and destiny. The words echoed off the rock and returned thinner, as if the mountain itself found them embarrassing.

Halfway through the paragraph the physicist stopped.

Dietrich froze mid-step. The surgeon's eyes lifted, focusing without understanding why.

"What?" Kammler asked.

The physicist stared at the paper as if it were breathing. "It's changing as I speak," he said.

"Describe."

The physicist swallowed. "The phrasing is hardening. It's becoming… more absolute. Where it said, 'expected resistance,' it now says 'insignificant resistance.' It's adjusting to the tone."

Kammler watched the line under the glass. The ink did not flow. The paper did not ripple. There was no theatricality. Only the undeniable fact is that the sentence was not the same sentence it had been ten minutes ago.

"Stop," Kammler said.

The physicist's voice cut off. Silence returned quickly, heavy with the sense that something had been interrupted.

For a moment nothing moved. Then a small change occurred anyway, almost spiteful in its subtlety: a punctuation mark in the lower column shifted position, a comma sliding as if to alter the rhythm of a lie.

The physicist let out a breath that sounded like he had been holding it for hours. "It doesn't need our voices," he whispered. "It changes regardless."

"It changes differently," Kammler corrected.

Dietrich resumed pacing, slower now. "You're saying it reacts to what we do."

"I'm saying it reacts," Kammler replied.

The surgeon flicked ash into a tin tray, his hand steady by habit. "Reacting suggests awareness."

Kammler's gaze remained on the papers, but his attention was elsewhere too, split the way it had been since the Black Forest. He thought of Schreiber's finger brushing the living interface, the way the lamp had flickered as if the craft resented illumination. He thought of the corridor that had not been there until it wanted to be. Of the empty harness, straps cut cleanly as though by a blade that understood human materials.

He did not believe in ghosts. He believed in mechanisms. But mechanisms could be designed by minds. And minds could watch.

"You have seen the shifts," Kammler said. "You have measured them. That is enough."

The physicist straightened slightly, hopeful that the night might finally end. "Then we have proof the future is unstable."

Kammler looked at him, and the physicist faltered. There was something in Kammler's expression that was not anger or triumph. It was a narrowness, a tightening around the eyes that signaled calculation under strain.

"Not simply unstable," Kammler said. "Unreliable."

Dietrich stopped again. "Those are the same thing."

"No," Kammler said softly. "Unstable is a bridge that sways but can be crossed if you know its motion. Unreliable is a bridge that chooses when you fall."

The surgeon watched him closely now. "And you think it chooses."

Kammler did not answer immediately. He reached under the table and pulled out the catalog sheet the physicist had been building, the one filled with contradictions like a ledger of competing realities. He laid it flat and ran a gloved finger down the column of dates, then across to the notes: Minsk encircled, Minsk fallen, Minsk contested. Kiev advanced, Kiev halted. Winter mentioned early, winter omitted, winter framed as irrelevant.

He stopped at a small entry from an issue they had not discussed aloud much, because it had felt like a splinter. A brief line about executions, denied. A rumor printed and immediately smothered.

Kammler's finger stayed on it.

Dietrich noticed. "Why does that matter? Rumors are always printed."

"This rumor exists in some versions and not in others," Kammler said. "Which means in some versions it became visible enough to require denial."

The physicist frowned, following the logic. "Visibility implies consequences."

Kammler nodded once. The denial was not about morality. It was about control. A regime denied only what threatened its own narrative. The future newspapers were not merely reporting outcomes. They were recording which lies held and which began to fracture.

"You said earlier we choose the version that serves us," Dietrich reminded him, as if repeating it could restore the certainty of it.

Kammler looked up then, and for the first time tonight his gaze left the papers and landed on Die Glocke itself. The bell chamber hung silent, massive and polished, its curve swallowing light rather than returning it. It had been built to contain and shape something that did not behave like matter. Yet it sat there with the calm of a weapon that had already been fired and was waiting to be fired again.

Kammler spoke, and his voice was quieter than before. "Serve us."

The phrase sounded strange in his mouth, as if he had tasted a word and found it less solid than expected.

The physicist shifted uncomfortably. "Herr Doktor?"

Kammler turned back to the papers. "These newspapers describe victories," he said. "Advance. Encirclement. Collapse. And still, they contain the seeds of failure. Not because the authors were honest, but because the future cannot erase everything without rewriting itself entirely."

The surgeon's cigarette paused on its way to his lips. "Failure."

Dietrich's face hardened. "That is defeatist talk."

Kammler's eyes flicked to him, cold and assessing. "It is arithmetic."

Dietrich's jaw clenched, but he did not speak. He was an SS officer, trained to fear ideology more than truth, but the papers on the table were not rumors. They were printed dates. They were columns of ink that moved when you watched them, yes, but they still carried a weight Dietrich could feel even if he could not name it.

The physicist leaned forward, voice strained. "If the future is shifting, then our actions now may influence which version becomes dominant. That is what you want. That is why we built the machine."

Kammler listened, then said something that made the cavern feel suddenly colder.

"And if our actions are not the only influence?"

Dietrich stared. "What else is there? The enemy doesn't have this."

Kammler did not look at him when he answered. His gaze stayed on a spot near the bottom of one of the pages where, earlier, the surgeon had claimed to hear paper turning by a careful hand.

"The future is not empty," Kammler said. "It contains observers. The moment we touched it, it began to react as if we were not alone in the room."

The physicist's throat bobbed. "That is conjecture."

Kammler nodded slightly. "So was time travel. Until the prisoner returned with blood on his mouth and syllables not his own."

The surgeon exhaled smoke slowly. "You think something is pushing back."

"I think something is correcting," Kammler replied. "And I do not know whether it corrects to preserve itself, or to mislead us, or simply because our presence disturbs a structure that was never meant to bear our weight."

Dietrich made a harsh sound. "You've never doubted a structure before."

The words escaped Dietrich before he could stop them. The surgeon glanced at him, surprised by the intimacy of the accusation. The physicist went still, as if expecting punishment.

Kammler did not strike Dietrich. He did not even raise his voice. He simply stood there with the papers and let the silence widen until it became a corridor in its own right.

Then he spoke, and the admission was so controlled it barely qualified as one.

"I do not doubt the need," Kammler said. "I doubt the promise."

The physicist blinked. "The promise of what?"

Kammler's gloved hand touched the edge of the catalog sheet, not quite trembling, but pressing harder than necessary. "That knowledge equals control," he said. "That if we can see the future, we can own it. These papers do not behave like property. They behave like bait."

Dietrich's eyes narrowed. "Bait for whom?"

Kammler looked back at Die Glocke. The bell chamber did not move. But the shadows near its base seemed, for a fraction of a second, to sit slightly wrong on the concrete, as if the light had decided to tell a different story.

"For us," Kammler said.

The physicist's face tightened with sudden understanding and fear. "If the future reacts to our observation, it could shape what we retrieve. It could show us victories to lure us into committing to them, or conceal the true points of collapse."

The surgeon's voice was quiet, almost bitter. "Or it could be indifferent and we are only watching ourselves break the world."

Kammler stared at the bell, and something in him tightened further, not with panic but with an unfamiliar constraint. He had always trusted systems because systems could be enforced. Concrete cured. Steel held. Men broke predictably if pressure was applied correctly.

But this was not steel. This was not men. This was a field that edited itself.

In the Black Forest, the craft had taken Schreiber without effort. In the Owl Mountains, Die Glocke had returned men with tomorrow's ink, and that ink had begun to rewrite itself as though ashamed of being seen.

Kammler's doubt was not moral. It was structural. It was the realization that the foundation beneath his certainty might not be bedrock. It might be something alive.

He reached for one of the papers, then stopped short of touching the glass, as if his fingertips had suddenly remembered the warmth of the hull and the pulse beneath it.

"Tomorrow," Kammler said, voice returning to command because command was the only language he trusted, "we retrieve again. Different date. Different location. We test whether the contradictions follow us, or whether they are being arranged for us."

Dietrich nodded automatically. The physicist hesitated, then nodded too, because he did not know how to refuse without becoming disposable.

The surgeon watched Kammler, eyes narrowed. “And if you find it is being arranged?”

Kammler’s gaze stayed on the bell. “Then we stop pretending we are the first to discover this,” he said. “And we plan accordingly.”

The surgeon held his cigarette, ash finally falling into the tray in a soft collapse. “Plan against what?”

Kammler did not answer at once. He listened again, and for a moment he thought he heard it: that faint rustle, paper turned by a hand that was not present.

He could not prove it. He could not measure it. And that, more than any contradiction on the table, was what unsettled him.

“Against being used,” Kammler said finally.

Then he turned away from the table and walked toward the edge of the central ring where the floodlights did not quite reach. Behind him, the papers lay under glass, their ink waiting.

In the shadowed corner of the cavern, Kammler paused, and for the first time since the Black Forest he allowed himself a thought he had always disciplined out of existence.

Not fear of death.

Fear of irrelevance.

If the future could rewrite itself, then it could also write around him. If something else was listening, then it might not care about the Reich, or victory, or any of the grand narratives men killed for. It might only care about the act of interference itself, and the way interference could be cultivated into a harvest.

Kammler's doubt did not soften him. It sharpened him.

He left the others in the light and stood in the dark long enough to feel the mountain's weight above him, the concrete and steel and secrecy he had built. He imagined Schreiber somewhere beyond corridors, somewhere outside coordinates, and felt nothing like guilt. Only the quiet understanding that the first men taken had not been punished.

They had been selected.

And selection meant criteria.

Kammler returned to the table without speaking, lifted the catalog sheet, and with a pencil he did not usually allow himself to touch, drew a single new column at the far right. He labeled it with one word.

Observer.

Then he set the pencil down as if it had burned him, and ordered the night shift to continue recording everything, including the smallest sounds, because now even silence had become suspect.

Chapter 5

The Vatican Ultimatum

Kammler left the Owl Mountains the way he had left the Black Forest: without ceremony, without farewell, and without allowing anyone to mistake departure for retreat.

The cavern remained lit behind him, the bell chamber hanging in its ribs of steel like a captive organ, the table of newspapers sealed beneath glass as if glass could keep a future from breathing. The physicist with wire-rimmed glasses had tried to speak when Kammler announced he would be gone for an indeterminate number of days. His mouth opened on a sentence that would have been half caution, half plea. Kammler silenced him with a look.

"You will continue," he said. "Catalog every shift. Every contradiction. And you will add to my new column."

The physicist's eyes dropped to the sheet where Kammler had written Observer in hard pencil. The word looked wrong among the measured headings, like a superstition smuggled into a laboratory.

Dietrich had followed Kammler into the corridor outside the central cavern, boots striking concrete with a soldier's impatience. He waited until the hum of machinery and the low murmur of technicians faded behind the bend of rock.

"You're going to Berlin," Dietrich said, already constructing the orders in his head. "To the Reichsführer. Or to the Chancellery."

"No," Kammler replied.

Dietrich slowed half a step, thrown off balance by a simple refusal. "Then where?"

Kammler's gloved hand rested for a moment on the cold wall, feeling the mountain's damp seep into the leather. It was not a gesture of fatigue. It was an act of calibration, as if he were making sure the world was still solid.

"I am going to Rome," he said.

Dietrich's mouth tightened. "The Italians?"

"The Vatican," Kammler said, and let the word settle.

Dietrich stopped walking entirely. In the corridor's harsh light, his face looked briefly unmasked, less officer than man. "Why?"

Kammler turned his head, eyes level. "Because the papers are moving," he said. "Because the future behaves like a witness that changes its testimony. And because there are institutions older than the Reich that have practiced controlling testimony for centuries."

Dietrich's jaw worked. "You think the Church can stabilize it."

"I think the Church understands leverage," Kammler replied. "And I think it understands fear. Not human fear. Metaphysical fear. The kind that makes men obey even when no rifle is pointed at them."

Dietrich hesitated, then said what he feared was disloyalty but sounded like it anyway. "Or you think they already know."

Kammler's gaze did not flicker. "I think if anyone has heard a voice in the dark and built a structure around it, it is Rome."

He resumed walking, and Dietrich fell in beside him again, still uneasy. They emerged into the outer tunnels where the air was colder and smelled of oil and wet rock instead of metallic sweetness. The closer they got to the surface compound, the more ordinary the world pretended to become: generators, trucks, shouted orders, the steady rhythm of forced labor. Ordinary violence. Familiar tools.

Kammler did not allow himself to feel relief at the familiar. The newspapers had cured him of it.

In his quarters aboveground, he prepared what he would take like a man assembling an indictment.

He chose three newspapers from the June 1941 cluster, each with the same date and the same bold headline, each with contradictions that could not be dismissed as editorial. He chose photographs of the pages taken before they shifted, the fossilized versions the camera had trapped. He chose the physicist's grids, copied onto clean sheets in careful hand, the list of divergences and triggers. He included one log entry from the living tests, the technician's phrase: "It already happened." Not because it proved anything, but because it showed pattern, the way men's perception had been dragged forward like a hooked fish.

He did not take the alien fragment. He did not take any part of the hull. That material had its own gravity, and he would not risk drawing that attention into the open world where it could not be contained by rock.

He packed the documents into a black case with reinforced corners; the kind of case used for engineering instruments and secret weapons prototypes. Dietrich watched from the doorway, arms crossed.

"And what do you tell them?" Dietrich asked. "The Pope does not take meetings because a German engineer has strange paper."

Kammler snapped the case shut. "I will not ask for a meeting," he said. "I will present a necessity."

Dietrich exhaled through his nose. "Rome is not occupied territory."

"No," Kammler said, and his voice held a faint edge. "That is why it is useful."

Before dawn, a convoy carried Kammler away from the mountain. The road down through the Owl Mountains was narrow and slick with frost, trees standing black and patient on either side. They passed villages still sleeping beneath curfew and poverty, the kind of places where men kept their heads down because lifting them invited attention. In the distance, the sky had the bruised color of an approaching winter.

Kammler rode in the back seat of a staff car, the case on the seat beside him like a second passenger. Dietrich sat in front, silent, eyes scanning mirrors and roadside shadows. The driver did not speak. No one joked. Jokes belonged to men who believed tomorrow would resemble today.

The Reich's infrastructure carried them efficiently at first: checkpoints that snapped to attention, roads cleared ahead, papers stamped without reading. Then, as they moved south and west, the world changed texture. Borders were not lines here but moods, each one demanding its own performance of authority. In occupied cities, posters shouted in multiple languages. In rail stations, soldiers slept sitting up with rifles between their knees. Women moved with their eyes lowered, clutching baskets that looked too light. Priests passed through crowds like dark stains, heads bowed, faces unreadable.

At a junction outside Vienna, the staff car joined a small column headed for Italy under diplomatic cover. Dietrich had arranged the documents with bureaucratic care: travel orders signed by men whose names carried weight, seals that implied consequences, a thin veneer of official necessity. Kammler did not enjoy the pretense, but he understood its function. Even the SS used costumes when the audience demanded it.

By the time they crossed the Alps, the air had changed. The cold sharpened, thin and clean, and for a moment the mountain passes felt like the Owl Mountains' older, quieter cousins. Snow clung to rock faces. Pine forests stretched down into valleys like dark wool. The world looked indifferent to war at this height, and that indifference irritated Kammler more than ruined cities ever had. It reminded him that human conflict was not the only scale of reality.

He slept for short periods with his gloved hand resting on the case, waking with the same image pressing behind his eyes: printed headlines sliding under glass, commas migrating like insects, the word Kiev changing from advance to halt as if a hand had reached back through paper and rewritten the sentence.

In northern Italy, the roads filled with different uniforms. Italian soldiers in gray-green watched convoys with expressions that hovered between pride and exhaustion. Fascist banners hung from buildings like declarations that had to be repeated because belief alone was not sufficient. Dietrich handled the interactions with practiced contempt masked as politeness. Kammler remained still, a man traveling not to negotiate but to deliver a problem.

Rome arrived in layers: first the outskirts where ancient stones and modern propaganda leaned uneasily against each other, then the crowded streets where motorcycles wove through traffic like insects, then the buildings whose facades carried the weight of centuries. War had not cracked the city the way it had cracked others. Rome carried itself with an old confidence, as if it had outlasted too many empires to fear this one.

Kammler looked out the car window as they moved toward Vatican City. He saw churches rising among apartments, their domes and bell towers asserting a geometry that predated the Reich's symbols and would likely outlast them. He saw priests walking in pairs, heads close together, speaking softly. He saw civilians kneeling in open doorways, lighting candles as casually as if the world were not on fire.

It was not piety that struck him. It was infrastructure. The Church had built an empire of ritual that functioned even under occupation, even under threat. It was a system designed to persist.

Dietrich leaned back slightly in his seat, voice low. "You're certain this is wise."

Kammler's eyes remained on the passing streets. "Wise is a word for men who have time," he said. "We have instability."

"And if they refuse to see you?" Dietrich asked.

Kammler's reflection in the window glass looked like a ghost superimposed over Rome's stone. "Then I will make refusal expensive."

The car approached the Vatican walls, and the atmosphere shifted again. The guards at the gates wore Swiss uniforms, small and crisp, almost theatrical in their precision. The sight of them should have been absurd against the SS escort behind Kammler. Instead, it felt like a reminder: there were still places in Europe where German authority had to knock rather than kick.

Dietrich presented papers. The Swiss Guards accepted them with the cool reserve of men trained to stand their ground without performing aggression. A Vatican official in dark clothing arrived, glanced at Kammler, then at the case, then back at Kammler's face with cautious disdain.

"You have requested an audience?" the official asked in German that carried a Roman accent like a blade wrapped in velvet.

Kammler stepped out of the car, boots on cobblestone. The air smelled different here, less exhaust, more stone warmed by sun and old incense lingering in porous walls.

"I have not requested," Kammler said. "I have come to speak with the Holy Father."

The official's eyes narrowed. "That is not how this works."

Kammler's hand rested on the handle of the case. He did not lift it. He did not open it. He simply held it as a fact.

"It will work," he said, voice level, "because what I carry is not a political matter. It is not even a military matter. It is a matter of time."

The official stared at him for a long moment, as if deciding whether this was arrogance, madness, or something more dangerous.

Then he said, coldly, "You will wait."

Kammler did not argue. He did not plead. He let them lead him into a holding room within the Vatican's outer administrative spaces, a room furnished with polite chairs and a crucifix on the wall that looked like it had watched men make threats for centuries and found them repetitive.

Dietrich remained with him, two SS men at the door like a warning. The Vatican official vanished down a corridor.

Minutes passed. Then more.

Kammler sat with his back straight, the case on the floor by his boot. He stared at the crucifix, not with reverence but with assessment. A man nailed to wood, an empire built on the story of it. If proof existed, the Church had made a profession out of deciding who was allowed to see it.

Dietrich leaned close, voice barely audible. "They're testing you."

Kammler's eyes did not move from the crucifix. "Let them," he said. "They will learn that I do not come here to be tested."

Outside, bells rang somewhere in the city, their sound drifting faintly through thick stone. For a moment it reminded Kammler of Die Glocke, of resonance building behind the teeth. Then the sound softened into something older and human.

Kammler's fingers tightened once on his knee, a small betrayal of tension. He could not shake the sensation that the Observer he had named on his grid might be listening even here, amused by the idea that he could hide his intentions behind Vatican walls.

He waited anyway.

Because this, he understood, was also an experiment.

If Rome delayed him, it meant Rome feared him, or did not believe him, or believed and wanted to control the terms. Any of those outcomes would tell him something. And if the future had become a field that shifted under observation, then this was the next question he would ask it with his own body.

How much would the oldest power in Europe move, when Kammler finally knocked hard enough?

The waiting room's politeness curdled with every passing minute.

Kammler sat without shifting, his posture so controlled it looked rehearsed. The crucifix on the wall held its fixed agony, a body made into a symbol by repetition. Dietrich stood near the window, hands behind his back, watching a slice of courtyard where Vatican personnel moved with contained urgency that never became haste. The two SS men at the door stayed rigid, the black of their uniforms an insult among the Vatican's muted cloth and stone.

A half hour passed. Then another.

The Vatican official returned once, not to escort them, but to deliver a message with the careful stiffness of someone handling a dangerous animal through glass.

"His Holiness is occupied," he said. "You will be received when it is possible."

Kammler did not look at him. "No."

The official's eyes narrowed. "Excuse me?"

Kammler's gaze remained on the crucifix. "It is possible now," he said. "You have decided it is inconvenient."

Dietrich saw the small movement at the corner of the official's mouth, the flicker of offended pride. "You are in Vatican City, Herr… Doctor. You are not in one of your mountain facilities."

Kammler finally turned his head. His eyes were calm, almost bored, and that calm made the sentence sharper than shouting. "That is precisely why I am here," he said. "Because you believe your walls create a different physics."

The official drew a breath as if to reply, then checked himself. He looked past Kammler to Dietrich, then to the SS men at the door, weighing the scene as a political equation.

"You will wait," he said again, and left.

Dietrich leaned in, voice low. "They'll stall until night if they can."

Kammler's hand rested on the case handle. "Then we remove their ability to stall."

Dietrich hesitated. He knew Kammler's vocabulary well enough to hear what was implied in that simple phrase. "In the Vatican?"

Kammler stood. The chair legs made a brief scrape on stone. The sound seemed to carry farther than it should have.

"Yes," Kammler said. "Here. In front of their saints. In front of their tourists. In front of their God."

Dietrich's jaw tightened. "You can't shoot your way into an audience with the Pope."

Kammler did not answer the sentence as asked. He gave Dietrich a different truth. "I do not need to shoot my way in," he said. "I need to make refusal cost something they cannot afford."

He moved to the door. The SS men straightened, expecting orders. The Swiss Guards at the far end of the corridor watched with statuesque composure, but their hands shifted subtly on their halberds, the movement of men trained to look ceremonial while preparing for violence.

A Vatican gendarme stepped forward. "You are not permitted beyond this point."

Kammler's gaze met his. The gendarme saw, in that look, the absence of negotiation. Not rage. Not excitement. Only a mind that had already placed him into a category of obstacle.

Kammler spoke in a tone that had sent men into pits and tunnels without ever raising his voice. "Bring your superior," he said.

"I can call—"

"Now," Kammler said, and the word cut.

The gendarme glanced toward the Swiss Guards as if seeking support, found none, then retreated quickly, footsteps clipped and offended.

Dietrich followed Kammler down the corridor, boots loud against stone. He kept close, protective by habit, but his expression carried a tension that was not fear for himself. It was fear of optics, of scandal, of how quickly a single misstep in Rome could turn into a diplomatic fire that burned beyond control.

They reached a threshold where the building opened into an outer administrative courtyard. Sunlight hit them with a warm weight, the air smelling of stone, wax, and something faintly floral from nearby gardens. Beyond an arched passageway, through layered gates, St. Peter's Square lay like a great pale bowl, already filling with afternoon visitors.

The Vatican official arrived at a near run, his composure strained. "What are you doing?"

Kammler stopped. “I am being received,” he said.

“You will not—”

Kammler glanced toward the arched passageway. “Open the gate.”

The official went still, as if the phrase itself were profanity. “Absolutely not.”

Kammler looked past him at the Swiss Guards, then back. “Then you will accompany me through it,” he said. “Or I will go through without your consent.”

Dietrich spoke for the first time, voice carefully neutral. “We are under diplomatic cover. We are not here to create disorder.”

Kammler did not look at him. “Disorder is already here,” he said, and lifted the case slightly, just enough to make the weight and purpose of it visible. “It is in this. You are all pretending you can decide when to hear it.”

The official’s eyes flicked to the case with visible discomfort. “You are threatening the Holy See.”

Kammler’s mouth tightened into something that was not a smile. “No,” he said. “I am threatening you with your own delay.”

Dietrich heard the difference immediately. Kammler was not bluffing with vague intimidation. He was positioning delay itself as the trigger, as though time were a fuse the Vatican had chosen to light by refusing him.

They moved forward. Not fast. Kammler never hurried. He advanced at a pace that forced the world to either make room or collide.

Two Swiss Guards stepped into the archway, halberds held diagonally, crossed to block passage. Their uniforms were vivid, an old pageant made serious by the men inside it. Their faces were composed, but their eyes tracked Kammler's SS escort with hard clarity.

"Halt," one said in German. "You cannot proceed."

Kammler stopped close enough that the guard could see the fine dust still ground into the seams of Kammler's gloves, the residue of a mountain that had become a laboratory. Kammler's voice stayed quiet.

"You are guarding a door," he said. "Not a world."

The guard did not flinch. "You will return to the waiting room."

Kammler turned his head slightly, addressing the Vatican official without raising his voice. "Bring me the Pope," he said, "or bring me the square."

The official's face flushed. "This is madness."

Kammler nodded once, as if confirming a diagnostic. "Then you understand."

He gestured with two fingers. Dietrich stiffened, then signaled the SS men behind them. Two more SS personnel, previously kept at distance to avoid drawing attention, emerged from the courtyard shadows where they had been waiting, dressed in uniforms that made Vatican stone look suddenly fragile.

They did not draw weapons yet. The restraint was deliberate. It made the threat clearer, not less. It said they had not come to explode into chaos; they had come with a plan.

The Swiss Guards tightened their stance. Halberds remained crossed. Their hands stayed steady. The old ceremonial blades, polished bright, looked suddenly useful.

Kammler looked toward the Vatican official again. "Do you know what the Reich does with delays?" he asked.

The official swallowed. "I know what the Reich does to civilians."

"Good," Kammler said, and began walking again, forcing the moment.

It happened quickly then, not in a cinematic rush but in the sudden alignment of men who had been waiting for permission to become dangerous.

One Swiss Guard shifted his halberd, not striking, but preparing to block with force. An SS man stepped forward in response, his hand going to his belt. The Vatican gendarme shouted something in Italian, more alarm than command. For a breath the courtyard filled with overlapping languages, a confusion of authority.

Kammler cut through it with a single sentence, spoken not loudly, but with enough clarity that it acted like a switch.

"Bring me witnesses," he said.

Dietrich's eyes flicked to him, startled. "Herr Doktor—"

Kammler did not explain. Explanations were for subordinates. He turned slightly, addressing the SS men. "Outside," he ordered. "Now."

They moved through the archway not by breaking the Swiss Guards, but by making the Swiss Guards choose. A halberd could block a man's chest; it could not block the inevitability of a scene in front of thousands. The Swiss Guards retreated a step, then another, not out of fear, but out of calculation. Their duty was to protect the Pope, not to stage a massacre in a courtyard.

The gate opened.

Sunlight widened. Sound changed. The square's ambient noise poured in: footsteps on stone, distant voices, the occasional laugh, the rumble of Rome beyond the walls. It was the sound of normal life pressing against sacred architecture, unaware of the violence that could be summoned with a word.

Kammler stepped out with Dietrich and the SS men.

St. Peter's Square sprawled before them, bright and open, lined with columns that held the sky like a disciplined crowd. Tourists drifted in clusters, priests moved like dark punctuation marks among lighter clothing, and civilians from Rome crossed the space with baskets and packages, using the Vatican's vastness as a thoroughfare.

Dietrich's voice dropped to a warning. "This is insanity. Cameras, foreigners—"

Kammler's eyes swept the square. He did not look for cameras. He looked for leverage.

"There," he said quietly.

Near the edge of the square, just beyond a line where Vatican guards typically blended into routine, a group of civilians stood waiting beside a side entrance: a man in a work jacket, an older woman with a scarf pulled tight around her hair, two younger women with paper-wrapped parcels. They looked like ordinary Romans, caught in some bureaucratic pause. Their faces turned as the SS men approached, first with confusion, then with immediate fear, the kind that arrived fully formed without explanation.

Dietrich's stomach tightened. He knew where this was going. He also knew that, once it began, nothing about it would be contained by the Vatican's walls.

The SS men moved with practiced efficiency, not rough but absolute. They herded the civilians away from the entrance, toward a blank stretch of stone near a low wall, where the background would be clean and visible to anyone watching. One of the younger women protested, voice rising. The older woman clutched her scarf and began to pray under her breath, her lips moving fast.

The man in the work jacket lifted his hands, palms out. "Che cosa volete?" he demanded, then switched to broken German. "What do you want?"

Dietrich stepped forward, as if he could intercept the moment by force of will. “Herr Doktor, stop. This is the Vatican.”

Kammler looked at him, and the look held no cruelty, only the cold arithmetic he had voiced in the mountain. “That is why it will work,” he said.

The civilians were lined against the stone, not as neatly as soldiers, but close enough that the message was unmistakable. One of the SS men raised his rifle, not aiming yet, but holding it at the ready, the posture of execution practiced in places where no one wrote down names.

The square noticed.

Voices shifted. A few tourists slowed, then stopped entirely. A priest in black froze mid-step, his face draining of color as he recognized the uniforms. A Vatican guard further away began to move faster, signaling with his hand, urgency spreading like a ripple.

The Vatican official stood behind Kammler now, breathing hard, his composure finally cracking. “You cannot do this,” he hissed. “You cannot bring that into the square.”

Kammler turned his head slightly. His voice stayed calm, pitched to carry just enough.

"I can," he said. "And I will, unless you bring me the Holy Father."

The official's mouth worked soundlessly, as if trying to form a response that could compete with a rifle.

Dietrich felt, with sudden clarity, why Kammler had come to Rome at all. Not simply for the Pope's help. For the demonstration of will. For the proof that even here, in the center of the Church's self-story, fear could still be installed like a device and turned on.

Kammler looked at the lined civilians. Their faces shone with a panic that made them more human than any of the men in uniform. The younger woman whispered something that sounded like a plea to the Virgin. The man in the work jacket stared at Kammler with hatred that was impotent, pure, and therefore heartbreaking.

Kammler did not care about the hatred. He cared about what it forced others to do.

He spoke again, quiet and deliberate, to the Vatican official.

"You have one minute," he said.

Then he raised his voice just enough to be heard by the nearest clusters of onlookers, by the priest frozen mid-step, by the Vatican guards now hurrying toward them.

"This is not a negotiation," Kammler announced. "This is an ultimatum. You will bring me the Pope. Or you will watch your sanctuary become another wall."

And as the words settled, Dietrich saw the oldest trick in Kammler's arsenal deployed in the most sacred place in Europe.

Procedure.

Countdown.

Fear made public.

The square held its breath, and the Vatican, forced into the open, had to decide whether it would meet him as a sovereign power or as a witness to an execution it could not undo.

The minute did not feel like a minute.

It felt like the air between a rifle and a ribcage, stretched thin and held there by will.

Kammler stood with the black case at his side, his posture unchanged. Dietrich kept his eyes moving, counting threats that were not soldiers: tourists with open mouths, a priest with hands half-raised as if blessing could function as a shield, Vatican guards converging from different angles with the disciplined speed of men trained for emergencies that were supposed to remain theoretical.

The civilians against the wall did not cry loudly. That would have been easier to endure. The older woman whispered, lips fluttering so fast her prayer became a hiss. The man in the work jacket stared at Kammler with an expression that contained no bargaining. Only the raw certainty that hatred could exist without effect.

Behind Kammler, the Vatican official's face had tightened into a mask of pale fury. He spoke in Italian to a gendarme who had arrived breathless, then switched to German as if choosing a sharper blade.

"You are in the heart of the Church," he said. "Do you imagine God will let you—"

Kammler cut him off without raising his voice. "God has allowed Rome to burn before," he said. "He has allowed popes to be dragged from their palaces. Do not threaten me with a history you have already survived."

Dietrich heard the implication and felt the square tilt slightly, as if the stone itself had become less reliable beneath their boots. Kammler was not performing for the civilians. He was performing for the institution. He was reminding it, with brutal efficiency, that sanctity was not immunity.

A Swiss Guard officer approached, his uniform immaculate despite the heat and the tension. He stopped a few paces away; halberd held not as a ceremonial prop but as a line. His jaw was set hard enough to crack teeth.

"This ends now," the guard said in German. "Release them."

Kammler looked at him with mild interest, as if assessing a piece of architecture. "It ends when I am received," he replied. "You are welcome to attempt to remove me. It will not be quiet."

The Swiss Guard's eyes flicked to the SS rifles, then to the civilians, then back to Kammler's face. The guard's discipline held, but there was a momentary darkening in his gaze, not fear, but disgust. The disgust was almost a relief. It meant the man was still human.

Dietrich leaned close to Kammler, voice so low it barely carried over the square's gathered murmurs. "If they storm us, this becomes blood. You will not get out."

Kammler did not look at him. "If they storm us," he said quietly, "then they admit that their walls are only walls."

The onlookers had begun to form a loose semicircle at a distance, held by instinct and by Vatican guards trying to contain panic without inflaming it. Someone shouted in English. Someone else answered in French. Words collided without forming a coherent plea.

A camera clicked.

Dietrich's stomach tightened. He glanced sharply and saw a tourist lowering a small device, hands shaking. No press badge. No official lens. Just an ordinary person trapping the scene in a form that could not be denied later.

Kammler noticed too. He did not flinch. If anything, his gaze sharpened. Evidence was a kind of currency. The Church understood that better than anyone.

The Vatican official's mouth opened again, but before he could speak, a hush moved through the nearest band of people like a sudden wind. It was not commanded. It simply happened, as if the square had collectively recognized a shift in gravity.

From the archway behind the Swiss Guards, a small procession emerged.

It was not the elaborate theater Dietrich expected. No gilded chair, no fanfare. Just a handful of clerics in dark cassocks and, at their center, an older man in white.

The Pope walked without hurry.

He was smaller than he appeared in photographs, more compact, as if the centuries of the office had pressed the body into a denser shape. His face was lined and pale beneath the white skullcap, but his eyes were clear, alert, and not at all soft. His hands were clasped lightly at his waist, and he moved like a man stepping into an argument he had already understood.

The Swiss Guards snapped to a stricter attention, halberds angling in a precise choreography, but the Pope lifted a hand almost impatiently, and the blades lowered.

He stopped several paces from Kammler.

For a moment the square's noise faded to a distant smear. Dietrich became acutely aware of his own breath, of the weight of his pistol against his hip, of the civilians' trembling behind him. The Pope looked past the rifles, past the uniforms, and fixed his gaze on Kammler with an expression that was neither outrage nor fear.

Curiosity.

It was not the gentle curiosity of a scholar. It was the cold curiosity of a man who had spent a lifetime watching power shift masks, wondering which mask this one wore.

"You are Dr. Kammler," the Pope said in German. His accent was light, controlled. He spoke as if he were naming a fact, not greeting a guest.

Kammler inclined his head by the smallest fraction. "Holy Father."

The Pope's eyes flicked to the civilians lined against the wall. He did not stare at them long, but Dietrich saw the subtle tightening at the corner of his mouth. Not panic. Not helplessness. Displeasure, as if something coarse had been dragged across polished stone.

Then he looked back at Kammler. "You have brought your war into my square," he said. "You have done so loudly."

Kammler's voice stayed even. "I was not received."

"You were not received on your timetable," the Pope corrected. His tone was almost conversational. "And in response you threatened to kill Romans in front of tourists."

A murmur rippled through the onlookers at the bluntness of it. The Pope had named the act without flinching. No euphemism. No diplomatic fog. He spoke like a confessor reciting sins to see whether the sinner would admit them.

Kammler did not deny it. "Yes."

Dietrich's jaw tightened. He expected the Pope to condemn, to invoke God, to call Kammler a barbarian. Instead, the Pope tilted his head slightly, studying Kammler's face as if looking for a seam.

"And yet," the Pope said, "you did not come here to kill them."

Kammler's gaze did not waver. "No."

"You came to force a door," the Pope continued. "Because you believe what you carry is greater than scandal."

Kammler lifted the black case a few centimeters, enough to make the gesture unmistakable. "It is greater than scandal."

The Pope's eyes followed the movement. "Then show me," he said simply.

Dietrich blinked. He felt the square shift again. The Pope was not bargaining. He was inviting demonstration, as if the threat had been a crude language and he had decided to answer in another.

Kammler did not move immediately. The hesitation was not uncertainty. It was calibration.

He was adjusting to an opponent who did not behave as expected.

Around them, Vatican gendarmes had formed a tighter perimeter, their presence a promise that the square would not be allowed to rupture. The Swiss Guard officer's knuckles had gone white on the halberd shaft. The civilians trembled against the wall, eyes locked on the Pope now with a desperate, disbelieving hope.

Kammler turned his head slightly toward Dietrich. "Release them," he said.

Dietrich stared, then signaled sharply. The SS men lowered their rifles. One stepped back. Another unclenched his stance as if it physically hurt to do so. The civilians were not untied from anything; their restraint had been psychological, installed by the geometry of weapons. As the rifles lowered, they stumbled away from the wall in a clumsy burst, the younger women half-running toward the nearest Vatican guard, the older woman collapsing to her knees with a sob that sounded like a prayer finally allowed to breathe. The man in the work jacket did not flee immediately. He stared at Kammler one last time as if trying to carve the face into memory, then turned away sharply, shoulders rigid.

A wave of sound moved through the onlookers, relief and anger tangled together. The Vatican guards pressed them back, restoring space.

The Pope watched the release without visible reaction. Only when the civilians were out of the immediate line did he look again at Kammler, and his expression returned to the same unsettling focus.

"Now," he said. "What is it?"

Kammler set the case on the stone and snapped the latches. The sound was small, but in the square's hush it landed like a nail.

He opened it.

Inside were papers sealed in a simple protective wrap: three newspapers, photographs, sheets of grids, a log entry. They looked absurdly ordinary against the backdrop of St. Peter's Basilica, like something a courier might bring for a bureaucrat.

The Pope's gaze narrowed. "Newspapers," he said, and there was a flicker of something like amusement. "This is your weapon?"

Kammler lifted one, careful, gloved hands holding the folded paper by its edges. He offered it forward without stepping closer, as if respecting an invisible boundary.

"Read the date," Kammler said.

One of the Pope's attendants stepped forward automatically, but the Pope lifted a hand again, stopping him. He reached out himself and took the paper.

Dietrich watched the Pope's fingers, expecting hesitation, the recoil of superstition. There was none. The Pope handled the paper the way a man handled a document he intended to interpret, not a relic he intended to venerate.

His eyes scanned the top line.

"June 23, 1941," he read aloud.

The square did not react. Most of them did not understand the significance. Dietrich felt the coldness in his own chest, the old unease from the Owl Mountains returning as if summoned by ink.

The Pope looked up. "And you are telling me," he said, "that this was printed in a year that has not yet come."

Kammler did not blink. "Yes."

The Pope's gaze returned to the page. He read the headline, then the first paragraph. His eyes moved quickly, not with the plodding pace of public reading, but with the practiced speed of someone accustomed to consuming information under pressure.

Then he stopped.

He turned the paper slightly, as if adjusting for light. His thumb held the fold. His eyes narrowed again, and Dietrich saw the moment the Pope noticed what the scientists had noticed: something subtle, a phrase that did not sit still.

The Pope looked up, not alarmed, not angry.

Interested.

"This text," he said softly, "does not behave like paper."

Kammler's voice remained controlled, but there was a faint tightness in it now, the strain of standing before a man who did not fear him. "It changes."

The Pope's eyebrows lifted by a fraction. "When?"

"When observed," Kammler said. "When spoken. When we attempt to fix it into certainty."

The Pope held the paper as if listening through it. He did not cross himself. He did not step back. He did not glance toward the sky.

Instead, he asked, with a calm that was almost clinical, "And what do you believe is doing the changing?"

Kammler heard, in that question, the same shape as the column he had written in pencil back in the mountain.

Observer.

Dietrich felt it too. His skin tightened under his uniform as if the air had become charged.

Kammler met the Pope's gaze. "That," he said, "is why I am here."

The Pope looked down at the newspaper again, then back at Kammler, and for the first time his voice carried a note of something that was not curiosity alone.

Hunger.

"You have torn open a window," the Pope said. "And you have found that the wind is not empty."

Kammler's eyes did not leave him. "I need access," he said. "To what you keep. To what you know."

The Pope's mouth tightened slightly. Not refusal. Consideration.

Around them, St. Peter's Square began to breathe again. People whispered. Guards tightened their perimeter. The civilians Kammler had threatened were being shepherded away by Vatican officials, faces still streaked with shock.

But the Pope did not look at any of that. He looked only at the paper in his hands and the man who had brought it to him.

"You have frightened my city," he said, almost idly, as if noting a secondary effect. "You have also brought me something I have never held."

He folded the newspaper carefully, preserving it as if it were fragile in a way that had nothing to do with age. Then he extended it back to Kammler.

"Come," the Pope said.

Dietrich's head snapped slightly. "Holy Father—"

The Pope's eyes moved to Dietrich for the first time, and the look pinned him with effortless authority. "You will keep your weapons outside," the Pope said. It was not a request. "And you," he added, returning his gaze to Kammler, "will speak to me not as a conqueror, but as a man who has discovered a problem he cannot solve alone."

Kammler closed the case with controlled motions, as if sealing a specimen. "I will speak as necessary," he said.

The Pope's expression did not change, but his eyes sharpened, amused by the attempt at dominance.

"Yes," he said quietly. "You will."

He turned, the white of his robe moving like a small flag through the darker cloth around him and began walking back toward the archway.

Kammler followed.

Dietrich signaled his men, keeping them tight and disciplined as they withdrew from the square's center. The Swiss Guards closed ranks, creating a corridor that was less about honor and more about containment.

As Kammler stepped under the archway into the Vatican's shade, the air seemed to cool. The stone swallowed the square's noise.

He had forced the door. But as he crossed the threshold, Kammler understood something he had not expected.

He had not dragged the Pope into fear.

He had dragged the Pope into interest.

And curiosity, he realized, could be as dangerous as any rifle, because it did not flinch when confronted with the impossible.

It leaned closer.

Chapter 6

A Covenant Forged

The corridor swallowed them the way the mountain tunnels had, but with a different kind of weight.

In the Owl Mountains, stone and concrete had pressed in with the blunt force of engineering. Here, the walls were older, smoother, worn by centuries of hands that had not been forced. The air carried a faint sweetness of incense embedded in porous plaster and an undertone of candle wax, as if the building itself had learned to remember prayers the way the bell chamber had learned to remember resonance.

Kammler walked at the Pope's shoulder, the black case in his left hand. Dietrich followed a step behind, unarmed now except for his posture. Swiss Guards formed a moving boundary, bright uniforms muted in the Vatican's shade, halberds held not to threaten but to declare that violence would not be permitted to pretend it was normal here.

They passed through an antechamber where clerics paused mid-conversation and fell silent. A monsignor's eyes flicked to Kammler's SS insignia, then to the case, and he made the sign of the cross as if against a storm. Kammler watched the gesture without expression. He had built storms.

The Pope did not take them to a grand hall. He led them into a smaller room lined with books and pale marble busts whose faces had been carved into permanence long before Kammler was born. A single window admitted a wash of Roman light. A crucifix hung above a desk that was scarred by use rather than ornament.

"Close the door," the Pope said.

A priest obeyed. The latch clicked softly, and with it the outside world became distant. The square's murmur vanished. Even the Vatican's own footfalls faded, as if the building knew the value of silence.

The Pope gestured to a long table. "Put it there."

Kammler set the case down. His movements were careful, not reverent but precise, like a man placing a detonator.

The Pope sat on one side of the table. He did not invite Kammler to sit first. He simply watched him until Kammler took the chair opposite. Dietrich remained standing behind and to Kammler's right, his gaze fixed on corners and door seams, performing vigilance even in a room that made it feel faintly ridiculous.

The Pope's eyes returned to the case. "Open it," he said.

Kammler snapped the latches and lifted the lid. The papers inside looked even more ordinary here than they had in the square, cheap pulp amid marble and old wood. Kammler laid out the three newspapers first, then the photographs, then the grids copied from the mountain's catalog. He placed the log entry on top, the single sentence in German: Es ist schon passiert. It already happened.

The Pope did not touch anything yet. He leaned forward, eyes moving, taking in the arrangement the way he might have taken in a confession: first the shape, then the detail, then the cracks.

"These are your exhibits," he said.

"They are the least dangerous pieces of it," Kammler replied.

"Least," the Pope repeated, tasting the word. "Then there is more."

Kammler took one of the newspapers and slid it across the table, the same June 23, 1941, issue the Pope had held outside. "Read the headline again," he said.

The Pope's mouth tightened faintly. "I read it already."

"Read it," Kammler said, and there was no threat in the tone, only insistence. Kammler had learned in the mountain that language could be a lever.

The Pope picked it up. He read the top lines aloud, calmly, giving the German the measured cadence of a man accustomed to Latin. As he spoke, his gaze slowed, then stopped.

Dietrich felt his skin prickle. The pause was the same kind of pause the wire-rimmed physicist had made when a sentence shifted under glass.

The Pope glanced up. "It changes," he said quietly. Not a question. A confirmation.

Kammler slid a photograph forward. "Compare."

The Pope held the photograph beside the paper. The differences were subtle enough to be denied by anyone determined to deny them, but the Pope's eyes were trained for subtlety. He had spent a lifetime reading meanings that hid inside punctuation.

He exhaled once. "So, the page does not merely come from the future," he said. "It behaves as if the future is still arguing with itself."

Kammler nodded. "Yes."

The Pope placed the paper down carefully, as if it might bruise. "Tell me how you obtained them."

Kammler did not begin with metaphors. He began with logistics, because logistics were a form of truth.

"In the Owl Mountains, we built a device," he said. "A chamber. Bell-shaped. It contains a fragment recovered in Germany, in the Black Forest. A crashed craft. Not ours."

The Pope's eyes did not widen. That, Kammler realized, was either discipline or prior familiarity with heresy. "Your scientists," the Pope said. "SS men playing at God."

Kammler's expression did not change. "Playing implies frivolity. We did not have that luxury."

Dietrich shifted slightly behind him but did not interrupt.

Kammler continued. "The fragment distorts time in proximity. Animals aged forward, then reverted. Men vanished and returned speaking syllables that did not belong to any known language in our lab. When we stabilized the field inside the chamber, we achieved displacement. Not through space. Through coordinate."

The Pope's fingers rested on the grid sheets. He did not pick them up, but his touch was close enough that Kammler wondered if the ink would react to him too. "And you sent men," the Pope said.

"We sent a prisoner first," Kammler said, and did not soften it. "He returned with blood and descriptions of newspapers with dates. Then we sent two SS men tethered together to retrieve physical copies."

The Pope's gaze lifted to Kammler's face, and for the first time something like distaste surfaced openly. "You used a human being as a probe."

"I used what I had," Kammler said. "The machine did not care what kind of man entered it. It only cared that he was alive."

The Pope's mouth moved as if he might say something about souls. Instead, he asked, "And the newspapers. They speak of war."

"They speak of our war," Kammler said. "Before it has happened. They describe an eastern campaign in 1941. They name it. They list movements."

"Barbarossa," the Pope said, and the word sounded like an old barbarian stepping into a church.

Kammler nodded. "They also contradict themselves. Two editions with the same date disagree on cities taken on unit designations. The contradictions multiply. And then something worse: the ink changes while we observe it. Not randomly. Responsive. We tested light. We tested handling. We tested reading aloud. The papers behave like a surface being revised to accommodate scrutiny."

The Pope finally lifted one of the grid sheets. His eyes tracked along the columns: Date, Publication, Divergence, Trigger. And at the far right, the new column Kammler had added in pencil, the word that looked like superstition forced into a ledger.

Observer.

The Pope's eyes paused on it. He looked up slowly. "You believe something is watching."

Kammler held his gaze. "I have no interest in belief. I have interest in behavior. The behavior suggests correction. Our interference produces adjustment."

The Pope set the grid down and steepled his fingers, the gesture of a man who had listened to countless men explain their own devils. “And you have come to me,” he said, “because you think I will recognize the watcher.”

Kammler’s jaw tightened slightly. “I have come to you because your institution has experience with phenomena that claim authority over time. Prophecy. Revelation. Relics. Miracles. You know how to control what a crowd is allowed to call true.”

The Pope’s eyes narrowed, not offended so much as sharpened. “You think this is a problem of narrative.”

“I think it is a problem of custody,” Kammler said. “The future is evidence. Evidence is power. And power must be held by someone who knows how to hold it.”

Dictrich’s breath caught quietly. Even he, loyal as he was, could hear the audacity of saying that to the Holy Father in a room full of crosses.

The Pope did not flinch. “And you,” he said, “have decided that someone should be you.”

Kammler did not deny it. Denial would have been a weak form of honesty. “I have decided it cannot be left to chance,” he said.

The Pope leaned back a fraction, his white robe whispering against the chair. His face, in the window’s light, looked carved from fatigue and will. "You brought me papers that rewrite themselves," he said. "You claim an instrument that can step into tomorrow. And you say the future is unstable."

"Yes."

"And still," the Pope said, "you threatened civilians in my square to deliver this confession."

Kammler's eyes remained level. "Because delay is also a kind of choice. I needed you to choose quickly."

The Pope's gaze held him. The curiosity was still there, but it had deepened, edged now with something colder.

"You are not afraid of sin," the Pope said. "You are afraid of losing."

Kammler did not answer immediately. In the mountain, his doubt had sharpened into a new kind of vigilance. Here, under the Vatican's stone, that vigilance felt justified.

"I am afraid of being misled," he said finally. "The papers show victory and failure in different versions. They shift. They react. If something can curate what we see, then our machine is not an advantage. It is a baited hook."

The Pope's fingers tapped once on the table, soft as a rosary bead hitting wood. "So, you want an anchor," he said.

Kammler nodded. "I want something that does not shift."

The Pope's eyes moved to the crucifix on the wall, then back to Kammler. "You came to the wrong place if you want the world to stop moving," he said. His tone was almost gentle, and that gentleness was more unsettling than anger would have been. "But you may have come to the right place if you want to know what moves it."

He leaned forward again and placed a hand on the newspaper, not as a scholar might, but as if listening for a pulse beneath pulp. "Tell me," he said, "what else did you bring back from your bell besides paper."

Kammler's gaze flicked briefly, involuntarily, to the far right of the grids in his mind. To the word he had written, half warning, half admission.

Observer.

"We brought back," he said, "the certainty that we were noticed."

The Pope's eyes did not leave the paper. "Then reveal to me," he said quietly, "what you believe noticed you."

And in that sealed room, with Rome outside and the future on the table, Kammler began to lay out not just the headlines of tomorrow, but the shape of the thing behind them, the presence that made ink behave like a living testimony.

He had come to the Vatican to show proof.

Now he found himself revealing the future as a crime scene and asking an old institution whether it recognized the hand that kept turning the page.

The Pope did not answer Kammler's last sentence immediately.

Silence in the Vatican had a different texture than silence in the mountain. In the Owl Mountains, quiet was always temporary, always threaded with the hum of generators and the distant scrape of labor. Here, quiet felt cultivated, layered, preserved. It had been practiced for centuries until it could be deployed like a curtain.

The Pope's hand remained on the newspaper. His fingers did not drum. They rested as if he were steadying something that might drift away. Kammler watched the hand more than the face, the way he watched instruments more than the men who read them.

"You say you were noticed," the Pope said at last. His voice was even, but it carried the weight of an accusation shaped into a question. "And you have come to me because you believe we will name what noticed you."

"I came because you understand custodianship," Kammler replied. "Because you have archives that outlast governments. Because you are not shocked by claims of miracles, only by claims you cannot control."

A faint tightening appeared at the corner of the Pope's mouth, almost amusement, almost irritation. "You confuse our patience with your cynicism."

Kammler did not flinch. "I confuse nothing. I am describing function."

The Pope lifted his eyes from the paper and looked directly at Kammler. The curiosity that had met him in the square was still there, but it had refined itself into something sharper: a scholar's focus coupled with a ruler's instinct.

"You threaten civilians to enter my city," the Pope said. "You bring me testimony that rewrites itself. You speak of an observer as if it is a problem to be engineered around. And you ask for access."

Kammler held the gaze. "I ask for cooperation."

"Cooperation," the Pope repeated, tasting the word as if it were a sacrament in a foreign language. He leaned back slightly in his chair, white fabric whispering against wood. "Very well. You will have an answer. But before you hear it, you will answer me without evasion."

Dietrich shifted behind Kammler, a quiet adjustment of a man who had spent his life recognizing the moment when a room became dangerous. Kammler did not turn. His attention stayed on the Pope.

"Ask," Kammler said.

The Pope's voice lowered, not in secrecy but in intimacy, as if he were pulling Kammler toward a confessional without granting absolution. "What is it you truly fear? Not defeat in Russia. Not the collapse of a plan. What do you fear in the shape of this phenomenon?"

Kammler's jaw tightened, almost imperceptibly. He thought of the newspapers changing under glass, of the sentence about Kiev halting as if the ink itself had learned caution. He thought of Schreiber vanishing into an alien corridor that had not existed until it did. He thought of the faint rustle the surgeon had heard, paper turned by a careful hand in a room with no draft.

"I fear that the machine is not neutral," Kammler said. "That what we call time is a medium with currents. That something in it corrects, edits, lures.

If it can choose what we see, then it can choose what we do."

The Pope nodded once, as if the answer matched something already filed away in his mind. "Then you are not asking for our help to win," he said. "You are asking for our help to discern."

Kammler did not grant the Pope the satisfaction of agreement. He kept his voice level. "I am asking for an institution that understands the difference between revelation and manipulation."

The Pope's gaze moved briefly to the crucifix on the wall above the desk, then returned to Kammler. "You assume we have always known that difference," he said quietly. "You assume the Church has been free of being used."

Dietrich's eyes flicked to the door, then back. Kammler remained still. "I assume only that you have survived long enough to have rules for it," he said.

The Pope's fingers came together, steepled, but the gesture was not prayer. It was calculation. "And in return for what?" he asked. "What exactly do you offer the Holy See?"

Kammler's answer came without hesitation. "Access to the instrument. Access to what it produces. And the ability to move people and material without question, across borders, with the protection of your networks."

Dietrich's breath caught, controlled but audible in the room's quiet. The Pope's eyebrows rose by a fraction, the smallest visible sign of surprise. Not at Kammler's audacity, but at the bluntness of his proposed transaction.

"You know of our networks," the Pope said.

"I know you have priests in every country," Kammler replied. "I know you have couriers that soldiers do not inspect because soldiers fear scandal. I know you have monasteries and convents that can hide a man better than a bunker if the men looking for him still believe in sin."

The Pope's eyes did not soften. "And you want those networks for yourself."

"I want them for the Reich," Kammler said. Then he added, because truth was a better weapon than politeness, "And for my work. If the future is unstable, then contingency becomes strategy. I will not build a machine that shows defeat without preparing an exit."

Dietrich's face went rigid. Kammler heard the tension without looking at him. To speak of exits was to speak of betrayal. But Kammler had never served ideology as a faith. He served it as an engineering brief.

The Pope sat very still. The air in the room seemed to settle.

"You have come to negotiate your salvation," the Pope said finally.

Kammler's eyes narrowed. "I have come to negotiate your relevance."

The Pope's head tilted slightly, and for a moment the old man looked less like a priest and more like a judge who had heard every form of arrogance and found some of it useful. "You mistake me," he said. "I do not need relevance. I need truth."

Kammler felt something cold and familiar lock into place. "Truth is expensive," he said. "You do not ask for it without intending to charge."

The Pope's gaze held him. "Correct," he said simply.

He reached forward and drew one of the grid sheets closer, the one with Observer written at the far right. He studied the column headings again as if reading a litany. Date. Divergence. Trigger. And then the word Kammler had written like a wound he could not cauterize.

"This is your confession," the Pope said. "You admit you have opened something and do not know who else is looking through."

Kammler said nothing.

The Pope's voice softened by a fraction, not into kindness but into clarity. "Then understand my position. If what you bring is merely tomorrow's war, I can refuse you. Empires fight. Empires fall. The Church buries them and continues. But if what you bring is an intrusion into the order of time, then it touches a domain the Church has claimed for two thousand years."

Dietrich's posture tightened further. Kammler could almost feel his objection forming, the reflex to insist on German authority. Kammler did not allow it space.

"You want access," Kammler said. "Name the price."

The Pope's eyes remained on the grid, but his attention was elsewhere now, somewhere behind his own eyes, where a man kept memories that were not written down.

"You believe your machine can bring back physical objects," the Pope said.

"It has," Kammler replied. "These papers. Photographs. Our men returned with them in sacks."

"And can it bring back something older than your war?" the Pope asked.

Kammler paused. A fraction of a second, just enough for honesty to move into place. "In principle," he said. "If the coordinates can be set."

The Pope nodded as if confirming what he had suspected. "Then here is my condition," he said.

The words did not come with drama. No thunder. No raised hand. Only a quiet statement spoken by a man who understood that the most dangerous decrees were the ones delivered calmly.

"You will bring me proof," the Pope said. "Not of your machine. Not of your future headlines. Proof that touches the foundation of my office."

Kammler's eyes narrowed. "Of what."

The Pope looked up, and when he spoke the next words there was no superstition in his tone. Only a kind of austere hunger, disciplined by years of ritual until it could be mistaken for serenity.

"Bring me truth," he said. "Not belief. Proof."

Dietrich's voice broke in despite himself. "Holy Father, what proof could possibly—"

The Pope cut him off with a glance, and Dietrich fell silent as if struck. The Pope returned his gaze to Kammler.

"You will go," the Pope said, "to the moment around which the world was built. You will take your bell and your science and your arrogance and you will place them where the Church has placed its altar."

Kammler's throat tightened. He already knew where the words were heading, but he waited because the act of making it explicit mattered. Agreements were built on explicitness.

"Prove to me," the Pope said, "that Jesus of Nazareth lived and died as we claim."

Kammler did not move. The air in the room felt suddenly denser, as if the stone itself were listening.

Dietrich stared at the Pope, disbelieving. "You want… you want him to go back," he said, struggling for German words that did not sound insane, "to the crucifixion."

The Pope did not look at Dietrich again. "I want the truth," he said to Kammler. "If your instrument can touch time, then it can touch that."

Kammler's mind moved quickly, not in panic but in engineering. Coordinates. Cultural variables. The instability they had already observed. The possibility that the Observer was not merely reacting to them but guarding something older than war. The danger of contaminating what the world called sacred history. The danger, also, of what could be extracted.

"What would you do with such proof," Kammler asked, "if I deliver it."

The Pope's expression did not change. "I will decide whether the Church remains a keeper of faith," he said, "or becomes a keeper of certainty."

Kammler felt, for the first time in the Vatican, the shape of a transaction that could not be undone. Not merely cooperation between institutions, but a covenant made over an altar neither of them fully understood.

"And in exchange," Kammler said, voice low, "you will provide what I asked."

The Pope nodded. "Routes," he said. "Custody. Silence where silence is required. And access to what we have kept hidden, if it assists you in setting your coordinates."

Dietrich's face had gone pale beneath its controlled discipline. "This is—" he began.

The Pope raised a hand, not in blessing but in command. "This is the only conversation worth having," he said. "You brought me the future of armies. I am asking you for the past of God."

Kammler leaned forward slightly, the movement so small it carried weight. "And if the truth is not what you want it to be," he asked. "If the machine reveals something that destroys your narrative."

The Pope's gaze held his. "Then it will destroy it," he said. "And I will have to decide what replaces it."

Kammler studied the old man across the table and realized, with a cold clarity, that the Pope was not afraid of revelation. He was afraid of revelation being controlled by someone else first.

The Pope's condition was not merely theological. It was strategic.

Kammler straightened. "You will have your proof," he said.

The Pope nodded once, satisfied not by the promise but by the inevitability in Kammler's tone. "Then we have an understanding," he said. "A covenant, if you like that word."

Kammler's eyes flicked briefly to the crucifix on the wall. A body suspended at the center of history, turned into an empire of meaning. If he could touch that moment, he could touch everything built upon it.

He looked back at the Pope. “One more question,” Kammler said.

The Pope waited.

“If I go,” Kammler asked, “and I find that something is watching there too, something that does not belong to your faith or mine… will your Church still call it God?”

The Pope’s face remained composed, but his eyes sharpened as if the question had cut through flesh to bone.

“We will call it what it proves itself to be,” he said. “And we will pray that you survive long enough to bring back the name.”

Then he rose from his chair, the audience ending not with dismissal but with purpose. The Vatican had made its demand.

Not for headlines.

For divinity, held in the hand like paper, dated and undeniable.

The Pope did not offer his hand.

He stood beside the table with the stillness of a man ending a meeting and beginning a policy. The room’s light had shifted while they spoke, Rome’s afternoon sliding toward evening, and the window’s pale rectangle now fell across the newspapers like a bar of cold illumination. Kammler watched the way the ink held steady under the light for the moment, as if even it understood that a decision had been made.

Dietrich remained behind Kammler's chair, rigid, his face set into the professional mask of a subordinate who had just watched two empires bargain over a corpse.

Kammler closed the black case with careful clicks, sealing the papers inside as though they might escape if left open. When he looked up, the Pope was watching him with that same composed attention he had shown in the square, curiosity turned now into something more formal.

"You understand what you have agreed to," the Pope said.

"I understand what I have purchased," Kammler replied.

The Pope's mouth tightened slightly. "This is not commerce."

Kammler met his gaze without blinking. "Everything is commerce," he said. "Some men trade in money. Some trade in obedience. You have offered me access and silence. I have offered you certainty. We are both paying in human lives, whether we admit it or not."

The Pope did not deny it. He moved around the table, the hem of his white robe whispering against the floor and stopped near the crucifix above the desk as if placing his words under its witness.

"You will not perform this act alone," he said. "If you go to that moment, you go with more than your SS."

Dietrich's jaw tightened. "Holy Father, this is German state business."

The Pope's eyes flicked to him, cool and final. "It is not a state that will be tested," he said. "It is reality."

Dietrich fell silent, the rebuke landing without the need for volume.

Kammler inclined his head a fraction. "You have someone in mind."

"I have several," the Pope said. "Men who have kept our secrets and survived the keeping. Men who do not require your uniform to remain disciplined." He paused, measuring Kammler. "They will not carry rifles into your mountain. They will carry memory, and they will carry authority. You will not discard them as probes."

Kammler's voice remained even. "I discard what fails."

"And so do I," the Pope replied, and for a moment the words sat between them like a blade laid gently on a table. "Which is why you will understand this: if your machine can take you to the crucifixion, then your machine can take you anywhere. The Church cannot allow such a mechanism to exist outside custody."

Dietrich's posture shifted, a subtle movement toward offense, but Kammler lifted one hand slightly, a silent order for restraint. He had heard the phrase behind the phrase: custody. Not assistance. Not partnership. Possession.

"You will not have the machine," Kammler said.

The Pope regarded him. "Do you think I mean I will take it from you with soldiers?"

"No," Kammler said. "You mean you will take it by necessity. By making yourself indispensable to its use."

The Pope's eyes did not soften. "Indispensable is a polite word," he said. "I mean accountable. You have shown me a future that changes when watched. You suspect an observer. You have begun to sense that there are intelligences that do not respect your Reich or my sacraments. Then you will accept oversight, because without it you are only a man with a door and no knowledge of what lives on the other side."

Kammler felt the familiar urge to dominate the room with command. He did not indulge it. He had forced doors all his life. Some doors, he understood now, did not break cleanly. They broke into obligations.

"What do you want," he said, "in operational terms."

The Pope turned slightly toward the door and spoke a name in Italian. It was not shouted. It was spoken with the certainty of a man accustomed to being obeyed. A beat later the latch clicked, and a priest entered, followed by another figure in dark clerical clothing whose face was older and sharper, his gaze assessing Kammler the way Kammler assessed machinery.

"This is Monsignor Orsini," the Pope said in German. "He will handle the practicalities. He will have access to your materials and will provide you with ours."

Orsini bowed minimally, not deferential so much as acknowledging a transaction. "Doctor," he said.

Kammler did not return the greeting with warmth. "Monsignor."

Orsini's eyes flicked to the case. "The papers."

"They remain with me," Kammler said.

"They remain under our observation," Orsini replied, and the subtle emphasis was not accidental. "If they change with attention, then they must be monitored by independent witnesses. Otherwise, you will claim stability where there is none."

Kammler almost smiled but did not. It was the logic of the lab applied with the moral language of confession. "Independent," he repeated. "In your city. Under your lock."

"In a sealed room," Orsini said calmly. "With controlled light. With transcripts. With photographs. You have already done these tests. You understand their value."

The Pope watched Kammler, letting Orsini's words land as a demonstration: the Church could speak the language of instruments when it chose.

Kammler nodded once, conceding what could be conceded without surrendering the core. "You will see copies," he said. "Photographs. Transcripts. Not originals."

Orsini did not argue. "We will see enough to verify," he said. "And in exchange you will see enough to act."

The Pope moved back to the table and placed one hand on the closed case, not touching it as a thief might, but as a judge might touch a sealed document. “We will open our archives,” he said, and Dietrich’s breath caught quietly at the bluntness of it. “Not the public shelves. The restricted collections. We have maps. We have calendars that predate your Reich. We have records of eclipses and comets and Roman census lists. We have descriptions of the sky on days your historians treat as myth. We will provide what you need to find your coordinates.”

Kammler’s mind moved immediately to the practical: anchor points. Astronomical events. The way his physicist had spoken of timing signals and coil phasing. The future newspapers had been bait. The past, if it could be reached precisely, would be a fixed pin in a field of shifting cloth. Or it would tear the cloth entirely.

“And the routes,” Kammler said. “The networks.”

The Pope’s gaze sharpened. “Those are not given,” he said. “They are granted, and they can be withdrawn.” He leaned slightly forward. “If you betray this covenant, you will find that the Church does not punish with gunfire. It punishes with absence. Doors close. Names vanish from ledgers. A man becomes untouchable not because he is protected, but because he is no longer acknowledged.”

Kammler understood the threat because it resembled his own methods, refined by centuries. "You are offering escape lines," he said, "while reminding me you can cut them."

"I am offering continuity," the Pope replied. "You fear irrelevance, Doctor Kammler. So does every empire. The Church does not fear losing battles. It fears losing its claim to interpret the world." His eyes flicked toward the crucifix. "You are bringing us an instrument that can rewrite interpretation into evidence."

Dietrich finally spoke, unable to keep the strain out of his voice. "Holy Father, you ask us to violate the most sacred moment in human history. To what end? To strengthen faith?"

The Pope looked at him for a long moment, and the silence felt like a lesson. "Faith," he said softly, "is what people call obedience when they want it to sound noble." He let the sentence stand, then continued, still calm. "I will not insult you with piety. I want what every ruler wants when the ground begins to move. I want an anchor. And if the anchor is not what we have claimed, I want to know that too before someone else weaponizes the truth against us."

Kammler felt the alliance solidify in that sentence, not as friendship but as mutual fear shaped into policy. The Church was not joining the Reich. The Church was joining the problem.

Orsini stepped closer to the table and produced a small notebook from inside his cassock, the movement precise. “There are immediate requirements,” he said. “If you intend to set coordinates to Judea under Roman occupation, you will need language preparation, currency replication, clothing, and an understanding of local calendars. You will also require… restraints.”

Dietrich’s brow furrowed. “Restraints?”

Orsini’s eyes stayed on Kammler. “If the phenomenon reacts to observation, then the presence of an outsider in that moment could provoke correction. You may not be able to speak. You may not be able to touch anything. You may not be able to remain long. A single act might alter your return corridor.”

Kammler heard, beneath the monsignor’s careful language, the practical theology of a man who had spent his life treating belief as a volatile substance. “You assume the past will resist us,” Kammler said.

Orsini did not hesitate. “I assume it already has,” he replied. “You speak of an observer. If the observer exists, and if it is intelligent, then there are moments in history it would guard more fiercely than your eastern campaign."

The Pope's voice entered quietly, and it carried the same hunger as before, disciplined by ritual into something almost serene. "That is why you will not go as a conqueror," he said. "You will go as a thief. Quick, silent, taking what you came for and leaving before the room knows it has been entered."

Kammler's eyes narrowed slightly. "You are already anticipating extraction."

The Pope did not deny it. "Do not pretend your interest is purely observational," he said. "You did not build a bell in a mountain to watch. You built it to take."

Kammler felt the words land as an accurate accusation, and he allowed himself no defense. Defense would be sentimentality. "Then we are aligned," he said. "You want proof. I want material."

Dietrich stiffened, but Kammler continued, voice steady. "The difference is that you want it to hold your world together. I want it to keep mine from collapsing."

The Pope regarded him, then nodded once, as if acknowledging the only honest basis for cooperation. "Then we will proceed," he said.

"Orsini will travel with you to your facility. He will be shown enough to understand your constraints, and he will deliver enough for you to aim your instrument."

Kammler's gaze flicked briefly to the door, as if calculating how quickly word of this could spread even within the Vatican. "And secrecy."

The Pope's expression sharpened. "This will not be spoken of," he said. "Not by me. Not by you. Not by the men you choose, and not by the men I send." He paused, and the next words were soft but absolute. "If this truth escapes uncontrolled, it will not only destroy kingdoms. It will destroy meaning. People cannot live without meaning. When meaning collapses, they do not become free. They become violent."

Kammler understood that too. He had built systems designed to keep meaning narrow and enforceable. The Church had done the same with different tools.

He snapped the case shut again, as if sealing the covenant inside it. "Then we have an unholy alliance," he said.

The Pope's eyes held his. "Unholy," he repeated, and for the first time there was a trace of something like dry amusement. "Do not flatter yourself, Doctor. Holiness has always been a matter of perspective."

He extended his hand then, not for comfort, but for the formal closing of a bargain.

Kammler looked at it for a moment, the hand that blessed armies and condemned men, the hand that could open archives and close roads. Then he took it, his gloved grip firm and brief.

The Pope's fingers were warm. The warmth did not make the act human. It made it real.

When they released, the Pope said, "Bring me truth. Not belief."

Kammler answered, "I will bring you proof."

Orsini opened his notebook again, already listing what would be required to send a man into the center of history and return him intact. Dietrich stared at the crucifix as if seeing it for the first time not as a symbol, but as a coordinate.

Outside the sealed room, Rome continued, unaware that its stones had just housed a transaction that reached beyond war.

And somewhere, in the Owl Mountains, beneath rock and concrete, Die Glocke waited like a mouth that had learned the taste of time and wanted more.

Chapter 7

Through the Veil of Time

The return to the Owl Mountains was not a retreat into secrecy so much as a descent into a place that had stopped pretending the world was stable.

Kammler traveled with fewer vehicles than before. Speed mattered now, but so did the shape of attention. He had left Rome with Orsini seated opposite him in the staff car, hands folded inside his sleeves, gaze fixed on the window as if watching the countryside not for beauty but for patterns of concealment. The monsignor carried no case. What he carried was smaller and more dangerous: a thin portfolio of copied tables, a handwritten list of dates rendered in multiple calendars, and a set of astronomical notes pulled from a Vatican archive that did not officially exist.

Dietrich sat in front as he had on the way south, but he had become quieter, as if speech might turn into admission. Once, near a checkpoint, he glanced at Orsini in the rearview mirror and asked, unable to hold it in, "You really believe this will work?"

Orsini did not look at him. "Belief is your word," he said. "I am here because your paper moved under my thumb."

Kammler watched the roads slip past and tried not to think of St. Peter's Square breathing again after his rifles lowered. The Pope's curiosity had been more unsettling than outrage. Outrage could be predicted. Curiosity had no ceiling.

By the time the convoy reached the outer compound above the mountain facility, the air had the familiar bite of damp stone and oil. Guards snapped to attention, then hesitated when they saw Orsini step from the car in black clerical clothing. The man looked wrong among SS insignia and concrete, a piece of old Rome carried into a modern wound.

Dietrich's irritation returned in a flash. "He stays with me," he told the nearest officer, as if stating custody could erase discomfort.

Kammler did not indulge the impulse to reassure anyone. He led them underground with the same lack of ceremony he had shown leaving. The tunnels smelled of metal and wet rock. Generators throbbed in the distance. Somewhere deeper, the bell chamber waited in its steel ribs like a restrained organ.

The physicist with wire-rimmed glasses met them at the threshold of the central cavern, eyes red from sleeplessness and the strain of watching ink behave like an animal. He looked at Kammler first, then at Orsini, and for a moment the physicist's expression revealed the simple, exhausted question that no longer fit into his grids: how many impossibilities could be carried into one room before the room stopped being a room.

"Herr Doktor," he said, voice thin. "The papers shifted again. Not only wording. Layout. An entire column vanished and reappeared in another issue as if it had been misplaced."

"Later," Kammler said, and the word was not dismissal. It was triage. He turned his head slightly. "Monsignor Orsini. This is the man who has been mapping our contradictions."

Orsini stepped forward and offered the physicist a small nod. His eyes moved over the cavern with swift assessment, taking in the glass-covered workbench, the drafting grids, the lines strung with drying photographs, the guards posted as if paper might attempt escape. He did not react with awe. He reacted with recognition.

"This is an archive," Orsini said softly. "A crude one, but an archive."

The physicist blinked. "It is a laboratory."

Orsini looked at him with mild sympathy. "Most archives pretend they are not laboratories," he replied. "That is their advantage."

Kammler did not let the exchange continue. He walked past the workbench toward the bell chamber itself. The polished curve of Die Glocke caught the floodlight and returned it wrong, as if reflection had been edited. The surgeon stood near the edge of the ring, cigarette in hand, eyes tracking Orsini with a suspicion that had nothing to do with religion and everything to do with intrusion.

"Doctor," the surgeon said, not quite a greeting. His gaze flicked to Orsini. "You've brought a priest into the machine room."

"I have brought a witness," Kammler replied. "A different kind than you."

The surgeon's mouth tightened. "And what kind is that?"

Orsini answered before Kammler could. "The kind your men cannot shoot without consequences," he said calmly. Then he looked at the surgeon's cigarette. "And the kind who has heard confessions from men who built slaughter with clean hands."

The surgeon's eyes narrowed, but he said nothing. Smoke rose in a straight line and then vanished into the harsh light.

Kammler stopped at the inner perimeter, close enough to the bell's frame that he could feel the subtle pressure that remained even unpowered, a memory in the air. He turned and addressed them all with the tone of an engineer announcing a change in specifications.

"We are setting coordinates," he said. "Not to 1941. Not to a battlefield. To Judea. Thirty-three years after their Christ is born, as their calendars count it."

The cavern did not react like a room of true believers. It reacted like a room of men asked to step off a cliff on purpose. Dietrich's jaw clenched. The physicist's hands flexed as if searching for a pencil that could catalog dread.

Orsini opened his portfolio and laid papers on the edge of the workbench. He did it with care, keeping his hands visible, as if aware that sudden motions might be interpreted as threat in a place built on paranoia.

"These are not miracles," he said, and his voice carried further than it should have in the cavern's cold acoustics. "These are anchors."

He slid forward a sheet filled with tight handwriting and small diagrams: the phases of the moon across spring weeks, a list of Roman consular years, references to a lunar eclipse noted by a provincial governor, and the timing of Passover according to a calendar that did not match the Reich's neat dates.

The physicist stepped closer despite himself. His eyes caught on the astronomical notes first. "An eclipse," he murmured.

Orsini nodded. "There are records of one visible in Judea within the window you want. Not all agree on the exact year. That disagreement is itself useful. You have already learned that contradictions indicate movement."

The physicist glanced at Kammler as if checking permission to take the papers seriously. Kammler gave none. He simply watched, letting the physicist's mind do what it always did when cornered: work.

"We need more than a year," the physicist said, voice gaining speed, grasping at the familiar. "Our displacement is sensitive. We have drift even at the scale of days. If we aim at a season, we could land in the wrong Jerusalem, the wrong Passover."

Orsini's expression did not change. "Then do not aim at a season," he said. "Aim at a sky."

Kammler felt the phrase settle into him with the weight of utility. The newspapers had taught him that ink could lie, that words could shift. The sky was older than their arguments, and if it could be measured, it could serve as a fixed coordinate in a medium that resented fixation.

The physicist pulled his own materials closer: coil-phase charts, field resonance logs, notes about the near clock drifting when men argued. He began sketching without being told, pencil moving with a hunger that looked like relief. "If we treat the target time as a set of astronomical conditions," he said, "we can align to a specific night. A specific horizon configuration. But we still need the local longitude relative to our displacement model."

Orsini turned another sheet over. "We have approximate topography," he said. "Descriptions of Golgotha's position relative to the city wall, relative to a gate. There are Roman records of executions. Not names, not always, but practices. And there are pilgrim itineraries from later centuries that preserved the geography before it was rebuilt into legend."

Dietrich made a sound of frustration. "Later centuries are useless. Legends are useless."

Orsini looked at him as if at an impatient child. "Everything you are doing is built on the assumption that material can persist through retelling," he said. "If you do not accept that, you should go back to your rifles and leave the rest to men who understand memory."

Dietrich's eyes flashed, but Kammler cut in before the argument could feed the clock drift. "Enough," Kammler said. "We use every source. We triangulate. We do not worship the data. We weaponize it."

He pointed at the physicist's charts. "What do you need from them, specifically."

The physicist swallowed and forced himself into clarity. "Three things. One: a time window tight enough to minimize drift. Two: a location anchor, because we do not only step into time, we step into a coordinate that includes space. The bell does not separate them cleanly. Three: a stabilization protocol, because the field reacts to observation. If the target moment reacts harder, we may not be able to remain long enough to see anything, let alone retrieve proof."

The surgeon finally spoke again, voice dry. "Retrieve. There it is."

Kammler did not deny it. “We do not come back empty-handed,” he said. Then he looked at Orsini. “Your Pope asked for proof. Proof is not a story. It is material. We will take what we can carry.”

Orsini held Kammler’s gaze. “And what will you take,” he asked, “that does not unravel what you touch?”

Kammler looked toward the bell chamber, then back to the table where the Vatican’s anchor notes lay beside German coil-phase logs. “A sample,” he said, and the room went subtly colder at the plainness of it. “Biological. Small. Enough for analysis. Enough for certainty.”

The physicist’s pencil paused. His voice came out hoarse. “From the crucifixion.”

Kammler did not correct him. Correction would have implied doubt. Instead, he asked the question that mattered to an engineer who had learned the future could listen.

“How close,” Kammler said, “can we place ourselves without being noticed.”

Silence held for a beat, and in that beat Kammler remembered the faint rustle in the cavern, paper turned by a careful hand. He watched the shadows near the bell’s base and saw nothing move yet still felt watched.

Orsini answered carefully. “There is no such thing as unobserved presence,” he said. “There is only presence that does not trigger response.”

The physicist nodded slowly, as if the sentence belonged in his grids under Trigger. “Then we need a protocol,” he said. “No speech unless required. Minimal light. Minimal contact. And an immediate extraction plan if the field destabilizes.”

Kammler’s eyes narrowed. “We will not abort because someone feels fear.”

“We may have to abort because the machine does,” the physicist said, and then looked at Kammler as if bracing for punishment.

Kammler did not punish him. He had learned in the mountain that the rules were not enforced by ideology. They were enforced by whatever lived in the structure they had disturbed.

“Then we build the protocol,” Kammler said. “We set coordinates by sky and calendar. We run simulations with near targets first. We test drift. We test whether the Observer reacts to the act of aiming.”

The physicist’s hands began moving again, sketching a grid that looked like the earlier contradiction catalogs but with new headings: Lunar phase, Eclipse visibility, Roman date, Field amplitude, Return corridor stability. At the far right, without being told, he drew a final column and wrote the word Kammler had introduced to the lab like a poison.

Observer.

Orsini watched him write it and said nothing. His silence was a form of agreement more disturbing than argument.

Kammler leaned in over the workbench. The Vatican's ancient notes and the Reich's modern charts lay together under the floodlights like incompatible scriptures forced into the same binding. For a moment, he felt the scale of what they were attempting: not a raid on a future headline, but an intrusion into the hinge of meaning.

He straightened and looked at them one by one. "You will give me a date you can defend," he said. "A night sky you can reproduce. And a corridor the bell can hold. Then we go."

The surgeon ground his cigarette out too hard, as if needing the small violence. Dietrich stood rigid, neither objecting nor agreeing, trapped between obedience and the sudden realization that obedience now included blasphemy as a technical procedure.

Orsini closed his portfolio, leaving the anchor sheets on the table as if laying out relics for dissection. "You asked Rome for stability," he said quietly. "You will not find it. But you may find something better. A point the world cannot deny, even if it tries to rewrite itself."

Kammler looked at Die Glocke, and in the polished curve he saw the faintest distortion of his own reflection, as if the metal could not decide which version of him was real.

"Then we aim," he said. "And we see whether the past holds still when we touch it."

The bell chamber was awake before it was powered.

That was what the physicist said later, when he tried to describe the way the air changed as soon as the coils were brought into alignment. But in the moment, standing inside the ring of steel ribs beneath the mountain, Kammler did not permit language like awake. He permitted numbers, readings, and checklists.

They had built a ritual out of their caution.

The central cavern had been cleared of everything not essential. The table of newspapers remained under glass on the far bench, but the floodlights over it had been dimmed, as if too much attention might call the ink into mischief again. The clocks had been moved farther from the bell's base. Even then, one of them gained four seconds while the men argued over whether four seconds mattered when they were about to cross nineteen centuries.

It mattered enough that Kammler ended the argument with a look.

Orsini stood beside the physicist at the console, the monsignor's dark clothing making him a vertical shadow among gray uniforms and steel. He had insisted on observing the settings, not because he understood coil phasing, but because he understood custody. Kammler had allowed it because the Pope's condition was now another constraint in the machine, and Kammler did not waste time pretending he could remove it.

Dietrich waited with two SS men at the perimeter, weapons stowed outside the inner ring as ordered. His hands were empty, but his posture still carried the weight of command. He looked at the bell chamber the way a soldier looked at a doorway that might open onto a trench.

The surgeon checked the harnesses one last time, fingers moving with professional calm that did not match his eyes. The harnesses had changed since the early jumps. No more heavy tethers meant to drag men back. The bell did not tolerate being treated like a winch. Instead, the physicist had designed a return protocol built on timed resonance pulses, as if calling something home with a sound rather than pulling it with a rope.

Two men would go through.

Kammler, because the Pope had demanded proof and Kammler did not delegate transactions at this scale.

And an assistant, chosen not for bravery but for silence. A technician with thin lips and an obedience born of fear, already pale from days spent watching the newspapers shift. Kammler had considered sending Dietrich, but the officer's anger had become a variable. Variables multiplied in unstable fields.

Orsini would not go.

He had not asked to. He stood at the edge of the ring like a man watching a door that might open onto revelation and deciding that the only sane role was witness from this side. Yet his presence was not passive. He had placed a small notebook on the console and written, in a precise hand, the date as their sources converged on it, then refused to treat it as a date at all.

"Do not think of it as a day," he had told Kammler earlier. "Think of it as a sky you are borrowing."

Now the physicist read the final parameters out loud, because they had learned that speech could accelerate change, and they wanted the machine to hear their intention once, clearly, and then be left alone.

"Field amplitude stable. Coil phase locked. Target conditions: lunar phase, waning; eclipse window aligns within tolerance; return pulse set at eight minutes after entry, with manual override at six if destabilization exceeds threshold." He hesitated, eyes flicking to Kammler. "No speech unless required."

Kammler nodded, already moving. He stepped into the harness, felt the straps tighten around his torso, and for an irrational heartbeat he thought of the civilians lined against the wall in St. Peter's Square. Another wall now. Another set of bodies. Another threat, this time directed at the fabric of history rather than flesh.

He did not allow the thought to become moral. Morality was noise. He allowed it to become instruction.

Do it quickly.

Do it precisely.

Do not linger.

The technician was strapped in beside him, shoulders rigid, eyes fixed on the bell's polished curve as if it might reflect something back that should not be seen.

The surgeon leaned close to Kammler and spoke quietly, because old habits insisted on last words.

"You bring back paper and blood," he said. "Now you're going for blood that two thousand years have prayed over."

Kammler met his gaze. "I'm going for what holds," he replied.

The surgeon's mouth tightened. He wanted to say something about consequences. He did not, perhaps because he had already seen enough of them in the mountain shadows.

Orsini stepped forward then, close enough that Kammler could smell faint wax on his hands, as if he had just extinguished a candle.

"One thing," Orsini said. His German was careful, his tone controlled. "You may be noticed."

Kammler's eyes narrowed. "We already are."

Orsini's gaze held him. "Not like this," he said. "If there is an observer, this is a hinge. You are not stepping into a battlefield. You are stepping into a liturgy."

Kammler felt the phrase settle in his mind with the wrong kind of weight. He did not like metaphors when steel and current were involved. But he understood hinges. He understood that a hinge carried the load of a door and decided how it swung.

"Then I will be careful," Kammler said.

Orsini nodded once, as if accepting that care was the only virtue Kammler had to offer. He stepped back.

The physicist's hands hovered over the controls. He looked at Kammler and did not try to hide the fear in his eyes. It made him look younger than his wire-rimmed glasses suggested.

"Herr Doktor," he said, and his voice almost broke, "if the field reacts, if it shifts around you, do not fight it. Do not force anything. Come back."

Kammler gave him a look that contained no reassurance. "Open it," he said.

The physicist swallowed and threw the switch.

Die Glocke did not hum. It did not announce itself with the satisfying noise of German engineering. The first sensation was pressure, as if the air had been made thicker by decree. The floodlights dimmed by a fraction, not flicker but a subtle surrender, as though photons did not want to cross the space.

Then the sound arrived, low and intimate, felt more in the teeth than the ears. A resonance that made the bones behave as if they were instrument parts. Kammler's vision narrowed, not into darkness but into clarity so sharp it felt like pain.

The shadows near the bell's base did something wrong. Not dramatic. Just enough that his mind registered misalignment, like a compass needle twitching when it should not.

The technician beside him inhaled sharply. Kammler did not turn his head. Turning felt like an act that might be interpreted as curiosity.

Curiosity, he remembered, was what had made the newspapers move.

The bell's interior space shimmered, not with light, but with the absence of stable reference. The steel ribs and concrete walls seemed to stretch, then compress, as if the room were being folded. Kammler's stomach lifted and dropped in a slow wave, and for a moment he felt weightless without moving.

He saw the console, the physicist, Orsini's dark silhouette, Dietrich's rigid stance, all of them flattening into a thin plane as if viewed through water.

Then even that plane was gone.

Silence arrived like a cut cord.

The pressure released all at once, and Kammler's boots met ground that was not concrete. His knees flexed automatically, absorbing shock. The harness straps bit into his shoulders. The technician stumbled, caught himself, and made a choking sound that would have been a shout if fear had not stolen his breath.

Kammler held still, forcing his body to become a statue. The protocol demanded minimal movement. He let his eyes take in everything without turning his head too quickly.

They were outdoors.

The air was warm, dry, and thick with dust and something organic, the smell of animal sweat and crushed herbs. The sky was brighter than he expected, a hard blue stretched over pale hills. Sunlight lay on the land with no hint of industrial haze, no smoke, no distant drone of engines. The world sounded wrong in its simplicity: wind, insects, distant voices, and the occasional bray of a donkey.

To their left, an olive tree stood twisted and patient, its leaves flashing silver-green when the wind moved through it. The ground beneath their boots was uneven, stony, littered with small shards of pottery that looked old and fresh at once.

The technician's breathing accelerated into a near-panic. Kammler's hand, gloved, moved fractionally and touched the technician's forearm. The touch was not comfort. It was command.

The technician froze, swallowing hard. His eyes were wide, darting across the landscape as if expecting soldiers to appear from behind every rock.

Kammler's own eyes narrowed.

In the distance, he could see a road, not paved, a thin brown line worn into the earth by feet and hooves. Along it moved people in loose clusters, their clothing pale, simple, draped. Some carried bundles. One figure led a small animal by a rope. Their movement had the slow rhythm of a world without machines.

Farther still, on a rise, a city wall. Stone, sun-bleached, with a gate where traffic flowed in and out like blood through an artery. Above the wall rose rooftops and a suggestion of a larger structure, a temple silhouette against the sky that seemed to hold the horizon with its own authority.

Jerusalem, Kammler thought, and the thought did not feel like a word. It felt like a coordinate locking into place.

He forced himself to listen.

The voices carried in fragments, a language he did not speak, consonants sharp, vowels unfamiliar. He heard another tongue too, rougher, perhaps Latin, from somewhere nearer the road, but it was indistinct.

The technician's lips parted, and Kammler saw the word forming, some involuntary German exhale of astonishment. Kammler tightened his grip.

No speech.

Not because words were forbidden by superstition. Because words were attention made audible. And attention, they had learned, was a lever.

Kammler shifted his gaze upward again, scanning the sky.

It was the same sky they had aimed at, but it did not feel like a neutral canopy. It felt like a surface. A taut membrane holding back something deeper. For a moment he thought he saw a faint distortion at the edge of his vision, as if the blue were not entirely uniform, as if it had a grain.

He remembered the newspapers under glass, ink changing when observed.

He remembered the column he had added: Observer.

His skin tightened under the harness as a subtle chill moved through the warm air, a sensation that did not match the sun.

The technician's eyes fixed on a point behind Kammler, and the man went very still.

Kammler did not turn quickly. He let the movement be slow, measured, as if he were rotating a gun turret without wanting the target to know.

Behind them, the air shimmered. Not like heat. Like the space itself could not decide whether it was empty or occupied. A faint oval of wrongness, almost invisible, hanging a few paces back, as if their arrival had left a bruise in the world that had not yet healed.

The return corridor, Kammler thought. The mouth of the bell, opened here.

He watched it for a heartbeat, then forced his eyes away, because staring at it felt like staring at a wound and waiting for it to bleed.

The technician's chest rose and fell in small, controlled movements now. He was trying to obey.

Kammler scanned the road again. The people moving along it did not look toward them. Not yet. They passed at a distance, unaware of two men in strange harnesses standing near an olive tree like misplaced pieces of another era.

But the animals did.

A donkey being led by a boy lifted its head abruptly and balked, ears twitching. The boy tugged the rope, annoyed, then followed the animal's gaze toward the hillside where Kammler stood. The boy's eyes narrowed, not in recognition, but in a kind of instinctive unease. He hesitated, then pulled the donkey harder and hurried on, head lowered, as if choosing not to see.

Kammler felt a slow, cold satisfaction.

They were here.

The machine had delivered them into the right century, the right geography, under the right sky. The Vatican's anchors had held. The physicist's numbers had aligned. For the moment, the world was not tearing itself into contradictions.

For the moment.

Kammler's eyes moved toward the city wall again, toward the gate, toward the flow of people.

Somewhere inside that city, or outside it, a hill waited with wood and iron and a body the Church had turned into meaning. A moment the Pope wanted trapped into certainty. A moment Kammler wanted stripped into material.

Eight minutes, the physicist had said.

Eight minutes before the return pulse called them back whether they were ready or not.

Kammler lifted his hand slightly and pointed, a small, silent gesture toward the road and the city beyond. The technician swallowed and nodded, his face pale but obedient.

They began to move.

Each step felt heavier than it should have, as if the ground carried an additional gravity not measured in mass but in consequence. Dust rose around their boots. The wind shifted, and the olive leaves flashed again like small blades.

Above them, the sky remained blue.

Yet Kammler could not shake the sensation that it was watching him back, not with eyes, but with the subtle responsiveness of a surface that remembered being touched.

He kept his head down and walked toward Jerusalem, the harness straps creaking softly with each movement, and behind them, the faint oval of wrongness shimmered like a door left slightly open in a world that did not want doors.

The road rose gently toward the city, and with every step Kammler felt as if he were walking against an invisible current.

The dust here did not behave like the dust of Europe. It lifted too easily, clung to his boots and the lower straps of the harness with a stubborn, almost oily intimacy, as if the earth resented foreign soles and wanted to mark them. The stones underfoot were sun-warmed and sharp-edged. They looked like the kind of stones that kept their shape for centuries because no one had ever bothered to move them.

Kammler kept his pace steady. He counted breath and footfall the way the physicist had counted seconds and coil phases. Eight minutes. A return pulse that would call them back whether they had accomplished anything or not.

Beside him the technician moved with the stiff caution of a man trying not to look around too much. His eyes kept sliding to the harness buckles and then to the people on the road, as if terrified someone would recognize the straps as weapons.

The first group they passed close enough to hear did not look at them directly.

Three men in simple tunics, belts of braided cord, sandals that slapped the ground. One carried a basket with a cloth thrown over it. Another had a bundle of sticks on his shoulder. Their conversation ran in quick, clipped syllables, punctuated by the dry laugh of men who had grown up under a sun that made humor necessary. As Kammler approached, one of them faltered mid-sentence.

Not stopped. Faltered. A tiny hitch in his voice, a hesitation that made the other two glance at him. The man's eyes flicked toward Kammler's chest, then to his face, then away again, as if something about the shape of Kammler's presence produced discomfort without producing comprehension.

They did not speak to him.

They simply moved to the side of the road, making room too early, too politely, their shoulders angling away as if from heat. As Kammler passed, he felt their attention cling to his back like a hand that would not touch but wanted to.

A few paces later, the technician's breath hitched.

Kammler did not turn his head. He only extended two fingers and caught the technician's sleeve, a reminder, a restraint.

"No," Kammler said quietly, and then immediately regretted it.

A single German word, barely audible, swallowed by wind and distance, and yet the air seemed to tighten in response. It was not a sound effect. It was a pressure change, the subtle sensation of a membrane flexing.

The technician's eyes went wider, fear and relief mixing because the word had been both permission and warning.

Kammler closed his mouth and forced his breathing to become shallow, controlled. He watched the road ahead as if staring hard enough would prevent the world from reacting to the mistake.

The men behind them did not turn. They did not shout. They continued walking. But their laughter did not resume.

A lizard on a nearby rock, motionless a heartbeat earlier, darted away so suddenly it looked like a piece of the landscape had been cut out and removed.

The animals, Kammler thought again. They felt them first. Not because animals were mystical, but because animals lived closer to raw trigger and response. The newspapers had shifted when read aloud. Here, the world itself seemed to listen for intention.

They drew closer to the city gate, and the flow of people thickened. The air carried more smells:

sweat, dung, crushed olives, bread, smoke from cookfires. A thin metallic tang drifted in too, faint but present, like old blood on hot stone. Somewhere inside the walls there was shouting, not the sharp bark of German command but the layered noise of a crowded place where friction was constant.

Kammler's harness chafed against his shoulders. He could feel heat collecting beneath the straps. The technician kept adjusting his grip on the small canvas bag they had brought, empty for now. It looked absurdly modern in this landscape, its seams too straight, its weave too uniform. Kammler hated it, but they needed a container that could close.

He watched the guard presence as they approached. Roman authority here was not subtle. A pair of soldiers stood near the gate, helmets catching sun, spears held with the lazy competence of men who had never needed to prove they could kill. Their faces were bored in the way only occupiers could be bored. One spoke to the other in a low voice, then spat to the side.

As Kammler and the technician joined the stream of bodies moving toward the gate, the soldier's gaze lifted.

It slid over the crowd and then snagged on Kammler as if caught by a hook.

The soldier stared for a beat too long. His expression did not become alarmed. It became puzzled, then faintly wary. His eyes dropped to the harness straps crossing Kammler's chest, then to the technician's bag, then up again, searching for context.

Kammler lowered his gaze slightly, not in deference but in concealment. He let his face become blank. If the soldier decided these were strange foreigners, there were a dozen ways this could end badly within the remaining minutes.

The soldier's hand shifted on the spear. His mouth opened as if to speak, to demand language or tax or explanation.

Then a child in the crowd cried out, a sharp wail from somewhere behind Kammler, and the soldier's attention snapped away, annoyance overriding curiosity. He barked a word at someone in the crowd. A woman apologized rapidly. The soldier waved them through.

Kammler and the technician passed under the gate.

For a moment the shadow of the wall cooled their skin. Then they emerged into the city's heat.

Jerusalem was not the clean geometry of Rome. It was dense, layered, irregular, built from sun-bleached stone and desperation. Streets narrow enough that bodies brushed. Market stalls crowded with fruit, cloth, clay jugs. Voices everywhere, overlapping like water. The ground was worn smooth in places and jagged in others. The air vibrated with the endless, low-level conflict of commerce and faith and occupation.

And yet, beneath it all, Kammler felt the same wrongness he had felt under the blue sky.

Not a wrongness of location. The coordinates had held. This was the place the Vatican's maps described, the place later centuries would fossilize into ritual. The wrongness was in the way attention moved.

People looked at him.

Not all. Not constantly. But often enough that it formed a pattern. A man carrying a tray of bread glanced up and then stumbled, as if his foot had struck an unseen step. A woman selling olives paused mid-haggle and watched Kammler pass with narrowed eyes, her hand tightening on a string of coins. Two boys on a corner stopped their game, their faces turning not toward the harness but toward Kammler's head, as if drawn by the feeling of being watched by him even when he did not look at them.

The technician's breathing began to speed again. Kammler felt it through the air, heard it in the small catches and releases. The man was close to breaking protocol.

Kammler leaned in as if to avoid a collision and spoke without moving his lips much, German shaped into the smallest possible sound. "Look down. Follow."

The technician swallowed and did as ordered.

Kammler forced himself to become part of the crowd. He let shoulders bump him. He adjusted his pace to match the flow. He kept his hands close to his body. The harness made that difficult; it announced itself with every strap. He hated it with a practical hatred. If they survived this, he would demand a different design. Something that could be hidden under cloth. Something that did not turn them into anomalies with buckles.

A shout rose ahead, louder than the market noise. The crowd shifted as if a current had moved through it. People began to angle in the same direction, their faces turned, their steps quickening.

Kammler followed the vector automatically, not out of curiosity but out of inference. A city had only so many reasons to move as one. A procession. A riot. An execution.

He felt the technician tense beside him, a tremor running through the man's forearm. The technician's eyes were wide again, darting from face to face. He looked as if he expected someone to point and name them.

No one named them. That was part of what made it worse. The attention was wrong, not direct accusation but a kind of instinctive avoidance, as if the crowd were adjusting around a defect in the fabric without admitting it existed.

They reached a wider street where the flow of bodies became harder, pressed by density. The sound sharpened. He heard weeping, low and continuous. He heard laughter too, the cruel laughter of men who had found entertainment.

Roman soldiers appeared again, pushing people back with the casual authority of practiced brutality. Their armor and helmets caught sun in hard flashes. One soldier's whip snapped, not striking anyone, only cracking the air to remind the crowd what power sounded like.

Kammler's eyes tracked the soldiers, then the center of the moving mass.

There was a line of condemned men.

He saw wood first, rough-hewn beams on shoulders. Then he saw bodies: stripped backs, blood dried and fresh, stumbling feet. A man fell to his knees and was yanked up. Another's head lolled as if he were already half gone.

And then, in the center of it, a figure carrying a crossbeam, surrounded by soldiers.

Kammler's mouth went dry.

He had read the gospels as a boy the way German boys read any story forced into them: with impatience, with distance. He had not believed. Belief was not in his inventory. But he knew the shapes of this scene. He knew the weight of it in Western architecture, in paintings, in Rome's rituals.

The figure lifted his head, and Kammler saw a face marked by exhaustion and blood, hair matted with sweat. The eyes were open.

The crowd surged, shouting, sobbing, spitting words Kammler could not understand. A woman pushed forward and was shoved back. A man laughed too loudly. The soldiers barked.

Kammler's world narrowed into pure task.

Eight minutes were not enough, the thought came, crisp and involuntary. Eight minutes to enter a city, find a hill, approach a death that had become an empire, and take something from it without tearing the world open.

He felt the technician's sleeve tug against his fingers as the man tried to draw closer, pulled by horror and the need to see. Kammler tightened his grip.

The condemned line moved forward, toward the gate leading out of the city.

Golgotha, Kammler thought. The place of the skull. The hill outside the walls.

As the procession passed within a few paces, the air changed again.

It was subtle. A coldness sliding under the heat like a thin blade. The market smells thinned as if someone had drawn a cloth over them. The sound of the crowd dampened for a heartbeat, not silenced but muffled, as if Kammler's ears had been pressed underwater.

For that heartbeat, Kammler had the unbearable sensation that everything paused to accommodate their presence.

Then it resumed.

The soldier with the whip glanced toward Kammler, eyes narrowing. Not recognition. Calculation. The soldier's gaze dropped to Kammler's harness, then rose again, suspicion tightening his face.

Kammler forced himself to look away first. He moved with the crowd, letting bodies press between him and the soldier, letting the city's chaos become cover.

But as he moved, he felt it again, stronger now: the sky was not simply above them. It was reacting.

He looked up just enough to confirm his fear.

The blue did not fracture. The sun did not dim. There was no miracle to point at.

There was only a faint, almost imperceptible shimmer, like heat distortion but wrong in timing, rippling across the upper air above the procession, as if the world were trying to decide whether to reject an intruder or absorb him.

A world out of joint, Kammler thought, and for the first time the phrase felt less like metaphor and more like a mechanical diagnosis. A hinge under strain.

The procession moved through the gate and out toward the hill.

Kammler followed, keeping close, measuring distance, calculating angles and access points, the technician at his side like a tether that could panic at any moment.

Behind them, unseen in the city's noise, the return corridor waited wherever they had left it, eight minutes away from pulling them back by force.

Ahead of them, history bled in the sun, and the fabric of time, already aware, began to tighten around the moment as if preparing to resist being touched.

Chapter 8

Witness to Crucifixion

Outside the gate the air widened, and the city's pressure released into a harsher openness.

The road sloped down and then up again toward a low rise of exposed stone and scrub where the land looked flayed by sun and wind. No trees offered shade. The dust here was finer, ground into powder by countless feet. It lifted with every step and hung in the air like a veil that could not decide whether to settle or flee.

The procession thickened as it moved, not because more soldiers joined it, but because people did. Jerusalem spilled outward to witness its own violence. Men in worn tunics and sandals, women with headscarves pulled tight, children running ahead until a parent yanked them back by the arm. A few figures in better cloth moved more slowly, faces set in hard lines, as if they had come not from hunger for spectacle but from obligation to observe.

Kammler let the crowd take him. He kept his head slightly down and his shoulders angled so the harness straps were less visible, but there was no hiding them entirely. The buckles caught sun. The webbing across his chest made him feel as if he were wearing the future on his body like a sign.

Beside him the technician moved with rigid, frightened obedience, eyes fixed on the ground just ahead of his own feet. The canvas bag in his hand swung too evenly. Fear had made him careful. Kammler did not trust that carefulness to last.

The condemned men staggered in a loose line ahead, each surrounded by a pocket of Roman force. The soldiers did not look strained. Their control was routine. A whip cracked again, and the sound traveled cleanly in open air, louder than it had inside the city because there were fewer walls to swallow it. The crowd responded like an organism flinching. Some laughed. Some hissed. Some spoke words that sounded like prayers, and others answered with insults that cut through the prayer like stones thrown at a chant.

Kammler watched the soldiers' hands. Watched their spacing. Watched the way they formed a moving corridor of threat. He could not afford to be stopped. Every delay was a theft from the eight minutes the physicist had given him.

Eight minutes. And he had already spent too much of them walking.

He felt the return corridor behind him like a phantom limb. He could not see it from here, but he could feel its presence, a subtle pressure at the back of the mind, as if a door stood open in a storm and the storm kept whispering its address.

Ahead the hill rose closer, and the crowd's sound shifted. Inside the city, noise had been constant, layered, commercial. Out here the noise became purposeful. It narrowed into a single topic, a single hunger. The words blurred, but the tone was clear enough that language was unnecessary.

Judgment. Blame. Relief that someone else was suffering instead of you.

The first birds appeared as they neared the rise. Dark shapes circling high, lazy and patient. Not a flock yet. A few scouts tracing wide arcs against the blue, as if testing whether the day would offer meat.

Kammler's throat tightened. He had seen birds circle battlefields in the east. But this was not a battlefield. It was an altar of civic discipline. Rome's method of teaching obedience by making death into theater.

The hill itself was uglier up close, not dramatic in the way paintings made it. It was simply exposed rock, broken stone, patches of hard soil where nothing but thorny scrub would grow. The ground bore shallow grooves worn by feet and dragged wood. Here and there were darker stains, old and new layered together, absorbed into the porous earth.

Golgotha.

The name was not spoken aloud in this crowd, or if it was, it vanished into the noise. Yet Kammler felt the place declare itself the way a machine room declared itself by smell. This ground had been used for one purpose too many times. The air carried the metallic tang more strongly now, and beneath it, something else: sour wine, sweat, the sharp herbal note of crushed plants underfoot.

Roman soldiers spread out at the base and along the sides, forming a perimeter. They shoved people back with the casual force of men who knew they could. The crowd complied, grumbling, pushing, pressing for a better view while pretending to obey. Children were lifted onto shoulders. A few women cried openly, their sounds raw and continuous like a wound being rubbed.

Kammler found himself pushed to the left by the crowd's current. He let it happen. Fighting it would draw attention. He needed position, not dominance. He needed proximity without confrontation, like a man setting a charge and stepping away before anyone saw him kneel.

The condemned line slowed, then stopped.

A soldier barked an order. Another answered. Their Latin was clearer here, but Kammler still caught only fragments. It did not matter. He knew what came next because execution was an engineering problem. It had steps. It had requirements. Wood on ground. Nails. Rope. Bodies lifted. Time measured by breath and blood loss.

The man in the center stumbled hard, knee striking stone. The crossbeam slid down his shoulder and thudded into the dirt. The crowd surged, sound spiking. A soldier grabbed him by the arm and yanked him up. The condemned man's head lifted, and Kammler saw the face again, closer now. Blood had dried in uneven lines along the brow and cheek. The skin around the eyes was swollen. Yet the eyes were open and present, not glazed.

For a moment Kammler felt a disorienting anger at the simple fact of the man's humanity. The Church had made this face into iconography. The Reich had dismissed it into history. But here it was, a living face inside a machine of death.

The condemned man straightened under the soldier's grip. The soldier shoved him forward. He stumbled but did not fall. He moved as if each step was a decision.

Kammler's mind attempted to reduce the moment into a task list.

Approach. Acquire sample. Avoid notice. Return.

But the air kept interfering.

It was not merely that people looked at him too often. Here at the hill the attention sharpened into something more physical. The crowd's gaze did not just slide over him; it snagged, then moved away, then snagged again, like a hand brushing a hot surface and withdrawing. A woman with red-rimmed eyes stared at Kammler's harness for a heartbeat too long, then recoiled as if she had seen a wound. A boy stopped chewing on something and simply watched Kammler with an expression that was not fear but bafflement, as though Kammler's outline did not agree with the rest of the world.

The animals reacted more cleanly.

A skinny dog near the edge of the crowd, ribs visible under its coat, trotted forward and then stopped abruptly, head lowered, hackles rising. It did not bark. It did not growl. It made a soft sound like a whine swallowed too quickly, then backed away, eyes locked on Kammler as if seeing not a man but a pressure in the air.

Kammler's skin tightened beneath the harness straps. The warmth of the sun no longer matched what he felt. A thin chill threaded through the heat, a sensation like walking through a shadow that did not belong to any object.

He looked up.

The sky was still blue. The sun still bright. But the earlier shimmer had intensified above the hill, a subtle distortion that made the air appear thicker in one region, as if the world were compressing itself around the execution site. The shimmer did not spread randomly. It seemed to hang over the center, hovering where the condemned men stood, as if the hill were the focal point of a field.

Kammler thought of the bell's resonance, of coil phases locking, of a field that reacted to observation. He thought of the newspapers, ink shifting when read, as if time itself responded to attention like skin responding to touch.

And he thought, again, of the column the physicist had written without being told.

Observer.

The technician's breathing became audible beside him, fast and shallow. Kammler glanced down just enough to catch the man's eye.

The technician looked near tears. His lips moved soundlessly, shaping German words he did not dare speak. His gaze flicked toward the condemned men, then upward to the sky's wrongness, then back to Kammler with a plea that had no language.

Kammler's gloved hand closed briefly around the technician's forearm. Not comfort. Control.

The technician swallowed and nodded once, violently, forcing himself into stillness.

A soldier pushed the condemned men toward the prepared area at the top of the rise. There, beams lay on the ground like tools laid out before a procedure. A few men with rough hands waited, not soldiers but laborers, their faces indifferent in the way men's faces became indifferent when paid to do violence repeatedly.

The crowd pressed closer until the soldiers shoved them back again. A man laughed loudly and said something that made those around him laugh too, a coarse ripple that traveled and then died when a woman's sob cut through it.

Kammler edged forward by half-steps, letting the crowd's pressure do the work. He did not shove.

He did not look eager. He kept his posture controlled, his movements minimal, as the physicist had instructed. Yet he could not avoid moving closer if he wanted any chance at contact.

The condemned man in the center was forced down onto the ground near one of the beams. His hands were grabbed. His arm was stretched. A laborer lifted a nail, thick and dark.

The crowd's sound changed again. Some leaned in, faces hungry. Others turned away, unable to watch but unable to leave. A few voices rose in what might have been prayers. The Roman soldiers watched with bored vigilance, their attention on the crowd more than the dying.

Kammler felt the hill tilt slightly, not physically but perceptually, as if the world itself shifted under the act. The shimmer overhead tightened, becoming almost a faint, invisible dome.

Then, in the midst of it, the condemned man lifted his head.

His eyes moved through the crowd with a slow, exhausted precision that did not match his condition. He looked, and for a moment it felt as if his gaze did not stop on faces but passed through them, measuring something else.

Kammler's breath caught despite his discipline.

Because the gaze reached him.

Not in the casual way a man's eyes might sweep across a mass. It found him. It held him. The condemned man's expression did not change into surprise. It did not change into fear.

It changed into recognition.

Kammler's pulse thudded hard once, and the sensation of being watched multiplied: the crowd watching, the soldiers watching, the circling birds watching, the sky itself reacting like a living surface.

The technician made a small, strangled sound.

Kammler did not silence him this time. He could not. His own body had become a variable.

The condemned man's lips moved.

The sound that emerged was quiet, nearly lost under the crowd's noise, yet it reached Kammler with an impossible clarity, as if the air chose to deliver it.

A German syllable, shaped carefully.

Not shouted. Not whispered.

Spoken as if it had been waiting.

Kammler stood frozen among dust and sweat and history's machinery, staring at the bloodied face turned toward him, and understood with sudden, cold certainty that his protocol had failed before he had even touched anything.

He had been noticed.

Not by Rome.

Not by the crowd.

By the man on the ground, pinned beneath hands and iron.

By the center of the moment the Pope had demanded.

And by whatever made the sky tighten above Golgotha as if time itself were holding its breath.

"Kammler."

The syllables landed with a precision that had nothing to do with volume. They were not carried on the wind so much as placed into his ear, as if the air itself had been instructed where to deliver them.

Dr. Hans Kammler did not move. Around him, Golgotha continued its work. Hands pinned a forearm to wood. The laborer's fist tightened around the nail. The crowd's murmur rose and fell like surf against stone. A Roman soldier laughed at something said behind him. None of it mattered in that instant, because the man on the ground had spoken a German name that did not exist in his century.

Kammler's first instinct was the one that had kept him alive in rooms where loyalty was a trap: deny the premise. Refuse surprise. Control the variables.

But surprise was already in his body. His pulse had betrayed him with a hard, single word, and the tight, cold sensation under his skin had sharpened into certainty. This was not coincidence. Not mishearing. Not a priest's trick. Not Orsini's mythology brought to life.

The condemned man's eyes held him.

Those eyes were not glazed with impending death. They were exhausted, yes, and ringed by swelling and blood, but there was an awareness behind them that did not fit the posture of a man being executed for the entertainment of an empire.

The technician at Kammler's side made a thin sound, almost a whimper, and clapped his lips shut as if afraid the world would punish him for noise. His knuckles were white around the canvas bag.

Kammler felt the harness straps bite into his shoulders as he drew a slow breath. He counted, automatically, as if numbers could lay a grid over the impossible.

One breath. Two.

Do not speak, the protocol whispered.

But the protocol had not accounted for this. The protocol had assumed the past would be dumb. That it would accept intrusion the way a landscape accepted footsteps. That attention was a one-way force.

The man on the ground shifted his head a fraction, the movement painful, and yet his gaze did not waver. A soldier yanked his hair back roughly to expose the arm again.

"Hold him," the soldier barked in Latin.

The condemned man's lips parted again, and this time Kammler saw that the effort cost him, that each word was an expenditure of breath. Still, the voice came with the same impossible clarity, threading through noise like a wire through cloth.

"You came too early," he said in German.

Kammler's mind tried to place the accent. It could not. The German was not Berlin, not Austrian, not Swiss, not any dialect he recognized. It was simply German, stripped of geography, as if the language had been learned without a homeland.

The technician's eyes flicked to Kammler, pleading for instruction. Kammler did not look at him. Looking felt like an admission of fear.

Kammler leaned forward slightly, letting the crowd's press disguise the movement, and kept his lips barely moving when he answered. "Who are you," he said, and hated the tremor he heard in his own voice because it sounded like a question rather than an assessment.

The condemned man's mouth tightened faintly, not into a smile, but into something that resembled sadness with its edges shaved off.

"You know," he said. "And you do not."

A laborer raised the hammer. The nail's point touched skin.

The shimmer above the hill tightened. Kammler felt it as pressure in the teeth, like the first resonance of Die Glocke building under the mountain. It was the same kind of wrongness, translated into open air. A field without coils. A tension that did not require machinery to exist.

The condemned man's eyes flicked upward, briefly, not as if he feared the sky but as if he recognized the pattern of what was happening to it.

Then he looked back at Kammler. "You have made a door," he said. "And you think you are the first to stand in it."

The hammer came down. The crack of iron into flesh and wood snapped through the crowd's noise. A gasp rippled. Someone cheered. Someone retched. The condemned man's body jolted, shoulders straining, breath tearing out of him in a sound that did not become a scream, because the pain was too deep for performance.

Kammler's stomach tightened hard. He had watched men die in manufactured ways. He had designed conditions that made death efficient. But this was not efficiency. This was Rome teaching an occupied people what it meant to be powerless.

And in the middle of it, the man still tried to speak.

"You will not take what you came for," he said, voice ragged now, and the words had to fight through pain.

Kammler forced himself to focus on the sentence, not the blood. "You do not know what I came for."

"I know," the man said, and a thin, wet breath followed. "You came to steal proof."

The technician flinched, as if the word steal had struck him physically. His gaze skittered across the laborers and soldiers, terrified someone else had heard the German. But no one reacted. The Romans did not turn. The crowd did not suddenly fall silent. It was as if the conversation existed in a narrow corridor of perception that did not belong to the rest of the hill.

Kammler felt, with cold clarity, that the Observer he had named in pencil was not a metaphor.

It could allocate attention. It could narrow it. It could allow two men to speak across centuries while an empire hammered nails and the crowd watched without noticing the theft of language happening a few paces away.

Kammler swallowed, the motion hard in his throat. "If you know," he said, "then tell me what you are."

A second arm was seized and stretched. The condemned man's face tightened, anticipating the next hammer blow.

"I am here," he said. "And you are not."

The answer was infuriating in its simplicity. It sounded like a priest evading a direct question. It sounded like Orsini, calm and precise, refusing to speak in the language of machines. Kammler felt anger flare because anger was easier than awe.

"I am here," Kammler said, and forced the words out, "as you are. Flesh. Time. Place."

The condemned man's eyes held him, and for a moment Kammler thought he saw something behind them that was not human knowledge but an immense, quiet attention, like a horizon you only noticed when you tried to run past it.

"No," the man said. "You are a wound moving through the world. And you think the world will not bleed."

The hammer fell again. Another crack. Another jolt of body. Blood ran down the forearm in a thin, bright line that looked too vivid against sun-bleached wood.

The condemned man's breath came hard, and Kammler heard the effort it took to shape syllables around pain.

"You built your bell," he said, voice raw. "And you think it is a tool."

Kammler felt his jaw tighten. The bell. Die Glocke. The Owl Mountains. The alien fragment sealed in steel. The newspapers shifting. Schreiber vanishing in the Black Forest wreck. Names and places that did not exist here, and yet the man spoke as if he had walked through the facility and read the grids himself.

"How," Kammler said, and the single word held more than a question. It was an accusation against the structure of reality.

The condemned man's gaze flicked toward the crowd, toward the soldiers, toward the circling birds. Then up again, briefly, to the shimmer above the hill.

"You have been seen," he said simply. "And you do not understand what sees."

Kammler's fingers flexed inside his gloves. He could feel the sweat trapped beneath the leather. The harness creaked as he shifted his weight, barely perceptible.

The condemned man's lips parted again, and the next words came softer, not because he lacked strength, but because he chose to spend what strength remained with precision.

"You want to bring proof to Rome," he said. "To a man in white who is hungry."

Kammler's eyes narrowed. The Pope. The sealed room. The hand on the newspaper. The bargain. The routes. The condition. None of it belonged here, and yet it was laid out in front of him as if time were a ledger and this man had read the entries.

Kammler's voice dropped further. "Do you know him."

"I know what he wants," the man said. "And I know what you want."

A Roman soldier stepped close and spat, the globule landing near the condemned man's cheek.

The soldier laughed and said something to another soldier that made him grin.

The condemned man did not look at the soldier. His attention remained on Kammler, as if the empire's cruelty was small compared to the intrusion standing in the crowd with straps across his chest.

"You will take what you think is mine," he said. "And you will call it proof."

Kammler's mind leapt to the canvas bag. Biological sample. Blood, tissue, anything that could be analyzed, cloned, verified. Something that could not shift like ink when watched. Something that could anchor the future.

"Yes," Kammler said, and there was no apology in it. "I will."

The condemned man's eyelids lowered briefly, not in surrender, but in the reflex of a man holding pain at bay long enough to speak.

"You are not stealing proof," he said, and the words came with a weight that made the air feel denser. "You are creating something that should never exist."

Kammler felt the phrase strike him in a place he did not like to admit existed. Not conscience. Not faith. Something closer to engineering instinct: the warning in a blueprint that certain stresses will collapse a bridge no matter how much ideology you pour onto it.

"What," Kammler said, and heard the edge in his own voice, the impatience of a man who demanded specifics. "What will exist."

The condemned man's gaze shifted again, up toward the shimmer, and this time Kammler followed it without meaning to.

The sky above Golgotha looked unchanged to the crowd. Still blue. Still bright. Still indifferent.

But Kammler saw it now as a surface under pressure. Fine fractures of distortion, almost invisible, not cracks of light but shifts in texture, as if something on the other side pressed close enough to make itself felt. Not God. Not weather. Something like attention given form.

The condemned man spoke again, and his voice was nearly a whisper, threaded through pain.

"There are things," he said, "that learn by watching."

Kammler's throat tightened. He remembered the way the newspapers behaved like testimony under interrogation. He remembered the word Observer on the grid. He remembered the sense, in the mountain facility, that the shadows moved wrong when the machine warmed.

He looked back at the condemned man. “Are you saying it is not you,” he asked, and for the first time the question carried something close to fear, because the alternative was worse than blasphemy. “Are you saying something else is speaking.”

The condemned man’s eyes held his, and in them Kammler saw recognition that was too old to be personal.

“I am speaking,” he said. “And you are being heard.”

A laborer and a soldier began to drag the crossbeam into position, preparing the lift. The condemned man’s body was hauled with it, shoulders wrenching, breath breaking. The crowd surged again, hungry for the next stage.

Kammler felt an internal jolt, a sudden awareness of time not as theology but as an eight-minute return pulse counting down regardless of revelation. He had come for proof. He had found a voice.

The condemned man’s lips moved one more time as he was pulled, and the words came out with effort, shaped around the tearing of flesh and the scraping of wood.

"Go back," he said in German. "Close your door."

Kammler stood in the dust, the crowd pressing, the Roman soldiers shouting, the hill vibrating with old cruelty, and above it all the sky held its shimmering tension like a lid held down by force.

He did not step back.

He did not run.

He watched the crossbeam rise, watched the body lifted with it, and in the condemned man's eyes he saw not a plea for mercy, but a warning delivered like a specification.

Close your door.

Kammler tightened his grip on the technician's sleeve and leaned close, lips barely moving. "Stay with me," he ordered.

The technician nodded too fast, eyes wet, shaking.

Kammler's gaze fixed on the blood running along the condemned man's arm, on the bright line collecting and falling in slow drops to the dirt.

Material, his mind insisted. Anchor. Proof.

Above them, the sky's distortion tightened again, and for a fraction of a second Kammler felt, unmistakably, that something had turned its attention fully upon him, not curious like the Pope, not weary like the dying man, but cold and measuring, as if deciding what kind of consequence to assign.

Kammler held his posture anyway.

He had not crossed nineteen centuries to be dismissed by a warning.

And if the past was speaking to him in German, then the past could be made to yield more than words.

The condemned man's body rose with the crossbeam, lifted by hands that treated him like a weight to be placed rather than a life to be ended. Rope creaked. Wood scraped against stone. The laborers swore softly to one another in a language Kammler did not understand. Roman soldiers barked in sharp Latin, ordering the crowd back, ordering the work forward, ordering the day to remain orderly.

The warning hung in Kammler's mind with a precision that made it feel less like prophecy and more like instruction.

Go back. Close your door.

He did not move.

He watched the body tilt as they aligned the beam with the upright post, watched the shoulders wrench, watched the arms stretch into angles no living mechanism should have to endure. The crowd surged and recoiled in waves, as if the human mass had its own respiration. Somewhere a woman's cry rose above the noise and then broke into sobbing that could not find words. A man laughed too loudly and was slapped by another, not in defense of mercy but in defense of decorum.

Kammler counted. Not seconds, because he had no instrument, but the internal rhythm the physicist had trained into them: the length of a breath, the span of a glance, the time it took for a drop of blood to gather and fall.

Blood.

It was running steadily now, bright against the condemned man's forearm where the nail had been driven, tracing a path down skin and wrist, pooling briefly in the shallow depression of bone before spilling in drops. Each drop struck the dust and vanished into it, absorbed too quickly, as if the ground had learned what to do with this particular offering.

The technician beside him made a small sound, and Kammler felt the man's sleeve pull taut under his grip. The technician's eyes were fixed on the lifted body, glassy with terror, and Kammler saw the exact moment the man began to sway, the body's instinct to faint as a way to escape what the mind could not endure.

Kammler tightened his fingers around the technician's arm until the man stiffened, pain cutting through panic.

"Stay," Kammler said, barely shaping the word, and hated himself for speaking again. The air responded with the faintest tightening, like skin reacting to a touch it did not want. He closed his mouth and forced his gaze forward as if discipline alone could undo the mistake.

The condemned man's head lolled forward, then lifted again. His eyes found Kammler once more with the same impossible precision. Not scanning. Not searching. Finding.

There was no pleading in that gaze. Only knowledge and something like sorrow, not for himself, but for what Kammler was about to do.

Kammler felt a surge of anger at that expression, because it assumed superiority. It assumed that the man on the wood had authority over the man standing free in the crowd.

"You want to bring proof to Rome," the man had said. "You want to steal proof."

Kammler's jaw tightened beneath the harness straps. He had not come here to be shamed by a dying man's calm.

Proof was not a hymn. Proof was matter.

His gloved hand slid down to the canvas bag the technician carried. The bag was absurd in this century, but inside it was the reason they had come prepared at all: a small glass ampoule sealed with wax, a folded strip of sterile cloth, and a thin metal implement the surgeon had provided without comment. The implement was not a knife in the usual sense. It was a narrow, sharpened tool meant to take a sliver cleanly, quickly, without tearing. The surgeon had designed it for the bell's earlier animal tests. Kammler had repurposed it for divinity.

He glanced at the soldiers. Two stood near the base of the upright post, spears angled lazily, watching the crowd more than the execution. One soldier's attention wandered to a group of men arguing near the edge; another turned his head toward a vendor who had appeared with a jug, as if even at Golgotha someone could be expected to sell relief.

The crowd's eyes were mostly on the lifted bodies and the laborers, not on each other. That, Kammler realized, was the only reason any of this was possible. Rome had created a theater so compelling it blinded the audience to the aisles.

He used the crowd's pressure to move, not forward in a straight line, but sideways, sliding along the slope until he found a pocket where bodies stood tightly enough to conceal small motions. He kept the technician close, not as a companion but as an extension of his own cover.

The technician shook his head once, a tiny, frantic refusal. His lips moved as if to repeat the warning they had just heard. He did not dare speak it.

Kammler leaned close, breath warm against the man's ear, and spoke in German with minimal movement, a line that sounded like command because it was.

"You will open the bag when I touch your hand," he said. "You will not look at me. You will not look up. If you faint, I will leave you here."

The technician's eyes widened. The threat worked. Fear always worked. It was the Reich's oldest equation, and it did not change even when the century did.

The laborers began to secure the crossbeam. One hammered wedges into the joint with quick, practiced blows. The sound rang through the hill. A second condemned man, not the one who had spoken, was dragged into place nearby, his body limp in a way that suggested he had already surrendered. The crowd responded to him with less interest. Their attention kept returning to the center, to the man whose pain seemed to pull the air toward it.

Kammler moved again, edging closer. The shimmer in the sky thickened as he did, and for a moment he had the disorienting sensation that he was wading into a field. Not wind. Not heat. Something like resistance, as if the space around the cross were denser than the space around the crowd.

His teeth ached faintly, the same intimate vibration he had felt under Die Glocke when the coils aligned. He had assumed that was the machine's effect. Now, under an open sky, he understood that the machine had not invented the sensation. It had merely taught his body what it felt like when reality was being strained.

He forced himself forward anyway.

The condemned man's chest heaved. His hands were fixed now. The wrists bled. The fingers curled and uncurled reflexively, seeking purchase against nothing. A Roman soldier stepped forward with a jar and a stick tipped with a sponge, offering it to the condemned man's mouth, not as mercy but as prolongation. The man turned his head slightly away. The soldier shrugged and pulled the sponge back with irritation.

Kammler saw his opening.

A strip of cloth or a sponge could carry blood. A droplet could be trapped before it vanished into dust. He did not need to cut flesh. He did not need to reach the wound itself. He only needed contact with the evidence of it.

He slid his hand down and touched the technician's knuckles.

The technician's fingers trembled as he loosened the bag's mouth. His gaze remained fixed stubbornly on the ground, as ordered, but Kammler could feel the man's terror vibrating through his arm.

Kammler's gloved hand dipped into the bag and found the folded strip of cloth. He pulled it free slowly, shielding it between his forearm and the bodies pressed around him. He unfolded it with small, controlled movements, the way he might unfold a blueprint in a room full of men who wanted to steal it.

Someone in the crowd jostled him, and Kammler stiffened, instinctive, ready to strike. He did not. He absorbed the impact and let the crowd think it was ordinary clumsiness.

He raised the cloth, hiding it behind the technician's shoulder, and stepped into the last few paces where the soldiers' corridor began.

A Roman soldier glanced toward him, brow tightening. Kammler lowered his head and angled his shoulders as if he were merely another onlooker pressing too close. The soldier's gaze flicked to the execution again, drawn by the theater. He did not stop Kammler. He was trained to manage crowds, not anomalies. He did not know what an anomaly looked like.

Kammler reached the base of the upright post.

The condemned man's feet were not yet fixed to the wood. The laborers were still adjusting the height and angle, still preparing the next nail. For a brief span, the body hung and strained, blood running down the arm in a steadier stream. Kammler lifted the cloth and brought it close, not touching skin, not touching the nail, but catching a falling drop as it slid free.

The first drop struck the cloth and darkened it.

Kammler felt a shock run through his hand, not electric, not pain, but a sudden sense of contact that was too intimate to be merely physical. As if he had placed his fingers into a current.

The shimmer above the hill tightened into something that felt like a held breath.

The condemned man's head turned a fraction, and his eyes met Kammler's again. Close now. Close enough that Kammler could see the fine tremor in the eyelids, the lines of strain around the mouth, the sheen of sweat on bruised skin.

"You will not take what you came for," the man had said.

Kammler watched the cloth absorb the second drop of blood and felt the old, rigid part of him that had built weapons and tunnels and camps answer the warning with the only language it respected.

I will.

The condemned man's lips moved, and although the crowd roared at a hammer blow elsewhere, Kammler heard the German anyway, as if the sound were being delivered directly through the air's resistance.

"Do not," the man said, and the word was not a plea. It was a verdict.

Kammler folded the cloth quickly, sealing the wet portion inside, and slid it back into the bag. His fingers moved on their own with practiced precision. He reached for the ampoule.

The technician flinched as Kammler's hand brushed his, a reflex of a man who wanted to run but could not. Kammler's grip tightened on the ampoule, feeling the cool glass through his glove.

Above them, the sky's blue held, but the texture of it looked wrong, as if something behind it pressed closer, curious in a way that had nothing to do with mercy.

Kammler did not look up again. Looking up felt like acknowledgment.

He brought the ampoule out, shielded by bodies and wood, and positioned it near the folded cloth as if preparing to seal the sample away from air and dust and time itself.

The condemned man's gaze did not leave him.

"You are creating something that should never exist," the man had said.

Kammler's mouth tightened. He had created many things that should never have existed. The world had not stopped him then. Why would it stop him now?

He sealed the cloth into the ampoule with movements so small the crowd could not read them as theft. He pressed wax into place with a thumb. He returned the ampoule to the bag and closed it.

For a heartbeat, the air loosened slightly, as if the world had registered the act and recalculated.

Then the cold pressure returned, sharper.

Kammler stepped back into the crowd, pulling the technician with him, and for the first time since arriving he felt the return corridor's distant pull like a hand beginning to tighten on a rope.

Eight minutes were nearly gone.

Behind him, the laborers lifted the hammer again for the next nail.

In front of him, the hill continued its work.

And somewhere above, in the tightened blue, something watched the theft complete and did not intervene like a god.

It observed like an intelligence deciding what consequence would be appropriate for a man who had been warned by the dying and had chosen, anyway, to take.

Chapter 9

The Theft of Divinity

Kammler let the crowd carry him backward, step by measured step, until the upright post and the laborers' hands were no longer within arm's reach. He kept one gloved hand on the technician's sleeve, not because the man would run, but because panic had its own physics. It pulled in the wrong directions at the wrong times.

The canvas bag bumped against the technician's thigh. Each time it did, Kammler felt the ampoule inside as a phantom weight, a tiny sealed certainty that should have calmed him.

It did not.

The blood was proof, yes. Material taken from the hinge of history, sealed in glass and wax like an insect pinned for study. It was enough to satisfy the Pope's hunger for something he could not pray into existence.

But Kammler's mind would not stop at enough. The newspapers had taught him that the world could revise itself when it was watched. A single sample could be challenged, dismissed as contamination, questioned by men who needed doubt to survive their own beliefs. Kammler had survived by redundancy. Two generators. Two couriers. Two copies of everything that mattered.

One proof could be lost.

Two proofs could be defended.

The return corridor tugged at him again, subtle as a change in pressure before a storm. Not a hand, not a rope in the literal sense, but a growing insistence behind his sternum, like a clock that had begun to vibrate instead of tick. He could not see the oval of wrongness from here. He did not need to. The machine had left a leash in the world, and the leash was tightening.

He angled the technician through a knot of bodies until they reached a patch of thinner crowd near a cluster of stones. From there, the view up the rise was still clear. The condemned men were being fixed into position. Hammer blows cracked across the hill with a rhythm too practical to be holy.

The man on the central cross lifted his head again.

Kammler felt the gaze touch him like a fingertip.

Not searching. Not pleading. Knowing.

The German words from moments ago remained in Kammler's ear with the clarity of an order: Do not.

He refused to let them become anything more than noise. He had listened to too many warnings given by men who wanted to keep power by disguising it as morality.

He opened his hand inside his glove, flexed his fingers once, then slid them toward the bag again.

The technician flinched immediately, as if the movement itself was a threat.

Kammler leaned close without looking at him directly. "Hold it open," he murmured in the smallest possible German. "And do not shake."

The technician swallowed hard, eyes fixed downward, and eased the bag's mouth open with trembling fingers. His obedience was brittle, but it held.

Kammler's gloved hand went in and found the thin metal implement the surgeon had provided. It felt wrong in his palm here, too precise, too cold, a tool that belonged under electric light rather than an ancient sun. He kept it hidden by turning his body slightly, letting the bodies around him form a living curtain.

He waited for an opening.

A Roman soldier on the left moved down the line, barking at spectators who pressed too close. The crowd shifted away from the soldier like grass bending before a boot. For a heartbeat, the soldier's attention was not on the upright posts. The laborers were focused on rope and leverage. Everyone's attention was where it had been trained to be: on suffering.

Kammler stepped forward into the brief slack in the perimeter.

The air thickened as soon as he moved uphill. He felt it in his teeth again, that intimate ache, a resonance without coils. The shimmer overhead sharpened at the edges of his vision, and he had the irrational certainty that he could hear it if he listened the way he listened to a generator under strain.

Do not look up, he told himself. Looking up was acknowledgment. Acknowledgment was attention. Attention was what made ink shift.

He kept his eyes on the wood.

At the base of the central post, the dirt had been churned by feet. Darker stains marred the ground where blood had already fallen and been swallowed. Near the post's foot, a small ridge of rock jutted from the soil, and on it lay a smear that caught sunlight with a wet sheen.

Fresh.

Not a miracle. Not a sign.

A mechanical fact: blood did not vanish instantly. It clung where it could.

Kammler lowered himself as if pushed by the crowd, a half crouch disguised as losing balance on uneven stone. His left shoulder bumped another man's hip. Someone grunted and shoved back. Kammler absorbed it, head down, posture ordinary in its clumsiness.

His right hand, hidden, brought the implement down toward the smear.

The technician's breathing hitched behind him.

Kammler pressed the tip to the rock and drew it along the surface in a slow, controlled motion, scraping a thin line of fluid and dust into the implement's shallow groove. The sensation was faintly sticky through the glove, a detail so mundane it almost broke the spell of where he was.

Then the air tightened sharply, as if the world disliked being harvested.

The hairs at the back of Kammler's neck lifted. The thickening around him became a focused pressure, local and intent, like a lens turning.

He froze mid-motion.

For a fraction of a second, he thought the soldier would shout, that a hand would seize his collar, that Rome would punish him for trying to pocket what belonged to gods.

No one touched him.

No one spoke.

Instead, the sound of the hill seemed to shift around him. The crowd's roar remained, the hammer blows remained, but they muffled at the edges, as if his crouched pocket of air had been wrapped in cloth. He could still hear everything, yet it felt farther away, less immediate. The same narrow corridor of perception the dying man had used to speak German.

Kammler's mind snapped to the word he had written in pencil like an infection.

Observer.

He could feel it now not as an idea but as presence, cold and measuring, close enough to alter the thickness of a moment. It was not stopping him. It was making sure he understood he was being watched while he committed the act.

Kammler finished the scrape. He lifted the implement and drew his hand back into the bag in one smooth movement, the way a pickpocket withdrew a stolen wallet.

He did not exhale until he had stepped backward into the crowd's safer density.

The technician's eyes were wide, wet with fear. His lips moved soundlessly, forming a prayer or a plea or a German curse. He could not decide which, so he said nothing.

Kammler opened the bag again with his own hand and pulled out a second ampoule, smaller than the first. It had been intended as a reserve. Kammler had not told anyone he planned to use it here.

He slid the implement into the ampoule, angled it so the scraped mixture slid off into the glass. A smear, a bead, a dark fleck that looked unimpressive against the clear curvature of the container. Kammler's fingers worked quickly, sealing wax over the mouth, pressing it firm with a thumb.

For a heartbeat, he felt something like triumph.

Then the return corridor's pull surged hard enough that his knees flexed.

The technician made a noise he could not hold back, a sharp breath that almost became a cry.

Kammler seized his sleeve and dragged him laterally, away from the posts, away from the soldiers, away from the hill's center. The crowd resisted, dense with bodies that did not understand urgency, but it parted as if the air in front of Kammler had been warmed. People leaned away from him, not because they knew why, but because their instincts recoiled from whatever field clung to him like odor.

The central figure on the cross lifted his head again, and Kammler felt the gaze strike him once more.

Not anger.

Not fear.

A kind of grief that did not fit the scene, as if the man were watching something happen that was larger than his own death.

Kammler did not look away first this time. He met the eyes with the stubbornness of a man who had never yielded once he decided an act was necessary.

The lips on the cross moved.

Even with the crowd's noise and the hammering and the Roman commands, the German reached Kammler with quiet precision.

"You will carry it back," the man said, voice stretched thin by pain, "and you will think it is contained."

Kammler's jaw tightened. He did not answer. Answering would have been admission that the corridor existed, that the conversation was real.

The return pull intensified again, and this time it was not only in his body. The world around him seemed to tilt toward an unseen point. Dust rose in a brief swirl that did not match the wind's direction. A child stumbled and began to cry. A dog near the crowd's edge bolted without barking, tail tucked, as if fleeing a sound too low for human ears.

The technician's feet began to slide as if the ground had lost friction. He grabbed at Kammler's arm with both hands, suddenly no longer capable of pretending calm.

Kammler held him upright, and in the same instant he felt the air behind them shimmer with familiar wrongness.

The corridor was opening again, or widening, or preparing to snap shut with them inside it.

Kammler had both ampoules now: one containing cloth darkened by blood taken directly from the living flow, the other containing scrapings from the ground at the cross's base, a second proof gathered from the spill of history.

In his mind, the samples were neat, categorized, sealed.

In his body, the sensation was not neat at all.

It felt like theft.

Not theft from Rome, or from a Church, or from a mythology.

Theft from a moment that had been holding something back, and that had now been forced to notice him.

As the pull reached its peak, Kammler's eyes flicked upward in spite of himself.

The sky above Golgotha was still blue to the crowd, still sunlit, still the ordinary canopy of day.

But along the edge of his vision he saw fine distortions tighten into hairline fractures, not in light, not in clouds, but in the texture of the air itself, like stress lines in glass that had been struck but not yet shattered.

Something pressed close from the other side.

Not a face. Not a form.

An attention.

And in the split second before the corridor took him, Kammler understood that the man on the cross had not been warning him about punishment from God.

He had been warning him about consequence from whatever watched the hinge of time and learned, patiently, whenever a door was opened.

The world lurched.

Sound cut out as if someone had closed a fist around it.

The last thing Kammler felt before the hill vanished was the cold certainty of glass ampoules against his palm and the unsettling impression that the air itself had memorized his touch.

The return corridor did not open like a door.

It clenched.

Kammler's last sight of Golgotha was not the cross, not the crowd, but the air itself tightening into those hairline stress lines he had seen at the edge of perception, as if the blue above the hill had become a thin sheet under too much pressure. Then the world folded.

Silence did not arrive gradually. It was cut.

The crowd vanished mid-motion, sound severed so cleanly that Kammler's ears rang with the absence, a phantom roar where the hill had been. His stomach lurched upward as if gravity had been reassigned. The technician's weight slammed into him, both hands locking on Kammler's sleeve with the desperation of a drowning man. The harness straps bit hard, suddenly too tight, as though the machine resented carrying bodies through a space that was not meant to be walked.

The corridor was not darkness. It was a thin, shimmering wrongness, the oval bruise in the air expanded into a tunnel of uncertain distance. There was no stable surface to look at. Every attempt to fix his eyes on an edge made the edge move, as if the corridor corrected for scrutiny.

Kammler kept the bag close to his torso. The glass ampoules pressed against his palm through cloth and leather, cold and too real. Proof did not belong in a place like this. Matter felt obscene inside a passage that was half idea, half violence.

The technician tried to shout. No sound emerged, but Kammler felt the man's throat working, felt the tremor traveling down his arm into Kammler's grip.

"Do not," Kammler mouthed, the habit of command persisting even when the air refused to carry it.

The corridor responded anyway.

Not with a voice. With a shift.

It tightened around them, and Kammler understood, with the same kind of clinical certainty he applied to concrete and steel, that the return pulse was no longer a summons. It was a restraint mechanism, a timed resonance trying to pull them back along a thread that was beginning to fray.

Ahead, or what his mind insisted on calling ahead, the tunnel's texture changed. The shimmering became granular. Fine specks of light appeared and vanished, not like stars but like static on film. The field's pressure rose in his teeth until it became pain.

Then the sky appeared again.

Not the sky of 1936. Not the sky of the Owl Mountains. The blue of Golgotha flashed across the corridor like an image projected too close, a surface pressed up against their faces.

And it broke.

Kammler watched, suspended between centuries, as the blue tore along the hairline fractures he had seen. It did not tear like cloth. It broke like glass under stress, a clean, branching network of cracks that ran outward from a point he could not locate, because the sky was no longer above. It was around. It was inside the corridor with them, a membrane dragged into the passage by the act of leaving.

Through those cracks came something that was not light.

A darkness deeper than absence, threaded with a faint, oily iridescence, as if it had color but refused to settle on any one wavelength. It pressed against the broken edges and made them flex. Kammler felt the pressure in his bones, the way he had felt Die Glocke's resonance, but this was not a machine. This was a reaction.

The technician convulsed, and a soundless scream finally found a kind of expression, not through air but through vibration. Kammler felt it in his own skull, a raw, panicked frequency.

Kammler's mind tried to label what he was seeing. He could not. There were no instruments here, no graphs, no controlled light. Only the visual fact of fracture and the physical fact of being held inside a corridor that suddenly felt like the narrowest part of a throat.

The broken sky pulsed once.

Not a heartbeat. Something more deliberate. Like attention shifting.

Kammler had spent weeks watching ink revise itself under a microscope. He had suspected a watcher. In this corridor, with the sky splintered, suspicion became confirmation in the only way that mattered: it became sensation.

He was being examined.

Not by a man. Not even by a mind that needed eyes. The feeling was of something touching the outline of his presence, tracing him the way a gloved finger traced the edge of a wound. It lingered on the bag, on the ampoules, on the sealed wax as if it recognized the obscene act of carrying blood out of a moment that had been meant to remain sealed.

A shape moved behind the cracks.

Not a body. A distortion in the darkness, an implication of geometry that made Kammler's vision blur when he tried to focus. The corridor's surface shimmered in response, as though it wanted to hide the thing from direct observation and failed.

The technician's grip tightened until it hurt. Kammler did not push him away. The man's panic was an anchor in a place where anchors were failing.

Kammler forced his eyes away from the cracks and down to the bag, as if refusing to look would reduce the reaction. It had worked, partly, with the newspapers. Staring made them move. Minimizing attention made them settle.

Here, minimizing attention felt like offering submission.

He did not submit.

He pulled the bag closer to his chest, arm tightening, and in that motion the waxed mouth of one ampoule scraped lightly against another through the fabric. A tiny, delicate clink in a world without sound.

The corridor flinched.

The cracks in the sky widened by a hair.

And from the darkness behind them came a sensation that was almost, but not quite, amusement. Not human amusement. Something colder, like a system recognizing a pattern it could exploit.

Kammler saw, in a flash, the condemned man's face and the German words delivered as if the air itself had been trained to translate.

"There are things that learn by watching."

He had thought it was metaphor. He had been wrong.

The fractured sky brightened at the edges of the cracks, not with sun, but with a thin, harsh glow as if the membrane was being forced apart. Something on the other side pressed closer. The corridor's pressure spiked, and Kammler's harness straps seemed to tighten further, constricting his ribs.

The technician's eyes rolled back for a moment, then snapped forward again, wide and unfocused. His mouth formed a prayer Kammler could not hear. Kammler saw the shape of Latin in his lips without knowing the words. The man had not been trained for this. He had been chosen for silence. Silence was not enough.

Kammler's own throat worked. He wanted to speak, to command the corridor to close, to order the past to repair itself, to shout at the broken sky as if it were a subordinate.

He did not. He remembered the way the air had tightened on Golgotha when he said "No." Here, even thought felt loud.

The corridor lurched.

For an instant, Kammler saw two versions of reality layered on top of each other. The Owl Mountains cavern flickered into existence: steel ribs, floodlights, the physicist's pale face behind the console, Orsini's dark silhouette at the edge of the ring. Then Golgotha flickered back: dust, wood, the cross lifting, the blue membrane of sky cracking.

Both images shuddered. The corridor was failing to decide which world to privilege.

The cracks spread across the Golgotha-blue like lightning in reverse. Kammler saw, through one widening split, the suggestion of depth that was not space as humans understood it. It looked like a place between pages, the dark gap you never see until you tear the book.

And then the darkness moved with purpose.

It did not reach for Kammler with hands. It reached by aligning.

The corridor's shimmer began to rotate subtly, the way field lines rotated around Die Glocke when the coils were out of phase. Kammler recognized the sensation with the fury of a man watching an enemy use his own engineering against him. Something had found the resonance that held the corridor open and was testing it, turning it, seeking the point where it could slip through.

The technician's body jerked, as if something had brushed his nervous system directly. His grip loosened for a fraction of a second.

Kammler seized his sleeve harder, yanking him back against his own side. The movement was violent, more violent than protocol allowed, but protocol had been written for a machine. This was no longer only the machine.

The fractured sky convulsed once more.

Kammler saw, at the center of one crack, a brief image that made his stomach drop: not a face, but an arrangement of angles and voids that implied observation without needing a pupil. It was like looking at a symbol that carried meaning directly into the brain.

He felt, for a moment, that the thing had recognized him personally.

Not Hans Kammler as a man. Hans Kammler as an opening.

As a method.

The condemned man's warning returned with brutal clarity: "Close your door."

Kammler had not closed it. He had widened it, then tried to carry something through it.

The corridor screamed without sound, a violent vibration that turned Kammler's teeth into instruments. The cracks in the sky flashed, and the Golgotha-blue shattered entirely, breaking into fragments that spun outward like splinters of glass. For an instant, those fragments reflected both centuries at once: Roman helmets and SS uniforms, wood and steel, blood and ink.

Then the fragments dissolved into pure brightness, harsh and clinical like arc light.

Kammler's vision whitened.

The pull snapped hard, like a rope finally yanked free of a snag.

And as the corridor collapsed behind them, Kammler felt, unmistakably, a last brush of attention at his back, as if something had leaned close to inhale the trace of him, and had decided it could find him again.

The world slammed into solidity.

Sound returned as a brutal rush: generators thundering, men shouting, alarms beginning to rise. The bell chamber's floodlights flared too bright, then dimmed, then flared again, as if the facility itself had been shocked by what had followed them to the threshold.

Kammler's boots hit concrete. His knees buckled. The technician collapsed to the floor and vomited, the heave loud in the cavern's acoustics.

Orsini's voice cut through the chaos, sharp for the first time. "What happened?"

The physicist was already shouting numbers, eyes locked on gauges that trembled violently. "The return corridor destabilized. The field amplitude spiked. It spiked beyond range. It's still spiking."

Kammler did not answer either of them.

He stood over the technician's shaking body, one hand still clenched around the canvas bag. He could feel the ampoules inside, intact. Wax unbroken. Proof preserved.

Above Die Glocke, the air shimmered.

Not heat. Not dust.

A faint, hairline texture like stress in glass, barely visible under the floodlights.

As if the sky they had shattered had left a memory of its fracture in the mountain's air.

Kammler looked at the bell's polished curve and saw his own reflection split for a fraction of a second into two overlapping outlines, one slightly delayed, one slightly ahead, as though time itself could not quite agree on where he belonged.

Behind him, the technician sobbed into the concrete. The physicist kept speaking faster, panic distorting his German into something almost unrecognizable. Orsini stood rigid at the edge of the ring, eyes fixed on the shimmering air with the pale composure of a man watching theology become physics.

Kammler tightened his grip on the bag until his knuckles ached beneath leather.

He had brought back proof.

And he had brought back a fracture.

The alarms did not begin as a single sound.

They rose in layers, reluctant at first, then insistent, as if the facility had to decide whether to admit that what it was registering belonged in any category it had been built to monitor. A klaxon stuttered, died, then caught again with a steadier pulse. A second tone joined it, higher and thinner, the kind used to announce pressure failures in coolant lines. Men shouted over one another, their voices sharpened by the cavern's acoustics into something that sounded like panic dressed in command.

Kammler remained still long enough to take inventory.

Concrete under his boots. The bell's steel ribs gleaming under floodlights that could not settle into a consistent brightness. The technician on his knees, retching again, the vomit splattering and sliding in a thin line toward a drain. The physicist hunched over the console, wire-rimmed glasses skewed on his nose, hands hovering as if afraid to touch the controls again. Orsini rigid at the edge of the ring, his dark clothing a vertical punctuation mark in a room of gray uniforms.

And above Die Glocke, the air that should have been empty had texture.

Not smoke. Not dust. A faint pattern like stress inside glass, hairline and shifting when the light caught it wrong. It was strongest directly above the bell's open interior, where the corridor had snapped shut. It moved when no current should have moved it.

Kammler tightened his grip on the canvas bag until the fabric creased. He could feel the ampoules through it: cold cylinders, wax seals intact. The smallest proof imaginable, carried out of Golgotha in a glass fist.

Orsini took a step closer, and for the first time Kammler heard it in the monsignor's breathing. Not fear exactly. Something more controlled and older: the recognition of a pattern he wished he had not been trained to see.

"What did you bring back?" Orsini asked. His voice was steady, but it did not belong to a man making conversation. It belonged to a man trying to place a name on a thing before it placed a name on him.

Kammler did not look away from the air above the bell. "Proof," he said.

"That is not what I mean."

Kammler's jaw tightened. He could have lied. A lie would have been easy in this room. But lying required a shared reality in which falsehood could remain stable. They no longer had stability.

"The corridor fractured," Kammler said. "The sky—" He stopped. The word sky sounded absurd underground. "The membrane did. Something pressed against it."

The physicist's head snapped up at that, eyes wide behind the lenses. "You saw it?" he demanded, voice cracking into a register that made the soldiers nearby glance at him with contempt.

Kammler's gaze remained fixed on the shimmer. "I felt it," he said. "And I saw enough."

The technician convulsed again on the floor, a sob forced out of him between heaves. The man's hands clutched at his own harness straps as if trying to peel them off, as if the buckles themselves were responsible.

"Get him out," Kammler said, and a guard moved at once, hauling the technician upright with little concern for gentleness. The man stumbled, gagging, and was dragged toward the tunnel.

As they passed under the lights, Kammler saw something that made his stomach settle into a colder place.

The technician's shadow did not match him.

It lagged by a fraction of a heartbeat, like a delayed film. When the man's head jerked to the side, the shadow followed, but not perfectly. For an instant, it seemed to hesitate, then snap into alignment.

A trick of the flickering lights, Kammler's mind tried to insist.

But he had watched shadows in the bell chamber before, and he knew the difference between faulty power and faulty reality.

Orsini saw it too. Kammler could tell because the monsignor's eyes flicked down to the floor, then back up without comment, as if refusing to give the phenomenon the gift of acknowledgment.

The physicist began speaking again, fast, hands finally moving over the console as if speed could force the numbers into obedience. "Field amplitude is not returning to baseline. It's oscillating. It's as if we have a standing wave in the chamber, but the coils are disengaged. They are disengaged." He said the last words louder, as if needing the room to confirm that machines were still machines.

The surgeon pushed through the perimeter with two guards behind him, cigarette gone, mouth tight. He took in the vomiting on the floor, the shaking gauges, the shimmer above the bell. His gaze landed on Kammler's bag and stayed there.

"You got it," he said, not a question.

Kammler nodded once.

The surgeon exhaled through his nose. "And you brought something else."

Orsini's head turned toward him. "You feel it too," Orsini said.

The surgeon's eyes narrowed. "I have been in this chamber when the air did not behave," he said. "This is worse."

Kammler stepped closer to the bell's inner perimeter, careful not to cross it. The ring of steel ribs felt less like containment now and more like a throat. The shimmer above the opening seemed to grow more visible the nearer he stood, not brighter, but more defined, as if it wanted him close enough to be sure he understood its presence.

He remembered Golgotha, the sense that the crowd's noise had muffled around him, that perception had narrowed into a corridor where German could be spoken without being heard by Romans. He remembered the cracks in the sky, the darkness behind them with its oily hint of color, the feeling of being examined.

Now he felt it again, but without sun, without dust. Here it had concrete and floodlight and steel to press against. Here it had the bell itself, a device built from alien material that healed when cut, a device that behaved as if it could remember a man's touch.

Orsini moved beside the physicist, leaning in to see the readings though he could not interpret them. His attention was on the air, not the dials.

"You called it an observer," Orsini said quietly, almost to himself. "As if it were merely watching."

The physicist swallowed. "It is watching," he insisted. "It responds to observation. The newspapers, the drift, the—" His voice faltered when the lights flickered again, hard enough that every shadow in the cavern jumped.

The shimmer above the bell pulsed.

Not like a heartbeat. Like a decision.

Every man in the chamber went still. Even the guards seemed to freeze, trained instincts recognizing that a sudden movement might become a target even if the target was unseen.

Kammler felt pressure in his teeth, sudden and intimate. The same low resonance as the bell's activation, but with no sound attached. He tasted metal.

The physicist's console screen, a small rectangle of green, warped. For a moment the numbers displayed there doubled and slid out of alignment, then snapped back as if corrected by an irritated hand.

And then something happened that Kammler could not reduce to equipment malfunction.

A shadow detached itself from the bell.

It was not dramatic. It did not leap. It simply separated slightly from the curvature of steel as if the steel and the darkness beneath it could no longer agree on where their boundary lay. The shadow stretched upward, thin as smoke, but it did not diffuse. It held shape, a narrow column of absence rising toward the shimmer overhead.

The surgeon took a half step back without realizing it. One of the guards made the sign of the cross so fast it looked like a twitch.

Orsini did not move. His face went paler, but his eyes stayed fixed, an archivist watching an entry write itself in the air.

The thin column reached the shimmer and stopped, as if meeting resistance. It pressed, and the shimmer pressed back. There was no explosion. No flash. Only a visible tension, a boundary made temporarily legible.

Kammler felt a thought that was not his own brush the edge of his mind.

Not a voice. Not language. More like the sensation of being counted.

He clenched his jaw until it ached. He did not look away. If it wanted him to flinch, he would not give it that.

The physicist whispered, barely audible, “It’s in phase with us.”

“Not us,” Kammler said. His voice came out rougher than he intended. “With the bell.”

The column of shadow wavered, and for an instant Kammler saw something inside it: a suggestion of geometry, angles that did not behave as perspective demanded. The sight made his eyes water, not from emotion but from the strain of attempting to render the impossible into vision.

Then it was gone. The shadow snapped back to the bell’s base as if yanked. The shimmer overhead softened by a fraction, but it did not vanish. It remained as hairline texture, a bruise in the air.

A guard at the far side of the cavern spoke, voice shaking despite discipline. “Herr Doktor… what is that?”

Kammler did not answer him. He looked at the physicist. “Shut it down,” he ordered.

“It is down,” the physicist said, almost pleading. “The coils are disengaged. The chamber is inert.”

Kammler’s gaze slid to Orsini. “Your Church has names for things that intrude,” he said. “What do you call this.”

Orsini’s throat worked once. When he spoke, his voice was low and careful, as if words themselves might attract attention. “We have many names,” he said. “Most of them are attempts to domesticate what cannot be domesticated.”

Kammler held his gaze. “Then give me the undomesticated one.”

Orsini looked back at the bell, at the shimmer, at the way shadows clung too tightly to the steel ribs. “Inhuman,” he said finally. “Not a demon from a painting. Not an angel from a hymn. Something that does not belong to our categories and does not care that we have them.”

The surgeon let out a short, humorless breath. “It followed you.”

Kammler’s gloved hand tightened around the canvas bag again. Proof pressed against his palm, cold and sealed. He had carried blood across centuries, and the act had not stayed contained.

He remembered the condemned man's eyes; the warning shaped like a specification: There are things that learn by watching.

Kammler had assumed learning was passive. Now he understood it could be active, adaptive, patient.

He stepped back from the perimeter, forcing himself to create distance as if distance could become safety. "No one enters the chamber," he said. "No one touches the bell. Not until we understand what we have brought into our facility."

The physicist shook his head rapidly, almost frantic. "We can't understand it," he said. "We can measure drift, we can measure amplitude, but this is not an output. This is an intrusion."

Orsini's eyes remained on the shimmer. "And it is not finished," he said quietly.

As if in response, the hairline texture above Die Glocke shifted again, just enough that it looked, for a heartbeat, like an iris narrowing. Not an eye in any human sense. A focusing. A recalibration.

Kammler felt the pressure in his teeth return, and behind it the unmistakable sensation of attention settling on him personally, weighing him the way a hand weighed a tool to decide how it might be used.

Then it lifted, not gone, only withdrawn, like a predator choosing not to strike yet.

The alarms continued their layered howl. Men moved again, cautiously, unsure what motions were permitted in a room where shadows had demonstrated the ability to disobey.

Kammler turned away from the bell and started toward the exit tunnel, bag still clenched in his hand, his mind already shifting into containment protocols and interrogations and damage control.

But as he walked, he saw it once more in the corner of his vision: his own shadow sliding along the concrete beside him.

For a fraction of a second, it moved first.

Then it fell back into place, obedient again, as if it had only wanted him to notice that obedience was now optional.

Kammler did not slow. He did not look down. He kept walking with the rigid discipline of a man refusing to grant significance to a threat he could not yet shoot.

Behind him, under the mountain, Die Glocke sat silent and gleaming.

Above it, the bruise in the air remained.

And somewhere in that bruise, something inhuman waited with the calm patience of an intelligence that had learned a new pathway into the present and had no need to hurry.

Chapter 10

Unintended Consequences

Kammler did not remember walking the length of the tunnel.

He remembered only the sensation of distance failing to behave like distance. Every step away from the bell chamber should have thinned the pressure in his teeth, should have let the air become ordinary again. Instead, it followed him in pulses, like a residual current in wires that had been cut but not discharged.

The canvas bag pulled at his hand with a weight that was almost nothing and felt like everything. The ampoules inside it clicked softly once as the tunnel sloped upward, and the sound made his stomach tighten. In the corridor behind him the alarms still layered their unwilling music, and he could imagine the shimmer above the bell persisting in the floodlights, patient as a bruise.

A guard hurried ahead to clear doors. Another kept close behind, boots too loud on stone. Their discipline was performative now. Men performed discipline when they did not know what else to offer the world.

Kammler's mind assembled procedures the way it always did when the universe misbehaved. Quarantine. Compartmentalize. Reduce witnesses. Separate the Vatican from the apparatus that had just demonstrated it could be followed.

And yet he could not stop seeing Golgotha's blue membrane breaking, the cracks widening, the darkness pressing close as if the corridor had been a throat and something had tasted the air at the back of it.

He reached the first security door. The guard spun the wheel. Metal scraped, then gave. The door swung open into a narrow antechamber where lamps burned with that steady yellow light the facility preferred, a deliberate refusal of softness.

Orsini was there already.

Kammler halted so abruptly the guard behind him almost collided. Orsini stood near a worktable that had been cleared in haste, his hands folded again inside his sleeves as if the posture were a kind of armor. He had moved with a speed that did not match his calm, as though he understood that custody of proof was meaningless if the proof altered the room it sat in.

The monsignor's eyes went first to the bag, then to Kammler's face.

"You are back," Orsini said.

Kammler heard in the words a layered meaning he did not like. Back from where, exactly. Back as what.

"I am here," Kammler replied, and the phrase tasted wrong because it echoed the condemned man's reply on the hill: I am here. And you are not.

Orsini took a half step closer. He did not reach for the bag. That was not his role. His role was to witness, and witnesses survived by keeping their hands clean.

"Is it intact?" Orsini asked.

Kammler placed the bag on the worktable. His glove left a faint dust smear from Judea on the wood, a pale line that looked like chalk.

"It is sealed," Kammler said. He opened the bag with careful movements, as if sudden motion might make the air pay attention. He withdrew the first ampoule, the larger one, and set it down. Wax glistened where his thumb had pressed it. Inside, the folded cloth was dark in two places where blood had soaked it.

Then he withdrew the second, smaller ampoule with the implement still inside, its groove smeared with a darker mixture of dust and dried fluid.

Orsini stared at them as though they were relics and weapons simultaneously. His breathing remained even, but Kammler saw a subtle tightening at the corners of his mouth.

"You took more than you agreed," Orsini said softly.

"I agreed to proof," Kammler replied. "I do not gamble a covenant on a single sample."

Orsini's eyes flicked to Kammler's gloves. "And what did it cost you to take it."

Kammler held his gaze. "We returned."

"That is not an answer," Orsini said.

Before Kammler could respond, the door behind them opened again with a burst of noise. Dietrich entered, face drawn tight, cap in his hand. Two soldiers followed him and stopped just inside the threshold, their eyes moving over Orsini, the table, the ampoules, as if trying to decide which was more dangerous.

Dietrich's gaze snapped to the glass cylinders. He did not ask what they were. He had heard enough in the bell chamber, and rumor traveled faster than electricity underground.

"You cannot keep it here," Dietrich said, voice low with controlled urgency. "Men are talking. The technician you brought… he is not coherent."

"Where is he," Kammler asked.

"Medical room," Dietrich said. "He keeps saying something is in the lights."

Kammler's jaw tightened. The facility had been built to keep secrets from the world, not to keep the world from noticing it was being altered. He looked at the ampoules again and felt a cold satisfaction beneath the unease. Proof was proof. Material had been taken from the hinge of history, and now it sat under a yellow lamp on a wooden table like any other specimen.

The lamp above them flickered once.

It was subtle, a brief tremor in brightness, but it drew every eye in the room upward like a reflex. The shadows on the wall shifted.

Kammler did not look at his own shadow. He refused. He had learned that refusing was not safety, but it was posture, and posture mattered when being counted.

He reached into the bag again and withdrew a third object: his own notebook, the one he had carried through the corridor because habit insisted on documenting even when documentation felt like sacrilege. Its cover was slightly warped as if exposed to heat that had not been heat. He set it beside the ampoules.

Orsini watched the notebook more intently than he watched the blood.

"You wrote," Orsini said.

Kammler gave him a brief glance. "I do not rely on memory."

Orsini's mouth tightened. "Memory may not rely on you."

Dietrich shifted, impatient. "Herr Doktor, the chamber is not settling. The physicist says the coils are off, but the gauges behave as if the machine is still running. And the men… the guards outside are refusing to stand watch alone."

Kammler's gaze stayed on the ampoules. He was thinking of transport, of containment. He was thinking of Rome, of the Pope's demand, of the moment when a white-robed man would be forced to confront glass and blood rather than scripture.

"We move it to a sealed room," Kammler said. "Steel cabinet. Two locks. No one enters without my permission. Not even you, Dietrich."

Dietrich's jaw clenched, but he nodded.

Orsini did not object. His objections were not operational. They were theological, and theology was useless if the air itself had begun to behave like a listening surface.

A faint sound came from the corridor outside, a scrape like a boot dragged rather than lifted. One of the soldiers by the door turned his head sharply.

"What was that," he murmured.

No one answered. The lamps flickered again, longer this time, as if the facility's power grid had been touched by an invisible hand testing its responsiveness.

Kammler reached for the larger ampoule.

As his gloved fingers closed around the glass, a sensation ran up his arm that made him go still. Not pain. Not shock. A subtle resistance, as if the ampoule had momentarily gained inertia beyond its mass. The feeling lasted less than a second, then vanished.

He did not look at Orsini. He did not look at Dietrich. He simply held the ampoule steady and waited to see whether the room would react to his attention the way ink had reacted on paper.

It did not. Not overtly.

But the soldier at the door inhaled sharply, and Kammler saw in his peripheral vision that the man's shadow had moved even though the man had not. It slid a fraction of an inch up the wall like a living thing climbing.

Dietrich saw it too. His face went pale beneath the hard planes of his discipline.

Orsini closed his eyes for one brief moment, not in prayer but in calculation, as if naming the phenomenon internally and choosing not to give it sound.

Kammler set the ampoule down again with deliberate gentleness.

"We are back," Kammler said, speaking to them as much as to himself, and the words were a declaration, an attempt to force the concept into solidity. "This is the present. This facility is ours. The machine is under control."

The lamp above them dimmed for a heartbeat.

In that heartbeat, the room's shadows thickened, deepening into something heavier than absence. For an instant Kammler thought he saw a narrow vertical smear of darkness detach near the corner of the ceiling, like the earlier column in the bell chamber trying to form again in a more ordinary room.

Then the light returned, and the smear was only a corner shadow behaving as a corner shadow should.

Dietrich swallowed audibly. “Herr Doktor,” he said, and the title sounded suddenly smaller than the situation, “you said it followed you.”

Kammler did not deny it. Denial was pointless now.

“It did not follow me,” Kammler said. “It followed the corridor.”

Orsini opened his eyes again. “Or it followed what you took,” he said.

Kammler looked down at the ampoules. Blood and dust in glass. Wax seals. A sample taken from a moment that had spoken his name in German.

Proof, he thought again, and felt the word wobble under strain.

He gathered the ampoules carefully and slid them back into the bag, padding them with cloth so they would not clink. The small, domestic act felt obscene after the way the sky had fractured, but Kammler had survived by committing obscene acts with clean hands.

He lifted the bag.

The soldier at the door stepped aside, almost too eagerly.

As Kammler moved toward the corridor, Orsini spoke, his voice low enough that it felt like a confession spoken into a stone.

"You are in the present," Orsini said. "But you have brought the hinge back with you. And hinges do not return to being only metal once they have been forced."

Kammler did not turn. He could not afford to give the monsignor's words the weight they wanted.

He walked out into the corridor, Dietrich and the soldiers flanking him, and with every step the lamps above seemed to hesitate before committing to illumination, as if even light now needed permission.

Behind him, in the bell chamber deeper in the mountain, the machine sat silent and gleaming.

But the air was no longer empty.

The present had accepted their return in the same way Golgotha had: outwardly indifferent, inwardly aware.

And Kammler, carrying a bag that held blood sealed in glass, understood with a clarity that made his skin tighten that returning was not the same as arriving home.

It was simply crossing the threshold again.

Whatever had counted him in the corridor between centuries had learned where to find him.

By the time Kammler reached the sealed room he had chosen, the facility's corridors felt narrower than they had been hours earlier, as if the mountain itself had learned to press inward.

The steel cabinet stood against a concrete wall that sweated faintly in the lamp's heat. Two locks, two keys, two guards posted outside the door with orders that allowed no interpretation. Kammler placed the canvas bag on the cabinet's bare surface and watched the lamp above it for a full ten seconds before he moved. The light held. It did not flicker. That alone felt like a concession.

He did not open the bag again. He had already verified the wax seals in the antechamber. Verification was a form of attention. Attention was a lever. He had learned that twice now, once with ink and once with sky.

"Doctor."

The voice came from behind him. The surgeon, uninvited as always, with Dietrich half a step behind and Orsini standing in the doorway like a man refusing to cross a threshold into contagion.

Kammler turned.

"What is the status," he asked.

The surgeon's gaze did not go to the bag. It went to Kammler's face, searching for the smallest crack that might suggest regret. He found none.

"The technician is sedated," the surgeon said. "He fought. Not us. The room. He kept striking the light fixture with his fist. He said his shadow was whispering."

Dietrich's jaw tightened, a muscle jumping once in his cheek. "He also said you left him on the hill."

"I did not," Kammler replied. "He returned. That is more than can be said for Schreiber."

Orsini shifted slightly in the doorway. The name Schreiber had a weight in this place, the first man to vanish into an alien wound in the Black Forest and not come back by any mechanism they understood. Orsini had never been told the full details, but he had seen enough in Kammler's eyes and the physicist's charts to understand that disappearances here were not always deaths. Sometimes they were transactions.

"Herr Doktor," Dietrich said, forcing himself into calm. "The bell chamber is not stable."

Kammler looked past them, toward the deeper tunnels. He could almost feel the chamber through rock and steel, a presence like a low fever in the facility's bones.

"The coils are disengaged," Kammler said. It was not a question. It was a requirement.

"They are," Dietrich replied. "That is the problem. It behaves as if they are not."

The surgeon added, "The physicist is calling it a residual field. He is also calling it impossible."

Orsini spoke quietly, his German careful and unnervingly neutral. "Impossible is what you call a pattern before you understand what it wants."

Kammler held Orsini's gaze for a moment, then turned back to the cabinet. He took out a key, unlocked the first lock, and then stopped with his hand resting on the second key. The metal felt cold enough to burn.

"I will not store it here long," Kammler said, meaning the bag, meaning the proof, meaning perhaps more than that. "Rome will receive it as agreed."

Orsini's eyes did not move to the cabinet. They remained on Kammler's hand. "If Rome receives it," he said, "it will not be the only thing you deliver."

Kammler closed the first lock again without opening the cabinet. The gesture was almost superstitious and he hated himself for it. He turned and walked past them into the corridor, and they fell in beside him as if the facility's hierarchy could still protect them from what had begun to loosen.

The deeper they went, the more the lamps hesitated. Not flickering constantly, but dimming by a fraction and returning, like eyelids narrowing and opening. Kammler kept his pace even. The sound of their boots struck the stone with the same rhythm as always, but the echoes seemed to arrive a heartbeat late, as if the tunnel needed extra time to decide whether to repeat them.

At the door to the main cavern, the guards posted there looked relieved to see Kammler and ashamed of their relief. One of them had a rosary looped around his fingers. Kammler pretended not to notice. Pretending was another form of control.

The door swung open.

The bell chamber was louder than it had been when Kammler left it.

Not with machinery. With voices.

Not shouting, not speech that carried meaning, but the layered murmur of men talking too close together, the kind of indistinct, communal sound that drifted through barracks at night. It filled the cavern like humidity. Kammler knew at once that it was wrong because the men present were not speaking. The guards stood rigid. The physicist and his assistants clustered around the console, faces pale, mouths closed.

Yet the murmur persisted, coming from no obvious direction.

The bell itself sat in the center of the ring, inert in its posture, polished steel catching floodlight. Above it, the hairline texture in the air had thickened into something more visible, like stress in glass seen from the right angle.

The physicist turned at Kammler's approach, relief and terror colliding in his expression. His wire-rimmed glasses were smeared as if he had rubbed his eyes too hard.

"It will not settle," he said at once, words tumbling out. "We shut down, we cut power, we isolated the coils, and the field remains. It is oscillating without an input. The amplitude is low, but it is coherent. That is the frightening part. Coherent means organized."

Kammler stopped just outside the inner ring. The pressure in his teeth returned immediately, faint but present, as if the chamber recognized him by resonance rather than by sight.

“What is the period,” Kammler asked.

The physicist blinked, grateful for a question that belonged to engineering. He gestured toward the console. “It cycles every forty-seven seconds. Exactly. For the last twenty-three minutes.”

“Exactly,” Kammler repeated. “No drift.”

The physicist shook his head. “None. And it is not the bell. When we took readings at the perimeter, the cycle attenuated, but it did not disappear. The cavern itself is participating.”

The surgeon, standing just behind Kammler, exhaled through his nose. “As if the mountain is in the circuit.”

Orsini stepped forward to the edge of the ring. He did not enter it. He looked at the bell as if looking at a confessional that had begun to speak back.

The murmuring sound thickened for a moment, then thinned. Kammler listened. He could not pick out words, but the cadence was wrong for German and wrong for Latin and wrong for Polish. It had the rhythm of language without the content, like a voice heard through a wall.

“One of the men claims he understands it,” the physicist said, voice strained.

Kammler’s gaze snapped to him. “Who.”

The physicist hesitated. “An assistant. He began repeating sounds from it. He said it was… familiar.”

“Familiar how,” Kammler asked, already knowing the answer would be useless.

The physicist swallowed. “He said it sounded like his mother calling him from another room. He said it sounded like memory.”

Orsini’s face tightened at the word memory. “It is not memory,” he said. “It is imitation.”

The murmuring shifted again, and this time Kammler felt it less as sound and more as vibration in his chest. The bell’s polished surface seemed to dull for a fraction of a second, the reflection of the floodlights blurring as if the metal were sweating.

A guard near the far wall jerked his head toward his own shadow. Kammler followed the motion, eyes tracking without wanting to.

The guard’s shadow on the concrete had lengthened.

Not because the light had changed. The floodlights remained fixed. The shadow simply extended itself, thin and precise, as if reaching. The guard did not move, but the shadow did, creeping toward the ring by perhaps an inch.

Then it snapped back to where it should have been, obedient again, leaving the guard staring at the floor with the expression of a man who had just seen his own body betray him.

The surgeon spoke under his breath. "It's happening in open light now."

Kammler looked at the bell. "Run the diagnostics again," he ordered.

"We have," the physicist said, and his voice cracked. "We are running them constantly. Herr Doktor, it is responding to us. When we increase monitoring, the cycle sharpens. When we stop and step away, it smooths. It behaves like the newspapers."

Kammler felt a cold line of understanding cut through him. The newspapers had shifted in response to observation, as if the future resented being pinned. The sky at Golgotha had fractured under the strain of their exit, as if time itself had a membrane that could be cracked. Here, under the mountain, the bell was behaving like an organ that had been infected and was now producing symptoms.

"The bell is not malfunctioning," Kammler said slowly.

The physicist stared at him. “Then what is it doing.”

Kammler did not answer immediately. He watched the hairline texture above the bell. For a heartbeat it looked like it tightened, the way it had in the corridor between centuries, not into a shape the eye could name, but into a focus.

“The bell is being used,” Kammler said.

Dietrich’s voice came out harsh. “By what.”

Kammler’s jaw tightened. He thought of the dark geometry behind the cracks in the sky, the sensation of being counted, the almost-amusement that had brushed him when glass clinked against glass. He thought of Christ’s words on the hill, delivered in German as if language were only another field that could be bent.

“There are things,” he said, and heard the faint change in the room when he repeated the phrasing, as if the air recognized the quote, “that learn by watching.”

Orsini’s eyes narrowed. “And now it has learned your machine.”

The murmuring rose suddenly, not louder, but nearer, as if it moved from the cavern air into the men’s heads. One assistant clapped both hands over his ears. Another backed away from the console until he hit the rock wall and stopped, trembling.

The physicist stared at his gauges and whispered, almost pleading, "It's going into phase."

Kammler felt it too. The pressure in his teeth intensified. The bell's reflection wavered. The hairline texture above the opening thickened into a faint oval, a bruise becoming a doorway.

No coils engaged. No switch thrown. No human input.

Yet the chamber behaved as if something had leaned its weight onto the same resonance they used to tear holes in time.

Kammler took one step back from the ring, not out of fear but calculation. "Evacuate nonessential personnel," he said. His voice was calm and that calm was a weapon, a way of forcing the men around him to remember obedience even when reality stopped behaving like matter.

Dietrich barked orders immediately, grateful for something he could do with his hands. Guards began moving, ushering assistants toward the tunnels.

The surgeon did not move. Orsini did not move. The physicist remained at the console like a man chained to his own curiosity.

"Herr Doktor," the physicist said, and his eyes were wet now, not from tears but strain. "If it can open the corridor without us..."

Kammler stared at the bell, at the faint oval of wrongness forming above it, at the shadows on the floor that seemed too eager to detach.

"Yes," Kammler said. "That is what a malfunction means. It is no longer under command."

The murmuring resolved, for half a second, into something almost like a single voice. Not words. Not any human language. But an intonation that carried intent the way a siren carried intent.

The lights dimmed a fraction. The oval above the bell sharpened.

And for a moment, in the bell's polished curve, Kammler saw his own reflection split again into two outlines: one standing still, one leaning forward as if listening.

He did not know which one was real.

He only knew that the machine, once their instrument, was now behaving like an invitation left open on a table.

And something, somewhere that had learned the pathway, was testing whether the invitation could be accepted.

The oval above Die Glocke sharpened and then softened again, as if whatever shaped it could not quite decide how visible it wished to be.

The murmuring did not fade with the evacuation. If anything, the thinning of bodies made the sound more distinct, like a choir heard better once the crowd left the nave. It drifted through the cavern without a source, gathering in pockets near the steel ribs, then sliding away as though it preferred movement to location.

Dietrich's men hurried the assistants out. Boots struck stone. Orders snapped. The last of the technicians vanished into the tunnel, and the heavy door rolled shut with a metallic finality that felt performative. As if steel could still settle the question of what belonged where.

Only a small circle remained at the ring: Kammler just outside the inner perimeter; the physicist at the console, hands poised over dials he insisted were disconnected; the surgeon a pace behind Kammler; Dietrich on Kammler's left, rigid with a pistol he had no use for; and Orsini at the edge of the ring, black against floodlight, watching the bell as if it were an altar that had begun to answer.

The murmuring tightened into cadence.

Not language yet. Not words. But a rhythm with pauses in the wrong places, like breath taken by something that had no lungs and was imitating the idea of speech.

The physicist swallowed audibly. His wire-rimmed glasses reflected the console's green glow, and his eyes looked trapped behind them. "It's stabilizing," he said, and the sentence came out as both report and plea. "The oscillation is… it's locking."

Kammler's jaw clenched. "On what frequency."

The physicist glanced down, then back up, as if afraid the numbers themselves might be listening. "The same forty-seven-second cycle," he said. "But the harmonics changed. It's… it's closer to the activation profile."

"The coils are dead," Dietrich said, forcing the words through clenched teeth.

"The coils are not required," Orsini replied quietly, without looking at him. His gaze never left the bruise in the air. "Not anymore."

The surgeon shifted his weight. "You should move the monsignor out," he muttered to Kammler.

It sounded like practical advice, but his eyes were on the shadows, not on Orsini.

Kammler did not answer. He was watching the floor.

Under the floodlights, the shadows cast by the steel ribs had always been clean. Hard lines. Predictable angles. In the bell chamber, darkness normally behaved like a subordinate.

Now it behaved like an animal testing a cage.

At the far edge of the inner ring, the shadow of one rib elongated by a fraction and then slid sideways, detaching from the geometry that should have anchored it. It moved like liquid poured on stone: slow, deliberate, without regard for the direction of light.

Dietrich saw it at the same moment and raised the pistol instinctively. The motion was too fast in the cavern's thickened air.

The shadow responded.

It snapped toward the movement, not touching Dietrich, not physically, but the air between them tightened as if a membrane had been plucked. Dietrich's arm jerked, and the pistol dipped, his hand suddenly heavy. His face went pale with the ugly realization that something could interfere with his body without crossing distance.

Kammler stepped slightly toward him, not to comfort, but to establish control with proximity. “Lower it,” he said.

Dietrich forced his arm down. His breathing was loud. “It reacted,” he said, as if trying to keep the event in the language of tactics. “It reacted to threat.”

“No,” the physicist whispered, and his voice shook. “It reacted to attention.”

As if in confirmation, the shadow that had slid away paused, then eased back into place beneath the rib, aligning itself again with perfect obedience, like a performer resetting after an unsanctioned improvisation.

Then the murmuring changed.

A single syllable surfaced in the sound, clear enough that all of them stiffened.

Not German. Not Latin. Not Polish.

A name.

“Hans.”

Kammler felt the word land with the same impossible precision as on Golgotha. Not loud. Not carried by air. Placed.

His fingers flexed inside his gloves. He did not turn his head. He did not grant the sound the satisfaction of reaction.

The physicist's face tightened. "It can't," he said, as if refusing a mathematical result. "It cannot know—"

"Hans," the murmuring repeated, and this time it was less like a choir and more like a single voice passing through many mouths without using any of them. It held no accent. It held no warmth. It was imitation stripped down to function.

Orsini's chin lifted slightly. "It heard him in the corridor," he said. "It heard him on the hill."

Kammler kept his gaze fixed on the bell's polished curve. His reflection in it was no longer stable; it shimmered at the edges, and for a heartbeat he saw a second outline of himself slightly behind the first, as though the bell could not decide which time-version to display.

The surgeon spoke quietly, almost to himself. "It's not speaking," he said. "It's performing speech. Like the papers performed truth."

The murmuring shifted again, and the next voice was not Kammler's name.

It was a woman.

Not present. Not in the facility. Not any of their staff.

The sound was small, strained, intimate. A voice calling from another room.

"Hans… Hans, komm."

Kammler's throat tightened so hard it felt like a bruise. The German was simple, domestic, and it was wrong in this cavern where German usually meant command, not childhood.

The physicist turned his head sharply toward Kammler, horror widening his eyes. "It's using memory," he whispered.

Orsini's gaze flicked to Kammler's face for the first time, and what Kammler saw there was not curiosity now but something like mourning, the expression of a man watching a boundary violated that had once been sacred even to cynics.

Kammler did not answer them. He forced the sensation down, compressed it the way he compressed guilt, the way he compressed fear: into something small enough to carry without letting it leak into posture.

"Do not respond," Kammler said, and his voice came out rougher than he intended. The moment the words left him, the air tightened again, like skin reacting to a touch.

The woman's voice paused, as though listening.

Then it changed.

It became almost the same, but not quite. A fraction too smooth. A fraction too precise. An imitation refined mid-performance.

"Hans," it said softly, "bring it back."

Dietrich made a choked sound, not quite a gasp, not quite a curse. His eyes were on Kammler, but he looked away almost immediately, as if afraid to witness whatever private invasion was occurring.

The physicist's hands hovered over the console, trembling. "It is correlating," he said. "It's testing stimuli. It uses the response to refine the output."

Orsini's voice cut through the rising panic like a blade. "It is learning how to be believed."

The shadows moved again, more than before. Along the floor, the darkness beneath the bell's ribs slid outward in thin tongues, reaching toward the men at the ring. They did not leap; they advanced with a measured patience that felt worse than aggression. It was the patience of something that assumed time was on its side.

The surgeon took an involuntary step back. His boot crossed into a darker patch.

The shadow under his foot thickened.

He froze. His face changed as if he had felt a touch through leather. "Something grabbed me," he said hoarsely.

"No," the physicist said again, voice rising. "It's not physical. It's phase interference. Your proprioception is being altered. It can—" He swallowed, struggling to keep the sentence coherent. "It can lie to your nerves."

The surgeon's eyes flicked to Orsini with sudden, ugly suspicion. "Is this what you brought," he demanded. "Is this Vatican—"

Orsini did not flinch. "This is not ours," he said. "If you still believe in ownership, you are behind."

The shadow under the surgeon's boot released, not by retreating, but by thinning, as if it had only wanted him to register that it could. The surgeon exhaled hard through his nosc and did not step forward again.

Kammler watched the bruise in the air above the bell. It pulsed once more, and with the pulse the murmuring resolved into several overlapping voices, each distinct, each intimate, each wrong.

A child crying. A man laughing quietly. A whisper in Latin that could have been prayer if it had not been so perfectly pronounced.

Orsini stiffened at the Latin. His lips parted, and for a heartbeat Kammler thought the monsignor might answer out of reflex. His hands tightened inside his sleeves, knuckles pressing against cloth.

"What is it saying," Dietrich asked, and the question was half demand, half fear.

Orsini's eyes remained on the bell. "It's not saying anything," he murmured. "It's reciting shapes that resemble confession."

The Latin whisper shifted, and a German voice appeared within it, closer now, like breath against an ear.

"Proof," it said.

Kammler's grip tightened into a fist. He did not move, but he felt the air around the bag he no longer carried—now locked away in another room—become present in his mind as if the thing could taste it at a distance. The samples. The wax seals. The cloth dark with blood. The scrapings taken from stone.

The bell's field had touched them. The corridor had counted them. The Observer had brushed its attention across their glass.

The shadows on the floor began to synchronize with the forty-seven-second cycle. They expanded, then contracted, as if breathing with the chamber.

The physicist made a small, strangled noise. He leaned closer to the console, then stopped himself, remembering too late that observation fed this. "It's entraining the room," he whispered. "It's making the environment participate."

Kammler spoke without looking away from the bell. "Step back," he ordered. "All of you. To the outer line."

Dietrich hesitated, eyes flicking to Kammler as if waiting to see whether Kammler himself would obey his own command.

Kammler stepped back first. One pace. Then another. The pressure in his teeth eased by a fraction, confirming the physicist's warning: proximity mattered.

The others followed. Even Orsini moved, reluctantly, like a man leaving a bedside. They reached the outer line of floodlights where the cavern widened and the shadows became more ordinary by force of distance.

For three full cycles, the murmuring continued, and the shadows continued their slow, synchronized breathing.

Then, abruptly, the voices stopped.

Not fading. Stopping. Like a switch thrown in a mind.

The chamber fell into a silence that did not feel like relief. It felt like a pause taken for emphasis.

The bell's polished curve reflected their small group at the perimeter, four men and a monsignor, all of them suddenly aware of how thin the idea of control had become.

In the quiet, a single voice emerged again, nearer than any before.

Not the woman. Not the Latin whisper.

A man.

A voice Kammler recognized from the facility's earliest days in the mountains, from meetings, from briefings, from the kind of disciplined speech that had never allowed fear into syllables.

Schreiber.

"Herr Doktor," the voice said calmly, as if speaking from just behind Kammler's shoulder. "It's open."

Dietrich turned violently, pistol lifting again before he remembered the last time it reacted. The surgeon's face drained of color.

Orsini's eyes went briefly unfocused, as if listening not with ears but with the part of him that cataloged disasters.

Kammler did not turn. He stared at the bell's mouth and the bruise in the air above it, and in that moment he understood the point of the performance.

It was not haunting.

It was invitation.

The shadows had learned to wear voices the way ink had learned to wear headlines. They were not trying to terrify them into retreat. They were trying to coax them into approach, to make the men with hands on the machine step forward and touch the wrong place again.

Kammler's voice was low and flat, engineered to deny the room any emotional purchase. "No one answers," he said. "No one follows. No one speaks back."

The bell's bruise pulsed once, faintly, like a disappointed acknowledgement.

Then the shadows on the floor slid, not toward the men, but inward, gathering beneath the bell's ribs as if withdrawing into a heart.

The murmuring did not return. The voices did not call again.

Only the forty-seven-second cycle persisted in the gauges, steady as a metronome, the chamber continuing to breathe without lungs.

Kammler turned to Dietrich. "Seal the cavern," he said. "Two guard shifts. No one alone. And if anyone hears a familiar voice, they report it and they do not answer it. Understood."

Dietrich's eyes were hard, but fear lived behind them like a second pupil. "Understood," he said.

Kammler looked at the physicist. "You will stop monitoring continuously," he said. "You will take readings at fixed intervals and you will leave the console dark between them. You told me it sharpens when watched. Then we will stop feeding it."

The physicist nodded too quickly. "Yes," he whispered, grateful for an instruction that pretended the situation could still be managed by protocol.

Orsini remained silent until Kammler began to move toward the tunnel. Then he spoke, his voice low enough that it felt like a confession offered unwillingly.

"It is wearing the dead," Orsini said.

Kammler paused, but did not turn. "It is using whatever it has," he replied.

Orsini's next words were careful, and colder than anything he had said in Rome. "No," he said. "It is using whatever you gave it."

Kammler resumed walking. The sound of their boots echoed once, then arrived a heartbeat late, as if the mountain itself needed extra time to decide whether to repeat them.

Behind them, in the sealed cavern, Die Glocke remained silent.

And in that silence, shadows waited with voices they could shape at will, rehearsing the sound of trust.

Chapter 11

Keckshurg's Bell

It began as a light that refused to behave like a light.

Over western Pennsylvania the late-autumn sky should have been settling into its usual bruised gray, the kind that made the ridges look closer than they were and turned bare branches into black veins. Instead, at 4:47 p.m., a blue-white streak tore across the cloud base with the smooth certainty of something that did not burn so much as cut.

Children in a yard outside Kecksburg looked up first because children always did. They saw the line appear, saw it brighten, saw it split into smaller sparks that trailed behind like shavings from a blade. One boy would later insist it made no sound at all until it was already over the trees. A girl would say it sounded like a distant radio tuned between stations, a hiss threaded with something that almost became a voice if you listened too hard.

The adults looked up second, because adults had to decide whether the sky deserved attention. A man unloading groceries paused with a bag half out of his trunk and watched the streak arc lower, slower than it should have been, as if it were deliberately choosing its descent. A woman on her porch shaded her eyes and felt, unexpectedly, her teeth ache. She would describe it later as the feeling you got standing too close to a transformer, except there were no power lines nearby, only the trees and the cold.

The line became a fireball. Not orange, not the familiar meteor flame, but an unsteady pearl color that made the cloud cover glow from beneath. It pulsed once, dimmed, then brightened again with a rhythm that made more than one person glance at their watches without knowing why. Forty-seven seconds was not a number anyone could have named in that moment, but the body knew pattern even when the mind did not.

Then it dropped behind the ridge, into the folded dark of the forest.

The first impact did not sound like an explosion. It sounded like a heavy object slammed into wet ground, a muffled thud that traveled through the hills as vibration more than noise. Dogs began barking not at the ridge but at empty air, spinning in circles, hackles up. A flock of birds rose from the trees in a sudden black wave and scattered without formation, as if whatever had fallen had disturbed something older than instinct.

In the minutes that followed, Kecksburg did what small towns did when the extraordinary arrived: it moved toward it in uneven ripples. Men grabbed flashlights and rifles out of habit more than intention. A volunteer fireman called the station and then hesitated, receiver still in his hand, because he did not know what to say beyond, "Something went down." A teenager pedaled his bicycle hard toward the woods, the cold air burning his lungs, the thrill of being first outpacing fear.

At the edge of the forest, the light was wrong.

It was not brighter. It was not dimmer. It was simply different, as if the air itself had acquired a faint, metallic sheen. The trees stood with their branches bare and rigid, and yet their shadows did not lie the way they should have with the sinking sun. They seemed to lag by a fraction, as if the forest could not decide whether it belonged to daylight or dusk.

The teenager reached the first line of trunks and stopped so abruptly he nearly fell. He did not know what he was seeing, only that it did not belong among the roots and rocks.

Between the trees, half embedded in a shallow gouge of churned earth, lay a shape that made the word bell surface in his mind before he had any language to justify it.

It was not large, not the size of a plane or a rocket, but big enough to dominate the clearing it had made. Smooth metal, dull bronze in the weak light, with a curve that seemed too deliberate to be debris. It sat at a slight angle, one side sunk deeper, the soil around it pressed down as if by tremendous weight. The ground was torn but not burned. There were broken branches and shredded moss, yet no scattering of parts, no obvious wreckage. It looked less like a crash and more like a placement.

The teenager took a step closer and felt a pressure in his teeth again, faint but undeniable. His flashlight beam swept the object's surface and returned oddly flattened, as if the metal refused to reflect in the normal way. Along one side were markings. Not letters. Not symbols he recognized. They looked like grooves cut by a careful tool, and as his light passed over them, he had the brief, irrational impression that they shifted, not moving like an animal but changing their relationship to his gaze. The boy lowered the flashlight slightly and the impression stopped. He raised it again and it returned.

He backed away, heart hammering, and almost collided with the first adult to arrive: a hunter with a rifle slung over his shoulder and a cigarette clenched between his lips. The man swore softly and pushed past, his confidence intact until he saw what the boy had seen.

"Ain't no plane," the hunter said, voice suddenly thin.

More people arrived. A cluster of men and boys on foot. A woman with her coat thrown on over an apron. Two volunteer firemen, one still wearing his station cap. They all formed a loose semicircle at the treeline, staring at the object the way people stared at a wound they could not decide whether to touch.

Someone said it must be a satellite. Someone else said the Russians had finally done it. A third voice insisted it was a movie prop, because in America the extraordinary often had to be explained as entertainment before it could be treated as danger.

Then the object made a sound.

Not a hum. Not a whine. A soft pulse, like a distant bass note you felt more than heard. The air in front of it thickened. The cigarette in the hunter's mouth trembled, ash falling off in a clean drop. The woman in the apron put a hand to her mouth and whispered, “Lord have mercy,” without knowing why.

The pulse came again, and with it came a smell, sharp and clean like ozone, threaded with something older, like wet stone split open in a cave.

The firemen exchanged a look that said they did not want responsibility for this, that this was beyond hoses and axes and first aid. One of them raised his radio and spoke into it anyway, voice cracking as he tried to describe the indescribable.

At the edge of the clearing, at the point where the gouge in the earth began, the ground shifted.

Not the whole forest, not a tremor, but a precise heave, as if the soil itself were exhaling. A seam of darkness opened beside the bell-shaped object, and for a moment the watchers thought a door was sliding out.

It was not a door.

It was a shadow where no shadow should have been, too dense, too clean-edged, as if the evening had become a material and someone had cut a piece out of it. It rose like a thin column, hesitated, then collapsed inward again, leaving the air glittering with faint specks that vanished before anyone could be sure they had seen them.

Several people stepped back in unison. No one spoke. Even the dogs, which had been barking from a distance, went silent, their bodies rigid with something that looked like obedience.

Then a shape emerged from behind the bell.

A man.

He stepped into the clearing with the careful balance of someone walking out of a moving vehicle, one foot testing ground before committing weight. He wore a dark coat that did not fit the era, the cut too severe, the fabric too heavy. He was bareheaded. His hair was short, brushed back. His posture was straight despite the cold.

What held the watchers was not that he was there, but that he looked wrong in the way the object looked wrong. Not monstrous. Not deformed. Simply misplaced, as if the forest had produced a figure from another room.

The man lifted his head and looked around.

His eyes moved over the people at the treeline without widening, without the automatic panic of someone escaping a crash. He did not look injured. He did not look disoriented. He looked, if anything, annoyed, like a technician stepping out to assess a malfunction.

A boy near the front of the semicircle whispered, "Who are you?" in the kind of voice that barely existed.

The man did not answer. He looked past them, toward the slope beyond the clearing, as if listening for something they could not hear. His hand was at his side; fingers closed around an object that was too dark to identify in the failing light. A case, perhaps. Small enough to carry easily. Held with the unconscious protectiveness of someone who knew exactly what value it contained.

The hunter found his voice again, rougher now. "You from the government?" he called, and even as he spoke he seemed to know how absurd it was, because the man did not look like any government he recognized.

The man's gaze flicked to him briefly, the attention sharp enough that the hunter's words died in his throat. The man looked away again.

Behind the man, the bell-shaped craft pulsed a third time. The air shimmered around its curve, and for a heartbeat the watchers saw the surface behave as if it were not metal at all but something else wearing metal's appearance. The markings on its side seemed to deepen, then soften, like scars adjusting under skin.

A woman began to cry, quiet and uncontrollable. The sound made two other people flinch as if it might provoke the object.

The man took a step farther from the craft. He moved into the center of the clearing, putting distance between himself and the bell, and now the watchers could see his face more clearly. The light caught his skin, and a murmur moved through the group, not words but the collective recognition that he did not look like a survivor.

He looked untouched by time.

There was no soot on him. No blood. No dust from the forest on his shoes. He might have walked out of a clean room into mud without carrying any of it on his body. The effect made the object behind him feel less like a crash site and more like a delivery.

The fireman with the radio tried again, voice strained. "We got… we got a craft, looks like a bell, and there's a man here." He paused, swallowing. "He's… he's just standing."

As if summoned by the sentence, the distant sound of engines began to thread through the hills. Not one vehicle but several, their approach coordinated in a way no local response ever was. Headlights flickered between the trees as trucks moved along the narrow roads faster than they should have, tires spitting gravel.

The watchers heard it and turned their heads. Relief and fear mixed in them, because the arrival of authority meant this might become explainable, containable. It also meant they might be told to forget what they were seeing.

The man in the clearing heard the engines too. He did not look toward them immediately. He looked instead at the bell-shaped craft one last time, and in the set of his shoulders there was something that could have been satisfaction, or calculation, or both.

He raised the dark object in his hand slightly, adjusting his grip, and for a moment his fingers tightened in a way that suggested the object mattered more than his own presence.

Then he turned toward the approaching lights.

His face remained composed, but his eyes held a cold focus that did not belong to a stranded civilian. It belonged to someone who had been waiting for this exact meeting across a span of years that should have broken any ordinary man into dust.

At the treeline, the teenager who had arrived first whispered something he could not stop himself from saying, not to anyone else but to the air itself.

"It's like it wants us to watch."

No one answered him.

But in the clearing, as the engines drew nearer and the bell-shaped craft sat half-buried like an artifact placed for discovery, the air shimmered once, faintly, in a way that made the trees' shadows hesitate.

As if the forest itself had heard the thought.

As if observation had already begun to change what was being observed.

The first soldiers arrived too fast for the roads.

A pair of olive trucks should not have made the ridge in that time, not with the narrow lanes and the late-autumn slick of leaves, yet they came anyway, engines straining and then easing as if the drivers had been given permission to ignore caution. Headlights swung between trunks. The beams caught faces in flashes at the treeline, turning the watchers into a line of pale masks.

A third vehicle followed, lower and darker, a sedan that did not belong to the volunteer firemen or the hunters. It moved with the unhurried certainty of someone who already knew exactly where the clearing was and exactly what waited inside it.

When the first truck braked, gravel spat. Doors slammed. The soldiers spilled out with that practiced half-run that was meant to look like urgency without becoming panic. Their rifles were carried low but ready. Their eyes moved across the people first, then past them, toward the bell-shaped object half buried in the gouged earth.

Several locals started talking at once, words tumbling over one another. "Came down like a meteor." "No explosion." "There's a man." "It's right there."

A sergeant with a hard jaw and a flashlight that seemed too bright for the forest lifted a hand, palm outward. "Everybody step back. Stay where you are." His voice held the kind of authority that assumed obedience was automatic, and for most of the treeline it was. People shuffled backward, arms held close as if trying to make themselves smaller.

The man in the clearing did not move.

He stood with the bell-shaped craft behind him, not using it as cover, not leaning against it, not even glancing at it now. The soldiers' flashlights swept over him and failed to find what they expected. No blood. No soot. Not even the damp sheen a man picked up from standing in cold woods.

One private's beam caught the man's eyes and lingered, and the private flinched as if touched. The light slid away. The private swallowed hard and said something to himself that sounded like, "Jesus."

The sedan stopped at the edge of the clearing. For a moment nothing happened. Then the rear door opened and a man stepped out in a dark coat that fit better than the soldiers' fatigues, his hat pulled low. He did not carry a weapon openly. That, somehow, made him feel more armed than any of them.

He spoke to the sergeant without looking away from the figure in the center. "Secure the perimeter. No photographs. No radios except on my frequency."

The sergeant's posture shifted instantly, as if the words had turned him from local authority to extension of a larger machine. "Yes, sir."

The soldiers began to move, forming a wider ring, ushering the locals farther back. The volunteers protested weakly, asking who the newcomer was, what branch, what agency, but their questions were met with the same repeated command: "Move back. Now."

The teenager who had arrived first found himself pushed behind a tree line with the others, his flashlight lowered, his breath visible in small puffs. He stared past shoulders and rifle barrels at the man in the clearing and tried to decide whether what frightened him was the craft, the sudden military efficiency, or the way the man stood as if he had been waiting for a cue.

The newcomer from the sedan stepped forward alone, boots crunching in leaves. He stopped several paces from the man, close enough that the flashlights caught the shape of his face beneath the hat brim. He was older than most of the soldiers but not old. His eyes were alert in a way that made him feel permanently awake.

"You're going to come with us," he said.

The man out of time tilted his head slightly, a movement of consideration rather than confusion. His gaze finally settled on the newcomer. Up close, the man's features were severe: narrow mouth, straight nose, cheekbones cut cleanly under pale skin. His hair was short and brushed back, and in the harsh beams it looked neither gray nor youthful. It simply existed, like everything else about him, without the usual signs of a life lived day by day.

The man held a case in his right hand. Now that the lights were steadier, the watchers could see it clearly: a dark, rigid case, small, the kind that might hold instruments or film. He gripped it with the unconscious protectiveness of someone who had carried it through places that wanted to take it.

The newcomer's eyes flicked to the case. "That too."

The man's mouth tightened, not into a smile, but into an expression that suggested he had expected this line. He spoke at last, and when he did his voice was controlled, low, and faintly accented in a way the locals could not place.

"It is for transfer," he said. "Not for handling in the field."

The newcomer paused. The sergeant behind him shifted, surprise rippling through his posture. The man's English was precise, not conversational, as if learned for command rather than comfort.

"And who are you to set terms?" the newcomer asked.

The man looked past him toward the soldiers, then toward the locals held back at the trees. His eyes moved the way a technician's eyes moved over gauges: cataloging, assessing, noting points of failure.

Then his gaze returned to the newcomer. "You already have your instructions," he said. "You would not be here so quickly otherwise."

The newcomer's jaw tightened. "You're in no position to—"

"I am," the man interrupted, and for the first time his voice carried an edge that made the soldiers' grips tighten on rifles. It was not loud. It did not need to be. It landed like a command placed directly into the space between hearts.

Behind the man, the bell-shaped craft pulsed again.

The sound was the same soft bass note the first witnesses had heard, but now it carried through the clearing with a clearer physical effect. Several soldiers blinked hard and swallowed as if their ears had equalized pressure. One put a hand to his mouth, eyes watering. The locals murmured in fear, but their voices were low, as if the air itself discouraged volume.

The newcomer did not flinch. His attention remained locked on the man as if refusing to acknowledge the craft's pulse would make it irrelevant.

"What is that?" he asked, nodding once toward the bell.

The man out of time did not look back at it. "A return," he said.

The answer did not help anyone, which made it feel deliberately chosen.

The newcomer exhaled sharply and glanced over his shoulder at the sergeant. "Get a cordon. Keep them all back. I want nobody within fifty yards of that thing."

The sergeant hesitated, as if fifty yards in dense woods were a suggestion rather than a command. Then he nodded and barked at his men. They began to push outward, moving the locals with increasing firmness.

The teenager heard someone behind him whisper, "It's government." Another voice said, "It's Russian." A woman said, "It's the end," and began to pray aloud until a soldier told her to be quiet.

In the clearing, the newcomer stepped closer again, reducing the distance in a way that was meant to intimidate.

The man did not yield ground.

In the harsh beams, it became impossible to ignore the wrongness of him. Not only his lack of dirt or injury. His skin held a stillness that did not match the cold. His eyes did not flick or dart. He did not perform the small involuntary movements of a man in shock. He seemed, if anything, more composed than the soldiers confronting him.

The newcomer said quietly, "We can do this easy, or we can do it hard."

The man's gaze dropped to the newcomer's hands, empty, then back up. "You will do it as you were instructed," he replied. "Bring a sealed vehicle. No unnecessary contact. No questions in the open."

The newcomer's mouth tightened. "You talk like you've done this before."

The man's expression did not change. "I have."

A flashlight beam swept accidentally across the bell's markings again, and the teenager saw the grooves shift for a heartbeat, like a pattern rearranging itself under observation. He blinked hard, and when he opened his eyes the grooves were still. He had the uneasy sense that the craft was aware of being watched, and that the watching mattered.

In the clearing, the man adjusted his grip on the case. The motion was small. Yet as his fingers tightened, several soldiers' shadows on the leaf-strewn ground seemed to lag, as if the light had hesitated. The locals did not notice. The soldiers did, and one of them looked down sharply at his own feet, face pale.

The newcomer noticed too. His eyes narrowed, not at the shadows, but at the man. "What are you?" he asked, the question escaping before he could dress it in procedure.

The man out of time held his gaze. For a moment something like amusement touched the edges of his expression, but it was not warmth. It was the reaction of a mind recognizing predictable fear.

"A courier," he said.

The bell pulsed again, and this time the air shimmered just above its curved surface, a faint hairline texture like stress in glass. The same kind of wrongness the teenager had felt in his teeth strengthened briefly and then eased. The trees' shadows at the clearing's edge hesitated, then snapped back into normal alignment.

The newcomer's composure tightened into something more rigid. "You're coming now," he said, and signaled to two soldiers.

They stepped forward.

As they approached the man, one of them raised a hand as if to take the case. His fingers hovered an inch away.

The man's voice cut through the moment, calm and absolute. "Do not."

The soldier froze; hand suspended in air. His face showed confusion, then fear, as if his body had obeyed an order before his mind decided whether to accept it.

The newcomer stared at the soldier, then at the man. “Touch it,” he said, more harshly.

The soldier tried. His hand moved a fraction, then stopped again, trembling, as if pushing against invisible resistance. His eyes widened, wet with sudden strain.

The man with the case did not move. He simply watched, and in that watching there was a cold patience, the same patience the craft seemed to carry in its silent presence.

The newcomer’s face hardened. He stepped forward himself, close enough now that the flashlights lit both their faces evenly. “Listen to me,” he said, voice low. “I don’t care what you are. You’re in American soil. You’re going to Wright-Patterson.”

At the mention of the base, the man’s eyes flickered for the first time, not with surprise but recognition. A point on a map confirmed.

He nodded once. “Yes,” he said. “That is where this goes.”

“And the case?” the newcomer demanded.

The man's gaze held steady. "The case does not open here."

The newcomer stared at him for a long moment, measuring the situation the way a man measured a fire he could not put out with water. Then he looked past him at the bell-shaped craft, half buried, humming softly in its own rhythm, and for a brief instant his eyes betrayed what his voice would not: uncertainty.

"What's in it?" he asked, quieter.

The man out of time answered with a precision that felt rehearsed.

"Evidence," he said.

He lifted the case slightly, not as threat, but as statement. "And a message that must be delivered intact."

The newcomer's mouth tightened. "To who?"

The man's eyes moved toward the forest line where the locals were being held back, toward the soldiers with rifles, toward the bell that shimmered under too many lights. Then his gaze returned to the newcomer, and the words came out flat, stripped of emotion.

"To Rome," he said. "And to those who think Rome can own what is taken from time."

The bell pulsed again, softer this time, as if satisfied the correct names had been spoken.

In the treeline, the teenager hugged his arms around himself and felt the cold settle deeper, not from weather but from the sense that the clearing had become a hinge between worlds. The man in the center did not look like a survivor. He looked like a man who had stepped out of a locked room after thirty years and found the doorknob still warm.

And as the soldiers began to guide him toward the waiting vehicles, careful now not to touch the case, the teenager had one final, irrational thought that felt less like imagination and more like something placed into his mind from outside.

The crash was not an accident.

It was an arrival arranged so others would witness it.

The vehicles that came for him were not the olive trucks.

Those trucks were noise and perimeter, rifles and flashlights and shouted orders that pushed the locals farther back until Kecksburg became a line of faces behind trees. The vehicles that came for him arrived after the first cordon was already in place, after the clearing had been claimed by men who did not use the word claim out loud.

A panel van rolled in without lights, its engine subdued, its paint so dark it looked like it absorbed the beams that struck it. Behind it came a second sedan, identical to the first in the way government liked things identical when it expected trouble. Two men stepped out of the van wearing plain coats despite the cold, their posture too calm for soldiers and too practiced for civilians. One carried a metal case the size of a suitcase, not the case in Kammler's hand but a container meant to swallow it.

The man from the first sedan, the one who had issued the orders, met them near the edge of the clearing. He spoke briefly, low, and the two men nodded without looking at the bell-shaped craft as if their training included not giving an object the dignity of attention.

Kammler watched without moving. He could feel the craft behind him pulsing in its measured way, a soft bass note that he did not hear so much as feel in the molars. The same ache he had once felt under a mountain in the Owl Mountains, the same wrongness that had turned air into a listening surface.

The newcomer approached again, this time with the plain-coated men behind him. He stopped at the same careful distance as before, eyes fixed on Kammler's hand.

"Here's how this goes," the newcomer said. "You come with us. You keep your hands where we can see them. And you give me the case."

"The case does not go to you," Kammler replied.

A flicker of anger crossed the man's face. "It goes to the United States."

Kammler let the sentence hang for a moment, not because he needed time, but because he understood the value of silence. Silence made other men fill gaps, and gaps were where mistakes happened.

"It goes to a secure facility," Kammler said, and watched the man's eyes tighten at the implication that Kammler knew the machinery behind him. "It will be logged by the correct personnel. It will be transferred without field exposure. You will not open it. You will not allow anyone else to open it."

One of the plain-coated men shifted his weight, impatient. The other looked past Kammler, finally unable to resist glancing toward the craft. He stared for a heartbeat too long, and Kammler saw the subtle change in the man's expression, the instinctive recoil as if the air had brushed him.

The craft pulsed again, and the man's eyes watered. He looked down quickly, almost ashamed.

The newcomer noticed. He followed the glance to the bell's curved surface and the grooves that caught the flashlight beams with a dull refusal. "We'll handle that," he said.

Kammler's mouth tightened. He could have said, You will not. He could have said, It will handle you. He did not. Americans did not respond well to being told their own limits, especially by a man in an unfamiliar coat standing beside something that did not belong to their sky.

"You are in charge here," Kammler said, giving the man what he wanted: acknowledgment of hierarchy. "Then you are responsible if it is compromised."

The newcomer narrowed his eyes. "Compromised by what?"

Kammler held his gaze. "By observation," he said.

The word meant nothing to the clearing, not in any precise way. Yet Kammler felt the air tighten slightly when he said it, as if the concept itself was a hook.

The craft pulsed again, softer, and the trees' shadows at the clearing's edge hesitated by a fraction before settling back into place. Several soldiers shifted uneasily, glancing at their feet as if they had sensed something moving that their eyes could not justify.

The newcomer exhaled sharply. “Put it in the transfer container,” he said, gesturing to the man with the metal suitcase.

The plain-coated man opened the suitcase. Inside was foam cut to shape, a sterile cavity with straps. It smelled faintly of chemicals and new metal. It looked, Kammler thought, like an American attempt to build a reliquary without admitting the word reliquary.

Kammler did not step forward immediately. He looked at the men’s hands, at the way their fingers hovered and then pulled back as if waiting for an instruction that would allow them to touch without consequence.

“You will not touch it,” Kammler said.

The newcomer’s eyes flashed. “We’re not going to let you—”

“I will place it,” Kammler cut in, calm and absolute. The calm was a weapon; it made other men feel their own rising emotion like a flaw. “And then I will close the container. That is the transfer.”

The newcomer's jaw worked. He glanced at the soldiers, at the locals in the trees, at the craft behind Kammler that refused to behave like wreckage. He was calculating the cost of forcing compliance.

"Fine," he said at last. "You place it."

Kammler stepped toward the open suitcase. The leaves under his boots were damp and soft. Yet when he crossed into the space near the foam cavity, he felt the pressure in his teeth sharpen, as if two fields had overlapped: the craft's pulse and something else, something that recognized the motion of surrender and wanted to see what would happen.

He lowered the case in his hand slowly. He did not look at the bell. He did not look at the soldiers. He kept his attention narrowed to the foam, to the rectangle of prepared emptiness.

As the case hovered over the cavity, the grooves on the craft seemed to deepen in the corner of his vision. He did not turn his head to confirm it. Confirmation was attention. Attention fed pattern.

The case settled into the foam with a muted thump.

Nothing exploded. No light burst from the seams. The world did not split open the way it had in the corridor between centuries.

Still, Kammler felt a subtle shift in the air, like a breath taken by something that did not have lungs. The craft pulsed immediately afterward, and the pulse came with a faint shimmer above its surface, a hairline texture that made the flashlight beams look briefly distorted.

One of the plain-coated men made a small sound of discomfort and looked away. The other did not move, his face held still by concentration. Kammler could see the effort in his eyes, the way he tried to keep his gaze on the suitcase, on procedure, on any part of the scene that could be made ordinary.

Kammler reached down and pulled the straps across the case inside the suitcase. He tightened them, not because the case would shift in transport but because tension reassured men who lived by locking things down.

Then he closed the lid.

The latches snapped shut with a clean, satisfying finality.

The newcomer stepped forward and put his hand on the suitcase handle. For a heartbeat his fingers hesitated, as if his nerves had offered him one last chance to avoid contact. Then he gripped it firmly, daring the world to punish him for touching.

The craft pulsed again.

The newcomer's shadow on the leaves lagged by a fraction. It moved a fraction too late, like an echo arriving after the sound. The newcomer did not look down. If he noticed, he hid it well. But one soldier near the tree line stiffened and stared at the ground, his expression turning pale as his mind tried to interpret what his eyes had not been trained to see.

Kammler watched the newcomer's face. He saw the tightening around the eyes, the shallow breath disguised as steadiness.

"You will take me to Wright-Patterson," Kammler said.

The newcomer's gaze snapped back to him. "You're coming," he confirmed, as if the sentence were a correction rather than an agreement. "But you're not calling the shots."

Kammler nodded once. "You think this is a crash," he said quietly. "You think you are collecting an object."

The newcomer's mouth tightened. "And you think you're not?"

Kammler let the question pass. There was no point explaining to a man who believed in rooms and locks that the most dangerous thing in the clearing was not metal.

Behind him, the craft pulsed again, the steady rhythm that made the body recognize pattern even before the mind could name it. Forty-seven seconds, Kammler thought, and felt an almost involuntary satisfaction at the confirmation. The number had followed him across time. Or it had been waiting in time, and he had merely stepped into its line of sight.

The plain-coated men lifted the metal suitcase and carried it toward the van, holding it level as if it contained fluid instead of evidence. The newcomer gestured, and soldiers moved with them, forming a moving corridor that pushed any stray flashlight beams away, discouraging eyes from lingering on the transfer.

At the edge of the clearing, the teenager watched, hugging his arms against the cold, and felt the peculiar frustration of being made into a witness and then denied the conclusion. The locals could see the bell-shaped craft, half buried, still and wrong. They could see men moving with a controlled urgency that did not belong to volunteer firemen or hunters. They could see the dark-coated stranger, now being guided toward the sedan, still untouched by mud.

What they could not see was the thing that mattered most to Kammler: the way the forest's shadows behaved as if they were listening.

The newcomer stopped beside the sedan and looked at Kammler one last time before the door opened. His voice dropped, pitched for only Kammler's hearing.

"What's in that case?" he asked.

Kammler's face remained composed. "A covenant," he said.

The newcomer stared at him, and for a moment Kammler saw the exact shape of the man's uncertainty, the instinctive sense that he had stepped into a story that did not belong to him. He masked it quickly with procedure.

"Get in," he said.

Kammler slid into the back seat. The interior smelled of cold vinyl and cigarettes. The door closed, sealing him in.

As the sedan began to roll, Kammler looked out through the rear window.

The bell-shaped craft sat in the clearing like a deliberate offering. Soldiers moved around it with flashlights and measured distance, careful not to touch. The van carrying the metal suitcase pulled out behind the sedan, its engine quiet.

At the treeline, the locals stood in a line of faces and breath, already being told by shouted orders that they had seen nothing, that they would go home and forget.

Kammler watched the craft recede between trunks.

Just before it vanished from view entirely, the craft pulsed one more time, and the air above it shimmered with that hairline texture, as if the forest itself had briefly become a membrane under strain.

Kammler did not look away.

He let the world know, in the only way he could, that he was still watching.

Then the trees swallowed the clearing, and Kecksburg became only dark road and engine hum and the steady forward motion of a convoy heading toward a base that specialized in taking the extraordinary and locking it into rooms.

In the van behind him, the case rode inside its metal coffin.

And in the case, sealed away from leaves and flashlights and frightened witnesses, the evidence waited, patient as blood in glass, ready to be delivered to men who believed they could own what had been taken from time.

Chapter 12

American Custody

The sedan's windows were dark enough to turn the outside world into a moving strip of muted color. Kammler watched it anyway, not because it offered information, but because it offered orientation. Road. Trees. Occasional farm lights that did not belong to any facility. For a time, the convoy moved without sirens, without the theatrics of an emergency. It behaved like something ordinary, and that ordinariness was part of the procedure.

In the front seat the driver said nothing. The newcomer who had taken control in the clearing sat beside him, hat still low, shoulders squared as if posture could keep the night from changing shape. In the rearview mirror, when the angle permitted, Kammler caught a sliver of the man's eyes. They did not relax. They did not stop measuring.

Behind them the panel van followed at a fixed distance, headlights dimmed. The metal suitcase with the foam cavity rode inside it, strapped down as if inertia were the enemy and not attention.

Kammler's hands were free. That, more than restraints, told him what kind of custody this was. They had not decided whether he was a prisoner or an asset. They were avoiding decisions until they were indoors, until the world around them belonged to them again.

The man in the front passenger seat finally spoke, voice low, pitched so it would not carry even inside the car.

"What's your name?"

Kammler did not answer immediately. Names were not neutral. Names were handles.

"You already know," Kammler said.

A pause. Then, "We have guesses."

Kammler let his gaze stay on the window. Outside, the road bent. The sedan followed it with a smoothness that suggested the driver had been trained for more than commuting.

"I am the one you were told would arrive," Kammler said. "That is the only name that matters to your chain of command."

The man's jaw tightened. "You're German."

"I am," Kammler replied.

"And you expect me to believe you just fell out of the sky in Pennsylvania with a bell-shaped craft and a case full of… evidence."

Kammler turned his head slightly, just enough to see the man's reflection rather than his face. "You do not need belief," he said. "You need containment."

The word did what Kammler intended. It pulled the conversation away from incredulity and toward procedure, where men like this were strongest.

"We'll contain," the man said. Then, after a beat: "You said it was for transfer. To Rome. That's not happening."

Kammler did not react. The car's interior smelled of cold vinyl, stale smoke, and something else underneath, a faint sharpness that reminded him of the bell chamber's ozone after a pulse. He wondered briefly if it was only memory, then felt it again in his teeth: a small pressure, rhythmic, as if his body still carried the imprint of a field.

"You will take it where you take things you do not understand," Kammler said. "And you will tell yourselves that is the same as control."

The man's eyes flicked in the mirror. "You talk like you've been here before."

“I have been in facilities like yours,” Kammler said. “They all smell the same. Disinfectant and fear.”

The driver’s knuckles whitened on the wheel. The passenger said nothing for a while, and the silence stretched until it began to feel like part of the transport protocol. Kammler watched the outside world drain away into flatter land, then into highway lighting, then into the harsher regularity of military infrastructure. Guard posts appeared. Fences. Signs. The kind of geometry that announced territory.

At the first checkpoint the convoy slowed. A floodlight washed across the sedan, bright enough that Kammler saw his own reflection in the glass layered over the guard’s face. For a heartbeat the reflection lagged. Not much. The kind of delay a tired mind might invent.

Kammler did not blink until the light moved on.

The guard leaned down to the passenger window. Papers were presented. Words exchanged too softly for Kammler to hear. The guard glanced into the back seat.

His eyes met Kammler’s.

The guard’s expression tightened in a way Kammler recognized. Not recognition of a face, but recognition of wrongness. The guard's gaze flicked toward Kammler's shoes, as if expecting mud and finding none, then back to Kammler's eyes. A brief instinctive recoil.

The passenger in the front seat spoke sharply, a tone that did not invite questions. The guard straightened, stepped back, and lifted the barrier.

The sedan rolled forward onto Wright-Patterson Air Force Base.

The base at night was a controlled constellation: pools of light separated by darkness, roads drawn in hard lines, buildings low and functional. There were hangars that looked like sleeping animals, their doors closed, their outlines too large to be entirely reassuring. Everything was quiet in the way a place was quiet when it had trained itself to hide activity rather than reduce it.

They did not go to a main building. They drove past administrative blocks, past a lit medical facility, past a row of parked aircraft whose shapes Kammler could not fully identify in the dark. The convoy turned onto a narrower service road and continued toward a section where the fence lines doubled, and the lights grew more deliberate.

At a second checkpoint, closer, more guarded, the sedan stopped again. This time men approached with weapons held with casual competence, not raised, but present. Another man arrived from a door in the fence line, wearing a coat despite the cold, his posture indicating authority without rank insignia.

He leaned toward the passenger window. The passenger spoke first, quick and clipped. "We have the package. We have the courier."

The man at the fence looked past him to Kammler. "Out," he said.

Kammler stepped from the sedan into air that tasted different, less like winter and more like machinery. Somewhere nearby a generator ran with a steady hum. As his boots hit pavement he felt the same faint pressure in his teeth strengthen, then settle, as if the base itself carried electrical tension the way mountains carried storms.

The new man, older, face lined with lack of sleep, watched Kammler with professional wariness. "You're not restrained."

"I am contained," Kammler replied.

That earned him a brief narrowing of the eyes, then a gesture. Two men flanked Kammler without grabbing him, close enough to be a message rather than a hold.

The panel van rolled through the gate behind them. It stopped near a low building with no windows at ground level. The building was unmarked. That was, in itself, a kind of marking.

The rear doors of the van opened. The metal suitcase was lifted out with care, held level as if it contained something unstable. The foam-lined cavity was inside it, and inside that, the smaller case Kammler had carried out of the clearing. A nested containment, like Russian dolls built by engineers.

A door opened in the building. Warm light spilled out, harsh and white, the light of clinics and interrogation rooms. The air that came with it was dry, filtered, stripped of weather.

They guided Kammler inside.

The interior corridor was narrow, painted an institutional gray that tried and failed to look neutral. The smell of disinfectant was stronger here, layered over metal and paper. The hum of ventilation was constant, a background insistence that the building was sealed from the world.

Kammler was led into a room with a table bolted to the floor, chairs bolted as well, and a single light overhead that did not flicker. That steadiness made Kammler uneasy. He had become accustomed to light hesitating.

The man from the fence line entered behind him and closed the door. A second door was visible in the far wall, heavier, with a keypad.

"We're going to ask you some questions," the man said.

"You already are," Kammler replied.

The man ignored that. He pulled a folder from under his arm and placed it on the table without opening it, as if the folder itself were a tool of authority. "Who are you?"

Kammler sat without being told. His posture remained straight. "You have files," he said. "Use them."

The man's mouth tightened. He did not sit. "You appear in no immigration record. No flight record. No passport record. And yet you arrive with something that came down like a meteor, except it didn't burn, and you walk out like you stepped from a hallway. So, I'll ask again. Who are you?"

Kammler looked up into the steady light, then back at the man. He decided, strategically, to give a truth that would sound like a lie. Truths that sounded like lies were useful. They delayed certainty.

"I am Dr. Hans Kammler," he said. "And I am late."

The man's eyes did not widen, but something changed around them, subtle as a pressure shift. A name had weight in rooms built for secrets. The man's gaze flicked to the folder on the table as if the paper inside it might suddenly rearrange itself to match what he was hearing.

"Kammler," he repeated. "As in SS. As in dead."

"Dead is an administrative word," Kammler said. "Not a physical one."

The man stared at him, and Kammler watched the moment the stare became an assessment. Not whether to believe, but what to do if belief became necessary.

The door in the far wall opened, and two men entered with the metal suitcase. They placed it on a second table against the wall, not the bolted one. That second table had a drain in its surface. Laboratory furniture. Something meant to be washed.

One of the men reached for the suitcase latches.

Kammler spoke sharply enough that even Americans heard command in it. "Do not."

The hand hesitated.

The older man turned his head slightly. "We can open whatever we want on this base."

Kammler did not raise his voice. He did not need to. "You can open it," he said. "And you will contaminate it. Not with fingerprints. With attention. With curiosity. With the assumption that a lock is the only boundary that matters."

The older man's eyes narrowed. "We'll decide what contamination means."

Kammler held his gaze. "You already felt it," he said. "In your teeth. In the air near the object. In the way the clearing behaved under your lights. That was not imagination. That was response."

For a moment the older man looked as if he might argue on instinct, the way men argued when threatened with the idea that their tools were inadequate. Then he did something that told Kammler more than any response.

He did not order the latches opened.

He ordered the room emptied.

"You two, out," he said to the men with the suitcase. "Wait outside."

They hesitated, then obeyed. The door closed behind them.

Only Kammler and the older man remained.

The ventilation hummed. The light stayed steady. Somewhere deeper in the building, another door closed with a sound too heavy to belong to ordinary offices.

The older man leaned forward slightly, lowering his voice. "If you're Kammler, you're a war criminal."

Kammler's expression did not change. "If I am," he said, "then you will still keep me alive, because I brought you something you cannot name."

The older man's gaze dropped to the metal suitcase, then returned to Kammler. "What is in the case."

Kammler answered with the same word he had used in the forest, because repeating a word made it a peg in a shifting wall.

"Evidence," he said. Then he added, carefully: "And instruction."

The older man's eyes hardened. "Instruction for who."

Kammler looked at the bolted table, at the folder untouched, at the steady lamp that pretended the building was immune to hesitation. He thought of a sealed cabinet under a mountain, of waxed ampoules, of shadows that learned voices, of a cycle of forty-seven seconds that had followed him like a signature.

He met the older man's stare. "For the Vatican," he said. "And for you, if you are wise enough to understand that custody is not ownership."

The older man's mouth tightened. He straightened slightly, as if his body needed distance from the implications. "Why should we do anything for Rome."

Kammler's reply came without hesitation, because it was the hinge on which his entire covenant turned.

"Because," he said, "Rome is already involved. And because I did not come here to ask permission."

The older man stared at him in a silence that felt like a calculation running behind the eyes.

Kammler waited.

He had learned patience from the Observer, if nothing else. There were forces that did not hurry because they did not need to. Kammler had survived by borrowing that calm when it suited him.

At last, the older man spoke. "You're going to tell me exactly what you think you've brought onto my base."

Kammler did not glance at the metal suitcase. He did not give it the courtesy of attention in this room. He kept his gaze on the man.

"I brought proof," Kammler said. "And I brought the consequence of taking it."

For a fraction of a second, the older man's eyes flicked down, not to the suitcase, but to the floor near Kammler's feet, as if checking something his body had sensed.

Kammler felt it too, faintly: a hesitation in shadow where no hesitation should exist, like a delayed echo waiting to decide whether to arrive.

Then it settled again, obedient.

The older man looked back up, his face set into the expression of a man who had just realized that secrecy was no longer only about what people knew.

It was about what the world itself might learn.

The older man did not sit. He remained standing as if gravity itself were a tool he could use, an advantage of height and posture in a room built for leverage.

Kammler kept his hands folded loosely on the bolted table, palms down. He had learned long ago that stillness unsettled men more than defiance.

Defiance gave them something to push against. Stillness made them wonder what else was moving.

The older man tapped the folder once with a finger. "Proof," he repeated, as if testing whether the word would hold its shape. "And consequence. You're speaking in riddles."

"I am speaking precisely," Kammler said. "Your language is inadequate."

A faint tightening passed across the older man's mouth. "You're in no position to insult me."

Kammler tilted his head a fraction. "You are the one who believes you are holding a man. You are not. You are holding a junction."

The ventilation continued its steady hum. The light remained steady. Kammler waited for the smallest betrayals of the room: the momentary dimming, the lag of shadow at the edge of vision. Nothing obliged him. Either the base was better shielded than the Owl Mountains facility, or whatever had learned the corridor preferred to wait until it was invited by attention again.

The older man walked to the second table where the sealed metal suitcase sat. He stopped short of touching it. The restraint was small, but it was there.

"You want me to call the Vatican," he said.

"I want you to relay a message," Kammler replied. "A message that informs them that the covenant is active."

The older man turned back. "Covenant."

Kammler did not smile. "You already accepted the word in the forest. You carried it here."

Silence stretched. It had weight now, not merely the absence of speech but a pause in which the next action would define the rules of the room.

At last, the older man spoke again, and his tone shifted. Less interrogation, more negotiation. "If I contact Rome, it will be on our terms."

"You cannot impose terms on an institution that predates your republic," Kammler said. He watched the older man's eyes narrow at the mention of history, at the reminder that time could be used as a weapon. "But you can choose how you are remembered by them."

The older man's face hardened. "Don't threaten me with memory."

Kammler's gaze remained steady. "I am not threatening you. I am describing what you have already involved yourself in."

The older man stared at him, then reached toward the door. He opened it sharply and spoke to someone unseen in the corridor. "Get me a secure line. Now. And I want a translator who understands ecclesiastical protocols."

A pause, a murmur of acknowledgment.

The older man closed the door again and faced Kammler. "You give me the message. I decide what gets transmitted."

"You will transmit it exactly," Kammler said. "Verbatim."

The older man exhaled through his nose. "We'll see."

Kammler waited. He could feel the faint, rhythmic pressure in his teeth again, like a memory of a pulse that had once belonged to a bell under a mountain. Forty-seven seconds. The number did not appear in this room, not yet, but his body still recognized pattern the way a wound recognized weather.

Minutes later, the door opened and a younger officer entered carrying a field telephone with a heavy handset and a small box of equipment. He set it on the table as carefully as if it were explosive. His eyes flicked to Kammler, then away. He did not know what he was looking at, only that his superiors had changed tone.

Behind him came another man, older, civilian dressed, with glasses and the weary expression of someone pulled from a desk into a situation that would not fit on paper. He nodded once to the older officer and did not look at Kammler at all, as if eye contact itself felt risky.

"We can route through an attaché channel," the younger officer said. "It'll take a few minutes."

The older officer's gaze remained on Kammler. "You speak Latin?"

Kammler did not bother answering the obvious. "German," he said. "Italian, if necessary. But the message is in English. It should not be softened by translation."

The civilian cleared his throat. "If this is to the Holy See, there are formal—"

Kammler cut him off without raising his voice. "There are realities that do not care about your formalities. You will not address a secretary. You will not leave a message. You will reach someone who understands what a private courier from a dead Reich implies."

The older officer's eyes tightened. He did not like being instructed, but the discomfort in his posture suggested he also did not like the alternative: improvisation with a man who spoke like a blueprint.

"Who exactly are we calling?" he asked.

“A man named Orsini will know where it should go,” Kammler said. He chose the name carefully. Monsignor Orsini was not a public official; his existence was a shadow in Vatican corridors. Speaking the name in this American room felt like dragging a thread across continents.

The civilian finally looked up at that, and the look was brief and startled, as if he had heard a name he was not supposed to hear. He opened his mouth, then closed it again.

The older officer noticed. “You know it,” he said to the civilian.

The civilian swallowed. “I… I’ve seen it in cables,” he admitted. “Not official ones.”

Kammler watched both of them. “Then you understand why this cannot be delayed.”

The younger officer adjusted dials on the equipment box. A light blinked, then steadied. The handset cord looked too thin for the weight of what it was about to carry.

While they waited, the older officer leaned slightly toward Kammler, lowering his voice. “You said consequence. What consequence.”

Kammler considered how much truth was useful. Too much would sound like madness and be dismissed. Too little would invite mistakes.

"We opened a corridor," Kammler said. "We took something from a fixed point." He did not say Golgotha. He did not offer them the relief of a name that could be categorized as delusion. "Something noticed."

The older officer's gaze flicked involuntarily toward the floor again. Not the suitcase. The floor. As if his body had begun to distrust shadows.

Kammler continued, because now that the door had opened even slightly, withholding would only make them fill the gap with less accurate nightmares. "It learns by watching. It refines its imitation. It wears voices. It uses familiarity to invite response."

The younger officer glanced up from the equipment, face pale. The civilian's fingers tightened around a notebook he had brought, knuckles whitening.

The older officer stared at Kammler for a long moment. "And you're telling me the Vatican is part of this."

"I am telling you the Vatican demanded proof," Kammler replied. "And I delivered it. Now they must receive the message that delivery has occurred."

The equipment box clicked softly. The younger officer lifted a hand. "We've got a line."

The older officer took the handset but did not speak immediately. His eyes remained on Kammler, the look of a man making a choice he would later describe as unavoidable.

He spoke into the handset in clipped phrases, requesting a connection through channels that were clearly not meant for casual use. The civilian leaned in slightly, listening to the faint voices on the other end, translating protocol into access.

Time stretched. Kammler remained still.

Then the older officer's posture shifted. He held the handset tighter. His voice changed, becoming more formal. "This is an encrypted United States military line. We require immediate contact with the Secretariat of State, Vatican City. Priority classification. Yes, now."

A pause. A murmur from the handset that was too faint to parse.

The older officer glanced at Kammler once, then spoke again. "We have an individual claiming to be Dr. Hans Kammler. He has requested transmission of a message to a Vatican operative, Orsini. The nature of the request involves… physical evidence."

Another pause, longer this time. The civilian scribbled notes he would later pretend were routine.

Kammler watched the lamp overhead. It did not flicker. The steadiness felt almost insulting, as if this room believed it could remain purely mechanical.

Finally, the older officer's eyes narrowed slightly, and he held the handset out toward Kammler without stepping closer. "You have one sentence," he said. "Make it count."

Kammler took the handset. It was warm from the officer's hand, a mundane detail that irritated him. He brought it to his ear and listened.

On the other end was silence, then a breath. Then a voice speaking Italian-accented Latin that slipped into English as if switching tracks on a record. Controlled, cautious, trained to sound neutral.

"This line is not secure for confession," the voice said. "State your purpose."

Kammler spoke without hesitation, and he spoke clearly, as if dictating to a stenographer.

"Tell Orsini," Kammler said, "that the covenant is fulfilled. I have delivered the evidence. And tell the Holy See this: I have risen."

The silence that followed was not disbelief. It was calculation.

The voice returned, quieter now. "Who is this."

Kammler did not answer the question as asked, because answering it would invite them to argue about identity, about death certificates, about administrative words. He gave them only what mattered: the hook that would pull the correct people into motion.

"The case is in American custody," he said. "If you want it intact, you will move quickly. And you will not come alone."

He handed the handset back to the older officer before the voice could ask another question. Conversation was a door. Doors invited attention.

The older officer took the handset and listened briefly, then ended the call with a decisive motion. He set the handset down as if it might bite.

The civilian looked at Kammler with something like horror now, stripped of professional detachment. "You just told the Vatican you've risen," he said softly, as if testing whether he had misheard.

Kammler's gaze drifted, for the first time, to the sealed metal suitcase. He did not look long. He did not feed it. But he allowed himself a single measured acknowledgment of what sat inside: film, samples, notes, and the shadow of consequence wrapped around them like a second seal.

"I told them what they need to hear," Kammler replied. "They asked for proof. Proof requires a messenger. A messenger requires myth."

The older officer's voice was flat. "And what do we get."

Kammler looked back at him. "You get to decide whether your custody becomes collaboration," he said. "Or whether you are merely the next set of hands that touches the wrong thing and learns too late that touch is a form of invitation."

For a heartbeat, the older officer's eyes flicked again to the floor near Kammler's feet.

Kammler felt it too, faint as breath: a hesitation where his shadow should have moved in perfect obedience. Not a dramatic detachment, not yet. Just a delayed echo, a reminder that something had learned patience, and that sealed buildings were not the same as sealed worlds.

Then it settled again.

The older officer straightened, his face set into the expression of a man who had just placed a call he could not retract. "Get him moved to a secure holding room," he said to the younger officer. "No windows. No contact with personnel unless authorized. And nobody touches that suitcase until we decide what protocols apply."

The younger officer nodded too quickly.

As they moved to open the door, Kammler spoke one last time, not loud, not dramatic, but with the careful emphasis of a man placing a final piece on a board.

"You will receive visitors," he said. "Not from Rome. Not at first. But you will receive them. You have announced the existence of the evidence. Now the world will behave as if it has been watched."

The older officer paused in the doorway, just long enough to show the words had landed. He did not turn back.

The door closed.

Kammler was left with the hum of ventilation, the steady light, and the satisfaction of a message delivered across an ocean to a city built on secrets.

Somewhere far away, in Vatican corridors that smelled of stone and incense and old paper, the name Orsini would be spoken with a new urgency.

And in the spaces between observation and response, something else would listen, patient and inhuman, counting the distance between doors.

The holding room was colder than the interrogation room, but the cold was a choice, not a failure. It lived in the air as a steady, dry bite that kept skin awake and made breath visible only in the mind. The walls were painted the same institutional gray, but here the paint looked newer, as if freshness could substitute for security. A single light sat behind a frosted panel in the ceiling, bright enough to deny corners any softness.

Kammler sat on the narrow cot with his back straight and his boots on the floor. They had taken his coat. They had not taken his composure. A camera watched him from a corner behind smoked glass, and the ventilation hummed with the same unbroken insistence, a mechanical lullaby for men who believed machines were immune to suggestion.

He waited.

Not for freedom. For movement. For the first sign that the message had reached the kind of ears that did not need to be told what a covenant implied.

Beyond the door, the base adjusted.

The older officer's order had spread through corridors like a voltage: restrict access, silence radios, log every hand that came near the package. The sort of containment Wright-Patterson was built to perform. But the package was not a crate of foreign metal or a pilot's body. It was evidence intended for Rome, nested inside an American shell, and the act of placing it on the base had already created a second network of interest that would never appear in official logs.

In a windowless lab two corridors away, the metal suitcase sat on a stainless table under another steady lamp. A red tag hung from its handle with a barcode and a time stamp. The foam inside still held Kammler's smaller case like a tooth in a jaw. Two guards stood outside the lab door with rifles carried low, eyes fixed on the corridor rather than the room, as if the room were the dangerous thing.

Inside, the older officer and a man in a white coat stood without touching it.

The white coat's name was on his badge, but the older officer did not use it. This was not the kind of meeting where names improved clarity. The scientist wore latex gloves anyway, out of habit, and that habit made the older officer's mouth tighten.

"Tell me again," the older officer said. "Why we're not opening it."

The scientist's gaze did not leave the suitcase. "Because the courier told you not to," he replied, then seemed to regret the simplicity of that answer. He added, quieter, "And because the men who handled the craft in the field reported sensory anomalies. Dental pressure. Light distortions. A perceived delay in shadow movement. Those are not typical stress responses."

"Perceived," the older officer repeated.

The scientist looked at him then. His eyes were tired and sharp. "We say perceived when we don't have instruments for it," he said. "That doesn't make it imaginary."

The older officer's jaw worked once. He turned his head slightly toward the one-way glass. On the other side, behind the wall, Kammler waited in his holding room, a man who claimed to have been dead and spoke as if he had the patience of something that did not care about clocks.

"We don't do theology here," the older officer said. "We do chain of custody."

The scientist gave a small, humorless exhale. "Then you should understand that custody is already compromised," he said.

Before the older officer could answer, the lab door opened and the younger officer stepped in, holding a paper strip in one hand and a telephone message form in the other.

"They called back," the younger officer said. His voice was controlled, but his eyes had the look of a man who had just been told a door existed in a wall he thought was solid. "From the same channel. Vatican State Secretariat. They said they cannot acknowledge the content of the previous transmission, but they request immediate liaison."

The older officer took the message form without touching the suitcase. "Request is a polite word," he said.

The younger officer nodded once. "They also asked if the courier is under physical restraint."

The scientist's gaze flicked to the older officer. A silent question: why would they care about that.

The older officer read the form, then looked up. "Who else got the transcript of what he said?"

"Just us," the younger officer replied. "And command."

The older officer stared at him a moment longer than necessary. Then, quietly, "And the other line?"

The younger officer hesitated. A fraction too long. The kind of hesitation that meant something had already happened.

"There was a second call," the younger officer admitted. "Not logged on the lab line. It came through the secure exchange in communications. A man from… another office took it."

The scientist's expression changed, subtle but immediate. "Another office," he repeated, as if translating the euphemism into something more concrete.

The older officer's face remained still. "What office."

The younger officer swallowed. "He didn't say. He just had access. He asked for the courier's name. He asked for 'Rome.' He asked if the package was intact."

The older officer took a slow breath, then released it through his nose. "Unseen transactions," he said, not as a title, but as a diagnosis.

He turned toward the lab door. "Stay with it," he told the scientist. "No one opens anything. No one runs light across it. No photographs. No microscopy. Nothing."

The scientist blinked. "No light?"

"Not unless I'm in the room," the older officer said. "And even then, only what is necessary. If Kammler is right about observation, then our curiosity is a tool we can't control."

The scientist's mouth tightened as if the order offended his profession. But he nodded once, because even scientists on bases knew when policy had become fear wearing a lab coat.

As the older officer left the lab, the younger officer followed. The corridor outside smelled faintly of disinfectant and warm wiring. The steady lights remained steady, but the older officer found himself looking at the floors anyway, catching his own shadow in peripheral vision and hating that he did.

"Who has access to comms exchange at this hour?" he asked.

The younger officer kept his eyes forward. "Certain agencies," he said.

The older officer stopped walking. The younger officer stopped too, shoulders tightening.

"What did the man say," the older officer demanded.

The younger officer's throat worked. "He said he was authorized to 'coordinate foreign ecclesiastical contact.' He said, 'We're not letting Rome walk into our vault and walk out with a relic.'"

Relic. The word made the older officer's skin tighten.

"And what did you tell him?" he asked.

The younger officer's eyes flicked once toward the lab door they had left behind, as if the suitcase could hear. "I told him the package was sealed and under guard. I told him the courier is isolated. I told him you were handling the Vatican communication."

The older officer stared at him for a beat, then nodded once, sharp. "You didn't lie," he said. "You just gave him enough."

The younger officer looked down briefly, a man realizing that there were traps that did not require malice to spring. "Sir," he said quietly, "what is it? Really."

The older officer's mouth tightened. He thought of Kammler's flat certainty in the interrogation room. Proof and consequence. A junction. The idea that a lock was not the only boundary.

He resumed walking. "It's leverage," he said. "And it's bait. And it's something our procedures aren't built to recognize as alive."

They reached a junction where two men waited in suits that did not belong on an Air Force base. One was broad-shouldered with a calm, practiced face. The other held a folder as if it were a passport into any room. Neither wore a name tag. Their eyes moved over the older officer and then, briefly, over the younger officer, measuring him as either useful or accidental.

"We need access to the courier," the broad-shouldered man said. His voice was polite enough to be a threat.

The older officer stopped. "This is an Air Force facility," he said. "You don't get access because you want it."

The man with the folder smiled without warmth. "We're not asking," he said. "We're coordinating. The Vatican call you made created ripples. Those ripples attract interest."

"So does the craft," the older officer replied.

The broad-shouldered man's gaze remained steady. "The craft is a separate matter," he said. "The case is the matter now. The case is portable."

The older officer felt something cold settle behind his ribs. Portable. Evidence as an object to be moved, traded, hidden. A transaction, not a discovery.

"What's your office," he asked.

The folder man's smile did not change. "The one that keeps your problems from becoming public," he said.

The older officer stared at them and understood, with a clarity that did not bring comfort, that the base had already become a marketplace for secrecy. Not money exchanged, not openly. But access.

Influence. The right to hold something first, to interpret it first, to decide which truths would exist and which would remain rumors.

"You won't interrogate him," the older officer said.

"We won't interrogate," the broad-shouldered man agreed smoothly. "We'll assess. We need to know what he is and what he brought."

The older officer's jaw tightened. "He's in isolation for a reason."

The folder man shrugged slightly. "Then we'll assess in isolation."

Before the older officer could answer, a wall-mounted phone at the corridor junction rang once, sharp and out of place. The younger officer flinched as if the sound had arrived inside his head instead of through air. The older officer looked at the phone, then at the two suited men, then back at the phone.

He lifted the receiver.

A voice came through, distorted by distance and equipment, but clear enough in tone. "This is communications. We have an incoming request on the ecclesiastical channel. They insist on speaking to whoever transmitted the message. They repeated a name. Orsini."

The older officer closed his eyes for half a second, not in prayer, but in irritation at how quickly the unseen lines had tightened around them.

He opened his eyes and looked at the suited men. "You see," he said quietly. "It's already a negotiation."

The folder man's smile thinned. "Then negotiate," he said. "But remember you're not the only party at the table."

In the holding room, two corridors away, Kammler sat perfectly still under the frosted ceiling light and listened to the ventilation hum. He could not hear the phone ring. He could not hear the suited men speak.

But he felt the change anyway, the subtle shift in the air that came when decisions were made elsewhere. A faint pressure in his teeth. A barely perceptible hesitation in the edge of his shadow as it lay against the cot frame.

The world was moving around his message now.

Hands he could not see were reaching for what he had delivered, not only the case, but the meaning inside it. Men who had never believed in relics were now bargaining over one. Men who had never spoken to Rome were now using Rome as a keyword in American corridors.

Kammler allowed himself a single, small breath that might have been satisfaction, or might have been acknowledgement of the thing Orsini had warned him about under the mountain: once a hinge had been forced, it never returned to being only metal.

Beyond these walls, the Vatican would respond. Agencies would intervene. Protocols would be rewritten on the fly.

And in the gaps between calls and signatures and orders that would never be recorded, something else would be listening too, learning not from what they said, but from what they reached for when they thought no one could see.

Chapter 13

The Vatican Envoy

The call reached Vatican City the way poison reached a bloodstream: through channels built for necessity, disguised as routine until the body began to react.

In a side office off the Secretariat's main corridor, a priest in a black cassock replaced the handset with a careful hand and did not sit down. He stood in the stale pocket of air between a filing cabinet and a window that had been painted shut decades earlier. He stared at the receiver as if it might speak again on its own, and for a few seconds the only sound in the room was the soft rasp of paper shifting under a fan that never quite moved enough air.

Monsignor Matteo Orsini listened without interrupting, hands folded inside his sleeves, eyes half-lidded in the posture of a man receiving a confession he could not absolve.

The priest who had taken the call cleared his throat. "He said it exactly like that. In English. 'Tell Orsini the covenant is fulfilled. I have delivered the evidence. I have risen.'"

Orsini did not ask how a dead man spoke on an American military line. He did not ask who had authorized the connection. He had learned, the hard way, that improbable access was not proof of safety but proof of pressure.

"Where is it," Orsini asked.

"Wright-Patterson Air Force Base," the priest replied. "They say they can arrange a liaison. They asked for… protocols."

Orsini's mouth tightened at the word. Protocols were what men clung to when they were already in water above their heads. He crossed the room and drew a thin folder from a locked drawer. It had no title on the spine, only a number written in pencil so faint it looked like a shadow. He opened it and scanned a page of notes he had written years earlier in a hand that now felt like someone else's.

Kammler had promised delivery. Kammler had delivered. And, as Orsini had warned him under the mountain, delivery was never only a movement of objects. It was a movement of consequence.

"The Americans will not give it to an attaché," Orsini said. "And they will not give it to a bishop."

The priest swallowed. "Then who."

Orsini closed the folder. "Someone they can justify letting into their vault without saying the word relic," he said. He turned his head slightly, listening. Not for footsteps. For the building itself.

For a moment he had the irrational sensation that the light in the room was hesitating. The window was shut, the lamp steady, yet the edge of his shadow on the wall seemed to arrive a fraction late, like an echo that had forgotten its cue. The feeling passed as quickly as it came, leaving behind only a mild tightness in his teeth.

Orsini did not mention it.

He stepped out into the corridor and walked with purpose that looked clerical and was anything but. He passed secretaries who lowered their eyes in automatic respect. He passed tourists shepherded at a distance by Swiss Guards who had been trained to smile without seeing. He moved through the public heart of the Holy See as if it were simply another hallway, and in a way it was. The real Vatican lived in locked rooms and unnamed ledgers and the understanding that salvation was often administered like intelligence.

In a small chamber two levels down, behind a door that required both a key and a whispered phrase, three men waited. One was an elderly cardinal whose hands shook slightly when he pretended they did not. One was a bureaucrat with ink stains on his fingers and a face trained into neutrality. The third wore a plain black suit without collar or insignia, the kind of suit that belonged to men who served the Church best when they did not look like servants.

Orsini greeted none of them with warmth.

“They have it,” Orsini said. “In America.”

The cardinal exhaled, the sound almost a prayer. “So, the German has kept his word.”

“The German has kept the part of his word that benefits him,” Orsini replied. He placed the thin folder on the table. “We must assume he has also kept the part that benefits whatever now accompanies him.”

The bureaucrat’s eyes flicked to the folder and then away as if reading a title would invite it to become real. “What do the Americans want.”

“Control,” Orsini said. “And time. And the right to be first to interpret what they cannot name.”

The cardinal lifted his chin. “We cannot allow them to keep it.”

Orsini's gaze remained steady. "We also cannot allow them to open it," he said. "Kammler said there is contamination by observation. Whether that is physics, superstition, or something else, it changes the risk. The Americans will treat it like a specimen. They will flood it with light."

The man in the plain suit finally spoke. His Italian was crisp, his voice low. "Send me."

The cardinal looked at him with the mixture of discomfort and reliance that powerful men reserved for necessary sins. "Ferretti," he said softly, as if the name itself belonged behind a curtain.

Father Gabriel Ferretti did not correct him. Father was the cover; the rest of his history was a ledger the Church did not display. He had served in places where confessionals were used for dead drops. He had heard last rites given with codes woven into the Latin. He had learned to carry sacred objects through crowds without letting the crowd notice their weight.

Orsini studied him. Ferretti was in his forties, clean-shaven, with a narrow face and eyes that did not linger on icons. Those eyes belonged to a man trained to assess exits before altars.

"You understand what this is," Orsini said.

Ferretti nodded once. “It is proof,” he said, and Orsini heard the careful skepticism in the word. “And it is leverage.”

“It is also bait,” Orsini replied.

The cardinal made a small, impatient gesture. “Enough. If it is in their custody, then we retrieve it. Quietly. Without scandal. Without… theater.”

Orsini did not smile. Theater was what Kammler had already created by crashing a bell-shaped craft into a Pennsylvania forest. Theater was what the Americans would create by trying to own the narrative. Theater was what the Vatican had mastered long before radios.

“We will not go through the nuncio,” Orsini said. “We go through a channel they believe they control. Their agencies. Their men in suits who speak of coordination. They will assume we are predictable if we appear cooperative.”

Ferretti’s gaze sharpened slightly. “And if they refuse.”

Orsini’s fingers tightened inside his sleeves. “They will not,” he said. “They are already negotiating among themselves. That is what fear does. It splits authority into factions. A split is a doorway.”

The bureaucrat licked his lips. "What authority do we give him."

Orsini reached into the folder and drew out a thin paper sealed with an old stamp, not the public seal of the Holy See but another one, pressed into wax so dark it might have been blood. He slid it across the table toward Ferretti.

Ferretti did not touch it immediately. "This will open doors," he said.

"It will," Orsini agreed. "And it will attach your name to the retrieval. If it goes wrong, you will be the one who went wrong."

Ferretti's expression did not change. "That is what you require," he said.

Orsini watched him a moment longer, measuring. Men like Ferretti were useful because they did not flinch from becoming disposable, but they were also dangerous because they did not flinch from noticing when they were being used.

"When you have it," Orsini said, "you will not open it."

Ferretti's eyes held Orsini's. "You believe the German."

"I believe the consequence," Orsini replied. "I saw what came back with him in the mountains. I heard voices where no mouths moved. I watched shadows rehearse familiarity."

The cardinal's hand tightened on the arm of his chair. "Voices," he repeated, as if the word itself might invite them in.

Orsini continued, because fear grew when it was left vague. "If the evidence is what Kammler claims, then it is connected to a fixed point in history. A hinge. Hinges attract pressure. And something is learning the paths between doors."

Ferretti finally reached forward and took the sealed paper. His fingers did not tremble.

"How do I approach them," he asked.

"Under the only cover they will respect," Orsini said. "Diplomacy framed as damage control. They will tell themselves they are managing a religious nuisance. Let them."

"And Kammler," Ferretti said. "Do they still have him."

Orsini's jaw tightened. "Yes."

Ferretti's voice was quiet. "Then he can speak."

"That is why you do not meet him alone," Orsini said.

The cardinal leaned forward. "You will bring the case to Rome," he said. "Directly. No detours."

Ferretti tucked the sealed paper into his inner pocket. “I will bring it,” he said. “If it can be carried.”

Orsini felt the old pressure in his teeth again, faint as a memory. For a second he imagined Wright-Patterson’s steady lights, the metal suitcase under a lamp that refused to flicker, and men in suits circling like carrion around the idea of a relic. He imagined Kammler sitting in a cold room, perfectly still, as if waiting were a sacrament.

“Do not let them persuade you to let them open it for you,” Orsini said. “Do not let them isolate you. And if you feel anything change in the light, if you notice your shadow lagging, if you hear a voice that uses your name as if it has always known it, you do not respond. Do you understand.”

Ferretti’s eyes narrowed slightly at the specificity. “That has happened to you,” he said.

Orsini did not answer directly. Answers were also invitations.

“I understand,” Ferretti said instead.

The cardinal made the sign of the cross, quick and instinctive, then seemed faintly embarrassed by the gesture in front of men who traded in secrets. “May God protect you,” he murmured.

Ferretti stood. "God is not the only thing watching," he said, and the bluntness of it made the bureaucrat flinch.

Orsini walked Ferretti to the door himself. In the corridor outside, the ordinary Vatican continued: footsteps, murmured Italian, the distant echo of tourists being redirected. The stone walls held centuries of prayer, and for a moment Orsini wanted to believe that weight could shield them.

As Ferretti turned to leave, Orsini spoke once more, low enough that only Ferretti could hear.

"If Kammler truly believes he has risen," Orsini said, "then he will expect resurrection to have witnesses. Do not become one willingly."

Ferretti inclined his head, neither agreement nor refusal, just acknowledgment of instruction.

He walked away down the corridor with the pace of a man heading for an airport and a vault and a bargain he already suspected was rigged.

Orsini remained where he was, watching until Ferretti vanished around a corner. Only then did Orsini allow himself to glance at the wall beside him.

His shadow lay there, narrow and obedient.

A heartbeat late, it seemed to settle into place.

Orsini turned away before he could be sure. In a world where observation changed the observed, certainty was a kind of arrogance.

Behind Ferretti's departing footsteps, behind the Vatican's public calm, the retrieval mission had already begun, not as a journey across the Atlantic but as a chain of hands reaching for a case they believed contained proof.

Orsini knew better.

It contained a hinge.

And hinges did not simply open doors.

They taught doors how to open themselves.

The flight to New York was ordinary in all the ways Ferretti preferred: a seat number, a passport stamped by a man who did not look at faces long enough to remember them, coffee served with a smile that belonged to routine and not belief. He wore a Roman collar because it opened some doors faster than any forged credential, and because it made Americans place him into a category they thought they understood.

On the tarmac at JFK an attaché from the Apostolic Nunciature met him with a car and a practiced expression of concern that did not reach the eyes.

"You were difficult to reach," the attaché said in Italian as they drove.

"I was meant to be difficult to reach," Ferretti replied, watching the city's geometry pass behind glass. He did not ask how many messages had been exchanged before the pickup. He assumed the answer would be more than he was told.

Two hours later, in a federal building that did not put its name on the directory, Ferretti sat across from men who introduced themselves with first names that were almost certainly not their first names. They spoke with the careful courtesy of people who believed courtesy could be a leash.

"You're here about a package," one of them said. Broad shoulders, clean haircut, the kind of calm that came from institutional immunity. "It's currently on an Air Force installation. We can arrange access under supervision."

Ferretti placed Orsini's sealed paper on the table without sliding it forward. He let them see the wax and the old stamp, let their eyes do the work of recognizing authority they would never admit existed.

"I am here to take custody," Ferretti said. "Not to arrange a viewing."

The other man, thinner, with a folder that looked like it had been assembled in the last twelve hours, gave a small smile. "Custody is a strong word on our soil, Father."

Ferretti held the smile with his eyes until it became uncomfortable. "Then call it transfer," he said. "You like that word."

A beat of silence. Ferretti felt the moment when they weighed refusing him against the inconvenience of keeping an object they could not describe, and the larger inconvenience of explaining to their superiors why the Vatican had been angered into speaking publicly.

The broad-shouldered man finally nodded once. "We'll fly you to Ohio," he said. "You'll be escorted. No photography. No independent communication once you're inside the facility."

Ferretti's expression did not change. "And the courier," he said.

The folder man glanced down at his notes. "He's being held. Isolated."

Ferretti watched the slight hesitation before the word isolated and filed it away. Isolation could mean caution. It could also mean bargaining.

"He does not travel with the package," Ferretti said.

The broad-shouldered man leaned back. “You don’t get to set every term.”

Ferretti’s voice remained mild. “No,” he agreed. “I get to refuse. And then you keep the relic and explain why Rome has begun asking questions your press will understand.”

Relic made the folder man’s mouth tighten, exactly as Ferretti expected. Americans did not like old words. Old words implied old claims.

By midnight Ferretti was on a military aircraft that smelled of fuel and recycled air, escorted by two men who did not speak to him unless necessary. They treated him like a nuisance that had acquired diplomatic immunity and teeth.

At Wright-Patterson, the secure building looked the same as every other secure building in every other country: windowless, lit too evenly, designed by people who believed smooth surfaces reduced risk. Ferretti was led through corridors where the hum of ventilation made a constant, patient sound. He thought of Orsini’s warning about observation, and he kept his eyes moving, never lingering on the same corner long enough for his mind to turn it into a question.

They brought him into a lab that was too clean, too bright. A stainless table, steady overhead lights, a drain built into the surface as if the room had been designed for things that leaked. A man in an Air Force uniform stood by the far wall, older, lined with fatigue. Ferretti recognized him from description before he spoke: the one who had taken Kammler's call and regretted it.

"You're Ferretti," the officer said.

"I am the envoy," Ferretti replied. He did not offer his first name. Names were handles. He had learned that in Rome long before Orsini said it aloud.

On the table sat a metal suitcase with a red tag hanging from its handle. The tag had a barcode and a time stamp, a modern attempt to make a sacred theft into inventory.

The officer did not touch it. He stood as if proximity alone was risk.

"You're going to sign," the officer said. "Chain of custody."

Ferretti looked at the suitcase, then at the officer's face. "You do not want chain," he said quietly. "You want a break."

The officer's eyes narrowed. "We want to know what the hell it is."

Ferretti removed a pen from his pocket. He did not like pens with logos, so his was plain and heavy. He signed the form they placed in front of him, not because the signature mattered to Rome, but because it mattered to the men who needed paper to justify their fear.

When the officer gestured toward the suitcase, Ferretti did not move immediately.

"Before I open anything," Ferretti said, "tell me the rules you have already broken."

The officer's jaw worked once. "We haven't opened it," he said.

Ferretti held his gaze, letting the silence do what it always did. The officer's eyes flicked, involuntarily, toward the ceiling light, then toward the floor.

A small admission, then. "We ran it through X-ray," the officer said. "We took external photographs. We logged weight. Nothing more."

"And did the room behave," Ferretti asked, "or did it hesitate."

The officer stared at him. The answer came after a beat, unwilling. "There were reports," he said. "Light distortion in the field. Men complaining about their teeth. One guy swore his shadow… lagged."

Ferretti felt his stomach tighten, not at the content but at the familiarity of it. Orsini's list had not been superstition. It had been field notes.

"All right," Ferretti said. "Dim the lights."

The officer blinked. "What."

"Dim," Ferretti repeated. "Not off. Not dramatic. Less."

The officer made a small gesture to a technician behind glass. A panel clicked. The room's brightness dropped by a few degrees, as if the building had exhaled. The corners became a fraction more honest.

Ferretti stepped closer to the suitcase.

The pressure in his teeth arrived like a remembered ache. Not painful, just insistent, a rhythm he could not quite count but could feel in the way his jaw tightened and released.

He did not look at his shadow.

He reached for the latches and stopped for half a second, allowing himself one controlled breath. Orsini had said do not respond. He had not said do not touch. If touching was invitation, then Ferretti would touch like a man disarming a bomb: minimal, precise, without emotion.

He opened the metal suitcase.

Inside was foam cut to shape. The foam held a smaller case, dark and rigid, strapped in place. There was nothing inherently strange about that.

The strange part was the way Ferretti's eyes wanted to linger, as if the case offered the promise of meaning if watched hard enough.

He unclipped the straps and lifted the inner case out.

The officer's gaze followed it with hungry caution. "Is it biological," he asked, unable to stop himself.

Ferretti glanced at him. "It is consequence," he said, and saw annoyance flare in the officer's face. Americans hated answers that sounded like sermons. Ferretti did not care. The words were not for the officer. They were for the room, for the pattern that might be listening for familiar shapes.

He placed the inner case on the table and opened it.

The smell came first. Not rot, not anything that would justify panic. A faint scent of old cloth, dust, and something metallic that reminded Ferretti of old reliquaries: iron and age and the ghost of blood.

Inside were several items packed with deliberate care.

A film canister, black, sealed with tape that had yellowed slightly as if it had not been made yesterday.

Two glass ampoules, wax sealed, cushioned in folded cloth. One contained a darker wad of fabric stained in two places. The other held a small implement, metal or stone, with a groove along its edge smeared with dried brown-red residue.

A notebook with a warped cover, edges slightly singed or heat-touched in a way that did not look like fire.

And beneath the notebook, a bundle of thin papers, folded, covered in lines of writing that made Ferretti's eyes shift away as if his mind refused to turn the marks into language. The characters were not Latin, not Greek, not Hebrew. They looked almost mathematical and yet too fluid, as if written by a hand that did not share human assumptions about curves.

The officer inhaled sharply. He took a step forward without realizing it, then stopped himself, as if a part of him remembered the courier's warning about observation.

Ferretti did not pick up the ampoules. Glass drew attention. Attention was a lever.

He lifted the notebook instead.

As his fingers closed around the cover, a faint resistance met him, like inertia briefly magnified. It was subtle enough that he could have dismissed it as nerves, but it was too precise in its timing. He felt it travel up his arm, then vanish.

He kept his face neutral.

The officer watched him with a rigid kind of patience. “Is it… him,” he said. “Is this Christ.”

Ferretti looked down at the ampoules again. Wax. Cloth. The small domestic obscenity of containing history in glass.

“I am not here to confirm your theology,” Ferretti said. He paused, then added, because lying would be too simple and too dangerous, “but someone believed enough to steal from a fixed point in time.”

He set the notebook down and reached for the bundle of papers with the inhuman script. He did not unfold them fully. He slid the top page forward, just enough to see the repeating shapes, the way certain strokes recurred like an algorithm learning its own signature.

His throat tightened. The marks made his eyes want to refocus, like looking at a pattern that refused to settle into foreground and background.

Behind him, the officer spoke quietly, almost to himself. “We found another set of markings,” he said. “On the craft.”

Ferretti’s hand stopped.

He did not turn his head quickly. Quick movement was attention, and attention made things sharper. He turned slowly to look at the officer.

"The bell-shaped object in Pennsylvania," Ferretti said.

The officer nodded once. "Yeah. Same kind of grooves. Our guys described them as shifting if you stared. Like they didn't want to be… pinned."

Ferretti felt the pressure in his teeth pulse once, a private metronome. In his mind, Orsini's voice: it learns by watching.

He turned back to the open case. The items lay there with innocent stillness, yet the room felt subtly altered, as if the air had become more interested.

Ferretti lowered his gaze to the film canister. He did not touch it. Film was a different kind of trap. Projection was observation multiplied.

He closed the inner case gently, not with finality but with restraint, and latched it again. Then he placed it back inside the metal suitcase without repacking it perfectly, because perfection invited additional handling. He wanted fewer hands, fewer glances, fewer reasons to reopen.

The officer watched every movement. "You're not even going to look," he said, frustration creeping in. "You came all the way here."

"I looked," Ferretti replied. "Enough."

He stood straight and met the officer's eyes. "Where is the courier," he asked.

The officer hesitated. "Why."

"Because if he truly is Kammler," Ferretti said, "he did not come to deliver objects. He came to deliver a story. And stories require witnesses."

The officer's mouth tightened. "You don't get to see him."

Ferretti said nothing for a moment. He listened instead, not with his ears but with the part of him Orsini had trained into caution.

In the softened light, the edge of his shadow beneath the table seemed to settle a fraction late.

Ferretti did not acknowledge it. He did not grant the room the satisfaction of recognition.

He placed his hand on the suitcase handle, feeling the cold metal through his skin, and said quietly, "Then you will keep him alive until I leave with this. If he dies before transfer is complete, Rome will assume you tried to keep the covenant for yourself."

The officer stared at him, weighing the threat, recognizing the truth inside it.

"Get him out of here," the officer said finally, not to Ferretti but to someone beyond the glass. "Escort. Direct to the airfield."

As the door opened and Ferretti lifted the suitcase, the pressure in his teeth eased slightly, as if distance reduced risk. Or perhaps, he thought, as if the thing that learned by watching had already taken what it needed from this moment.

He did not look back at the table. He did not look at his shadow. He walked out with the evidence in his hand, a portable hinge wrapped in modern metal, and he could not shake the certainty that the most dangerous item in the suitcase was not blood, not film, not alien script.

It was the attention that followed it, patient and unseen, counting doors.

The escort did not speak to Ferretti on the way out. Two men in uniform walked flanking him at a distance that was not quite guard and not quite courtesy, their hands empty but their posture full of remembered weapons. The corridor lights remained steady, too steady, as if the building had been designed to refuse superstition by refusing any visible flaw.

Ferretti carried the metal suitcase in his right hand. It was not heavy, not by weight, but by implication. Every step made the handle cut a slightly deeper line into his palm, and he found himself grateful for the small pain. It kept his attention anchored to something physical.

At the last interior checkpoint before the airfield, a sergeant stopped them with a clipboard and an unnecessary question. "Destination?"

One of the escorts answered without looking up. "Direct transfer."

The sergeant's eyes slid to the red tag hanging from the handle. Barcode. Time stamp. It was the kind of label that made men believe an object had become manageable.

The sergeant's gaze lifted toward Ferretti's face. "Father," he began, and then stopped, as if the word itself was an error in the script.

Ferretti did not offer help. He let the pause widen until it became discomfort.

The sergeant cleared his throat. "You really taking it to Rome?"

Ferretti nodded once. "That is why I am here."

The sergeant wet his lips. "What is it?"

Ferretti could have said evidence. He could have said relic. He could have said a case full of film and blood and a notebook. Instead, he said what was truest and least useful.

"It is a language," he replied.

The sergeant blinked. "A language."

"A way of speaking," Ferretti said, and walked past him before the question could become a conversation.

Outside, the air was colder and tasted of fuel and night. The base lights spread across the tarmac in white pools that turned the parked aircraft into hard silhouettes. A transport plane waited with its rear ramp lowered, engines quiet, the kind of readiness that suggested someone had been told to expect a problem even if no one had been told what the problem was.

Ferretti paused at the base of the ramp, forcing himself to breathe evenly. The pressure in his teeth was faint now, almost gone, and that absence felt like a warning rather than relief. Inside the lab, under the softened lights, the sensation had been a metronome he could feel in his jaw. Here, in open air, it receded like a tide, and he suspected the tide could return without notice.

One of the escorts gestured. "Up."

Ferretti climbed the ramp. The plane's interior smelled of webbing, oil, and old metal warmed by steady use. A small compartment near the front had been prepared: two canvas seats facing each other, a fold-down table bolted to the wall, straps for cargo. They were giving him the illusion of privacy because illusions made transfers smoother.

The door ramp began to lift, hydraulics whining softly. Ferretti watched the gap of night shrink until it became a sealed seam. The moment the aircraft enclosed him, the sound changed. The world became a contained hum: engines, ventilation, the subtle tremor of a machine that pretended it was only a machine.

He set the suitcase on the table and did not open it.

Not yet.

Across from him, one of the escorting men sat and looked anywhere but at the case. The other remained standing near the compartment entrance, posture rigid, eyes forward. Ferretti recognized the stance. It was the stance of men assigned to guard something they had been told not to understand.

The standing man spoke without turning his head. "You can't open that in here."

Ferretti glanced up. "Who ordered that."

The man's throat bobbed. "They said no unnecessary exposure."

Ferretti rested his fingers on the suitcase lid without touching the latches. "Then they believe the courier," he said.

The man did not answer. He did not need to. His silence was an admission that the building's confidence had been damaged by a single sentence: contamination by observation.

Ferretti leaned back slightly and let his eyes close for a moment, not in prayer but in cataloging. Orsini's warning. Kammler's calm. The strange marks on paper that refused to settle into meaning. The shifting grooves on the bell-shaped craft. The way the lab's steady lights had suddenly felt like a fragile decision.

He opened his eyes and looked at the suitcase again.

A language, he thought. Not only the script. The whole mechanism. Voices that wore familiarity. Shadows that rehearsed trust. Objects that responded to attention the way an animal responded to a gaze.

If something could learn by watching, then perhaps the most dangerous thing in that case was not the blood, but the pattern that had begun to speak through it.

The engines deepened. The aircraft shuddered slightly and began to move.

Ferretti waited until the vibration became constant, until takeoff had committed them to the air. Only then did he unlatch the suitcase.

The sound of the latches was too loud in the compartment, two small snaps that seemed to declare intention. The seated escort tensed, shoulders tightening, eyes flicking toward Ferretti's hands and then away again as if looking directly would count as participation.

Ferretti opened the lid.

The foam cavity presented the inner case like an offering. He lifted it out with both hands and placed it on the table. The aircraft's vibration made the table tremble faintly; the case remained still, unconcerned.

The standing escort took one step forward, then stopped himself, as if the movement had been involuntary. "Father," he said, voice lower now, "they really told us not to look at it too long."

Ferretti glanced up. "Then don't."

He opened the inner case.

The smell rose again, faint and intimate: old cloth, dust, the metallic ghost of blood. It did not belong in a modern aircraft compartment. It belonged in a stone room, behind glass, behind prayer. The anachronism made his skin tighten.

The items lay where he had left them in the lab. Film canister. Ampoules. Notebook. And the folded papers with the inhuman script.

Ferretti did not touch the film or the ampoules. He reached for the papers.

His fingers hesitated an inch above them.

Orsini had not said do not read. He had said do not respond. Ferretti told himself reading was not responding. Reading was private, internal. Yet he knew that was a comforting lie. To interpret was to engage. Engagement was a kind of reply.

He lifted the top page.

Under the aircraft's overhead light, the marks seemed less like writing and more like a set of instructions for the eye. Lines that curved too smoothly. Angles that implied depth where the paper had none. Repeating shapes that looked almost consistent until he tried to count them and realized the repetition was not exact, but iterative, like a thought adjusting itself.

Ferretti felt his gaze trying to lock onto a symbol. The symbol resisted, not by moving but by refusing to become stable in his perception. His eyes refocused. The symbol seemed to sharpen, then immediately soften, as if clarity itself were the trap.

His teeth ached faintly.

He lowered the paper a fraction, and the ache eased. He raised it again, and it returned, a subtle pulse that seemed to match the rhythm of the plane's vibration until he realized it was not the plane at all. It was independent. It had its own cadence.

Forty-seven seconds, he thought, uninvited. The number came to him like a memory that was not his.

Ferretti's throat tightened. He did not want the number. He did not want to share a rhythm with something that had been counting doors since a mountain facility in Poland.

He forced his gaze to a different part of the page, away from the symbol that had tried to anchor him. He began to look for structure instead of meaning: spacing, alignment, the way the marks clustered.

There was structure.

Not like human paragraphs or lines. More like a diagram of relationships. Certain symbols sat beside others repeatedly, as if signifying adjacency rather than sequence. The writing did not feel like a story. It felt like a mapping.

Ferretti realized, with a quiet lurch in his stomach, that perhaps it was not meant to be read left to right at all. Perhaps it was meant to be seen as a whole, like a circuit. An arrangement that created effect simply by being observed in the correct way.

He looked away sharply, as if breaking eye contact with an animal.

The standing escort made a small sound, not quite a cough. "You okay?"

Ferretti kept his voice steady. "Yes."

He set the page down, but his fingers did not release it immediately. The paper felt ordinary. It was the marks that were not.

He reached for Kammler's notebook instead, because the notebook was human, however warped. He opened it carefully.

Inside, Kammler's handwriting marched across the pages in tight German lines, disciplined and controlled. Diagrams of coils. Notes on field behavior. Observations of the sky's fracture. A brief line in the margin that made Ferretti's breath catch: Er sprach meinen Namen. He spoke my name.

Further down, another line, underlined once: Nicht stehlen. Erzeugen. Not steal. Create.

Christ's warning, translated into Kammler's private logic. Ferretti felt his skin prickle. The implication was not simply that Kammler had taken something. It was that the act of extraction had altered what could exist afterward.

Ferretti turned a page.

There were sketches he could not fully understand: the bell chamber's layout, the oval bruise in the air, and beside it, an attempt to draw something Kammler had apparently seen in reflection. Not a face. Not a body. A geometry that looked like layered absence. Kammler had written one word near it in block letters: BEOBACHTER. Observer.

Ferretti closed the notebook slowly.

Now he understood why Orsini had not wanted this opened in bright rooms by men who would flood it with curiosity. Curiosity was fuel. Kammler had known it. Orsini had learned it. Ferretti could feel it now in his own body, the way the papers seemed to tug at his attention like a hook in cloth.

He glanced at the folded inhuman pages again and did not look long enough to let the marks settle.

He thought of language again, but differently. The script was not simply a record. It was an interface. A partially alive method of contact, like the interface in the crashed craft in the Black Forest that responded to touch. Like a thing built to recruit perception as a component.

Ferretti began to put the items back without rearranging them perfectly. The more he handled, the more he participated. He closed the inner case. He set it into the foam. He latched the outer suitcase.

The seated escort exhaled, as if the closing had eased pressure he did not know he was holding. The standing escort relaxed by a fraction, though his eyes still avoided the case like it might speak.

Ferretti rested his palm on the closed lid. Through the metal he felt nothing, but he knew better than to trust the absence of sensation.

He leaned back and looked at the compartment's overhead light. It remained steady. The aircraft hummed around him. Everything appeared controlled.

In the lower corner of his vision, his shadow lay along the floor seam near the table leg.

It looked obedient.

Ferretti did not stare. He did not test it. He refused the impulse to verify, because verification was attention, and attention was how the unknowable learned the shape of belief.

Instead, he spoke quietly, not to the escorts, not to the case, but to the air, as if reminding himself of a rule that had become more important than any prayer.

"I will not answer," he said.

The standing escort frowned. "Answer what?"

Ferretti did not explain. Explanation would make it real in the wrong way. He simply sat with his hands folded, waiting for the long flight to unspool.

Outside the sealed aircraft, the night stretched over America, and beyond it, across an ocean, Rome waited with its stone corridors and its secret decrees.

In the suitcase, the language of the unknowable lay quiet, not dead, not alive in any human sense, but ready.

And somewhere in the gap between reading and response, something listened without ears, learning the shape of Ferretti's restraint the way it had learned Kammler's ambition.

Not all languages needed words.

Some only needed witnesses.

Chapter 14

Orders from the Holy See

In Rome, dawn did not arrive all at once. It seeped through the Vatican's high windows in pale layers, turning stone from black to charcoal to the color of old bone. The city outside woke in ordinary rhythms, but inside the walls the day began the way it always did when something unholy had slipped into the machinery of faith: quietly, with paper.

Monsignor Matteo Orsini had not slept. He sat at a narrow desk in a room that was not on any public map, the kind of room that existed because the Church had learned long ago that confession was not the only thing that needed privacy. A single lamp burned with a careful steadiness. Orsini kept it low.

On the desk lay the thin folder with the penciled number, opened to a page he had written years earlier after the Owl Mountains, after the first time he had watched a shadow behave as if it had an opinion. The notes looked smaller now, as if time itself had tried to reduce them to superstition. But the call from America had made them heavy again.

I have risen.

A phrase designed to provoke, to hook. Kammler understood myth the way engineers understood load-bearing arches. Orsini understood something else: if Kammler could weaponize resurrection as a message, then the thing that learned by watching would weaponize whatever it could get.

A knock came at the door, soft and precise. Orsini did not answer immediately. He listened for the shape of the sound, for anything in it that felt rehearsed. The knock came again, identical.

He rose and opened the door.

Father Gabriel Ferretti stood in the corridor, coat on, collar visible, a small travel bag in one hand. He looked as if he had returned from a long walk rather than a transatlantic retrieval under armed escort. His eyes, however, were too focused, the way eyes became when they had spent hours refusing to look directly at something that wanted to be read.

"You're early," Orsini said.

“I’m on time,” Ferretti replied. “Which means something went wrong in their schedules.”

Orsini stepped aside, letting him in. The corridor light behind Ferretti framed his shadow against the threshold for a fraction of a second. Orsini felt his teeth tighten. The shadow arrived as it should, but he could not shake the suspicion that it arrived by choice.

Ferretti set the bag down and did not sit. “They tried to negotiate,” he said. “They wanted to keep copies. Photographs. A reel duplicated. They used words like cooperation and shared custody.”

Orsini’s mouth tightened. “And you refused.”

“I refused without making it theatrical,” Ferretti said. “They respond poorly to theater when they are not the ones producing it.”

Orsini watched him, measuring. “You opened it.”

Ferretti’s gaze flicked once, a controlled admission. “Yes,” he said. “Briefly. In dim light.”

“And the script,” Orsini asked.

Ferretti’s jaw worked once, the only visible crack in his composure. “It is not writing,” he said. “Not in the way we mean it. It behaves like an interface. Looking at it feels like… participation.”

Orsini's fingers tightened inside his sleeves. "And you did not respond."

Ferretti held Orsini's eyes. "I did not answer," he said quietly. "Not even in my head."

Orsini believed him. Not because Ferretti was incapable of fear, but because Ferretti had learned to treat fear as information instead of instruction.

A second knock sounded at the door, louder now. Orsini felt irritation flare. The hour was early, and only certain men knocked on certain doors before sunrise.

He opened it to find the ink-stained bureaucrat from the previous night's chamber, face pale with lack of sleep. Behind him stood the elderly cardinal, hands tucked into his sleeves as if warmth could be stolen from ritual.

"We have convened," the bureaucrat said.

Orsini glanced once at Ferretti. "He's back," Orsini said. "So, the case is in motion."

The cardinal stepped into the room without waiting to be invited. His breath smelled faintly of wine and mint. "It should not have been in motion at all," he said. "It should never have left the custody of the Holy See."

"It never entered it," Orsini replied.

The cardinal's eyes sharpened. "Do not correct me with technicalities, Matteo. We are beyond technicalities."

Orsini did not argue. He had learned which arguments were permitted and which ones simply marked you for later removal.

The bureaucrat closed the door behind them and produced a sealed envelope, thick paper, the seal not the familiar keys and tiara but the darker stamp Orsini had given Ferretti before he left. Seeing it returned made Orsini's stomach tighten, not with pride, but with the uncomfortable recognition that the stamp now carried more weight than it had two days ago.

"From the Secretariat," the bureaucrat said. "Not the public one."

Orsini did not take the envelope immediately. "Who dictated it," he asked.

The cardinal's expression became the careful neutrality of a man stepping away from responsibility while claiming authority. "The necessary offices," he said. "It has been reviewed. It has been agreed."

Agreed was another word for decided without dissent.

Ferretti remained still, eyes on the envelope. He did not reach for it. Orsini recognized the restraint as the same restraint he had shown with the inhuman pages. Ferretti understood that paper could be bait too.

Orsini took the envelope and broke the seal with his thumbnail. The sound was small, but in the quiet room it felt like a blade drawing across cloth.

Inside was a single sheet, densely typed, with a handwritten signature at the bottom that Orsini recognized even before he let his eyes fully settle. He read quickly, then again, slower, because the mind always tried to soften what it did not want to accept.

When he looked up, Ferretti's gaze met his and Orsini saw a question there that did not need words.

Orsini handed the paper to Ferretti.

Ferretti read it without changing expression. Halfway down, his eyes narrowed slightly. At the end, he lifted his gaze.

The cardinal watched both of them. "You understand," he said. "There are moments when the Church must protect the faithful from truth. This is one of them."

Orsini kept his voice controlled. "This decree is not protection," he said. "It is containment through erasure."

The bureaucrat shifted uncomfortably, as if the word erasure had scraped too close to what he did for a living. "It is a security directive," he said. "A necessary one."

Ferretti held the paper between two fingers as if it might stain him. "It orders silence," he said, voice flat. "Not only from outsiders. From insiders."

The cardinal's hands tightened inside his sleeves. "There must be no witnesses," he said. "No records. No testimony. No second narrative."

Orsini's teeth ached faintly. He could not tell if it was stress or the remembered pressure that came when something listened.

"And the envoy," Orsini said softly.

The cardinal did not look at Ferretti. He did not have the decency. "The envoy has seen too much," he said. "He has touched the hinge. He has read a language that is not ours. Even if he is loyal, he is compromised."

Compromised. A modern word used as a sacramental knife.

Ferretti folded the decree once, then again, precise creases. He did not tear it. He did not throw it. He treated it like something that would outlive all of them.

"You sent me to retrieve it," he said.

"Yes," the cardinal replied. "And you did."

Ferretti's voice remained even. "And now you issue an order that ensures I do not return with it."

The bureaucrat spoke quickly, as if speed could make it less cruel. "You will return," he said. "You will deliver the package to the designated vault. You will follow the handling protocols. And then… arrangements will be made."

Arrangements. Another euphemism that pretended murder was only scheduling.

Orsini felt a thin, unexpected anger cut through his fatigue. "You cannot do this," he said. "Not to him. Not now."

The cardinal's eyes snapped to him. "Do not moralize to me," he said. "We are not discussing sin. We are discussing survival."

Orsini held his ground. "You are making the Church into an accomplice of fear," he said. "You are doing what Kammler wanted. You are behaving like men who believe control can be achieved by removing witnesses."

The cardinal's expression tightened. "Witnesses create saints," he said. "Witnesses create schism. Witnesses create cults. Do you want pilgrims lining up for a film canister? Do you want blood in glass to become an icon? Do you want the world to tear itself apart over proof."

Proof. The word hung there, and Orsini heard in it the echo of the Pope's condition from years earlier: Bring me truth. Not belief. Proof.

Orsini looked down at the decree again, at the signature that had made it law in shadows. He understood, with a cold clarity, that this was not simply about avoiding scandal. It was about ownership. If the evidence could not be controlled, then it would be buried. And if a man could not be controlled, then he would be removed.

Ferretti placed the folded paper on Orsini's desk. "Who executes this," he asked.

The bureaucrat's eyes slid away. The cardinal answered instead, voice calm with the horror of certainty. "The Order will," he said.

Orsini's stomach tightened at that phrasing, old and simple. Not the Church. Not the Secretariat. The Order. A mechanism inside the mechanism, invoked only when the Vatican wanted to pretend it had not acted.

Ferretti nodded once, as if he had expected it. "Then there will be no appeal," he said.

The cardinal leaned forward slightly. "There is always appeal," he said, "but not to me."

Orsini felt the room's air shift, barely perceptible, as if the conversation had attracted attention, it should not. He glanced, against his better judgment, at the edge of his shadow on the wall beside the desk.

For a heartbeat it seemed to hesitate, not lagging like a mistake, but pausing like a listener deciding whether to step closer.

Orsini looked away immediately.

Ferretti's gaze remained steady on Orsini. "You warned me not to become a witness willingly," he said.

Orsini swallowed. "Yes."

Ferretti's voice did not rise. It did not need to. "And now you're telling me the Holy See has decided I will be one unwillingly," he said. "And then they will erase me so no one can testify that the Church ordered it."

The bureaucrat opened his mouth, then closed it again. There were no good words left.

Orsini felt, in that moment, the true shape of the decree. It was not merely an order to silence. It was an attempt to cut a thread before something could follow it back into Rome. They believed that by removing eyes and mouths they could stop the watching.

But Orsini had seen what learned by watching.

It did not require witnesses who spoke.

It required only witnesses who existed.

"The package goes to the vault," the cardinal said, final and cold. "It is to be sealed. Logged only in the private ledger. Access by unanimous consent of the necessary offices."

Ferretti's eyes did not leave the cardinal. "And Kammler," he said. "The courier in American custody."

The cardinal's mouth tightened as if tasting something bitter. "If he is still alive, he is to remain where he is. He is not to be brought to Rome."

Orsini heard the unspoken addition: if he is not alive, then let him be a problem for Americans.

Ferretti turned his gaze back to Orsini. "So, this is the secret decree," he said. "No witnesses. No survivors."

Orsini did not deny it. Denial would have been another kind of lie and lies were also languages.

Ferretti picked up his travel bag again. "Then I should assume I have enemies waiting in the corridors I just walked," he said.

The bureaucrat flinched. The cardinal did not.

Orsini stepped closer to Ferretti, lowering his voice. "You must not confront them," he said. "Do you understand. Do not let them force you into drama. Drama is how stories stick."

Ferretti's expression softened by a fraction, not into warmth, but into something like grim recognition. "And silence," he said, "is how bodies disappear."

Orsini's teeth ached again, sharper now. He could not tell if it came from fear or from the sense that somewhere, in the folds of the Vatican's ancient stone, something had heard the shape of the decree and filed it away.

Ferretti moved toward the door.

The cardinal spoke once more, as if granting a blessing without calling it one. "You have served," he said. "Be at peace."

Ferretti paused at the threshold. He did not look back at the cardinal. He looked at Orsini instead.

"Peace is what you offer when you have already decided the ending," he said quietly. "I will not answer. But I will not cooperate."

Then he stepped into the corridor and walked away, the rhythm of his footsteps measured, controlled, as if he could keep the world from learning him by refusing to give it any sudden movement to remember.

Orsini remained in the room with the decree on his desk and the cardinal's calm authority filling the air like incense that burned the lungs.

When the door finally closed, the bureaucrat exhaled shakily, and the cardinal's shoulders relaxed as if a burden had been transferred rather than increased.

Orsini looked down at the folded paper again.

A directive written in the language of preservation, executed in the grammar of murder.

He wondered, not for the first time, whether the Church understood that by issuing a decree in secret, it had still spoken aloud in the only realm that mattered.

Not to the faithful.

But to whatever listened between shadows, learning how institutions behaved when they were afraid.

The corridor swallowed Ferretti the way corridors in the Vatican always did, with a practiced indifference that made every footstep feel anonymous. He kept his pace even, neither hurried nor slow. Hurry drew eyes. Slowness invited questions. He walked like a man who belonged, because belonging was the safest disguise in a place built on ritual.

Behind him, in Orsini's room, the cardinal and the bureaucrat remained. Ferretti could feel their decision at his back like a hand that had already begun to close.

He did not carry the metal suitcase openly. He had learned, long ago, that objects with weight attracted the wrong kind of attention. The evidence, nested inside American metal and foam, had been transferred through Vatican channels before dawn, moved by hands that would never sign a ledger. The only thing Ferretti carried now was his small bag and the memory of the script's refusal to settle in the eye. That memory felt more dangerous than any physical case.

He turned once, not his head but his path, angling into a side passage that led away from the Secretariat offices and toward the older parts of the Apostolic Palace. The stone here was older, the air cooler. Saints in alcoves watched with painted calm.

As he passed a window cut into thick wall, he caught a reflection: his own face, pale under the early light. For a heartbeat, he thought the reflection arrived late.

He did not stop to verify.

Verification was attention. Attention was reply.

He kept walking.

In Orsini's room, the cardinal spoke in a tone that assumed the world would obey because it usually did.

"It is done," he said.

Orsini looked at the folded decree on his desk as if it were a specimen. The signature at the bottom did not tremble. Authority never did, not on paper.

"You have ordered the death of a priest," Orsini said.

The ink-stained bureaucrat flinched as if the word death had been spoken too loudly. The cardinal did not change expression. "I have ordered the removal of a liability," he corrected. "And the prevention of scandal."

Orsini lifted his gaze. "No witnesses," he said, tasting the phrase again. "No survivors."

The cardinal's eyes narrowed slightly. "Do not dramatize it."

"It is already drama," Orsini replied. "You are simply choosing the ending."

The bureaucrat cleared his throat. "Monsignor," he began, voice thin, "the Order will handle it. You do not need to—"

"The Order," Orsini repeated softly. He hated how the words made the air feel. Not because they were mystical, but because they were efficient. Men in the Church liked to pretend holiness guided their hands. The Order did not pretend. It was a tool used when piety became inconvenient.

The cardinal stepped closer to the desk, lowering his voice as if walls could be trusted. "Ferretti has looked at what should not be looked at," he said. "He has been in proximity to a hinge. He has read marks that are not ours. He has been in American rooms that have now learned our names. If he speaks, we are finished."

Orsini's jaw tightened. "If he dies, we may still be finished," he said.

The cardinal's gaze sharpened. "You fear superstition," he said.

"I fear pattern," Orsini replied. "I fear a thing that learns by watching. You think removing witnesses removes the watching. But the watching is already here. It heard you the moment you decided."

The bureaucrat's face turned slightly paler. "We are not children," he said. "This is not—"

Orsini cut him off. "This is exactly what it is," he said. "Only the child's name for it is different."

The cardinal did not argue theology. He did not need to. He had power and procedure, and those were enough to kill men quietly.

He turned toward the door. "You will return to your duties," he told Orsini. "You will not interfere. And you will not contact Ferretti again. Do you understand."

Orsini did not answer immediately. Silence here was a risk; it could be interpreted as dissent. Yet he had learned that obedience offered no safety either.

"I understand what you are ordering," he said at last. "I understand what you think it will accomplish."

The cardinal's mouth tightened at the distinction, then he left the room with the bureaucrat trailing him like a shadow that had chosen the wrong master.

Orsini remained alone with the steady lamp and the folded decree.

He felt, faintly, the old pressure in his teeth.

He stood and walked to the wall near his desk, the place where his shadow fell at an angle when the lamp was low. He did not stare at it directly. He let it exist in the corner of his vision.

It lay there, narrow and obedient.

Still, he had the irrational impression that it was listening, not moving, just attentive in the way a predator could be attentive without shifting a muscle.

Orsini turned away.

In another part of the Vatican, behind a door that opened only for certain knocks, the Order received its instructions without the drama of a decree.

Three men stood around a table in a room with no icons. One was in clerical black, collar immaculate. One wore a suit with the cut of Italian bureaucracy. The third wore neither. He was older, hair cropped close, hands plain. His face held no expression that could be appealed to.

A folder lay open on the table. Ferretti's name appeared only once, typed, clinical. Beneath it were locations, times, routines. The kind of knowledge gathered not by prayer but by watching.

"He is to be removed before he can become a narrative," the man in the suit said.

The older man nodded once. "And the case."

"The case is to be sealed," the clerical one replied. "The case is not the immediate problem. The envoy is."

The older man's eyes flicked to the folder. "No survivors," he said, not as an echo, but as a rule.

The clerical man hesitated a fraction. "Minimal exposure," he said. "No spectacle. No blood where pilgrims can find it."

The older man closed the folder with a flat sound. "He will vanish," he said. "People vanish all the time in Rome. They call it sin, or scandal, or an accident. They do not call it policy."

He stood, and the others stood with him. In that room, the air felt ordinary. Yet the older man paused by the table as if listening for something he could not name.

For the briefest moment, the overhead light seemed to dim, not flicker, just soften as if a hand had passed between bulb and world.

The older man did not look up. He simply waited until the light returned to its steady state.

Then he walked out.

Ferretti reached the small courtyard near the Belvedere with the posture of a man who had just made himself invisible by refusing to react. The air outside carried the smell of stone cooling and distant incense, the Vatican's favorite combination of ancient and immediate. A Swiss Guard stood at a gate with ceremonial stillness, halberd upright, gaze forward.

Ferretti nodded as he passed. The Guard's eyes did not move.

That was not normal. They always moved, even if only slightly. Guards watched. That was their purpose.

Ferretti's steps did not change, but something in his spine tightened.

He turned down a narrow passage that led toward a service stair. The stair was used by maintenance, by delivery men, by those who knew which routes to take when they did not want to be seen by tourists or noticed by officials.

Halfway down, a voice spoke behind him.

"Father Ferretti."

The voice was calm, respectful. Italian, Roman cadence. Familiar enough to invite a turn.

Ferretti did not turn.

He kept walking, one step, then another, as if he had not heard.

"Father," the voice repeated, slightly closer now. "A moment."

Ferretti felt the old warning rise in him like a reflex. Do not respond. Do not answer.

He continued down the stairs.

Behind him, footsteps began, measured, not rushed, not trying to catch him quickly. The pace was chosen to keep him from panicking. Panic created mistakes. Panic created scenes.

Ferretti reached the lower landing and pushed open a door that led into a corridor lined with storage rooms. The hinges squealed softly. The sound echoed more than it should have, as if the corridor was longer than its geometry allowed.

He closed the door behind him without slamming it. Slams were invitations. He walked faster now, not running, but decisive.

A second door opened behind him. The same squeal.

Footsteps entered the corridor.

Ferretti passed a row of locked cabinets and an unmarked door with a small brass plate. He knew what was behind it: an electrical closet, a place where the building's wiring could be accessed. He also knew such places were often empty.

He stopped at the door, inserted a key from his pocket, and turned it. The key was not labeled. It never was.

The door opened.

Inside was darkness and the smell of dust and warm copper.

He stepped in and closed the door behind him, leaving it unlatched so it could be pulled open from inside without sound. He stood still, breath controlled, bag held in one hand.

In the darkness, his mind tried to produce images: the inhuman script, the way it pulled at the eye, the uninvited thought of forty-seven seconds. He pushed them away.

He listened instead.

Footsteps reached the corridor outside. They stopped.

For a moment there was only the building's hum. Ventilation. The faint distant murmur of the Vatican waking.

Then the door handle to the electrical closet moved, slowly, testing.

A pause.

A voice, close now, spoke through the gap with gentle certainty.

“Father Ferretti,” it said. “You don’t need to make this difficult. It will be quick. No one will see.”

Ferretti felt his teeth ache faintly, as if the air itself had tightened.

He did not answer.

In the darkness, he became aware of his own shadow on the floor, cast by a thin line of corridor light under the door.

It lay there like a black ribbon.

And then, impossibly, it seemed to shift a fraction, not away from him but toward the crack beneath the door, as if it wanted to leave first.

Ferretti’s stomach tightened. He kept his eyes on the concrete instead of the shadow’s edge. Looking would make it real in the way the script became real when read.

Outside, the handle moved again, firmer this time.

The door began to open.

Ferretti’s free hand slid into his coat, not for a weapon, but for a rosary. Wood beads. Familiar shape. Weight. A tool for focus.

Not a charm.

Not protection.

Just something human to hold while men from his own institution came to erase him.

The gap widened. Light spilled into the closet in a thin blade.

In that blade, the shadow on the floor seemed to hesitate, as if waiting to see who would enter.

And Ferretti understood with a cold, lucid clarity that the decree was not only an order to kill.

It was an order to ensure there would be no one left who could say, later, that the Church had chosen control over truth.

No witnesses.

No survivors.

The door opened another inch, and a figure filled the crack of light.

Ferretti stayed silent, breathing shallowly through his nose, refusing the simplest human impulse: to speak his own innocence, to plead, to name the betrayal out loud.

He would not give the world his voice.

He would not give the thing that listened a clean sample of fear.

If he survived, he would do it the only way left.

By disappearing before they could make him a story.

The door opened another inch, and the thin blade of light widened across the concrete floor.

A man stood in it, close enough that Ferretti could see the line of his jaw and the plainness of his hands. Not a Swiss Guard. Not a priest. He wore a dark coat with no insignia, no collar, no small signals of belonging. His shoes were practical, the kind meant for silence on stone.

Behind him, half-hidden in the corridor, another figure waited. Ferretti caught a glimpse of a clerical sleeve, black and clean, as if the Church could launder complicity until it looked like obedience.

The man in the coat did not rush in. He let the door hang partly open, letting the light do the work of intimidation. His eyes moved once over the closet's interior, measuring. When his gaze reached Ferretti's face, it did not change.

"Come out," the man said. His voice was not angry. It was procedural. "This doesn't need to become unpleasant."

Ferretti kept his back near the electrical panel, shoulders squared, rosary beads nested in his palm like a weight meant to keep him anchored. He did not answer. Not because he believed silence could negotiate, but because Orsini's warning had become a rule more important than social instinct.

Do not respond. Do not answer. Do not let familiarity turn into a handle.

The man's eyes narrowed a fraction, as if the lack of dialogue annoyed him. He shifted his stance, and the light from the corridor moved across the floor.

Ferretti felt it before he let himself see it: the line of shadow under the door, the black ribbon he had refused to look at, changed shape.

It did not jerk. It did not leap. It simply behaved like something that had been waiting for permission to move.

A subtle slide toward the threshold, as if it wanted to be in the corridor more than in the closet. As if it wanted to meet the men outside first.

Ferretti's throat tightened. He kept his gaze on the man's shoes instead of the shadow's edge. He forced his breathing to stay even, shallow and quiet, refusing the body's urge to spike into panic.

The man in the coat took a step forward. The door opened wider. Light flooded the closet's mouth and revealed dust in the air like suspended ash.

The second figure in the corridor spoke, the voice softer, the accent unmistakably Roman. "Father Ferretti. You have carried out your task. There is no shame in obedience now."

Obedience. The word was chosen carefully, the way a confessor chose words meant to bend without breaking. Ferretti felt a brief, bitter clarity: they were not only here to kill him. They were here to make him accept the shape of his own erasure. To make the ending look like consent.

Ferretti's fingers tightened on the rosary beads until the wood pressed crescents into his skin. He did not speak. He did not even let his lips part. He had seen the inhuman script tug at attention; he had felt the way looking became participation. Perhaps speech was the same. Perhaps a single sentence of pleading would be enough to teach whatever listened the precise frequency of his fear.

The man in the coat stepped into the closet.

He moved with the calm of training, weight distributed, shoulders relaxed, hands low but ready. He was not holding a gun. Ferretti understood why: guns were noisy, and noise created stories. The Order wanted no story. Just absence.

The man's eyes flicked to Ferretti's hand. "Rosary," he said, almost amused. "That won't help you."

Ferretti lifted his gaze just enough to meet the man's eyes. Not long. Not an invitation. A measurement.

Then, without warning, Ferretti reached behind him and yanked down on the main breaker handle.

The closet went dark with a blunt finality that felt like a slap.

For a half-second, there was only the building's hum and the sharp intake of breath from the corridor. The darkness was not complete; a thin wedge of light still entered through the open door, but the sudden loss of illumination made the men outside hesitate, instinctively recalibrating.

Ferretti used the hesitation.

He moved to the left, slipping past the door's edge, shoulders turned sideways to minimize contact. The man in the coat lunged, but his hand closed on air, his reach misjudged in the changed light. Ferretti felt fabric brush his sleeve, then nothing.

In the corridor, the clerical figure swore under his breath, the sound small and shocked, as if profanity had escaped him like blood.

Ferretti did not run. Running drew pursuit into certainty. He moved quickly, silently, the pace of someone who belonged to the corridor and had merely remembered an appointment.

The corridor was darker now, emergency lighting faint and uneven. The Vatican did not like true darkness; it suggested things it could not catalogue. Small red exit lamps glowed at intervals, turning stone corners into shallow pockets of shadow.

Ferretti turned right, then left, then down a short service stair he had used years earlier. He heard footsteps behind him, faster now, no longer pretending to be polite.

The first man called out once, anger breaking through the calm. “Stop!”

Ferretti did not answer. The word stop was a hook. A response, even refusal, would tighten the line.

He descended into a lower passage that smelled of damp stone and old wiring. The walls here were rougher, older, less curated. This was the Vatican beneath the Vatican, the parts that existed because centuries of additions had created seams.

At the bottom of the stairs, Ferretti reached a junction with two doors. One led toward storage and maintenance. The other led toward a narrow corridor that, on paper, did not exist. Orsini had shown him once, long ago, when Ferretti had still believed loyalty was a simple thing.

Ferretti chose the corridor that did not exist.

As he pushed through, the air changed, cooler, with a faint mineral smell like water trapped in rock. The emergency lights were fewer here. Shadows lay thicker. Ferretti felt the pressure in his teeth return, faint but distinct, as if the building's older bones held different rules.

Behind him, the pursuing footsteps slowed at the junction, confused. He heard them speak in low, urgent Italian.

"Where did he go?"

"Find him. Before he reaches—"

Before he reaches what, Ferretti wondered and felt the answer form without words: before he reached a place where the Church could no longer pretend the disappearance was accidental.

The realization arrived not as a single thought but as a joining of pieces that had been waiting to lock.

Orsini's warning about witnesses. The cardinal's calm. The decree's language. The way the Americans had said relic like it burned their tongues. The insistence on no survivors, as if the danger was testimony and not the thing that learned by watching.

It had never been about faith.

Not in the way the faithful meant it. Not even in the cynical way bureaucrats meant it. The covenant Kammler forged, the one the Pope had accepted with a condition, had rotted into a simpler truth. Proof was a tool. Evidence was leverage. If the evidence could be owned, it could be used to command belief instead of serve it.

And if the evidence could not be owned, then it would be buried.

Including everyone who had touched it.

Ferretti kept moving down the corridor, hand brushing the wall for orientation. His mind ran ahead, cold and efficient. The case was already in a vault. He did not have it. He had only knowledge: the film canister, the ampoules, Kammler's notebook, the inhuman pages that behaved like an interface. He had seen enough to understand that opening the suitcase was not merely examination. It was contact.

If the Church sealed it away and killed every witness, it would not be protecting the world from scandal. It would be protecting itself from losing monopoly over meaning.

Ferretti's teeth ached again, timed with his steps. He slowed for half a breath, listening.

In the darkness ahead, his shadow should have been a simple smear on stone, governed by emergency lights and geometry.

Instead, it seemed to gather itself, to press closer to his feet.

Not lagging now.

Keeping pace.

A thought came, unwanted and sharp: what if the shadow was not his, not entirely. What if the thing that learned by watching had already learned the shape of him in the aircraft compartment, the way his eyes had skimmed the script without settling, the way he had refused to answer even in his head.

What if it had learned that he was difficult to read, and therefore valuable.

Ferretti forced the thought away. Giving it shape made it a kind of invitation.

He reached a small iron door at the corridor's end. It was old, the kind of door that still used a key because electronics had not yet colonized everything. Ferretti pulled the key ring from his pocket, selected the correct key by touch, and inserted it.

His hands were steady. He took pride in that, though pride was dangerous too.

He turned the key. The lock clicked. The sound echoed down the stone passage like a signal.

Behind him, at the junction he had left, voices rose again. They had found the corridor's mouth. Footsteps began to follow, faster, less careful. One of them called his name, trying to make the sound personal.

"Ferretti!"

He did not answer.

He pulled the iron door open and slipped through into a narrow stairwell that rose toward a higher level, the air warmer above. As he closed the door behind him, he caught a final glimpse of the corridor's darkness and the seam of shadow along the floor.

For a heartbeat, it looked as if the shadow hesitated at the threshold, deciding whether to follow him up.

Then it flowed after him, smooth and patient, as if it had already learned where all the doors were.

Ferretti climbed the stairs two at a time, breath controlled, rosary still in his fist.

He understood now, with a clarity that made his stomach feel hollow, that the betrayal was not an exception.

It was policy.

And if the Church was willing to erase its own envoy to protect ownership of proof, then there was no safety in returning to anyone who still sat under Vatican lamps and believed stone walls could keep consequence contained.

Ferretti reached the top of the stairwell and paused at the next door, listening for footsteps on the other side, for the rhythm of a world that still pretended to be ordinary.

He opened it a crack.

Light spilled in. Morning light, soft and indifferent. The sound of distant voices, normal Vatican voices. Tourists, guards, staff beginning their day.

The contrast was almost obscene.

Ferretti stepped into it, becoming again what he had always been on the surface: a priest moving through holy space with purpose. He adjusted his coat. He loosened his grip on the rosary enough to hide it within his sleeve.

And as he walked into the waking Vatican, he made one final internal vow, not spoken, not shaped into prayer.

If they wanted no witnesses, he would become the kind of witness they could not locate.

Not in their ledgers.

Not in their decrees.

Not even in their shadows.

Chapter 15

Escape into Shadow

Ferretti did not go back to Orsini's corridor. He did not go back to any corridor that belonged to names.

He moved through the waking Vatican as if he were only another cleric late for a meeting, letting the surface rituals carry him. He passed a cluster of tourists guided by a man holding a small flag, their cameras raised like offerings. He passed two Swiss Guards at a turn, their uniforms too bright for the private ugliness that now lived in the stone. He gave them a nod that said nothing and meant less.

No one stopped him.

That was the most frightening part. The Order was not a net thrown over crowds. It was a hand placed on a shoulder in an empty hallway. It was a door that opened at the wrong time. It was the careful disappearance of a single man after the paperwork had already explained why no one should look for him.

Ferretti kept his pace even. He had learned, in other countries and other wars, that the first instinct to run was often what made a pursuer confident. Confidence made them fast. Uncertainty made them cautious.

He turned down a public stairwell with marble steps polished by centuries of shoes and knees. At the bottom, he let himself drift into a small flow of staff: men in dark suits, women carrying files, a nun moving with downcast eyes. Ferretti adjusted his collar, lowered his chin, became part of the building's bloodstream.

His teeth ached faintly. Not sharp, not constant. A pulse that arrived and vanished as if testing whether he would notice. He refused to reach for it mentally. He refused to name it. Orsini had taught him the rule, and Kammler had proven why it mattered: attention fed patterns. Patterns fed imitation.

Outside, Rome was already loud with normal life. Mopeds whined past the walls. Vendors argued over crates. Somewhere a bell rang, the unthinking echo of a thousand other bells. Ferretti crossed through a service exit used by deliveries and minor officials, showed a credential that no guard read properly, and stepped into the city's ordinary light.

The air smelled different immediately: exhaust, coffee, damp stone, cigarette smoke. He took one breath and felt his body loosen by a fraction. In the Vatican every footstep belonged to architecture. In Rome, footsteps belonged to chaos.

He did not hail a car. He walked.

He moved south, away from the immediate gravity of the Apostolic Palace, through streets that bent and changed names without warning. He kept to the edges of crowds, not because crowds were safety, but because crowds were noise. The Order operated best in quiet.

At the first corner he used a shop window to check his reflection without looking directly at himself. A habit learned from surveillance, from the old discipline of not making your own face an object of scrutiny. He saw a priest, mid-forties, pale, composed. Behind him, the street continued with its indifferent commerce.

And in the lower portion of the glass, his shadow lay at an angle that did not quite match the sun.

He looked away before his mind could start counting degrees.

A few blocks later, he made his first call.

Not from a phone booth. Phone booths were too obvious now, and too romantic. He found a tobacconist with a payphone bolted to the wall near the back, the kind that still existed because old men still mistrusted new systems. He fed coins into it with slow fingers and dialed a number he had memorized years ago and hoped he would never need again.

It rang four times.

Then a woman's voice answered, bored and slightly irritated. "Pronto."

Ferretti did not use his name. Names were handles.

He said, "The choir is missing its tenor."

Silence. A soft shift in breathing.

"Who is this," the woman asked, and the boredom vanished, replaced by cautious precision.

"The man who carried a sealed letter to Ohio," Ferretti said.

Another pause, longer. "You're supposed to be back inside."

"I was," Ferretti replied. "Now I'm outside. I need a room that isn't on a map."

The woman's voice lowered. "If they're hunting you, you don't come here."

"I'm not asking to come there," Ferretti said. "I'm asking you to tell me where to go."

A faint sound in the background, like a chair moving. "Who is 'they'."

"The Order," Ferretti said.

The word landed. Even over a cheap phone line, he felt it change the air.

"Stay where you are," the woman said.

"I can't," Ferretti replied. "Tell me."

A breath. Then, "Via Giulia. Number forty-eight. There's a tailor shop. Ask for Paolo. Tell him you need your collar adjusted."

Ferretti hung up without thank you. Gratitude was a kind of attachment. Attachment was a line that could be followed.

He left the shop and walked again, using the city as cover. He changed direction twice, not in dramatic turns but in gradual drifts, the way a man might wander when thinking. At a small piazza he sat on a bench for two minutes, watched a street cleaner push water and trash into a gutter, watched a couple argue softly under an umbrella. No one looked at him longer than a glance.

His teeth stopped aching.

The absence felt like attention.

He stood and kept moving.

The tailor shop on Via Giulia did not look like a sanctuary. It looked like commerce: fabric rolls visible behind glass, a mannequin in a suit that had never known a human body, a bell above the door that rang with a tired sound when he entered. The air inside smelled of wool, chalk, steam, and old cologne.

A man behind the counter looked up and immediately looked away, as if seeing Ferretti too clearly would implicate him. He was in his sixties, with thick hands and the posture of someone who had spent a life bending over cloth and listening.

"Yes," the tailor said, not a question.

Ferretti approached the counter and kept his voice low. "I need my collar adjusted."

The tailor's eyes flicked to Ferretti's face, then to his hands, as if searching for tremor. He found none.

"Priests never stop complaining," the tailor muttered, playing his part. Then, more quietly: "Back room."

Ferretti followed him through a curtain into a narrow space filled with half-finished garments and a table scattered with measuring tape. In the corner was a door that should have led to a storage closet. The tailor opened it to reveal a second corridor, dimmer, narrower, smelling of damp stone and electricity.

Rome was built on layers. So were the Church's habits.

"Down," the tailor said, pointing to a stair.

Ferretti descended.

The stairwell led to a basement room with rough walls and a single bare bulb. A cot stood against one wall. A small table held a metal kettle, a loaf of bread, and a radio that looked older than the last war. Another door in the far wall was closed, its frame reinforced, as if someone had once been afraid of what might come through.

"Sit," the tailor said. His voice carried a weight now, no longer shopkeeper, but caretaker of a secret.

Ferretti sat on the cot without removing his coat. He kept his bag beside him, though it contained nothing but ordinary travel items now. Still, the habit of guarding what you carried was difficult to break.

The tailor poured water into a cup and handed it to him. Ferretti drank. It tasted of metal, but it anchored him.

"Who told you," the tailor asked.

"Orsini didn't tell me," Ferretti said. He chose his words carefully. "He warned me. The decree told me."

The tailor's mouth tightened at decree. "They issued it."

"Yes."

A silence stretched between them, filled by the faint electrical hum from somewhere behind the walls. Ferretti became aware, again, of his shadow. The bulb above made it fall on the floor in a clean shape. It looked obedient.

He did not look at it directly.

The tailor spoke again. "They'll say you ran. They'll say you panicked. They'll say you stole something."

"They already have what matters," Ferretti replied. "The case is in their vault."

"Then why hunt you," the tailor asked, genuinely confused.

Ferretti stared at the wall behind the tailor's shoulder, focusing on chipped plaster instead of the edges of darkness. "Because I saw it," he said. "Not enough to interpret, but enough to describe. Film. Ampoules. Notes in German. And writing that isn't writing."

The tailor swallowed. "Writing."

"It behaves like an interface," Ferretti said, and felt his teeth ache at the memory. "Looking at it feels like participating in something that can see you back."

The tailor's face tightened, half disbelief, half recognition of fear he did not want but could not avoid. "And Orsini sent you anyway."

"He thought Rome would act like Rome," Ferretti said. "He misjudged which Rome would answer first. The one built on faith, or the one built on control."

The tailor did not ask which had answered. He already knew.

Ferretti leaned forward slightly, lowering his voice. "I need a second place," he said. "Not this one. They will look for me where they can justify looking. A tailor shop. A safe room. They'll search in patterns."

The tailor hesitated. "There are routes," he said. "Old ones. People who still owe favors."

"I'm not asking for favors," Ferretti replied. "I'm asking for distance."

The tailor nodded once, decision made. He moved to the radio and turned a dial slowly until it settled on a station broadcasting music so soft it was almost only static.

"That's for upstairs," the tailor said. "If someone comes in. If they ask questions. If they listen."

Ferretti watched him. The man's hands were steady, too. Steady hands were rare in a world that survived on anxiety.

"Who else knows you're here," Ferretti asked.

"No one," the tailor said. Then, after a beat: "If Orsini comes asking, I'll deny it."

Ferretti did not flinch. "Good."

The tailor looked at him sharply. "You don't trust Orsini now."

"I trust Orsini's fear," Ferretti said. "I don't trust what the Vatican will do with it."

The bulb overhead buzzed once, almost imperceptibly, as if the filament had been touched by a thought.

Ferretti did not look up.

The tailor stepped closer. "They'll keep hunting," he said.

"Yes," Ferretti replied.

"And if they catch you."

Ferretti closed his fingers around the rosary inside his sleeve, not as a prayer, not as superstition, but as a reminder of what remained human in his hands. "Then I disappear," he said. "But not the way they want. Not as an erased witness. As a living one they can't locate."

The tailor stared at him for a long moment, then gave a single, slow nod. "You want to go underground," he said, and the phrase sounded less like metaphor in that basement room.

Ferretti's mouth tightened. "I already am."

He sat back on the cot and listened. Above them, Rome moved, unconcerned. Inside the Vatican, men with clean sleeves and sealed decrees would already be shaping the story of his absence into something tidy. Somewhere else, perhaps, in spaces that were neither Rome nor the Vatican, something patient and inhuman might be listening not to words but to choices, learning what a frightened institution did to prevent witnesses.

Ferretti kept his breathing even and his gaze away from his shadow.

He had made his vow in the Vatican's morning light.

Now he began the work of keeping it.

Outside, the city's bells continued to ring, and this time he could not tell whether they were marking an hour or counting doors.

Footsteps passed above the basement ceiling with the casual rhythm of customers and clerks, but Ferretti heard them as messages anyway. In the dim room beneath the tailor shop, every sound filtered through stone and plaster arrived softened, stripped of detail, and that made the mind invent detail to compensate.

Paolo moved quietly, pausing at the bottom of the stairs as if he could taste the air for danger. He listened with his head angled, eyes half closed. He had the face of a man who had learned to read the city not by sight but by vibration.

Ferretti remained seated on the cot, coat still on, collar still visible, hands resting where they could be seen. He did not fidget. He did not make prayer into theater. The rosary beads stayed hidden in his sleeve, a private weight against the irrational impulse to plead with the ceiling.

After a minute Paolo came back down, shutting the stair door gently.

"Two men came into the shop," Paolo said. "Not police. Not priests. Clean shoes. No interest in fabric."

Ferretti felt his teeth tighten, a small pressure as if his jaw had decided to brace itself.

"What did they ask," he said.

Paolo's mouth twisted. "They didn't ask about you. Not directly. They asked if I had seen anyone from the Secretariat this morning. They used names like they expected me to react. They were fishing for fear."

"And you gave them boredom," Ferretti said.

Paolo nodded once. "I gave them the look I reserve for men who don't pay. Then they left."

Ferretti exhaled slowly. He did not let it become relief. The Order did not test once. It tested until it found the seam.

He stood, rolling his shoulders once as if loosening fatigue. Movement was necessary now, but it had to be the right kind. Suddenness created a story. The Order thrived on stories because stories guided hands.

Paolo watched him with a frank, uneasy respect. "They'll come back," Paolo said.

"Yes," Ferretti replied. "But not here first. Not again. They will check who I might trust. They will check Orsini."

Paolo's eyes narrowed. "Orsini won't give you up."

Ferretti did not answer immediately. He had served long enough to understand that loyalty and survival were not always aligned, especially in Rome. Orsini had warned him. Orsini had also helped send him into the American vault. Orsini was not the enemy, but he was inside the structure that had decided Ferretti's death was administrative.

"They won't need Orsini's consent," Ferretti said at last. "They'll watch him. They'll follow who visits him. They'll trace who makes calls he shouldn't. The Vatican is excellent at prayer. It is also excellent at surveillance."

Paolo's hands flexed once, a tailor's hands that now held a different kind of craft. "Then you can't stay in the city."

Ferretti looked at the far door with the reinforced frame, the door that looked like it had been installed by someone who expected pressure from the other side. "I can't stay in one version of it," he said. "Rome is many cities layered together. We use the layers."

Paolo hesitated, then moved to a crate near the wall and pulled out a folded garment bag. He unzipped it and lifted a suit jacket and trousers, dark and unremarkable, the sort of clothing that did not invite interpretation.

"You'll change," Paolo said. "No collar."

Ferretti took the clothes and felt a brief, sharp irritation at how quickly identity became costume. The collar had been useful on American soil. In Rome it was a target.

He changed without ceremony, hanging the cassock and Roman collar on a hook as if he might return for them later. When he stepped back, he looked like a bureaucrat. A man with errands. A man who belonged to the machinery rather than the altar.

Paolo handed him a small envelope. "Keys," he said. "A room near Trastevere. Not this one. And a second address, outside the walls, if the first one burns."

Ferretti took the envelope and did not open it yet. "Who knows these places," he asked.

Paolo's gaze held his. "Only men who understand that knowing too much gets you buried," he said. Then he added, quieter, "And one woman who doesn't ask names."

Ferretti nodded once. Names were handles. He had repeated that rule so many times it had become a kind of liturgy.

Paolo turned the radio volume up slightly, then down again, a small gesture of habit, as if sound levels could seal rooms. "Wait five minutes," he said. "Then leave by the back corridor. The alley is empty right now."

Ferretti did not sit again. Waiting on a cot felt too much like surrender. He stood beneath the bare bulb and kept his gaze off the floor. The shadow would be there, clean and obedient, and his mind would want to test it. He refused the impulse. Verification was how the script on the inhuman pages worked. It invited a gaze, then used that gaze to become more real.

Above them, the shop bell rang. A muffled exchange of voices followed. Paolo went still, head tilted.

Ferretti heard it too: two male voices, polite, controlled, the tone of men who understood how to make threats sound like questions.

Paolo climbed the stairs without looking back.

Ferretti remained in the basement, breathing evenly. He counted nothing. Counting invited rhythms. Forty-seven seconds was not his number, and he would not let it become one.

The voices above grew clearer as Paolo spoke louder than necessary, letting the words bleed through the floorboards with deliberate innocence.

"No, I have not seen any monsignor today. No, no deliveries. This is a tailor shop."

A pause. A second voice, closer now. "You're certain."

"I'm a tailor," Paolo replied. "Certainty is my job."

Ferretti's jaw tightened. The Order had returned sooner than expected, or a second team had arrived, which meant the net was already being adjusted. They had spoken to someone. Or they had simply decided to squeeze.

He moved to the reinforced door and placed his hand on the knob. The metal was cool. The building's hum felt louder suddenly, as if the walls were listening.

A thud sounded upstairs, not a blow but a drawer closed with impatience. Paolo's voice stayed calm, but Ferretti heard the change in it, a fraction too sharp.

"Gentlemen," Paolo said, "you can't go back there. Private."

Private. Another word that meant nothing to men like these.

Ferretti opened the reinforced door and stepped into the narrow corridor beyond. The air was cooler here, damp stone and old dust, the smell of Rome's buried history. He moved quietly, closing the door behind him without letting it click.

He walked down the passage with the confidence of someone who had walked it before, even though he had not. Paolo had said Rome was layers. This was one of them: a service artery running between buildings that pretended they had no connection.

Behind him, the shop bell rang again. Louder. The kind of ring that was not customer and not commerce. It sounded like a signal.

Ferretti did not quicken his pace. He let his steps remain even, measured. In the tight corridor his shadow, cast by a distant utility light, stretched ahead of him in a long smear. It moved as he moved. It behaved.

But he could not shake the sensation that it was not merely following.

That it was leading, by half an inch.

He kept his eyes on the corridor's end.

At the far side, a metal hatch opened into a small alley behind the shop. Ferretti paused with his hand on the latch, listening.

He heard nothing at first. Then he heard it: a muffled voice from the shop above, Paolo's, raised in annoyance, and beneath it, the softer, colder cadence of a man who did not need to raise his voice.

"You're nervous," the man said.

"I'm annoyed," Paolo snapped.

"Nervous and annoyed often share a tailor," the man replied.

Ferretti swallowed. The line was almost humorous. Almost. It carried an awareness of roles, of masks, of performance. It was the kind of sentence a man used when he wanted to unsettle by sounding observant.

Ferretti opened the hatch and stepped into the alley.

The city smelled like wet stone and cigarette smoke. A motorbike passed at the far end of the alley, its engine a brief snarl. Two women spoke from a window above in a stream of Italian that meant nothing to Ferretti beyond its ordinariness.

He walked out as if he belonged there.

At the corner he turned left, then right, choosing a route that would look aimless to anyone watching casually. But he assumed no one would watch casually now. The Order watched with intent. And intent changed the watched.

Half a block away, he caught his reflection in a dark window. The suit fit him well enough. His hair was neat. His face was composed.

Behind him, in the reflection's depth, a man stepped out of the alley.

Not rushing. Not obvious. Just present, as if he had been part of the street all along and Ferretti's movement had simply revealed him.

Ferretti did not turn his head. He kept walking, letting the reflection slide out of view.

The pursuit had begun, not with a shout or a gun, but with the simplest Roman method of erasure: a man appearing at the right distance, at the right time, ready to become closer whenever Ferretti made the mistake of acknowledging him.

Ferretti adjusted his pace by a fraction, just enough to test.

Behind him, in the next window's reflection, the man adjusted too.

Not matching stride like a novice, but maintaining the same spacing, the same calm interval. The distance was deliberate. It was meant to suggest inevitability.

Ferretti felt, faintly, the pressure in his teeth pulse once, like a private metronome waking.

He did not answer it with fear. He did not answer it with prayer.

He turned into a crowded street where vendors were setting up tables, where voices overlapped and bodies moved unpredictably. He let the crowd swallow him.

As he moved, he caught one more glimpse in a shop window of his shadow at his feet.

It looked ordinary.

Too ordinary, as if it had learned how to behave in public.

Ferretti kept walking, eyes forward, mouth closed, refusing to give his pursuers what they wanted most: a reaction that could be used as proof he was afraid.

If the Vatican wanted no witnesses, then the Order would try to make him disappear cleanly.

But Ferretti had spent a night staring at a language that acted like an interface, and he understood now that clean lines were a lie.

Everything left residue.

Everything taught something else how to follow.

Ferretti let the crowd do what stone corridors could not: break lines.

He moved with the current of morning commerce, past crates of oranges and stacks of folded cloth, past a coffee bar where the air smelled of burnt sugar and impatience. He kept his shoulders loose and his face set in the mild fatigue of a man with appointments. If he looked hunted, he would become a signal. If he looked calm, he became background.

In the next shop window he caught it again, not his face this time but the spacing behind him. The man who had emerged from the alley remained there, threaded into the flow with practiced ease. A second figure, farther back, appeared briefly in the glass as the angle changed. Ferretti did not need to see their faces clearly to understand what the Order had decided.

Not one hand on a shoulder in an empty hallway.

A net.

His teeth pressed together. The faint pulse in his jaw tried to return, as if the city itself had remembered a rhythm. He refused to count it. Counting was surrendering a part of himself to pattern.

He turned into a narrower street where scooters choked the curb and laundry hung between windows like flags of domestic life. Halfway down, he stopped at a newspaper kiosk and pretended to scan headlines. He let his eyes move like any other Roman's: bored, judgmental, half awake.

The vendor glanced up. "You want one, signore?"

Ferretti gave him a distracted nod and paid for the first paper his hand touched. The vendor smiled the way men smiled when they thought they had done nothing that mattered.

Ferretti stepped away, folded the paper under his arm, and continued.

In the paper's glossy photograph of the Pope, the eyes looked serene. The caption spoke of peace in the world, of unity, of hope. Ferretti felt a bitter, precise clarity form behind his ribs. The Church's public face was always peace. Its private face was procedure.

He reached a small intersection where a bus rumbled past, coughing exhaust. He timed his steps with the bus's bulk, letting it cut the street in half. When the bus moved on, Ferretti was already on the opposite sidewalk, swallowed by a cluster of tourists looking at a map.

He did not look back. He did not test whether the cut had worked. Testing was attention, and attention was the first step toward answering.

He kept walking until the streets began to tilt toward Trastevere's older tangles. Here the buildings leaned closer together, as if sharing secrets, and the crowd thinned into locals and delivery boys. Ferretti slowed at an unremarkable doorway with a brass number dulled by years of fingers. He passed it once without pausing, then looped around the block and approached again from the other side.

This time he went in.

The stairwell smelled of cooking oil and damp plaster. A dog barked behind a door on the second floor, then stopped as if corrected. Ferretti climbed to the third floor and found the lock Paolo's key fit. He turned it without haste, stepped inside, and closed the door with the softest click he could manage.

The room was small, furnished with the minimum required for plausibility: a narrow bed, a table, a chair, curtains that did not quite close. A sink in the corner with a cracked mirror above it. Nothing on the walls. Not even a crucifix.

That absence was a kindness, or a warning.

Ferretti set the newspaper down and listened. The building's sounds arrived as they always did in Rome: water moving through pipes, footsteps above, distant voices through a window that did not seal properly. Ordinary life, unbothered by decrees and disappearances.

He waited a full minute before moving again, letting his breathing settle into something that did not sound like pursuit.

Then he opened Paolo's envelope.

Inside were two keys on a ring. A scrap of paper with an address in Trastevere, which he was already using, and a second address farther out, written in a hand that tried to be casual and failed. And beneath those, folded twice, a thin sheet of stationery with no letterhead, only a line of typed words and a number.

Do not return to Orsini. He cannot protect you now.

Below it: a telephone number, and under that, another line, this one handwritten.

Proof is not for belief. Proof is for ownership. Remember the Pope's condition.

Ferretti stared at that last sentence until he felt his jaw tighten. The Pope's condition. Bring me truth. Not belief. Proof.

At the time, perhaps, it had sounded like courage. A demand for clarity in a world of myths. Ferretti had served around men who used the language of faith the way bureaucrats used stamps: to make decisions look sacred. He had assumed the Pope's condition was a safeguard, a line in the sand.

Now he understood it had been the opposite.

A lever.

Proof did not end arguments. Proof ended rivals.

Ferretti sat on the edge of the bed without removing his coat and let the implications arrange themselves with the cold efficiency he had learned in confessionals that doubled as dead drops.

If the Vatican possessed proof of Christ, not legend, not relic, but direct evidence, then the Church would no longer be an institution of interpretation. It would be an institution of possession. Control of the artifact would become control of the narrative, and control of the narrative would become control of any government, any rival faith, any scientist, any skeptic.

And if the artifact could not be controlled, if it behaved like the inhuman script behaved, like an interface that used attention as a component, then the most dangerous outcome was not disbelief.

It was a competing ownership.

Americans had wanted copies. Agencies had wanted to be first. The Vatican had wanted the case sealed and the witness erased. Every hand that reached for it did so with the same instinct, clothed in different words.

Not reverence.

Claim.

Ferretti's teeth ached faintly, then eased. He realized with a small internal chill that the ache did not always correspond to fear. Sometimes it arrived when his mind brushed too close to the thing itself, to the idea that proof could be a lure.

He stood and went to the cracked mirror above the sink. He looked at his own face without lingering. His eyes were tired, but steady. He turned slightly to check the room's angles in the reflection, not because he expected to see a man behind him, but because he had learned that the most dangerous visitor was not always physical.

His shadow fell behind him on the wall in a soft wedge.

It looked correct.

He refused to feel relieved.

He moved away from the mirror and sat at the table. The room's single window looked out onto a slice of street where a woman hung clothes from a line. She shook out a sheet and pinned it with quick, practiced movements. Ferretti watched her hands, grateful for the simple humanity of the gesture.

Then, downstairs, a door opened and closed.

Footsteps on the stair.

Slow, unhurried, as if belonging.

Ferretti's body did not jolt. He had trained it not to. He listened instead, letting the sounds build a picture without forcing them into certainty. The footsteps stopped on the first landing. A murmur of voices. A short laugh, almost friendly.

A neighbor being asked a question.

Ferretti's mouth tightened. They were doing it carefully. No spectacle. No blood where pilgrims could find it. The same language the Order used in its instructions. The same instinct the decree wore like a mask.

No witnesses. No survivors.

The footsteps resumed, climbing.

Ferretti reached into his pocket and felt the rosary beads there, wood worn smooth. He did not pull them out. He did not pray with them. He simply let the familiar weight remind him that he was still himself, still not a mechanism.

His gaze slid to the telephone number on the note. He considered calling. Calling was a line. Lines could be traced. But staying silent was also a line, and silence, he had learned, did not prevent pursuit. It only made the pursuer bolder.

The footsteps reached the second floor. A door opened, a woman's voice answered, irritated, then softened into politeness. A question asked, a name mentioned. Not his, perhaps, but enough to stir attention.

Ferretti's teeth pulsed once.

He looked down at the paper and read the sentence again. Proof is not for belief. Proof is for ownership.

He saw, suddenly, how Kammler had played them. He had offered proof as bait because he knew the Vatican could not resist the temptation to possess it. And once they possessed it, once they committed themselves to secrecy and violence to keep it, they became predictable. An institution that had chosen ownership would keep choosing it, even when it became a noose.

Ferretti folded the note and put it back into his pocket. He stood and moved to the door, listening with his ear close to the wood.

On the stairwell, the footsteps climbed again.

Now, directly above him, the third floor.

A key ring jingled faintly, deliberate, meant to be heard. A pause. The soft scrape of metal near a lock.

Not his lock yet.

A neighboring door.

Another question, another polite exchange. The voice in the stairwell was calm, male, Roman. It sounded like a man who belonged in this building. It sounded like someone who could ask after a missing cousin, a visiting friend, a priest who had come to deliver papers.

It sounded like familiarity.

Ferretti's throat tightened. The inhuman script had behaved like an interface, tugging at the eye. Voices could do the same, tugging at reflex, at social instinct, at the need to answer when spoken to.

Do not respond. Do not answer.

He stepped away from the door and crossed to the window. He tested it. It opened, stiffly, as if reluctant to change. A narrow exterior ledge ran along the building, the kind used by men who repaired shutters and regretted their jobs.

The footsteps in the stairwell stopped outside his door.

Silence.

Then, a soft knock, measured and precise.

Ferretti did not move.

The knock came again, identical.

A voice, polite, close enough to be intimate through the wood. "Scusi. I'm looking for Father Ferretti."

The voice used the title gently, as if offering respect.

It also used his name as if it had every right.

Ferretti felt the pressure in his teeth rise, then ebb, like something listening to see whether he would answer. He did not let his eyes drift toward the floor; toward the shadow he could feel without seeing. He kept his attention on the window, on the ledge, on the fact that escape routes were only useful if taken before the net tightened.

The voice spoke again, warmer now. "Father, I know you're inside. We only want to talk. There's been… confusion."

Confusion. Another euphemism. Another stamp.

Ferretti placed one hand on the window frame. He opened it wider, letting Rome's noise spill in: scooters, voices, a distant bell. Ordinary sound, indifferent and alive.

Behind him, the doorknob turned slowly, testing.

Ferretti did not look. Looking would make it a moment, a scene, a memory for whatever watched between moments.

He stepped onto the ledge, closed the window as much as he dared without latching it, and began to move sideways along the building's face.

Behind the glass, inside the room, the lock clicked.

And in the thin strip of reflected light on the windowpane, Ferretti caught one last glimpse of his shadow on the wall.

For an instant, it did not seem to belong to the angle of the room at all.

It seemed to lean toward the opening door, as if eager to see who entered first.

Ferretti slid past the next window, breath controlled, fingers gripping stone that had been shaped by centuries of hands. He did not allow himself to think about falling. He thought only about the truth that had finally become simple enough to carry.

The Vatican had not wanted proof to end doubt.

It had wanted proof to end competition.

And now, because he had touched the edge of that truth, the Church had decided he must become the kind of missing person Rome produced without effort.

No witnesses.

No survivors.

Ferretti moved along the ledge into the city's bright, indifferent morning, understanding at last that what he was fleeing was not only the Order, not only the decree, not even only the case sealed in a vault.

He was fleeing an institution that had mistaken possession for salvation.

And something else, patient and unseen, had been listening closely enough to learn the difference.

Chapter 16

Seeds in Argentina

The safe house in Argentina did not look like a laboratory. That was the first rule, written nowhere but enforced in every decision that followed the war: nothing that could be photographed should resemble what it was.

From the road it was simply a ranch compound outside San Carlos de Bariloche, a low sprawl of buildings pressed against the edge of pine forest. The main house had a veranda, a battered radio antenna, and windows that reflected sky so cleanly they looked like empty squares. Cattle moved in slow, indifferent knots across the pasture. A traveler could pass and file it away as another remnant of European stubbornness transplanted to South American soil.

But the men who lived there had not come for cattle.

The access road was rutted, half-mud, half-gravel, the kind of inconvenience that discouraged strangers and slowed vehicles enough to be heard long before they arrived. A gate marked by no sign, watched by no uniformed guard, opened only after a long pause in which someone unseen decided whether the visitor's face belonged to memory.

The visitor this afternoon was a man who had once been called Obersturmbannführer and now answered to "Herr Doktor" with a practiced humility that never reached his eyes. His hair had been cut differently, his posture softened to resemble civilian age, but the bones of him retained their old certainty. Papers in his pocket said he was Austrian. The papers were excellent. They always were.

He stopped his car before the gate and left the engine running, as if the sound itself were a declaration of normality. He waited. The pressure of waiting had been the only punishment the world could still reliably impose on men like him.

A voice came from a speaker recessed into a fence post. Not tinny, not theatrical. Just controlled.

"Name."

The man looked at the gate as if it were an inferior officer. "You know my name."

"Say it."

A pause. A small correction in his jaw, the faintest movement that suggested he still did not like being instructed. Then he complied.

"Vogel," he said. "Dr. Ilse Vogel expects me."

A second pause, longer. Somewhere behind the fence, a mechanism clicked. The gate swung inward with a slow, heavy confidence.

The ranch swallowed the car.

Inside the compound, the air smelled of resin and wet earth and, beneath that, the faint chemical cleanliness of a place that fought constantly to remove the trace of what it did. A man in work clothes stepped out of a shed carrying a wrench, then kept walking without looking up, his role performed with the kind of disinterest that was never real.

The visitor parked near the main house and walked toward the side entrance, not the front. The path had been chosen to keep important faces away from casual sight. He did not knock. He pressed his thumb to a small metal plate set into the doorframe.

The lock released with a quiet shiver.

Inside, the house was warm in the way old houses were warm: heat trapped in wood, lingering smells of cooking and tobacco. A hallway led past a kitchen where a woman peeled potatoes without haste, her movements steady, her eyes avoiding the man as if looking too directly might require acknowledgment of who he was. A child's laughter came from somewhere deeper in the building, quickly muffled, as if someone had remembered to close a door.

The visitor followed the corridor to a room that had been presented, carefully, as a study. Shelves of books in German and Spanish. A desk with papers. A framed photograph of mountains. Nothing that screamed refuge. Nothing that confessed.

At the desk sat Dr. Ilse Vogel.

She was younger than he had expected, or perhaps she simply looked younger because she carried herself without the exhausted caution of men who had spent decades hiding. Her hair was pinned back severely. She wore no jewelry. Her face was precise, almost austere, as if she had trained it not to leak emotion that could be used against her. On the desk lay a small tray with a cup of coffee that had gone cold and a notebook filled with neat, narrow handwriting.

She did not rise as he entered.

"You're late," she said in German.

The visitor shut the door behind him. "Your clock is impatient."

"My clock is accurate," Vogel replied. She glanced at his hands, as if checking for tremor or stain, then returned her gaze to his face. "You came alone."

"I always come alone," he said.

Vogel's expression remained unchanged. "That is not what I meant."

He knew what she meant. Alone did not only refer to physical escort. It referred to the invisible chains of surveillance and obligation that followed men who moved through ratlines and false passports. It referred to handlers. To debts.

"I was not followed," he said, and in his voice was the faint offense of a man asked to prove competence.

Vogel leaned back slightly, measuring him. She did not say I believe you. Belief was a luxury. She simply moved on.

"Sit," she said.

He sat in the chair opposite the desk. It was an ordinary chair, slightly uncomfortable. Deliberately so. Comfort made people linger. Linger made them familiar. Familiar made them careless.

Vogel opened a drawer and removed a folder. No markings. No names. Only a thickness that suggested photographs and reports. She placed it on the desk but did not slide it toward him.

"The route from Genoa is compromised," she said. "One of the priests who used to arrange papers is gone."

The visitor's eyes narrowed. "Gone."

Vogel nodded once. "Vanished. Not arrested. Not found. His replacement speaks too much about loyalty. That kind of speech is either fear or theater."

The visitor felt a faint tightening in his mouth. "Rome is cleaning its own house."

"Or being cleaned," Vogel said. She paused, then added with a cold practicality: "Either way, it changes the flow."

He did not like hearing the Vatican discussed this way, not out of reverence, but because institutions that large were useful. Useful institutions were safer when they were predictable.

Vogel's fingers tapped the folder once. "We have what we need for now. The last shipment arrived."

His gaze sharpened. "The case?"

Vogel did not answer immediately. She reached instead for her notebook and opened it to a page of figures and dates. “Not a case,” she said. “A fraction. Enough to work with. Enough to ruin us if it becomes public.”

He leaned forward slightly despite himself. “Where is it.”

Vogel’s eyes lifted. “Not here,” she said. “Not in one place. Not in anything that can burn all at once.”

He sat back again, irritated. “So, you are afraid.”

Vogel’s mouth tightened. “I am cautious,” she corrected. “There is a difference. You of all people should understand it.”

He did not reply. The last time he had been accused of fear by a woman, it had been in a concrete facility in the Owl Mountains, and the accusation had been followed by screaming that did not come from any mouth.

Vogel watched him, perhaps noticing the flicker in his eyes. She leaned forward slightly and lowered her voice.

“They told us, in Poland, that time was a corridor,” she said. “A machine you could walk through. But what we have is not only time. It is attention. It reacts. It remembers.”

The visitor's jaw shifted. "You speak like a priest."

Vogel's gaze stayed steady. "No," she said. "I speak like someone who has seen records from the Black Forest. Like someone who has read Kammler's notes without letting her eyes settle too long on the wrong page."

The name Kammler landed in the room like a weight. Even here, even in Patagonia with mountains behind the windows and cattle outside, the name carried its own gravity. The visitor looked away for a fraction of a second, a reflex of old hierarchy.

Vogel continued, relentless in her calm.

"The material we have does not behave like ordinary tissue," she said. "It persists. It resists decay in ways it should not. It expresses markers that do not correspond to human inheritance. And when it is placed near certain fields, electromagnetic or otherwise, it changes. Not randomly. As if responding."

The visitor's fingers tightened on the chair arms. "You are describing adaptation."

"I am describing learning," Vogel replied.

She stood and walked to the bookcase. For a moment she looked like she was selecting a volume. Instead, she pressed her palm against a particular section of wood. The shelf clicked and swung inward, revealing a narrow passage and a stair descending into darkness.

The visitor's posture stiffened. He had expected it, and still the reveal made something in him recoil. Doors that opened into hidden space always reminded him of rooms that did not let men leave.

Vogel turned back to him. "You came to see," she said. "So, you will see. But you will follow instructions."

He gave a thin smile. "You sound like Kammler."

Vogel's expression did not change. "Then you should listen," she said, and stepped into the passage.

The air down the stair was colder and drier, stripped of domestic smell. The walls changed from plaster to concrete. A hum grew stronger, the steady vibration of generators and refrigeration. Lights came on in narrow, controlled strips, not bright enough to flood the space, bright enough to prevent accidents.

The lower level was larger than the house could have justified. It extended under the compound like a second architecture, built not for comfort but for containment. Metal cabinets. Work tables. Sealed doors with rubber gaskets. A surgical sink. A row of incubators along one wall, each with a small observation window. The room smelled of antiseptic and something else, faint and metallic, like old coins warmed in a hand.

Two men in white coats looked up briefly as Vogel entered, then returned to their work. Their faces were European, their eyes too tired to be new. They did not greet the visitor. That was another rule: names were not used unless necessary. Names created threads.

Vogel stopped beside the incubators and placed her hand on one of the warm metal housings, not tenderly, not reverently, but with the clinical familiarity of someone touching a machine she did not entirely trust.

"You wanted refuge," she said to the visitor without looking at him. "This is what refuge buys. Time. Quiet. Isolation."

The visitor stepped closer, drawn despite himself by the low, steady beeping of a monitor. "And what does it grow," he asked.

Vogel's eyes flicked toward him. "Not belief," she said. "Not salvation. A weapon, if you are naive. A successor, if you are ambitious. And a disaster, if you are honest."

She pointed to the nearest observation window.

Inside, beneath dim light and careful warmth, something moved.

At first glance it could have been a fetus in an ordinary medical photograph. A small curve. A suggestion of limbs. But the movement was wrong, too coordinated for the stage, as if the thing inside understood rhythm before it had nerves to justify it. The monitor beside the incubator recorded a heartbeat that was too steady, too untroubled by the world.

The visitor's mouth went dry.

Vogel's voice remained level, almost bored with the horror of it. "They called it proof," she said. "The Vatican wanted it sealed. America wanted copies. Kammler wanted leverage. We want a future that cannot be taken away from us again."

She leaned closer to the glass.

"And what we have," she said quietly, "is a seed."

The visitor stared at the movement behind the window until his eyes began to ache, a faint pressure in his teeth that he had not felt in years. He forced himself to look away, suddenly afraid not of what he saw, but of what seeing might teach it.

Vogel noticed the flinch. For the first time her expression shifted, not into kindness, but into something like grim satisfaction.

"You felt it," she said. "Good. Then you understand why this place exists."

He swallowed. "How many," he managed.

Vogel did not answer immediately. She gestured instead toward the far end of the room, where a second sealed door stood with warning labels in Spanish and German. Through a small reinforced window in that door, the visitor saw another chamber beyond, darker, lit by a slow pulsing glow that did not resemble any standard lamp.

A shape hung in the center of that chamber, suspended by cables and brackets. Not a machine exactly. Not yet an organism. A bell-like contour of metal, smaller than Die Glocke but suggestive of its geometry, as if someone had tried to recreate a memory with imperfect materials.

Vogel watched his eyes track it and said, very softly, as if speaking too loudly might count as attention.

"We have enough," she said. "Enough to change what comes next. Enough that there is no going back to hiding in other men's institutions."

Upstairs, above concrete and humming refrigeration, a child laughed again and was silenced again, the sound muffled by distance and deliberate walls.

The visitor stood between incubators and a half-born machine and felt the word refuge lose its ordinary meaning. This was not a hiding place. This was an ark built by people who did not believe the flood had ended.

Vogel turned away from the glass and looked at him with eyes that were no longer merely scientific. They were political. Hungry. Patient.

"You came here because Germany lost," she said. "Because the world decided you were a story it wanted to end."

She stepped closer until he could smell the coffee on her breath, cold now, stale.

"But stories do not end," she continued. "They migrate. They change language. They find new hosts."

Somewhere in the compound above, a door closed. Footsteps crossed a wooden floor. Ordinary sounds. Domestic. Carefully staged.

The scientists' refuge held its breath and continued its work in the dark under the ranch, planting what it believed were seeds of divinity into a soil that would not ask questions until the harvest.

The first birth happened on a Tuesday, which was how Dr. Ilse Vogel knew it would become a problem.

If it had happened on a night of storm or during one of the compound's staged celebrations, the story might have carried its own camouflage. A dramatic event could be buried under more dramatic noise. But Tuesday was plain. Tuesday was routine. Tuesday was the day the ranch hands repaired fences and the cook made stew and the men in white coats wrote figures in ledgers that had no names.

Upstairs, in the house that smelled of potatoes and tobacco and deliberate normality, the woman they called Marta went into labor just after dawn.

She was not one of them. That had been the rule from the beginning. No children of the scientists, no pregnancies that could be traced to familiar faces, no bloodlines that led back to Germany like a map drawn in veins. Marta had come down from the north with a husband who drank and a history that contained the right kind of holes. She had been paid well to stay quiet. She had been told she was carrying the child of a man who could not be named. She had accepted that with the practiced resignation of someone who had learned long ago that men with money always wanted the same thing: silence that looked like consent.

They had prepared her for pain. They had prepared themselves for complications.

They had not prepared for the way the air changed when the child finally arrived.

In the hidden level under the ranch, Dr. Vogel stood behind a glass panel with two other doctors and watched the monitors the way a priest watched the elevation of the host: with stillness that hid hunger. She did not go into the room unless necessary. Observation, she had learned, was not passive. It was contact. Kammler's notes had taught her that, even at the cost of making her skin crawl with the idea that attention could leave residue.

Still, she watched.

Marta screamed once, long and raw, and then the sound cut off as if a hand had closed around it. Not a hand on her mouth. Something else. The scream simply ended mid-breath, leaving the room in an abrupt quiet that made the midwife look up in shock.

The midwife was Argentine, older, competent, brought in because she had delivered hundreds of children in rural places where doctors were a luxury. She was paid enough not to ask questions about the locked doors and the lack of windows. She wore her suspicion like a shawl and kept it wrapped tight.

Now her eyes widened, and she made the sign of the cross without thinking.

Marta's lips moved. No sound came.

Vogel leaned closer to the glass. She did not touch it. Touch was an invitation.

"What happened?" one of the men beside her murmured in German.

Vogel did not answer. She watched Marta's throat work, watched the muscles of her chest strain against the silence, and felt the familiar pressure in her teeth, faint as a remembered ache. It arrived when the instruments spiked, when the lights seemed just a fraction too steady, when the world behaved as if it were listening.

Inside the room, the midwife bent over Marta and spoke rapidly, soothingly, in Spanish. Her voice emerged normally. Only Marta's voice was missing, as if the room had decided one sound was too sharp to allow.

Then the child crowned.

The midwife froze for half a second, her hands still, her breath caught. Vogel saw her glance toward the ceiling light as if expecting it to flicker. It did not.

"Dios mío," the midwife whispered, and for once the whisper carried fear without shame.

The child came out slick with blood and fluid, ordinary in size, the head dark with hair.

But the eyes were open.

Not the unfocused, reflexive opening of newborn eyes that saw light and nothing else. These eyes fixed.

They found the midwife's face.

Marta's mouth opened again, another silent scream, and the child's gaze slid toward her with a calm that did not belong to an infant fighting for its first breath.

The monitors chimed. Heart rate steady. Oxygenation normal. No sign of distress.

The midwife lifted the baby carefully, almost reluctantly, as if she were handling something that might break the rules of her hands. She rubbed the back briskly, expecting the cry that was supposed to follow.

The baby did not cry.

It inhaled, and the room's silence deepened, as if sound itself had been pressed down by an unseen palm.

Behind the glass, one of Vogel's men swallowed. "It isn't crying," he said, the observation coming out like a confession.

"It is breathing," Vogel replied. Her voice was flat. She hated the faint tremor in the air, the way the instruments seemed to hum with a quiet satisfaction. "It doesn't need to announce itself."

The baby's skin, still wet, caught the light oddly. Not luminous, not glowing, nothing so theatrical. It was more like the light did not quite decide how to sit on it. The same fractional hesitation Vogel had seen in field reports from Poland, described in ugly, careful German: a distortion that made the eye want to blink and then feel foolish for blinking.

The midwife carried the child to a small scale on a side table. As she set it down, Marta made a sound at last: a thin, broken gasp, like air escaping a puncture.

The midwife looked at Marta's face, then at the baby, and said softly, "No."

It was not denial of what she saw. It was refusal. A human attempt to push back against a reality she had not agreed to.

The baby turned its head.

It looked toward the glass.

Vogel felt her throat tighten.

For a heartbeat she was certain it could see her through the panel, could fix those steady eyes on her face the way Christ had fixed his eyes on Kammler's and spoken his name. The absurdity of the comparison did not weaken the fear. It strengthened it. It suggested continuity.

The baby did not blink.

One of the doctors beside Vogel stepped back, his chair scraping softly. The sound seemed too loud in the silence, and Vogel saw the baby's eyes flick toward it, registering. Tracking.

Learning.

"Remove the child," Vogel said.

The words came out clipped, controlled, but her hand had tightened into a fist without her noticing. She did not like giving orders when she could not pretend they were routine.

A nurse in a white coat moved into the room, her expression carefully blank. She did not look at Marta's face for long. She did not look at the baby for long. She did as she had been trained to do here:

act like a machine so the machines they built would not recognize a human mind to play with.

The baby did not resist when it was taken. It did not reach for Marta. It did not cry.

Marta's voice returned in fragments, hoarse and terrified. "What is it?" she rasped in Spanish. "What did you do?"

The midwife hesitated, caught between professionalism and the desire to flee. The nurse ignored the questions and carried the child toward the inner door that led down, away from domestic lies and into the humming concrete belly of the refuge.

As the door opened, a faint draft moved through the room.

Marta's hair lifted slightly off her forehead as if stirred by breath.

The midwife's eyes filled with tears she did not seem to understand. She whispered something like a prayer.

Vogel watched the child pass through the doorway and felt the pressure in her teeth ease by a fraction, as if proximity mattered.

Behind her, the visiting man who called himself Vogel had been silent for most of the birth, his face a mask of controlled interest. Now he spoke quietly. “That was only the first,” he said.

Vogel did not look at him. “No,” she replied. “That was the first that survived.”

They moved below into the room of incubators and antiseptic and machines that pretended to be medical rather than ideological. The baby was cleaned, weighed, tagged with a number instead of a name. Names were handles. Numbers were control.

They placed it behind reinforced glass.

The baby’s eyes followed them.

Not in the drifting way of infants. In the precise way of a cat watching a hand that might feed it or strike it.

A second birth followed three weeks later.

That one was not a Tuesday. It was at night, and they thought perhaps that would make it easier, as if darkness was a kind of mercy.

It was worse.

The mother, another local woman paid into silence, hemorrhaged during labor. She should have died. The doctors prepared blood, prepared clamps, prepared procedures they had used a hundred times.

Then the bleeding stopped.

Not slowly. Not by clotting. It stopped as if the body had obeyed an instruction.

The woman sobbed in confusion, hands gripping the sheets. The doctor who had been holding a clamp stared at his own fingers as if they had betrayed him by being unnecessary.

Vogel watched the monitors and saw the numbers normalize with an obscene calm. She thought of the biological sample in an ampoule, wax sealed, and the way she had been told it did not behave like ordinary tissue. She thought of Kammler's scribbled note: not steal. create.

The baby arrived with closed eyes this time.

Vogel almost felt relief.

Then, as the doctor leaned in to clear the airway, the room's overhead light dimmed by a fraction and returned. Not a flicker. A softening, like a hand passing between bulb and world.

The doctor froze. "Did you see that?"

No one answered. Answering gave shape to fear.

The baby inhaled.

And every shadow in the room shifted the wrong way, as if the light had moved when it had not.

The third birth produced twins.

They had hoped for twins. The project's old theories, dragged from German notebooks and Vatican whispers, suggested that mirrored development might stabilize what was otherwise too volatile. A divided expression of whatever they had planted. Two vessels sharing one origin.

The twins were identical in face.

They were not identical in behavior.

The first cried, loud and ordinary, the sound almost comforting in its normality. The staff exhaled. Someone even laughed, a short, disbelieving bark that sounded like relief trying on joy.

Then the second twin turned its head, eyes opening immediately, and the crying stopped mid-wail.

Not only the first twin's cry. The air itself seemed to dampen, as if a blanket had been thrown over the room's acoustics. The first twin's mouth remained open, face red, lungs straining, and yet no sound came.

The nurse holding the first twin panicked and began to rock the infant, whispering frantic Spanish endearments.

The second twin stared.

The first twin quieted, breath returning to normal as if soothed. The nurse's whisper slowed. Her shoulders loosened.

She looked at the second twin and smiled.

Vogel felt cold climb her spine.

She had seen this before, not in infants, but in adults around certain artifacts: the way the mind slid toward compliance when it was offered a shape that felt familiar. Voices that used your name. Shadows that rehearsed trust.

The second twin did not cry.

It did not need to.

It watched the room settle around it like dust falling after a door closed.

Afterward, when the mothers were moved back upstairs to heal under the ranch's polite lies, when the midwife was paid and sent away with a warning wrapped in gratitude, Vogel sat alone in the lower lab and opened a ledger.

She wrote the births as data. Dates. Times. Weights. Heart rates. Unusual phenomena.

She did not write what she felt, because feeling was not useful and because she suspected, more and more, that even writing could be a kind of invitation.

Still, in the margin beside the twins, her pen hesitated.

She thought of Rome and the envoy who had vanished into the city rather than be erased. She thought of the Vatican sealing the case and believing secrecy could prevent consequence. She thought of Americans wanting copies, as if duplication made ownership neutral.

She wrote one word anyway, in German, small enough that it looked like a scratch.

Ankunft.

Arrival.

Then she closed the ledger and stared at the row of incubators where numbered children lay behind glass, their breathing too steady, their eyes too attentive.

Above, the ranch continued to pretend at domestic life. A child's laugh. A door closing. Potatoes boiling.

Below, the unusual births accumulated like a quiet inventory of future power.

And with each new infant, Vogel felt the same unsettling certainty sharpen: the project was no longer only replication. It was adaptation. Whatever had been taken at the crucifixion and dragged through time had not remained passive in blood and film and ampoules.

It had learned.

And now it was being born.

By the time the fourth child arrived, Dr. Ilse Vogel stopped telling herself she was watching biology.

Biology had curves and error bars. Biology bled when it was cut and healed when it was stitched and did not care who held the needle. What she was seeing in the lower level beneath the ranch behaved less like a body and more like a decision.

The infants were kept in a row of reinforced cribs behind glass that was thicker than any nursery required. That thickness had begun as security theater, a gesture to make grown men feel as if they had built a wall between themselves and the implications of what they were doing. Now, months into the first cohort, it felt like the only honest response the facility had ever produced.

The firstborn, Tuesday's child, had been given the number 1-7 in the ledger, the seventh trial of a line that finally held. In the first weeks it slept too quietly and woke without fuss. It did not cry for hunger. It did not cry for discomfort. It watched the room with a steady interest that made the nurses avoid meeting its gaze, as if eye contact were a contract.

On the surface, the ranch still performed normality. Marta recovered upstairs and was paid and sent away with a new story to tell her husband if she was ever asked. The midwife was paid more, and then more again when she started to ask the wrong questions. Cattle were moved between pastures. A fence was repaired twice so a passerby could see men sweating over wood and wire and believe the compound's greatest concern was livestock.

Below, the pattern began.

It did not announce itself with a single miracle. It emerged the way cracks emerged in stone: repetition, pressure, and the quiet insistence of physics refusing to obey the old rules.

Vogel sat at her desk in the lower lab and laid out the logs. Vital signs. Feeding schedules. Sleep cycles. Temperature. Electrical activity in the rooms. Reports of staff headaches. Teeth pain. Complaints about lighting. Notes on shadows that "did not align" and "settled late," phrases that had started as jokes and ended as whispered superstition.

She disliked superstition. Superstition was imprecise. But she had learned, reluctantly, that precision did not protect you from things that used attention as a component. In Kammler's old notes, copied by hand into her private notebook because she would not trust a camera near them, there had been a line that returned to her more often than any equation.

Nicht stehlen. Erzeugen.

Not steal. Create.

Creation implied intent. Intent implied pattern.

The first clear pattern arrived not in the infants' bodies but in the people around them.

It started with the nurse named Estela, an Argentine woman in her thirties who had taken the job because the pay was good and the questions were few. Estela had steady hands and the practiced emotional distance of someone who had worked in rural clinics where survival depended on not breaking in front of families who needed you calm. She had been useful because she did not pray over the infants and did not gossip about them.

Then, one morning, she began to hum.

Not loudly. Not consciously, it seemed. A thin, repetitive melody that followed her down corridors and through doors. When asked, she blinked as if waking.

"I didn't realize," she said, frowning. "It's stuck in my head."

"What is it," Vogel asked.

Estela hesitated, then shrugged. "A hymn my grandmother used to sing," she said. "I haven't thought about it in years."

That night, one of the German technicians, a man who had survived the war by becoming forgettable, was heard whispering the same melody under his breath as he checked the incubator seals. When confronted, he flushed and denied it too quickly.

Vogel wrote it down. Not the notes, just the fact of it.

Familiarity, she thought. An offer of something remembered, something comforting. A way of making the mind loosen.

The infants did not need to speak to shape behavior. They only needed the room to behave as if it had already been shaped.

A week later, the pattern moved from mood to matter.

A ratline shipment arrived; a small wooden crate marked as medical supplies. Inside were vials and reagents and a coil assembly meant for field testing, all routed through hands that never met the same eyes twice. The crate was carried down into the lab by two men who complained about the weight and joked about the "holy children" below, laughing the way men laughed when they were trying to prove they were not afraid.

They set the crate down near crib 3-2, one of the twins, the one that cried loudly and seemed, for lack of a better word, more human.

The crying stopped.

The men froze, surprised by the sudden quiet. One of them looked toward the glass where the twin lay red-faced and tense, mouth open, but no sound emerged. The other man chuckled, relieved.

"See," he said. "Even it knows when to be quiet."

Crib 3-2's chest rose and fell. The infant did not appear distressed. It simply existed in the silence as if silence were the natural state and noise the anomaly.

Then crib 3-1, the twin that never cried, shifted its gaze.

Vogel watched from behind the observation panel as the infant's eyes settled on the crate. Not on the men. Not on the room. On the crate.

The air in the lab changed. Not dramatically. A slight thickening, the way humidity changed before rain. One of the overhead lights dimmed by a fraction, then steadied again.

The men did not notice the lights, but they both touched their jaws almost simultaneously.

"My teeth," one muttered.

The other laughed, forced. "You need a dentist."

The crate's lid creaked.

It did not spring open. No hinges snapped. It simply shifted, as if the wood had expanded and a nail had loosened. The top lifted by the width of a finger.

The men stared. The laughter died.

One reached forward, instinctively, to press it shut.

Vogel's voice cracked through the intercom, sharper than she intended. "Don't touch it."

The man flinched back as if burned. He looked toward the observation panel, then away, unsettled by being observed himself.

Vogel instructed them to carry the crate out immediately. When they did, the silence in the room eased and crib 3-2 began to whimper again, the sound returning gradually as if sound had to be reintroduced.

Afterward, the men tried to explain the lid as humidity, as poor craftsmanship, as anything that preserved their sense of a world that did not respond to an infant's attention.

Vogel did not correct them. She had no interest in arguing with denial. Denial was not ignorance; it was a coping mechanism. She needed the staff functional.

But she wrote a new line in her private ledger, one that she did not show to anyone.

Object response to gaze. Possible field effect without apparatus.

If this was power, it was not power like a gun. It was power like an instruction embedded in the environment.

As the months progressed, the infants developed at an uneven pace. They grew in fits rather than increments, as if time did not always move with the same smoothness around them. One week their measurements would track close to normal. Then, after a night when the power generators had hummed with an odd, syncing vibration, an infant would wake with longer fingers or a stronger grip or eyes that seemed to focus too sharply.

The staff began to report dreams.

A ranch hand named Luis, a man who had never been inside the lab, came to the kitchen pale and sweating and said he had dreamed of a bell shape lying in snow, its surface covered in grooves that moved when he tried to look directly at them. He had woken with his teeth aching.

"How do you know about snow," the cook demanded, half amused, half wary. "You've never left Patagonia."

Luis stared at her. "In the dream, it wasn't here," he said. "It was… elsewhere. Cold. Old. Like history."

Vogel heard of the dream through two intermediaries and felt the familiar chill settle in her stomach. The children were under the ranch, sealed behind reinforced glass, and still their influence was leaking upward, threading into people who did not even know they existed.

Not through words. Through associations. Symbols. A bell. Grooves. Snow. Things that belonged to the origin story the scientists carried like a secret scripture.

It was spreading through attention the way mold spread through walls.

The visiting man who called himself Vogel returned twice more over the following year. He sat in the study upstairs, drank coffee, and asked questions that were framed as administrative but carried hunger underneath.

“How many are stable,” he asked.

Vogel answered with numbers and probabilities, because that was the only language she trusted. “Stable is not the correct term,” she said. “Some are quieter. Some are louder. None are inert.”

He smiled faintly. “None of us are inert,” he said, and she heard in it the old ideology, repackaged into something that could survive defeat.

On his third visit, she walked him below and made him stand behind the observation glass.

The children were no longer newborns. They were toddlers now, small bodies that moved with an unsettling deliberation. They played without toys. They did not need them. Their games were with each other, with the space between them, with the room’s rules.

Crib 1-7 sat on the floor and watched a droplet of water hover above its palm. Not floating like a magician’s trick, not defying gravity with spectacle, but suspended as if gravity had been asked, politely, to wait. When the droplet fell, it fell in a straight line as if released from a thread.

Across the room, one of the later children pressed its hand to a cut on a technician's finger. The cut closed. The technician jerked back, breath catching, and then laughed too loudly, as if laughter could reassert normality.

The twins were the clearest and worst example of the pattern.

Twin 3-2, the one that cried, was affectionate. It reached for hands and clung to sleeves, and when it was frightened, it made ordinary noise. The staff liked it, and that liking frightened Vogel more than any hovering droplet. Liking made carelessness.

Twin 3-1 watched. Always watched. When it stared at someone long enough, the person would begin to mirror its posture, subtly, like a pendulum aligning with another pendulum in the same room. People stood straighter. Breathing slowed. Voices softened.

Compliance without orders.

The man beside Vogel shifted uneasily. "They're not just anomalies," he said.

Vogel kept her eyes on twin 3-1. The child's gaze touched the glass, and for a moment Vogel thought of Ferretti on the aircraft, refusing to answer even in his head. She thought of Rome sealing the case as if sealing could stop the watching.

"They are not miracles," Vogel said. "They are functions."

The man frowned. "Of what."

Vogel's answer came slowly, because speaking it gave it weight. "Of whatever learned from the crucifixion," she said. "Whatever crossed the hinge with Kammler. Whatever was brought back when the sky fractured."

Twin 3-1 turned its head slightly.

Not toward the staff. Toward Vogel.

The pressure in her teeth arrived, sharp and brief. Her tongue pressed against the back of her incisors as if instinctively bracing.

Vogel did not look away. She did not flinch. She would not give it the satisfaction of teaching her fear.

Behind the glass, the child's expression did not change. It did not smile. It did not threaten.

It simply watched her the way a scientist watched an experiment, patient and unblinking, as if learning which parts of her were controlled and which parts might someday be used.

Vogel forced her breathing steady and lowered her voice to the man beside her.

"Patterns of power," she said. "Not random. Not divine. Not even human. They are repeating, refining. They are discovering what works."

The man swallowed. "And what works," he asked, "is what."

Vogel's eyes stayed on the child. "Familiarity," she said. "Attention. And the human need to answer when called."

Above them, in the ranch house, a door closed. Someone laughed at a joke that had nothing to do with what was happening underground. Normal life, staged and fragile.

Below, behind reinforced glass, the children continued their quiet experiments with the world, and the world, without realizing it, began to adjust around them.

Vogel closed her notebook and understood, with a clarity she did not share out loud, that the project had already passed the point of containment. Not because the children were too strong, but because their strength did not rely on force. It relied on the simplest mechanism in any room.

The room's willingness to respond.

Chapter 17

Mengele's Doctrine

The file did not arrive as a file.

It arrived as a smell.

Old paper, oil from fingertips, the faint sweetness of cheap tobacco that had soaked into cardboard over years. It came wrapped in butcher's brown and tied with string that had been knotted and unknotted too many times. The man who delivered it to the ranch called himself a courier, but he had none of the careless speed of men who moved ordinary contraband. He drove a truck with produce crates stacked high, and when he stepped into the study he took off his hat and held it with both hands like a penitent.

Dr. Ilse Vogel did not offer him a chair. She did not ask his name. She had learned that names were handles, and handles were how the world pulled you back into notice.

He set the package on her desk and slid an envelope across the wood. “From Europe,” he said in Spanish, voice low. “From the old routes.”

“Which old route,” Vogel asked in German, not because the courier understood it but because she did not like speaking her fear in the language of her refuge.

The courier shrugged, eyes down. “A priest in Genoa handed it to a man who no longer wears a collar,” he said. “It passed through hands that don’t write.”

Vogel felt her teeth ache faintly at the word priest. Rome was a wound that kept bleeding into the rest of their network. She thought of the vanished envoy and the Vatican’s sealed vault, of orders written in calm language and executed in corridors that did not exist. She had never met Monsignor Orsini or Father Ferretti, but their absence had become a condition of the world, like humidity.

She cut the string with a letter opener and peeled back the paper. Inside was a thin binder and, beneath it, a small metal box no larger than a cigarette case. The box was heavy for its size, as if it contained more than paper should.

The binder's cover held no title. Only a typed inventory number and a stamp that had been pressed hard enough to bruise the fiber.

Vogel opened it.

The first page was a photograph. A man in a white coat standing in a room that had been blurred at the edges, as if the photographer had been instructed not to capture too much context. The man's face was unmistakable even through the grain: narrow, handsome in the way some predators were handsome, eyes too bright, smile too polite.

Mengele.

The name did not need to be written. The world had done the writing for them.

Vogel stared at the photograph until she felt the faint pressure in her jaw, then turned the page quickly, as if the act of looking too long could be its own mistake.

The binder contained transcripts. Letters copied by hand. Receipts for reagents, mislabeled. A list of clinics in Buenos Aires and Córdoba and Mendoza, each with a false name beside it, each with a number of "cases" tallied like livestock. There were notes on twin births, on "mirror stability," on developmental anomalies that read less like medical observation and more like a man trying to reverse-engineer heaven with calipers.

At the bottom of one page, in a cramped, familiar script, was a line that made Vogel's stomach tighten.

Zweieinigkeit bevorzugt. Spiegelung reduziert Rauschen.

Duality preferred. Mirroring reduces noise.

It echoed what she had already learned in the lower lab, what the twins had confirmed with their divided nature: the loud one, the quiet one, one human enough to draw affection, one watchful enough to shape rooms. Mengele had not discovered it first, but he had taken it as doctrine, the way he took anything useful and turned it into an excuse.

Behind her, the window reflected Bariloche's clean sky, too bright for what she was reading. Vogel closed the binder and sat still for a full minute, listening to the ranch's ordinary sounds through the walls. A pot clinked in the kitchen. Footsteps crossed the hall. Someone laughed at something harmless.

Below, the generators hummed.

She opened the metal box.

Inside were microfilm reels in plastic sleeves and, wrapped separately in waxed paper, a single key. Not a key to a door. A key to a cabinet, perhaps, or a safe, or a drawer that had never been meant to open again.

Vogel picked it up by the edge. It was warm, as if it had been held recently.

She called down into the lower level and told the staff to maintain protocol. No visitors near the children. No unnecessary contact. She did not explain why. Explanation was another kind of attention, and attention traveled.

Then she went down herself.

The stair behind the false bookcase swallowed her into concrete cold. The lower lab smelled as it always did: antiseptic, warmed metal, the faint metallic tang that lingered near the incubators no matter how often they cleaned. The children were no longer confined to cribs. Some were kept behind glass when necessary, but most of the cohort moved through a controlled playroom, its corners rounded, its cameras hidden behind tinted panels. They were watched by adults trained to behave as if they had no inner life.

Vogel stood behind the observation glass and held Mengele's binder against her chest like an unwanted relic.

Twin 3-1 was sitting on the floor. The quiet twin. The watcher. It was older now, hair darker, eyes steady in a small face that rarely displayed what most people would call emotion. Across from it, twin 3-2 leaned against a nurse's leg, mouth open in a half laugh, a normal child's noise that sometimes soothed the staff into forgetting what normal meant.

The moment Vogel entered the corridor, twin 3-1's head turned.

Not toward the door. Toward the air. Toward the fact of her presence.

The pressure in Vogel's teeth arrived, sharp and brief. She stopped walking, not because she feared the child, but because she did not want her own hesitation to become part of a pattern the room could learn.

The nurse glanced up, then lowered her eyes quickly. "Doctor," she murmured.

"Continue," Vogel said.

Twin 3-1 watched her through the glass. Its gaze did not feel like a child's curiosity. It felt like assessment, like a mechanism checking whether a component had changed.

Vogel opened the binder on a metal table behind the glass, angled so the children could not see it clearly. She did not know if they could read yet. She did not even know what "read" meant in a world where language behaved like an interface and attention itself could be used as a tool.

One of her German technicians, Heller, approached quietly. He kept his hands in his coat pockets, a gesture he had adopted after one of the children reached for him and he felt, for days afterward, as if his thoughts were not entirely private.

"What is it," he asked.

Vogel tapped the photograph of Mengele without looking at it again. "Confirmation," she said. "And escalation."

Heller's face tightened. "He's here."

"Not here," Vogel replied. "But in the network. He has been running parallel work. Clinics. Midwives. Women paid to carry children they don't understand. He's been collecting twins."

Heller swallowed. "Like before."

"Yes," Vogel said. "Like before. Except now he believes he has found a new justification for the old appetite."

Heller leaned closer, eyes scanning the list of locations. "Some of these are near Buenos Aires."

Vogel nodded once. “Which means he has access to doctors, labs, paperwork that can disappear. He can hide in noise. We hide in isolation. Different strategies. Same purpose.”

Heller looked past Vogel to the observation glass. Twin 3-2 was laughing at something trivial, chasing a rolling ball that no one had placed there. Twin 3-1 watched the ball’s path without moving. When it reached the wall it stopped as if it had hit an obstacle that did not exist. Then it rolled back in a straight line to the child who had laughed.

Heller’s mouth went dry. “Are they doing that,” he asked.

Vogel did not answer immediately. She watched the ball’s return, the way it traced the same line as if repeating was safer than improvisation.

“They are learning what works,” she said at last, echoing her own conclusion from weeks earlicr. “And Mengele is learning from them.”

Heller’s eyebrows pulled together. “How.”

Vogel turned the binder to a page with a hand-copied letter. The German was formal, almost courteous, and beneath the courtesy was a feverish certainty.

He writes about resonance, Vogel thought. About reducing noise. About training conditions.

As if the children are instruments and the world is something you tune.

She read aloud quietly, translating only enough for Heller to follow: “He calls it doctrine. Not research. Doctrine.”

Heller flinched at the word. “Doctrine belongs to priests.”

“It belongs to anyone who wants obedience,” Vogel said. She closed the binder with a soft slap. “Mengele has always wanted obedience. From bodies. From blood. From the idea that suffering is a kind of proof.”

Heller glanced down the corridor as if expecting a man in a white coat to appear at the end of it, smiling politely, hands clean. “What does he want from us.”

Vogel looked through the glass again. Twin 3-1 had not moved, but its gaze had shifted. It was no longer watching her. It was watching the binder on the table, though it could not see the words. It was watching the object as if objects carried intention.

“Access,” Vogel said. “Samples. Data. And legitimacy. He wants to claim he is the architect of what comes next.”

Heller’s jaw tightened. “We won’t.”

Vogel did not answer with reassurance. Reassurance was a form of belief, and belief made people sloppy. Instead, she slid the binder into a drawer and locked it, then pocketed the key from the metal box without telling Heller what it fit.

"Hidden experiments," she said softly, tasting the phrase as if it were a contamination. "He's been doing them for years. Not just births. Conditioning. Exposure. He's testing the children's response to fear, to affection, to confinement."

Heller's hands clenched in his pockets. "That could destabilize them."

"That is the point," Vogel replied. "A stable miracle is a sacred object. An unstable miracle is a weapon."

Through the glass, twin 3-2 ran to the nurse and threw its arms around her waist. The nurse's face softened, the human reflex to love what clung to you. Vogel felt a cold irritation at the softness. Softness was how rooms began to respond.

Twin 3-1 rose to its feet and took one slow step toward the glass.

It placed its palm against it.

The sound was gentle. Not a slap. Not a demand. Just contact.

The pressure in Vogel's teeth flared, then steadied, like a signal finding a frequency.

Heller stepped back involuntarily, and the overhead light dimmed by a fraction and returned, as if the building itself had inhaled.

Vogel kept her expression flat. She would not perform fear. She would not teach the room what her fear looked like.

Behind the glass, the child's eyes held hers.

Not pleading.

Not threatening.

Watching.

And in that watching, Vogel understood what the binder truly meant. Mengele was not merely alive in the network. He was attempting to formalize what they were doing into a creed, to wrap it in a story sturdy enough to survive leadership changes and geographic moves. He was turning anomaly into ritual, experiment into sacrament.

He was building a gospel for the laboratory.

Vogel leaned toward Heller and lowered her voice until it was almost a breath. "We have to assume," she said, "that he has produced others. Not just here. Not just under our glass."

Heller's eyes widened slightly. "How many."

Vogel's gaze stayed on twin 3-1's hand against the glass. "Enough," she said. "Enough to create a lineage outside this ranch. Enough that, even if we burned everything we've built, the doctrine would keep walking in other bodies."

The child's palm slid down the glass a few centimeters, leaving no mark.

But the air felt marked.

Upstairs, someone called a name in Spanish, laughing. A door opened. The ranch continued its theater of ordinary life.

Down here, in concrete cold and humming power, a different theater was taking shape, one that did not need applause. It needed only repetition, only the human need to answer, only men like Mengele who believed suffering was a necessary ingredient in creation.

Vogel turned away from the glass at last and felt the ache in her teeth fade by degrees, as if distance still mattered, as if proximity was still a kind of language.

She did not feel relief.

She felt a grim clarity settle into place.

If Mengele had doctrine, then what they had was no longer merely a project.

It was a movement.

And movements did not stay hidden forever.

The key in Vogel's pocket felt heavier as the day wore on, as if metal could accumulate meaning through proximity.

She did not return upstairs. She did not need the study's clean lies or the cook's careful normality. She stayed in the lower level where the air was regulated and the hum of refrigeration never stopped, where the smell of antiseptic tried and failed to erase the faint metallic tang that clung to everything connected to the children.

At a workbench in the small records room, she threaded one of the microfilm reels into a viewer with hands that did not shake. She forced her breathing into a slow, shallow rhythm and kept her eyes from lingering on the black spaces between frames. The inhuman pages Kammler had brought back, the writing that behaved like an interface, had taught her an unpleasant rule: attention did not merely observe. Attention participated.

The first frames were shipping manifests and medical invoices, the kind of bureaucracy that gave atrocity a receipt. False clinic names in Buenos

Aires. Reagent orders. Suture kits. Sterile packs, logged as if cleanliness were the point. Then the images changed to photographs.

Women on narrow beds with their faces turned away from the camera. Infants held up by gloved hands. A series of twins photographed in identical poses, as if the photographer believed symmetry could tame the unknown. There were notes beside them, written in neat German, the handwriting so careful it looked rehearsed.

Mirror reduces noise.

Twin anomalies stable when separated at birth, reunited at first cognition.

Exposure to holy stimulus increases compliance.

Vogel's jaw tightened at that phrase.

Holy stimulus.

It was an old habit to name what you wanted to control in the language that made it seem less obscene. In Poland they had called it the Bell and spoken of physics while soldiers hallucinated the future. In Rome they had called it proof. Here, Mengele called it holy.

She advanced the reel again and found the first mention of the thing she had been dreading and expecting in equal measure.

The Source.

Not Christ, not Jesus, not any name that would have implied reverence or fear of blasphemy. The Source was clinical, proprietary. The language of a man who had spent his life treating bodies as containers and had simply upgraded the contents.

There was a diagram of a vial, the kind used for blood draws, and beside it a cross-section of tissue annotated with precise measurements. Below that, a paragraph in German that made Vogel feel the faint pressure in her teeth, an ache like an old wound remembering itself.

Material does not decay under standard conditions. Cellular division persists beyond expected limits. When placed in field proximity, expression changes, not random, responsive. Suggests adaptive memory. Not human inheritance.

She sat back slightly, letting her gaze settle on the edge of the viewer instead of the words. She could almost hear Kammler's warning from the notes she had read and re-read until the paper felt thin: not steal. create.

Mengele, it seemed, had taken creation as an instruction.

A door opened behind her with a controlled softness. Heller entered and shut it again. He carried two cups of coffee, both black, both too strong, as if bitterness could serve as armor.

"You've been here for hours," he said quietly.

Vogel took the cup but did not drink. The coffee smell mixed with antiseptic and made her think, absurdly, of Rome mornings and Orsini's lamp and the way decrees were written in the same calm tone as prayers.

"Mengele is not chasing miracles," she said.

Heller's eyes flicked to the viewer. "He's building them."

"No," Vogel corrected, and the word came out sharper than she intended. She softened her voice. "He's manufacturing a lineage. He is taking what was supposed to be proof and turning it into stock."

Heller's mouth tightened. "He always did that. With twins."

"Twins were methodology," Vogel said. "This is theology, and he has translated it into a production plan."

She rewound the reel to a section marked with a handwritten number. The images that followed were not photographs. They were pages, filmed from a binder like the one she had received. The writing was Mengele's. She recognized the precision, the arrogant neatness that wanted to make cruelty look like discipline.

There were headings.

Doctrine of Replication.

Conditions of Divinity.

Failure Modes.

Heller leaned closer, and Vogel felt him hesitate as if proximity to the words could stain him.

"What does he mean," he asked, "divinity. He cannot believe in it."

Vogel watched the microfilmed text shift into clarity. "Belief is not required," she said. "Only utility."

She read aloud, translating as she went, because Heller needed the content but she did not want him to study the phrasing too long, did not want the words to settle in his mind the way hymns settled in Estela's throat without permission.

"Divinity is not a spirit," she murmured. "It is an instruction set. It propagates through flesh when flesh is made receptive. The crucifixion was not only an event, it was a transmission."

Heller exhaled once, short and sharp. "That's insane."

"It is coherent," Vogel replied, and hated herself for the honesty. "Which is worse."

She advanced again.

Mengele's doctrine continued in the same tone, as if writing a lecture to students who would inherit his work. He described the Source material as if it were yeast. A catalyst that could be introduced into a host genome, coaxed to express, then refined through selection. He wrote about failures, about infants who "collapsed into ordinary mortality," and he wrote about successes with a cold pride that made Vogel's skin prickle.

Successes were not merely living children.

Successes were behaviors.

Calming rooms. Inducing compliance. Stopping bleeding. Quieting sound.

Making the world respond.

Vogel felt the pressure in her teeth intensify for a moment, then ease, a pulse that did not correlate with fear so much as with recognition. It was as if the environment itself reacted when she came too close to the idea that the children were not only anomalous bodies, but nodes in something larger.

She reached the end of one section and stopped.

A single sentence had been underlined twice, the only visible emotion in the otherwise controlled script.

Divine replication requires a witness.

Heller frowned. “A witness.”

Vogel nodded slowly. “He understands what Kammler understood,” she said. “That observation is not neutral. It is an ingredient.”

She could not help thinking of Father Ferretti refusing to answer, mouth closed, eyes careful, because he suspected that response itself was a hook. The Church had ordered him erased not because he lacked loyalty, but because he had become a witness.

Mengele wanted witnesses, but not for testimony.

For effect.

The doctrine continued below the underlined sentence.

Witness must be conditioned. Fear is useful but destabilizing. Affection increases binding. Ritual reduces resistance. Use familiar forms. Hymn, prayer, touch. Create obedience without coercion. The subject must choose compliance.

Vogel's fingers tightened around the coffee cup until heat pressed into her palm. "He is building liturgy," she said quietly.

Heller's face went pale. "For them."

"For the world around them," Vogel replied. "The children don't need ritual. People do. Ritual makes surrender feel voluntary."

Heller looked toward the door, as if he could hear the children through concrete. "What does he want us to do."

Vogel reached into her pocket and put the small metal key on the table between them. It landed with a neat sound, too crisp for the weight it carried.

"This came with the microfilm," she said.

Heller stared at it. "What does it open."

"I don't know yet," Vogel replied. "But Mengele doesn't send keys as gifts. He sends them as invitations."

Heller did not touch it. Good, Vogel thought. Touch was also attention. She was glad he had learned that much.

She returned to the viewer and advanced to the last segment on the reel. The frames revealed a label, filmed at close range.

CÓRDOBA STORAGE. CABINET 12.

Under the label was a sketched outline of a cabinet door and a lock. The lock matched the key's cut.

Heller swallowed. "So, he has something stored."

"Yes," Vogel said. "And he wants us to retrieve it, or he wants us to know he can make us retrieve it."

She rewound and watched the cabinet sketch again. Cabinet 12. A physical location. A trail. A choice.

Heller's voice lowered. "It could be more Source material."

Vogel's eyes stayed on the viewer. "Or it could be something worse," she said. "A refinement. A variant. Evidence that he has already succeeded elsewhere."

Heller hesitated. "If we go, we expose ourselves."

"If we do nothing," Vogel replied, "we let his doctrine spread without friction."

She stood and walked to the small window cut into the adjacent observation corridor. From there she could see into the children's playroom. The toddlers moved with their quiet deliberation, their games still without toys, their attention still too focused. Twin 3-2 was sitting on a nurse's lap, laughing at a private joke that had not been spoken aloud. Twin 3-1 stood a short distance away, watching them with an expression that was neither envy nor cruelty, only study.

As Vogel watched, the nurse's laughter softened and slowed, becoming almost sleepy. Her shoulders dropped. Her face relaxed in a way that looked like relief but made Vogel's stomach clench.

Compliance without orders.

Vogel turned her head slightly to keep twin 3-1 in her peripheral vision rather than directly in her gaze. She did not want to lock eyes. She did not want to teach it what confrontation looked like.

Heller came to stand beside her, hands still in his pockets. "They can feel you," he said.

"They can feel anyone," Vogel replied. "Mengele is trying to turn that into a system. He thinks divinity can be replicated the way bacteria can be cultured."

Heller's mouth twisted. "Can it."

Vogel's answer took too long, and she hated that it did.

"We have already replicated something," she said at last. "We have children behind glass who make the air behave differently. We have shadows that settle late. We have grown adults humming hymns they haven't remembered in decades."

She picked up the key again and closed her fingers around it.

"But that doesn't mean we replicated Christ," she continued, voice low enough that even the corridor's cameras could not pretend to hear. "It means we replicated an effect. An instruction. A thing that responds to attention and uses familiarity to make itself welcome."

Heller stared at the children and spoke with a careful dread. "So, Mengele's doctrine is wrong."

Vogel shook her head once. "No," she said. "That's what scares me. It's not wrong enough."

The pressure in her teeth returned, brief and sharp, and in the playroom twin 3-1's head turned slightly, as if the ache had been a signal it could read.

Vogel forced her jaw to relax. She would not perform fear. She would not give the room the satisfaction of a learned reaction.

She kept her eyes on the glass and let the truth settle into the only form that mattered: a plan.

If divine replication required a witness, then Mengele would create witnesses until the world itself became a choir trained to respond. He would use prayer as conditioning, affection as restraint, ritual as a cage that people stepped into willingly.

And somewhere, in Córdoba, behind cabinet 12, he had stored something he wanted the movement to inherit.

Vogel slipped the key back into her pocket and turned away from the observation window.

"We go," she said.

Heller's eyes widened. "To Córdoba."

"To see what he thinks is worth locking away," Vogel replied. "And to learn how far his doctrine has already traveled."

She paused at the door and glanced back once more at the playroom.

Twin 3-1 was watching her now through the corridor glass, not smiling, not pleading, not threatening. Just watching, patient and unblinking, as if it understood that every decision made in this facility would eventually become part of its world.

Vogel opened the door and stepped out into the hum of the lower level, the key warm against her leg, the microfilm's words still etched into her mind.

Divine replication requires a witness.

She had spent years believing the danger was the sample itself, the tissue that did not decay, the blood that behaved like a material rather than a relic.

Now she understood the more precise horror.

The danger was not what they had in vials.

It was what the world became when men like Mengele taught it how to answer.

They left at dusk, because leaving at dawn looked like urgency and urgency left a trail.

Vogel wore a plain wool coat and kept her hair pinned back the way she always did, as if the severity were camouflage rather than habit. Heller drove, hands steady on the wheel, his face turned into something neutral enough to pass through checkpoints that existed more in memory than law. The car was not theirs. Nothing on the ranch was truly theirs, not even their names.

Bariloche fell away behind them in a slow dissolve of pine and lake and clean mountain air. The road east flattened, the sky widened, and Patagonia became what it always pretended to be: empty. Vogel watched the horizon and tried not to think of the children under the ranch, sealed behind reinforced glass, learning the world by watching adults pretend they were not afraid.

In the back seat, wrapped in oilcloth and tucked beneath a spare tire, the microfilm reels rode like a second heart. In her coat pocket, the key warmed against her thigh with each vibration of the road.

Heller did not speak for a long time. When he finally did, his voice was quiet and controlled, as if he were afraid sound might carry farther than it should.

"If this is a trap," he said, "it is a clever one."

Vogel kept her eyes on the road's pale ribbon. "It doesn't need to be clever," she replied. "It only needs to be inevitable."

Heller's jaw tightened. "You think he wants us to find it."

"I think he wants us to choose to find it," Vogel said. "Doctrine requires participation. He wrote that himself."

They drove through the night, stopping only once at a roadside station where the coffee tasted like metal and the attendant stared too long at Vogel's accent when she asked for change. Heller bought cigarettes he did not smoke, because buying nothing looked suspicious. Vogel watched their reflections in the station's dark window and did not let her gaze settle on the shape of her shadow beneath the fluorescent lights. She had learned, in

Poland and then through years of secondhand reports, that some patterns sharpened when you tried to measure them.

At a bend in the road near Río Colorado, Heller rubbed his jaw briefly and then dropped his hand as if embarrassed.

“My teeth,” he muttered.

Vogel did not look at him. “Don’t start counting,” she said.

He gave a short, humorless exhale. “I wasn’t.”

The ache passed. The car kept going.

By the time Córdoba’s outskirts appeared, the sun was up and the city wore its morning noise like a mask: buses, shouted greetings, metal shutters opening, street vendors setting up crates. It was ordinary. That ordinariness made Vogel’s skin crawl.

Mengele had always preferred ordinary surfaces. Ordinary surfaces made extraordinary acts easier to deny.

They parked three streets away from the address embedded in the microfilm label, in a neighborhood that looked neither wealthy nor desperate, the kind of middle that discouraged questions. A clinic sat on the corner with peeling paint and a hand-lettered sign advertising vaccinations and prenatal care.

Next to it was a narrower building with barred windows and a locksmith's shop on the ground floor.

"Cabinet storage," Heller said, reading the street the way he read instruments. "It fits."

Vogel adjusted her coat and stepped out into the heat. Córdoba was warmer than Bariloche, heavier, as if the air carried more human breath. She walked beside Heller, not too close, not too far, two strangers aligned by coincidence rather than intent.

Inside the locksmith's shop the smell of oil and metal was sharp enough to sting. A man with thick fingers and a graying mustache looked up from a workbench. His gaze moved over them with the slow caution of someone whose business depended on not being surprised.

"Estamos cerrados," he said automatically. Closed.

Vogel did not answer in Spanish. She answered in the flattest German she could manage, because language itself could be a test.

"I need cabinet twelve."

The man's eyes narrowed. For a fraction of a second something like recognition flickered, then vanished behind practiced blankness. He wiped his hands on a rag and gestured toward a door behind the counter.

“No tools back there,” he said in Spanish, for anyone listening through walls. Then, quieter, in accented German that sounded learned rather than native: “You’re late.”

Vogel did not correct him. In a world of hidden routes, late was often another word for alive.

The back room held a narrow corridor and a second locked door. No sign. No name. The kind of door that existed to make plausible deniability easy. Heller stood slightly behind Vogel, eyes scanning corners.

The locksmith produced a key ring and began to unlock the door. Vogel stopped him with a small movement of her hand.

“I have it,” she said.

The man hesitated, then stepped aside.

Vogel took the small metal key from her pocket. It looked harmless. It was not. She inserted it into the lock and turned.

The click was clean, too smooth, as if the mechanism had been oiled recently in anticipation. The door opened into a room lined with tall metal cabinets, each numbered in black paint. The air inside smelled of dust and paper and a faint chemical sweetness that reminded Vogel unpleasantly of the lower lab's antiseptic.

Cabinet 12 stood in the back row.

For a moment Vogel did not move. She listened.

The building's hum was ordinary: distant street noise, the faint vibration of a refrigerator somewhere, the creak of a ceiling fan. Nothing else. No footsteps. No voices. No obvious trap.

Heller stepped in beside her and shut the door behind them. The sound was small but final.

Vogel walked to cabinet 12 and placed her palm against the cold metal, not because she believed in sensing danger through touch, but because the gesture kept her hands steady. She slid the key into the cabinet's lock.

Heller's voice dropped. "If this is what he calls The Source…"

"It won't be that simple," Vogel said. "He doesn't give away origins. He gives away leverage."

She turned the key. The cabinet opened.

Inside were three things.

A stack of files, tied neatly with string, each file marked with a number instead of a name.

A padded metal case holding vials, the glass dark, the caps sealed with wax that had been stamped with a symbol Vogel did not recognize: not a cross, not an SS rune, but something geometric that looked uncomfortably like a simplified bell outline.

And, beneath those, a small reel-to-reel tape recorder wrapped in cloth.

Heller stared at the tape recorder as if it were the most frightening item of all. "Sound," he said quietly.

Vogel felt the faintest pressure in her teeth and forced her jaw to loosen. "Ritual," she corrected. "He's making a liturgy you can carry."

She pulled out the first file and opened it.

The paper inside was clean and clinical. Photographs, dated. Measurements. Observations. The first page showed a child, perhaps eight years old, sitting on a bed with hands folded, gaze turned slightly away from the camera. The child's face was ordinary enough to be missed on a street. The eyes were not.

They were too calm. Too aware of being observed.

The next photograph showed a second child, similar age, similar face structure. The caption beneath them was in German.

Pairing successful. Mirroring reduces noise. Subject A draws affection. Subject B enforces compliance.

Vogel felt cold settle behind her ribs.

“It’s our twins,” Heller whispered.

“No,” Vogel replied, flipping to the next pages. “It’s his.”

The files were full of them. Not one cohort. Several. Children photographed in pairs, children photographed alone. The locations stamped in the margins were not all Córdoba. Buenos Aires. Rosario. Mendoza. A few references to Europe, names of ports and a clinic in Spain.

Mengele had been building an archipelago of hidden nurseries, connected by routes that moved not only men and paperwork but doctrine.

Heller reached for one of the files and stopped himself halfway, as if remembering that touch was a kind of attention. “How many,” he asked.

Vogel did not answer with a number. The number would have been a lie anyway, because what mattered was not quantity. It was distribution.

She opened another file. The photograph showed a teenage girl this time, perhaps thirteen, standing in a plain room. Her hair was braided. Her posture was straight with the brittle discipline of someone trained to be watched. There was a small cut on her forearm in the second photograph. In the third photograph the cut was gone.

Bled. Healed. Controlled. No scar.

Underneath, Mengele's handwriting noted: Healing response escalates under witness condition. Use familiar prayer to stabilize.

Vogel's mouth tightened. "He's not only breeding anomalies," she said. "He's teaching them how to perform."

A faint sound came from somewhere beyond the cabinet room, so subtle it might have been imagined: a small scrape, like a chair leg shifting on tile.

Heller froze. Vogel held her breath without meaning to, then forced herself to exhale slowly. Panic was a language. She would not speak it.

The locksmith's shop was silent. The street noise continued outside like a river flowing past a sealed door.

Then the scrape came again, closer.

Heller's eyes flicked toward the cabinet room door. "We're not alone," he said.

Vogel closed the file and slid it back into the cabinet, not because she was finished, but because she had learned that lingering was an invitation. She reached for the padded metal case of vials. It was heavier than it should have been. She did not open it yet.

"We take what we can carry," she said. "We leave nothing that forces us into a scene."

Heller nodded, already moving to lift the tape recorder. The cloth around it slipped slightly, and Vogel saw the tape label.

A hymn title, written in careful German script.

Not sacred music as comfort. Sacred music as conditioning.

The scrape beyond the door became a footstep.

Then another.

Slow. Unhurried. As if whoever approached did not fear being stopped.

Vogel's teeth ached, sharp and brief. Not fear this time. Recognition. The building's air seemed to thicken by a fraction, the way the lower lab's air changed when the children fixed their attention on an object.

Mengele's doctrine returned to her in a line she had read aloud only hours earlier.

Divine replication requires a witness.

She had assumed he meant adults.

The footsteps stopped outside the cabinet room.

A voice spoke in Spanish, young and soft, so ordinary it would have been harmless anywhere else.

"Hola," it said, as if greeting family.

Heller went pale. "A child," he whispered.

Vogel's hands tightened around the metal case until her knuckles hurt. In her mind she saw twin 3-1 behind glass in Bariloche, palm resting against the panel, watching as if learning what doors were. She saw the nurse's face slacken into compliance. She saw Estela humming a hymn she hadn't remembered in years.

A new breed, Mengele's files suggested, did not begin and end under their ranch.

It walked.

It traveled on routes made of attention and ritual. It waited behind ordinary doors. It used familiar greetings to make the world answer.

The cabinet room door handle moved slightly, a gentle test.

Vogel leaned close to Heller and kept her voice low enough that it was nearly breath. “Do not respond,” she said. “Not to it. Not to anything it says. If it uses your name, you do not answer.”

Heller’s eyes were wide, but his hands were steady. “It doesn’t know my name,” he whispered.

Vogel did not look at the door. She did not want the impulse to measure shadows or angles. “It doesn’t need to,” she said. “It only needs you to behave like someone who can be spoken to.”

Outside, the voice spoke again, still soft, still polite, as if it had all the time in the world.

“Doctor Vogel,” it said, in careful German.

Heller flinched as if struck.

Vogel felt the pressure in her teeth flare, then settle into a cold, steady ache.

Mengele’s invitation was not only a key.

It was a meeting.

And whatever stood outside that door had not learned her name from paperwork alone.

It had learned it the way the children learned everything now: by listening for the moment the world revealed itself and then stepping into that revelation as if it belonged there.

Vogel lifted the metal case of vials and held it close. She did not answer the voice. She did not grant it the simplest human courtesy of acknowledgment.

But in the silence, she understood with brutal clarity that the doctrine had already succeeded.

The new breed did not need to be smuggled in crates or hidden under ranches forever.

It could be placed in a city and taught how to knock.

Chapter 18

The New Gospel

Vogel kept her mouth closed and her eyes on the cabinet's interior, as if the files were the only reality in the room.

Outside the door, the young voice waited with the patience of something that had never been punished for waiting.

"Doctor Vogel," it repeated, gently. The German was careful, nearly accentless, as if the speaker had learned the language from a mouth that demanded correctness. "You have my property."

Heller's fingers tightened around the cloth-wrapped tape recorder. His throat worked. Vogel heard the smallest sound of it, the instinctive human preparation to speak, to answer a claim with denial or defiance, to negotiate.

She leaned closer to him without looking away from the cabinet and breathed, almost soundless, "Do not."

The door handle moved again, not forcing, just testing the mechanism the way a child tested a toy to learn where it resisted.

Vogel slid the top stack of numbered files deeper into the cabinet with a single smooth motion and closed the metal door without locking it, as if the action were merely tidying. She shifted the padded case of vials into the crook of her arm and let her other hand hover near her coat pocket where a small pistol lay cold and unconvincing. A gun was a language these things did not have to respect.

The locksmith had left them in here and shut the outer corridor door. That had been the arrangement. Give them privacy. Maintain deniability. It meant there was only one way out now, and it went through the voice.

The voice spoke again, softer, almost conversational. "I know you were told not to answer. That is an old rule. It belonged to frightened men."

Vogel felt her teeth ache, sharp and brief, then settle into a steady pressure. The ache had become a kind of weather report in her body. It said: attention is near. It said: something is leaning into the room.

A third sound joined the voice, faint but unmistakable. Bare feet on tile. One step, then another, positioned close to the door as if the speaker had placed itself there and was now listening to the humans breathe.

Heller's eyes flicked toward Vogel, pleading without words for instruction.

Vogel turned her head just enough to see him in her peripheral vision and shook her head once. Small. Final. No response.

From the corridor, the child's tone changed, losing its polite warmth and gaining a practiced cadence, as if reciting something memorized.

"Mengele taught that the world cannot be taken by force for long," it said. "Force makes enemies. Enemies make stories. Stories make resistance."

A pause, and then, with quiet satisfaction, "But worship makes a cage people enter willingly."

Heller went very still, as if the air had thickened around his lungs.

So, Vogel thought. It wasn't simply here to retrieve the vials or the files. It was here to deliver the doctrine.

Not a trap. A sermon.

She forced herself to focus on details that kept her human: the smell of dust in the cabinet room; the faint oil tang seeping from the locksmith's shop through the walls; the texture of the cloth around the tape recorder. Grounding was a defense. If attention was a component, then so was discipline.

The voice continued, almost pleased to hear no interruption. "You are not his enemy," it said. "You are his continuation. Your children in Bariloche are only late."

Vogel's jaw tightened. The words landed with an accuracy that was not guesswork. It knew about the ranch. It knew about the cohort beneath the cattle and pine trees. It knew about twin 3-1's watching, about the way rooms softened and complied.

It had either been told, or it had learned by the same mechanism the children used to learn everything now: by listening for the moment the world revealed itself.

"What he built," the voice said, "is not a laboratory. It is a ladder."

A small sound like fabric moving, as if the speaker had leaned in close enough that its breath might reach the door's edge. "The old Reich wanted territory. That was childish. Territory is a map. A map can be redrawn. This is not a map. This is ascent."

Vogel felt the urge, fierce and stupid, to demand its name. Not out of courtesy. Out of the old human belief that naming something reduced it.

Names were handles.

It wanted her to reach for it.

She tightened her grip on the padded metal case until her forearm muscles burned and let the pain anchor her.

From the corridor the voice shifted again, leaving recitation and returning to intimacy, as if it could sense the shape of their silence and was adjusting its tool.

"Do you know why he called it The Source?" it asked. "Because people argue about God. They do not argue about sources. A source is a thing you can own."

Vogel's mind flashed to Rome, to the phrase Ferretti had carried like a wound: proof is not for belief. Proof is for ownership. She had never met him, and yet she felt, in the pressure behind her teeth, the same chain linking the Vatican vault to this cabinet room. Different institutions. Same hunger.

The voice continued. "The Church wanted proof so it could close the world's mouth. America wanted copies so it could keep its hands clean while holding the same power. Mengele wanted something more honest."

Heller's eyes narrowed slightly at that, as if even now some part of him wanted to reject the idea of honesty in a monster.

The child outside the door sounded almost amused. "He wanted heirs."

The handle moved once more. The door did not open. The movement was not a break-in. It was a reminder: I can try whenever I like. You will flinch whenever I like.

Vogel's teeth ache spiked, and then she felt something else beneath it, something she had only experienced twice before: a gentle pull at her attention, like a hook catching fabric.

Not a command.

An invitation to look.

She stared at the cabinet's blank metal face and refused the pull with the same stubbornness she used against panic. She would not let her gaze slide to the floor. She would not look for a shadow, would not measure angles, would not give the room a reaction it could store and reuse.

The voice softened. "He said you were practical," it said. "He said you understand function. You keep your children behind glass and call them numbers. That is good. It means you do not lie to yourself."

Vogel tasted bitterness in her mouth and realized her tongue had pressed hard against her teeth. She forced it to relax.

Outside, the child began to speak again in that memorized cadence. Now it sounded less like persuasion and more like reciting an oath.

"The Doctrine of Ascendancy," it said.

Heller's breath hitched. The phrase was clean, formal. A title. A thing meant to be written at the top of a page and repeated until it became a reflex.

The child continued, and with each line the air in the cabinet room seemed to adjust, not in temperature or pressure, but in mood, as if the building itself was listening and learning the rhythm.

"First: Divinity is a pattern. It can be induced."

"Second: The pattern does not require faith. It requires witness."

"Third: The witness must be guided. Ritual is guidance."

"Fourth: Miracles are not gifts. They are demonstrations. Demonstrations create submission."

"Fifth: Submission is the doorway. Through it, the world becomes receptive."

A pause, then, more quietly, as if savoring the final line. "Sixth: The receptive world will call us holy. And when it does, it will no longer be able to call us human."

Vogel felt, with cold clarity, what the doctrine was designed to do. It did not merely explain their abilities. It positioned those abilities as a hierarchy, a staircase: from anomaly to miracle, from miracle to worship, from worship to rule.

Not political rule. Existential rule. A rewrite of what the word human meant.

The child outside the door spoke again, almost tender. "This is why you were always going to come here," it said. "You cannot resist a locked cabinet. You cannot resist a key. You cannot resist the urge to know."

Vogel's fingers tightened around the tape recorder's cloth for a moment, surprising herself. She did not want the recorder. She wanted the vials. But the recorder mattered because it was portable ritual. A liturgy that could be played in any room. A voice that could be broadcast into the minds of people trained since childhood to soften when they heard prayer.

A gospel you could press into someone's hands.

The voice continued. "You have his vials now. That is your proof of participation. He wanted you marked. He wanted you carrying."

Vogel's skin prickled. The words were too precise. She thought of the padded case's weight, of the wax seals stamped with that bell-like symbol and felt as if she had been made into a courier for something more than material.

It was doctrine made physical: take the source, carry it, become invested in it.

Heller's gaze darted to the door again, and this time Vogel saw a reflection on the cabinet's metal surface: a sliver of the corridor light under the door, and within it, the faint shape of small feet positioned close enough that the toes nearly touched the gap.

The child was right there.

Listening.

Waiting for them to do what humans always did when confronted by a voice using their language: answer.

Vogel lowered her chin slightly and whispered, for Heller alone, "When we move, we do it fast. No speech."

He swallowed and gave the smallest nod.

Outside, the voice spoke again, and now the politeness returned fully, as if the sermon had simply been an introduction.

"Open the door," it said. "Let me see what you have taken. You do not need to fear. We are not here to punish."

A pause, and then, with gentle certainty that made Vogel's stomach turn, "We are here to elevate."

The word landed with the same function as a hymn hummed by accident: familiarity offered as a tool.

Vogel did not answer. But she understood the shape of what was rising around them.

Mengele's work had not been only clinics and hidden births. It had been language. It had been doctrine designed to turn anomalous children into a priesthood and ordinary people into an audience trained to surrender. The New Gospel was not written on paper alone. It was spoken at doors. It was carried on tape. It was encoded into rituals that made compliance feel like relief.

And in that moment, with the padded case heavy in her arm and a child's bare feet inches from the threshold, Vogel saw the true purpose of ascendancy.

It was not to become God.

It was to make the world ask you to.

The door handle turned slowly from the other side, not forcing, just demonstrating control. The latch clicked, not fully disengaging, but enough to make Heller flinch.

Vogel tightened her grip on the vials and prepared to move, silent and decisive, because the only defense she had left was the oldest one.

Refuse the invitation.

Do not answer.

Do not become the witness it wanted.

Vogel moved first.

Not toward the door. Not toward the cabinet. Toward Heller, closing the small distance between them so she could guide him without speaking. She shifted the padded case of vials higher against her ribs, the way you carried something fragile through a crowd, and with her free hand she took the tape recorder from Heller's grip by the cloth, careful not to let the bare machine touch her skin. Touch was attention. Attention was participation.

Heller's eyes were fixed on the thin bar of corridor light beneath the cabinet-room door. The small feet were still there, toes nearly aligned with the gap as if the child outside had positioned itself to feel the room's breath.

The handle turned again from the other side, slow and patient. It was not forcing entry. It was teaching them the rhythm of inevitability.

Vogel leaned close enough that her breath warmed Heller's ear and gave him the only instruction she could risk. "Now," she said, the word barely a vibration.

Heller's shoulders tightened. He nodded once.

They did not open the door.

They opened the cabinet-room window instead.

Not a window in the wall, a window in the plan: a narrow maintenance panel set into the back corner, half hidden behind cabinet 14, the kind of access that existed for wiring and cleaning and men who needed to believe there was always another way out. Vogel had seen it when she entered, had filed it away without looking at it too long. If the doctrine required witness, then even noticing exits too eagerly could become part of the lesson.

She slid her fingers into the panel's recessed latch and pulled. Metal rasped softly. The sound felt too loud in the small room, and for a moment she was certain the child outside would react the way the twins under the ranch reacted to any shift in attention.

The corridor beyond the panel was dark and smelled of old plaster and oil. It ran behind the cabinets like a spine behind ribs.

Heller hesitated, gaze darting back to the door as if his body wanted to verify whether the child had heard. Verification was exactly what the thing outside wanted.

Vogel did not allow the hesitation to settle. She pushed the tape recorder through first, then the padded case, then slid her own shoulders into the narrow opening. Heller followed, breath tight, moving with the careful urgency of a man trying not to make his fear into a signal.

Behind them, from the cabinet room, the door handle stopped moving.

Silence.

Then the child's voice came through the metal, no longer polite, no longer warm. Still soft, still controlled, but stripped of the theatrical tenderness.

"You refuse elevation," it said, in German that carried no accent at all. "You refuse the role that makes you useful."

Vogel did not answer. She did not even let her face change, because she had begun to suspect these things read not only words but the small movements that preceded words. The way a throat prepared to speak. The way a jaw clenched. The way fear tried to become visible.

The corridor behind the cabinets narrowed and then widened into a small service room filled with pipes and dust. A second door led out into the locksmith's back corridor. Vogel tested it and found it unlocked.

The locksmith was nowhere in sight.

That absence was not reassuring. It was confirmation of orchestration. Mengele had not left them a key and a cabinet to stumble upon. He had left a stage.

They stepped into the back corridor and moved quickly, still silent, toward the outer shop. Vogel's eyes stayed forward. She resisted the urge to scan for shadows, for reflections, for anything that would turn this into a scene they could not stop replaying in their minds.

The locksmith's shop looked normal, oil-smeared and cramped, its front door open to the street. A customer stood at the counter, a woman holding a bag of vegetables, speaking in rapid

Spanish about a broken lock. The locksmith himself leaned forward and nodded as if listening.

His posture was too careful. His hands were too still.

Vogel registered, with a cold certainty, that he was pretending for the woman's benefit. He was performing ordinariness the way the ranch performed ordinariness, the way Rome performed holiness.

The woman's voice rose, impatient. She wanted to be heard.

The locksmith's gaze flicked toward the back corridor, just for a fraction of a second. Not a look of warning. A look of apology.

Vogel and Heller stepped out anyway, becoming, in the woman's peripheral vision, just two customers leaving a back room. They did not hurry. They did not act like prey. They moved with the measured pace of people who belonged.

The heat of Córdoba hit them like a hand. Sunlight made the street look too sharp, too real, and for a moment Vogel felt something inside her relax at the ordinary chaos: traffic, shouting, the smell of exhaust and bread.

Then she heard it.

Not behind her. Not on the street. Inside the tape recorder in her hands, as if the machine had become eager.

A faint clicking, the spools shifting in their housing.

Heller heard it too. His head turned slightly toward the cloth-wrapped device, a reflexive glance.

Vogel tightened her grip and hissed, low and harsh, "No." Not as an answer to a voice, but as an order to Heller's instinct. "Do not look."

His eyes returned forward.

They reached the car without running. Heller unlocked it and opened the doors. Vogel put the padded case under the seat, not in the trunk where it could be searched easily, and wedged the tape recorder beside it. The microfilm remained wrapped and hidden. Nothing visible. No proof in the open.

Heller slid behind the wheel and started the engine.

As they pulled away from the curb, Vogel did what she had been avoiding since the cabinet room. She allowed herself one glance into the side mirror.

In the shop doorway, framed by hanging keychains and metal tools, stood a child.

Small, barefoot, wearing a pale shirt and dark shorts as ordinary as any summer clothing. Its hair was combed neatly. Its posture was straight with a discipline that did not belong to childhood. The locksmith stood behind it with his hands on the counter, face blank, eyes lowered.

The child did not wave.

It did not smile.

It simply watched the car recede as if watching were a kind of possession.

Vogel looked away and kept her face forward, refusing the mirror the way she refused the interface-like script. Refusing did not erase what she had seen, but it denied the child the satisfaction of being acknowledged as an actor in their minds.

Heller drove two blocks in silence before he spoke, voice low, German clipped by fear he was trying to disguise as professionalism.

“It used your name,” he said.

Vogel kept her hands in her lap to stop them from shaking. They did not shake anyway. “Yes,” she replied.

“How,” he demanded, and then caught himself as if the question itself was dangerous. “How does it know.”

"Mengele," Vogel said. "Or the mechanism. Or both."

Heller's jaw worked as if he were chewing on something bitter. "It spoke like a priest."

"It spoke like doctrine," Vogel corrected. "That's the point. The New Gospel isn't only a justification for what they are. It is an instruction for how the world should respond to them."

Heller's knuckles whitened on the steering wheel. "Ascendancy," he said. "Elevation. Worship."

Vogel leaned her head back against the seat and closed her eyes for one second, only one, and saw twin 3-1's palm against the glass in Bariloche, the way the nurse's laughter had softened into something like surrender. She thought of Estela humming her grandmother's hymn. Familiarity offered as a tool. Ritual as guidance.

"They're taking the old human habit," Vogel said, "and weaponizing it."

"What habit," Heller asked.

She opened her eyes and watched the street ahead, the traffic, the pedestrians, the ordinary people whose lives still belonged to ordinary fears. "The habit of kneeling," she said. "And the habit of wanting someone else to be responsible for the impossible."

Heller swallowed. "You mean God."

"I mean the role," Vogel said. "They are replacing the role."

The words from the child at the door returned with a clarity that felt like contamination. A receptive world will call us holy. It will no longer be able to call us human.

Vogel kept her voice steady. "This is the part Mengele understands better than the Church ever did," she said. "The Vatican thought proof would consolidate belief under their control. They believed ownership of evidence could make them unchallengeable."

Heller glanced at her. "And it couldn't."

"Because proof doesn't end hunger," Vogel replied. "It redirects it."

They passed the clinic on the corner again, now farther away. A pregnant woman stood outside holding paperwork. A nurse spoke to her gently and touched her arm in reassurance. A simple gesture, ordinary, human.

Vogel felt the ache in her teeth try to rise and forced her jaw to unclench.

"This is the new gospel," she said. "Not that God became man. That man becomes God."

Heller let out a short, incredulous breath. "That's blasphemy."

"It's strategy," Vogel said. "If you tell people you are divine, you create resistance. People argue, deny, fight. But if you demonstrate something they have been taught to associate with divinity, healing, miracles, knowledge that shouldn't exist, and you let them draw their own conclusion, the surrender feels like their idea."

Heller stared at the road. "So, the doctrine isn't for the children."

"It's for everyone around them," Vogel said. "A script for the witness."

Her gaze dropped toward the space under the seat where the tape recorder and the vials were hidden. She could almost feel the machine's weight through the floorboard. A portable sermon. A liturgy in spooled magnetic tape. Something that could be played in a room and make the room behave.

"Mengele isn't only breeding anomalies," she continued. "He's breeding interpretation. Training people to read their abilities as holiness. Training them to call it salvation. And once people call it salvation, they will accept anything done in its name."

Heller's voice was rough. "And the children. Do they believe it."

Vogel remembered the child in the doorway, the calm, the patience, the way it said property without shame.

"They don't need to believe," she said. "Belief is for humans who are trying to make sense of pain. They're beyond that. They're learning function. How to move through the world without force. How to make doors open because someone wants to open them."

Heller drove faster now, not reckless, just eager to put distance between their bodies and that cabinet room. "What do we do," he asked.

Vogel did not answer immediately, because answering felt too much like promising control.

Outside, Córdoba continued to shine in the sun, full of people who did not know they had already been included in someone else's doctrine.

Vogel's voice, when it came, was quiet and cold. "We go back," she said. "And we stop thinking of this as a project under a ranch."

Heller looked at her sharply. "What is it then."

Vogel stared ahead, past traffic lights and storefronts, past the world as it was, toward the world the doctrine wanted to build.

"A religion," she said. "With laboratories instead of cathedrals. With miracles that can be repeated. With witnesses trained to surrender."

She felt, for the first time since the Black Forest reports she had read in secret, the shape of the true ambition. Not survival. Not escape. Not even revenge for a lost war.

Replacement.

Humanity as God was not a philosophy. It was a takeover of the oldest human reflex: the desire to bow before power and call it meaning.

And now, because they had opened cabinet 12 and carried away its contents, Vogel understood they had been drafted into the gospel whether they wanted it or not.

Not as believers.

As witnesses.

Heller kept them on highways longer than necessary, then took smaller roads when the sun began to tilt west, as if distance could be bought in kilometers and turns. He drove with the rigid caution of a man trying to hold his fear in his wrists. Vogel watched the landscape flatten into scrub and field and the long straight lines that made Argentina feel, for hours at a time, like a country built for forgetting.

They did not speak about the child in the locksmith's doorway. Naming it too often felt like summoning the texture of its voice back into the car. The silence between them was not peace. It was discipline.

When they stopped for fuel outside Villa María, Vogel went inside the station alone and bought a bottle of water and a packet of crackers she did not want. The cashier looked at her passport, then at her face, and smiled with the bored kindness of a man who saw travelers all day.

"Buen viaje," he said.

Good trip.

Vogel nodded and walked out with the items in her hands, and as she crossed the forecourt she felt, faintly, the pressure in her teeth begin and then vanish, like a weather vane twitching in a wind that hadn't reached ground level. She did not turn. She did not look for reflections. She got into the car and shut the door with a controlled click.

Heller glanced at her. "Did you feel that," he asked quietly.

"No," Vogel said, and meant: do not make it true by agreeing.

They reached Bariloche on the third night after Córdoba, arriving before dawn when the ranch still wore darkness like a blanket. The gate opened after the familiar pause, the unseen assessment. The compound looked the same: the veranda, the radio antenna, the windows reflecting nothing. Cattle shifted in the pasture, indifferent. Somewhere upstairs in the house, a kettle began to whistle and then was silenced.

The normality held for exactly as long as it took Vogel to step through the hidden bookcase and descend into the lower level.

The hum of refrigeration welcomed her like a confession. Lights came on in narrow strips. The antiseptic smell met her, and beneath it, that faint metallic tang that never left, as if the walls themselves had been exposed to a substance that rewrote what metal meant.

Heller carried the microfilm and the tape recorder down with care. Vogel carried the padded case of vials as if it could bruise through her ribs.

The children were awake.

That in itself was not unusual. Their sleep cycles had never matched ordinary schedules. But as

Vogel entered the corridor outside the playroom, she saw the staff standing differently: shoulders tight, eyes avoiding the glass, mouths held in expressions meant to look neutral and failing.

Twin 3-2 sat on the floor with two of the other toddlers. It was laughing softly at something no one had said. The sound was almost comforting, and that was how Vogel knew it was dangerous. Affection increased binding. Mengele's words came back as if he had whispered them in her ear.

Twin 3-1 stood apart, as it always did, closer to the glass. Its hands were at its sides. Its posture was straight. Its gaze was fixed on the corridor, not on the staff, not on the room.

On her.

The pressure in Vogel's teeth arrived immediately, sharp enough to make her tongue press instinctively against the back of her incisors. She forced her jaw to relax and kept her eyes from settling on the child's eyes too directly. Peripheral vision. Angles. Do not grant it the satisfaction of an exchange.

Heller muttered, "It knows you're back."

"It knows I exist," Vogel replied. "That's enough."

They went to the small records room. Vogel shut the door and set the padded case on the metal table. It made a dull sound, like something heavier than glass and liquid should be.

Heller unwrapped the tape recorder and placed it beside the case with the same careful reluctance. The machine was old, portable, sturdy. Its spools were still. Its switches were simple. That simplicity made it more frightening. Complex devices had failure modes. Simple ones just worked.

Vogel reached for the microfilm viewer, then stopped herself. “Not yet,” she said.

Heller frowned. “We need to know what we stole.”

“We already know what we stole,” Vogel replied. “We stole an invitation.”

She opened the padded case.

The vials lay in fitted foam cutouts. Dark glass, sealed caps, wax stamped with the geometric bell symbol. No labels in Spanish, no clinic codes. These were not meant to be hidden in bureaucracy. They were meant to be recognized.

Heller’s face tightened. “More Source.”

“Or a variant,” Vogel said. She lifted one vial by the foam edge and held it up to the light. The glass absorbed the illumination rather than reflecting it.

The wax seal seemed too pristine for something that had traveled through networks and hands. It looked prepared.

She put it down again without letting her fingers linger.

Heller stared at the tape recorder. "And that."

Vogel looked at the label on the tape spool, the hymn title in German script. She did not read it aloud. She had learned, with the children's presence, that language was not only meaning. It was rhythm, memory, conditioning.

"Mengele is building an army," she said.

Heller's jaw tightened. "Children aren't an army."

Vogel's gaze drifted, unwillingly, toward the door, toward the faint sounds of the playroom: a child's breath, a soft footstep, a laugh that could become a lever. "Not soldiers," she said. "Miracles."

Heller opened his mouth, then shut it again as if uncertain which kind of objection was safest.

Vogel continued, voice low. "An army of miracles doesn't need uniforms. It doesn't need orders shouted across a field. It needs rooms. It needs witnesses. It needs small demonstrations repeated until the world stops calling them impossible."

She reached for the tape recorder and turned it over without switching it on, checking for markings, for additional labels. Her fingers touched only cloth and metal edges. She refused to let skin meet the plastic casing. Touch was attention. Attention was participation.

Heller watched her hands. "You think the tape is instruction."

"It's ritual," Vogel said. "He doesn't want a message delivered once. He wants something that can be played in a clinic, in a church basement, in a nursery, anywhere people gather. Music bypasses argument. Hymns are already shaped like surrender."

Heller's eyes flicked to the vials again. "And the vials are… what. Ammunition."

Vogel's mouth tightened. "Not ammunition," she said. "Seeds."

The word hung in the air, connecting itself to what she had called their own work beneath the ranch, and she hated the symmetry of it. Seeds implied growth. Growth implied inevitability. It implied that even if they locked their doors and erased their records, what had been planted would find new soil.

Heller rubbed his jaw once, then dropped his hand quickly as if ashamed of the gesture. “My teeth,” he muttered.

Vogel felt her own jaw tighten in response, the echo of the ache rising, then easing. The building was quiet, but it was not inert. The children did not need to be in the room for the room to remember them.

She looked at Heller. “He has produced older ones,” she said. “Not just infants. Not just toddlers. The files. Adolescents. Some already trained.”

“To do what,” Heller asked, and his voice carried the kind of dread that tried to be skeptical and failed.

Vogel answered with images rather than abstractions, because abstractions were how men lied to themselves. “To heal in public,” she said. “To stop bleeding at the right moment. To quiet a crowd without speaking. To make a man feel forgiven so he will do what he’s asked next.”

Heller swallowed. “That’s not war.”

“It is war,” Vogel said. “Just not the kind with trenches.”

She moved to the microfilm viewer at last, threaded one reel with hands that remained steady by force of will, and advanced to the photographs again. She did not linger on faces. She focused on captions and patterns. Pairing successful. Mirroring reduces noise. Subject A draws affection. Subject B enforces compliance.

"This is the structure," she said. "It's always two. One to attract. One to control. One makes people want to protect it. The other makes protection feel like obedience."

Heller stared at the frames. "Like our twins."

Vogel nodded once. "And it scales."

She heard, through the wall, a soft thump and then laughter, and for a moment the laughter sounded too synchronized, too timed, like a choir rehearsing without being told it was rehearsing.

Vogel advanced the reel again and stopped on a page of notes: exposure to holy stimulus increases compliance. Use familiar prayer to stabilize.

"Mengele is not simply building miracles," she said. "He's building a delivery system."

Heller leaned back in his chair as if the metal had gone suddenly cold beneath him. "An army of miracles," he repeated, voice flat.

“Yes,” Vogel said. “Each one a demonstration. Each demonstration a recruitment. Not recruitment into a party. Recruitment into a belief that obeying them is the same as being saved.”

She shut off the viewer and sat still for a moment, listening to the lab’s hum.

In her mind, she saw the Vatican vault, the sealed case Ferretti had carried into Rome’s machinery. She saw the Pope’s curiosity turned into leverage. Proof as ownership. She saw Kammler’s Bell in the Owl Mountains, time distortion and hallucinations, and the way soldiers had come back speaking unknown languages. She saw the crucifixion not as an altar piece but as a hinge, and the warning Kammler had ignored.

You are creating something that should never exist.

“What do we do,” Heller asked again, quieter this time, as if volume itself might count as attention.

Vogel stood and picked up the tape recorder, still unpowered. The machine’s weight was ordinary. The danger in it was not weight. It was the ease with which it could be used.

“We don’t play it,” she said.

Heller exhaled once, relieved by at least one clear instruction. “We destroy it.”

Vogel shook her head. “Not yet.”

His eyes snapped to hers. “Why.”

“Because I need to know what hymn,” Vogel said. “I need to know the pattern. If he has built a liturgy, then he has built a predictable sequence. Predictability is the only weakness doctrine has.”

Heller looked as if he wanted to argue, then glanced toward the door as the sound of laughter changed pitch. His shoulders tightened again.

Vogel lowered the tape recorder onto the table without turning it on. “We listen with instruments first,” she said. “Not with our ears in the room. Not with human bodies.”

Heller nodded, already thinking like a technician. “We can isolate it. Shielding.”

“Yes,” Vogel said. “And we keep the vials sealed.”

Heller stared at the wax stamps. “And if they aren’t meant to stay sealed.”

Vogel felt the pressure in her teeth flare briefly, then settle. She thought of the child in Córdoba calling the vials property. She thought of the phrase: your proof of participation.

"We are already marked," she said. "But we don't have to cooperate."

A knock came at the records room door, gentle and precise. Not urgent. Not fearful. The kind of knock that expected to be answered.

Heller froze.

Vogel did not move for a heartbeat. Her mind wanted to fill in a shape behind the door: small feet on tile, a soft voice, her name spoken with careful German.

Then she forced herself to breathe out slowly and walked to the door. She opened it.

Estela stood there, face pale, eyes avoiding Vogel's directly as if eye contact had become a kind of confession. Behind her, through the corridor glass, Vogel could see the playroom. Twin 3-1 was closer to the observation window than before, its head angled slightly, watching the door. Watching who entered and who left. Watching like a clerk recording transactions.

Estela's lips moved. She spoke in Spanish, voice strained. "Doctor… they've started forming lines."

Vogel felt her stomach tighten. "Lines," she repeated in German, not because Estela understood, but because she needed the word to stay hard and clinical.

Estela gestured helplessly toward the playroom. "When the nurses bring food, they stand. They wait. They… they put their hands together. Like prayer." Her eyes darted to the glass. "No one taught them."

Vogel looked past Estela to the children.

Twin 3-2 had stood. Two of the other toddlers stood beside it, hands pressed together, faces tilted upward in imitation of something they had never been shown. It should have looked like play.

It did not.

It looked like rehearsal.

Twin 3-1 did not join the posture. It simply watched the others do it, the way a conductor watched a choir learn its first notes.

Vogel felt the faint pressure in her teeth return, and this time it carried not fear but a cold understanding.

The army of miracles did not begin when they were old enough to walk into cities and knock on doors.

It began here, underground, in the smallest gestures that trained a room to respond.

Hands together. Heads bowed. A line formed without being ordered.

Ritual reducing resistance.

A witness being guided.

Vogel closed the records room door behind her without taking her eyes off the playroom.

"They're building the gospel into their bodies," she said quietly, to no one in particular.

Heller's voice came out rough. "And the staff."

Vogel watched Estela's hands. They were clasped together at her waist, fingers interlaced tightly. Not prayer, perhaps. But close enough to be mistaken by a child learning shapes.

"Into everyone," Vogel corrected.

She looked at Twin 3-1. For a moment, just a moment, the child's gaze met hers through layers of glass and corridor light. It did not smile. It did not threaten. It simply held the look with patient certainty, as if it already knew what the world would become once enough people learned to stand in line and call it reverence.

Vogel forced her eyes away first, not in submission, but in refusal.

"Double the protocols," she said to Estela. "No hymns. No prayers near them. No lullabies. No singing. No familiar rituals at all. Feed them without ceremony."

Estela's face tightened. "They get upset," she whispered. "When we don't."

Vogel felt the coldness settle fully into place. Upset. A child's word. A human word. Too gentle for what it meant.

"They aren't upset," Vogel said. "They're conditioning you to think you've done something wrong."

She turned and walked down the corridor toward the observation glass, toward the room where the toddlers stood in a quiet line, hands together, waiting. She kept her jaw loose and her breathing controlled, and she refused, with each step, to let her fear become a lesson they could memorize.

Behind the glass, the line held.

An army did not need weapons first.

It needed devotion.

And devotion, once taught, could be aimed.

Chapter 19

The Envoy's War

He learned to track them the way you tracked a disease outbreak, not the way you tracked men.

A man had routes: ports, safe houses, the habits of hunger and money. A man left fingerprints on paperwork and women and rooms. These children left something else. They left the aftertaste of ritual in places that did not know they had become altars.

Monsignor Luca Ferretti had not used his own name in years. In Buenos Aires, where he arrived on a passport that said he was a freight clerk from Montevideo, he answered to "Señor Ferrán" when someone insisted on an honorific. He kept his accent muffled, his collar absent, his rosary buried at the bottom of a bag like contraband. He had learned, in the hours after the Vatican's decree was delivered in a calm voice and sealed with an older kind of authority, that the Church's most dangerous weapon was not a gun.

It was a sentence spoken with certainty: No witnesses.

That sentence had been meant for him as much as anyone else.

So he became the thing Rome could not tolerate. He stayed alive, and he watched.

He did not begin with miracles. Miracles were theater; theater was unreliable. He began with data, because he still trusted numbers the way a priest trusted scripture: not because they were holy, but because they repeated.

The first clue was twins.

Not the folklore kind, not the soft human superstition that gave twins a shared soul. The other kind, the bureaucratic kind. Twin births were registered. They created forms. They required signatures. Even in places where money smoothed paperwork into silence, the pattern of twin deliveries left dents in ledgers.

In the city's civil registry, Ferretti bribed a clerk with cigarettes and the promise of a favor that would never be claimed. He sat under a buzzing ceiling fan and copied entries by hand, careful not to stare too long at any one name. Names were hooks. He had learned that too, though he could not have explained how, only that some part of him tightened whenever a name was offered with too much confidence.

He made lists: clinics with unusual spikes in twin registrations; midwives who appeared too often; doctors who signed with different hands. He cross-referenced addresses with parishes, not for prayer, but for access. Churches heard things. They collected gossip like dust.

In the confessional of San Ignacio, behind a screen that smelled of old varnish, he listened to a woman sob about her sister's baby who had been taken away by "people from the clinic" because the infant was "different." She did not mean jaundiced or sickly. She meant different in the way people meant when they wanted to spit and pray in the same breath.

"They said it was a blessing," the woman whispered. "They told her to be grateful. They said the child would help many."

Ferretti kept his voice low, neutral, the way he had learned to speak around land mines. "Who said this."

The woman hesitated. "A doctor. German, maybe. Or Austrian. He spoke Spanish like it hurt him."

Ferretti felt a familiar coldness settle in his stomach. Men from the old routes. The ratlines had carried more than fugitives; they had carried habits, methods, appetites.

"Where," he asked.

She gave him a clinic name and crossed herself so hard her knuckles cracked.

When he left the church, he did not look back at the altar. He had stopped doing that. Altars were supposed to watch you with mercy. Lately, he had begun to suspect the world watched with something else.

The clinic was in a neighborhood that pretended not to see its own hunger. Ferretti entered as if he belonged, carrying a clipboard he had stolen from a municipal office and a gray jacket that made him look like a man who measured things for a living. He had learned to wear dullness the way he used to wear vestments: as a claim to invisibility.

A nurse at the desk smiled automatically. Her smile did not reach her eyes.

"We're full today," she said.

"I'm not a patient," Ferretti replied, and showed a stamped paper with a seal that meant nothing but looked official enough to discourage questions. "I'm here about licensing."

The nurse's smile tightened. Her gaze slid past him toward the hallway, and for a fraction of a second her expression softened into something like relief, as if she expected someone else to handle him.

That was when Ferretti felt it: a faint pressure in his teeth, not pain exactly, more like a weather change inside his jaw. He stopped walking. He kept his breathing steady.

The nurse's eyes flicked back to him and then away. She said, too quickly, "Wait here."

He waited, and in the waiting he watched the room's shadows.

He had promised himself he would not become superstitious. Superstition was a door that opened inward. But he had seen enough in Rome, enough in the film frames he had glimpsed before he ran, enough in the envoy reports he had stolen and burned and then tried to forget, to know that attention itself could be used like a hand on a latch.

A child's laugh came from the hallway, bright and ordinary. It should have made the clinic feel alive. Instead, it landed like a cue.

The nurse returned with a doctor.

The man was not Mengele. Ferretti knew that face from photographs, from the world's simplified myth of evil. This doctor was younger, hair neatly combed, shirt sleeves rolled with practiced competence. But his eyes were too calm in a way Ferretti had begun to recognize. Not tranquil. Assured.

"Señor..." the doctor began and paused as if tasting the air. His gaze settled on Ferretti's face with a slight tilt of the head, the way you watched a lock you intended to open.

Ferretti kept his expression empty. He did not offer his name. He did not answer the invitation in the doctor's pause.

After a beat, the doctor continued anyway. "You said licensing."

"Yes," Ferretti replied.

The doctor's smile held for a second too long. "We have all our papers."

"I'm sure you do," Ferretti said. He kept his eyes on the doctor's forehead, not the eyes. He had learned that trick from a man in Naples who trafficked in forged passports and, quietly, in advice. "Don't give them your gaze," the forger had said. "Some people collect it."

Ferretti did not know if that was literal or metaphor. He no longer cared. He only cared that it worked.

"I will need to see your delivery records," Ferretti said.

The doctor's smile faded. Not into anger. Into something like disappointment, as if a rehearsed scene had failed to go as scripted. "Those are private."

"Not if your license is in question," Ferretti replied, tapping the meaningless seal on his paper.

Behind the doctor, down the hallway, a small figure appeared. A child, perhaps seven, wearing a clean shirt and shorts, barefoot on tile as if shoes were unnecessary. The child's hair was neatly cut. The posture was too straight. The eyes, even at a distance, seemed to fix on Ferretti with calm interest.

The pressure in Ferretti's teeth sharpened.

The child did not smile. It did not wave. It simply stood there, and Ferretti felt the room subtly adjust as if everyone had, without thinking, begun to breathe in time with the child's presence. The nurse's shoulders dropped. The doctor's jaw unclenched. A man in the waiting chairs stopped fidgeting.

A room becoming receptive.

Ferretti did not move. He did not speak. He did not let his attention snag on the child like fabric on a nail. He stared at the doctor's shoulder instead and forced himself to think of something profane and heavy, something that anchored him to ordinary reality: the smell of diesel at the port, the taste of cheap coffee, the ache in his feet after walking too long.

The doctor glanced back at the child and then returned his gaze to Ferretti, and now there was a subtle warning in it, an implication that the conversation could become something else if Ferretti insisted.

Ferretti understood with brutal clarity that this was not simply a clinic. It was a demonstration room.

He stepped back once, as if reconsidering, letting his body language suggest retreat without surrender. "I'll return with proper authorization," he said.

The doctor's smile returned, gentler now. "Of course."

As Ferretti turned to leave, the child spoke.

Not loudly. Not theatrically. Just one word, in Italian, in the accent of Rome.

"Luca."

The sound of his name in that place was like a finger inside an old wound.

Ferretti kept walking.

His throat tightened with the reflex to answer, to deny, to demand, to pray. All the human responses that made a man feel real. He swallowed them. He did not look back.

Outside, in the street's heat, he walked three blocks before allowing himself to breathe deeply. His teeth still ached. The ache did not fade immediately. It lingered like a mark.

He understood now what he was truly tracking.

Not children, not exactly. Not even miracles.

He was tracking a method that moved through bodies: the use of familiarity as a solvent, the use of ritual as a cage, the use of a witness as an ingredient. Someone had taught them this. Someone had written it down as doctrine and then made it portable, repeatable, scalable.

And they had learned the other lesson too: names were handles.

That night, in a rented room above a bakery, Ferretti spread his notes on the bed and drew lines between clinic addresses, registry entries, confessional whispers. A web emerged, ugly and coherent. Córdoba sat in it like a knot. Mendoza. Rosario. Smaller towns with one midwife who suddenly drove a better car.

And farther south, like a quiet seed pressed into pine-shadowed soil, he marked Bariloche.

He had heard that name from two different mouths in two different months. Once from a German expatriate priest whose hands shook when he held the chalice. Once from a frightened nurse who said there was a ranch where the doctors never went into town and the children never came out, and that the air around that place felt wrong, like a storm that refused to arrive.

Ferretti stared at the name until his jaw tightened.

He did not know Dr. Ilse Vogel. He did not know Heller. He did not know what had happened in a locksmith's shop in Córdoba, only that something had moved there with bare feet and a voice trained to sound like mercy. But he could feel the shape of the war clarifying.

It was not a war of armies clashing.

It was a war of witness against conditioning, of silence against invitation, of a human mind fighting not to become a component in someone else's miracle.

Ferretti folded his notes, extinguished the lamp, and lay in darkness listening to the city breathe.

He did not pray. Not because he had stopped believing, but because he had begun to fear that even prayer could be used as a lever if the wrong thing was listening.

In the morning he would travel south, toward Bariloche, toward the pine forests and the ranch that pretended to be ordinary.

He would go not as a priest and not as a soldier, because neither role fit this war.

He would go as what Rome had tried to erase.

A witness who refused to kneel.

The bus south carried him through hours of flat land that looked like it had been scraped clean by wind and time. Ferretti sat alone near the back, a canvas bag at his feet, his hands folded in his lap as if he were trying to convince his own body it still belonged to a disciplined life.

He watched the other passengers with the detached attention of a man who had spent too long listening to confessions. A mother shushed a child with a piece of bread. Two men argued softly about football. An old woman held a cage with a canary that sang whenever the bus hit a bump, as if the bird believed motion was permission.

Ordinary life, and under it the quiet question that had started to haunt him more than Rome's decree.

What if the children were not the enemy?

The word children had become slippery in his mind. It no longer meant small bodies and scraped knees. It meant a voice at a clinic saying his name in the accent of his birthplace. It meant bare feet on tile and a room falling into rhythm. It meant doctrine spoken as if it were comfort.

He tried to tell himself that it did not matter whether they were innocent. The Vatican had not cared about innocence when it issued No witnesses. Kammler had not cared when he reached into history with a gloved hand. Mengele had not cared, because caring had never been a useful tool for him.

But Ferretti was not Kammler, and he was no longer a priest permitted to outsource cruelty to doctrine. He had to choose his own sins now. That was what it meant to be outside the Church's protection: you did not get to call anything obedience.

At a fuel stop in a town whose name he did not bother to learn, passengers spilled out into bright heat and the smell of diesel. Ferretti stood near the bus's side, stretching his legs, and felt the familiar faint pressure in his teeth, like a storm warning that came without clouds.

He froze, not moving his head. He had learned that the first instinct, to search, to confirm, was exactly what made him useful to whatever wanted witnesses.

A girl walked past him toward the station shop, perhaps twelve or thirteen, hair braided tight, a dress too plain to be fashionable. She carried a small bag of oranges. On her wrist a strip of gauze was taped down, clean and fresh.

She glanced at him once, not lingering, not staring. But the glance landed with the same careful weight he had felt from the child in the clinic.

Assessment.

Ferretti lowered his gaze to the ground near her shoes, avoiding her eyes the way he had trained himself to do with dangerous relics. His teeth ached, then eased as she moved away. When he looked up again she was in the shop doorway, speaking to no one, lips moving without urgency.

A prayer, he thought, and hated that his mind went there first.

On the bus again, she sat three rows ahead of him. She peeled an orange slowly, offering segments to a younger boy beside her. The boy's hand trembled when he took them. He did not look at anyone else.

They got back on the highway. The canary sang. Ferretti tried to return to watching the landscape, but after half an hour the girl stood and walked down the aisle. She stopped beside his seat.

"Is this taken?" she asked in Spanish.

"No," Ferretti said.

She sat without waiting for invitation. That alone was not unusual. Buses filled, seats became shared. But she sat too neatly, her shoulders squared, her hands in her lap like a student waiting to be examined.

Ferretti kept his eyes on the seatback in front of him. "You're traveling with family?"

The girl's mouth tightened. "With him," she said, and nodded toward the boy. "They said I must not leave him."

"They," Ferretti repeated softly.

The pressure in his teeth returned, faint, and he wondered if it was her, or his own fear reacting to the shape of the conversation.

She did not answer his repetition. Instead, she said, in careful Italian, "You are from Rome."

Ferretti's throat constricted. He did not look at her. He felt the reflex to deny, to ask her who she was, to demand how she knew. He swallowed it down until it became a dull ache in his chest.

"People guess," he said in Spanish. "Accents travel."

She turned her head slightly, as if listening to the bus's engine, as if listening to something else beneath it. "You were in a church," she said. "In Buenos Aires. You listened to a woman behind a screen. You didn't pray after."

Ferretti's hands tightened together until his knuckles ached. He forced them to loosen. He had not told anyone that detail. He had not written it. It had been private, and privacy had been the last thing Rome had ever allowed him to believe in.

"Why are you talking to me?" he asked.

The girl hesitated, and for the first time her discipline faltered. Something like fear moved behind her eyes, quick and real.

"Because I think you are not with them," she said.

Ferretti almost laughed, a short sound of disbelief at the absurdity of being identified as a safe thing by a child who could reach into his past. Instead he said, "Who are they."

She looked down at her hands, and he saw the gauze on her wrist again. The tape was perfectly applied. Clinical. A mark of someone else's care.

"The doctors," she said. "The ones who make you stand in lines."

Ferretti felt cold slide down his spine at the phrase, because it echoed what he had heard whispered in Buenos Aires and what his own mind had turned into a map: ritual, repetition, witness guided into surrender.

"Where are you going?" he asked.

The girl's lips moved as if she were choosing each word from a list of permitted ones. "South," she said. "To the place with pine trees. To the ranch."

Bariloche.

Ferretti kept his expression still. The bus's windows reflected sunlight in hard flashes. He felt suddenly as if he were inside a moving mirror.

"Why," he asked.

Her eyes lifted toward him. He did not meet them directly, but in his peripheral vision he saw their steadiness. Not a child's steadiness. A trained steadiness. The kind that came from being watched so often you learned to perform watchfulness back.

"They said the ones there are late," she said. "They said they need to be brought into the gospel."

Ferretti tasted metal in his mouth. "And what do you think."

That question was dangerous. It invited confession. It invited story. It invited the very thing that doctrine used to bind people: the belief that speech itself made you real.

For a moment the girl said nothing. The bus hummed. The canary sang once and went quiet.

Then she whispered, so softly he almost missed it, "I don't want to be holy."

The words were not doctrine. They were hunger. They were a child's desire to be ordinary, voiced like a sin.

Ferretti's jaw clenched, and he felt the pressure in his teeth spike, then fade. Not from her this time, he realized. From him. From the moment his mind tried to make meaning out of her fear.

"You don't have to be," he said, and immediately hated the instinctive comfort in his voice. Comfort was also a ritual. Comfort was a kind of prayer.

The girl shook her head, a small, sharp motion. "You don't understand," she said. "They don't ask. They demonstrate. And when people see, they change. They look at you like you are a door."

Ferretti went still. Demonstration. Witness.

He pictured the clinic waiting room settling into quiet. He pictured a crowd being softened by a miracle performed at the right moment. He pictured the way people in churches looked at relics, not with skepticism but with the relief of being given something to kneel to.

The girl's voice tightened, and the discipline returned, but now it was threaded with panic. "Sometimes I do something and I don't mean to," she said. "Sometimes a cut closes. Sometimes someone stops crying because I want it to stop. And they smile like I saved them. And then I can't make them unsmile."

Ferretti felt his chest constrict. He had heard men confess to sins that sounded like that, except the men had wanted the power and called it temptation afterward.

"You can control it," he said, more question than statement.

The girl's mouth twisted. "They teach control," she said. "They teach it like prayer. They say, 'Think of the hymn. Think of the words. Let the room receive you.'"

Hymn. Tape. Liturgy.

Ferretti's mind flashed to the thought that had made him stop praying: that even prayer could become a lever. Here was proof in a child's mouth, spoken without reverence, only fear.

The boy beside her shifted, making a small sound. The girl's head turned instantly toward him. The movement was automatic, protective. The boy's eyes were wide and wet, his hands clenched. He looked like a child who had been told that noise was dangerous.

Ferretti watched the girl's shoulders lower, watched the boy's breathing slow as if someone had placed a hand on his chest without touching him.

The air around their seats felt subtly different. Not colder. Not warmer. Quieter, as if the bus itself had agreed to carry them gently.

Ferretti's instinct screamed at him to look away, to withdraw attention, to refuse participation. But the boy's fear was a raw human thing, not theater. And the girl's calming of him did not feel like conquest. It felt like a sister soothing a brother because no one else would.

Good, evil, and fear, Ferretti thought. The categories blurred here, because the same mechanism could be mercy or weapon depending on who held the script.

He forced his gaze to stay on the seat fabric, not their faces. "Listen to me," he said quietly. "If they use your name, do you answer."

The girl's laugh was small and broken. "They already know my name."

"That's not what I asked," Ferretti said.

She hesitated. "Sometimes," she admitted. "Sometimes I answer because it feels like relief to stop fighting."

Ferretti nodded once, more to himself than to her. He understood that relief. He understood why people knelt. He understood why Rome killed witnesses. Witnesses complicated obedience.

He took a breath, steadying himself. "When we reach the south," he said, choosing the word carefully, "you and the boy do not go to the ranch."

The girl turned toward him. The steadiness in her eyes fractured again into something young and desperate. "Where else is there," she whispered. "They have clinics. They have priests. They have songs. They have people who open doors."

Ferretti felt the weight of that truth press into him. A network that moved through ritual was harder to cut than a network that moved through money. Money could be traced. Ritual could be inherited.

He did not promise safety. Promises were a form of worship, an attempt to become the thing someone else could rely on.

Instead he said, “There are still places that do not know your story. There are still people who have not been taught to stand in line.”

The girl watched him as if trying to decide whether he was real. Then she asked, gently, almost curiously, “And you. What are you.”

Ferretti’s teeth ached faintly, the old warning. Names were handles. Roles were handles too. If he called himself priest, soldier, rescuer, he would be giving her a ritual shape to submit to.

“I am a witness,” he said at last, hating the word even as he claimed it. “And I am trying not to be used.”

The girl nodded slowly, as if that answer fit something she had been taught and something she had never been allowed to say out loud.

Ahead, the road narrowed. Pine-shadowed hills began to rise in the distance like a remembered promise. Bariloche waited somewhere beyond them, with its clean mountain air and its ranch pretending at domestic life.

Ferretti looked at the window and saw his own reflection faintly overlaid on the landscape: a tired man with controlled eyes, carrying secrets Rome wanted buried.

Beside him sat a girl who did not want to be holy, and a boy who had learned fear as a first language.

Ferretti understood, with a clarity that tasted like grief, that his war was not only against monsters.

It was against the temptation to simplify.

If he called them evil, he could justify anything done to stop them. If he called them innocent, he could be turned into a choir member by pity.

So he chose the only honest middle ground left.

He watched them, carefully, without kneeling to what they could do, and without denying what had been done to them.

And he prepared, quietly, to steal two frightened children out of a gospel that wanted them as proof.

The bus rolled into the southern towns the way a slow confession rolled toward absolution: inevitable, quiet, and heavy with what could not be unsaid.

Ferretti watched the pine line thicken on the horizon, the land rising into darker greens and sharper air. The girl sat rigidly beside him, hands folded, braid tight, eyes flicking toward the front of the bus every few minutes as if she could sense a change before it arrived. The boy leaned against the window with the exhausted stillness of someone whose fear had finally run out of fuel.

When the driver announced the next stop, a handful of passengers stirred. The canary's cage rattled as the old woman lifted it. A couple of men reached for their bags. Ordinary movement, ordinary sounds.

The pressure in Ferretti's teeth began as a faint ache and grew into something steadier, like a finger pressing from the inside of his jaw.

The girl's posture changed. Not dramatically. Just a subtle straightening, a readiness that looked like discipline until you recognized it as training.

"They're close," Ferretti murmured in Spanish, eyes on the seatback in front of him.

The girl did not ask who. "We can get off here," she said.

"And go where," he replied, keeping his voice low. "You said they have clinics. Priests. Songs."

"They don't have everywhere," she said, and for a moment her voice lost its rehearsed calm. It sounded like a child's urgency. "Not the places that don't want to see."

Ferretti felt the weight of that sentence settle in him. A gospel did not need to convince everyone. It only needed enough rooms that responded, enough witnesses who softened, enough people who mistook relief for holiness.

The bus slowed. Gravel crunched beneath tires. Through the window Ferretti saw a small roadside station, a sign advertising fuel and empanadas, a row of parked cars angled toward the road like patient animals.

And a van.

White paint, clean, no markings. But the cleanliness was wrong in this dust. The van looked like something that expected to be noticed and also expected that noticing would be interpreted as harmless.

The girl's breath shortened. The boy's fingers curled into the fabric of his shirt.

Ferretti stood as the bus door hissed open and reached for his bag. He did not look at the van directly. He did not give it the dignity of his full attention. But in the edge of his vision he saw movement near it, small and unhurried.

A child. Maybe ten. Barefoot on gravel as if pain was optional. A pale shirt, dark shorts. Hair combed. Posture straight.

The pattern, repeated.

The child did not wave or call out. It simply turned its head as if listening to the bus's breath, and Ferretti felt a ripple of quiet move through the passengers behind him. Conversation dimmed. The old woman stopped speaking to her canary. The driver's hands steadied on the wheel as if something had told him, gently, to be still.

A room becoming receptive, except the room had wheels.

Ferretti stepped into the aisle and moved as if he were only stretching. He leaned down toward the girl. "Do not answer," he whispered in Italian, close to her ear so the words would not carry.

She nodded once, sharply.

He looked at the boy. "Stay behind her," he said in Spanish. "No matter what you hear."

The boy's eyes widened. He did not speak.

Ferretti guided them forward. Not rushing. Not drawing attention with urgency. He remembered, with a sick clarity, the Vatican decree delivered in calm language. No witnesses. The Church understood something Mengele understood too: panic made theater, and theater created stories. Stories created resistance.

At the bottom step, the bus driver cleared his throat.

“Everyone off,” the driver said, too quickly. “Mechanical check.”

A lie, and a poor one. The engine sounded fine. But the driver’s eyes were unfocused, softened.

Ferretti felt anger rise in him, hot and useless. The driver was not collaborating. He was being guided.

They stepped into the station’s heat. The air smelled of fuel and fried dough. A man in an apron watched from the doorway with a blank expression that looked like shock and might have been submission.

The child by the van turned fully toward them.

Ferretti kept his gaze on the child’s shoulder, not the eyes. “Keep walking,” he murmured.

The girl’s hand drifted toward her braid, gripping it like a rosary.

The child spoke, in Spanish, voice mild. “You can rest. We will take you the rest of the way.”

It did not say Ferretti’s name. That was almost worse. It meant it did not need to. It assumed compliance as a default condition of the room.

Ferretti did not answer. He guided the girl and boy toward the station shop, toward the press of ordinary bodies and shelves, toward a place where the gospel's neat stage might blur into noise.

They entered. A bell above the door jingled, bright and too loud. The sound made Ferretti flinch, then he was grateful for it. Noise, for once, was a shield.

Inside, fluorescent lights buzzed. A radio played softly behind the counter, a tango song broken by static. The clerk, a young man with acne and tired eyes, stood frozen with his hands on the register as if waiting for permission to move.

Ferretti leaned toward him. "Señor," he said, gentle but firm. "We need to use your back door."

The clerk's eyes flicked to Ferretti's face, then past it, toward the station windows.

The pressure in Ferretti's teeth sharpened again.

The clerk's lips parted, but before he could speak, the girl beside Ferretti whispered, barely audible, "No."

The word was not addressed to the clerk. It was addressed to the air.

Ferretti felt it like a change in humidity, a small shift in the room's weight. The clerk blinked as if waking. His shoulders rose, a breath returning.

He looked at Ferretti again and seemed to actually see him.

“Back,” the clerk said quickly, hoarse. “Hurry.”

They moved behind the counter, past sacks of flour and crates of oranges, into a narrow corridor that smelled of damp cardboard. At the end was a metal door leading to a storage yard fenced with corrugated sheet.

Ferretti pushed it open.

Outside, the yard was empty except for a stack of broken pallets and a stray dog lying in the shade. The dog lifted its head and watched them with weary suspicion.

Ferretti turned right, along the fence, toward the road behind the station. If they could reach the trees, if they could reach any place where the gospel’s vehicles could not follow easily, they might gain time.

Behind them, the storage door clicked shut.

A voice spoke from the corridor, very close. Not loud. Not angry.

“Do you know what you are doing?” the voice asked in Italian.

Ferretti stopped.

He did not turn around. He felt the girl and boy stop behind him, their presence warm at his back, fragile and real.

The voice continued, calm as prayer. "You are stealing what was already chosen."

Ferretti swallowed, forcing his throat to stay closed. Names were handles. Dialogue was a handle. Argument was a handle shaped like dignity.

He did not answer.

The girl's breathing sped up, then steadied again as if she had gripped some internal rhythm. Ferretti realized she was doing something deliberately. Not a miracle performed for witnesses. A refusal, practiced.

The pressure in his teeth eased by a fraction.

The voice shifted to Spanish. "Little sister," it said, and the tenderness in it made Ferretti's stomach tighten. "You don't have to be afraid. We will make you clean."

The girl's hand clenched on her braid. "I am clean," she whispered, not to the voice, but as if reminding herself of a fact. Then, louder, in Spanish, she said, "Stop."

Ferretti felt the air tighten again, not as submission, but as resistance, like a room holding its breath to avoid inhaling smoke.

A footstep sounded behind the fence line, slow, testing gravel. A second step. The sound did not hurry. It did not need to.

Ferretti's mind flashed to the child in the clinic saying his name. He remembered how his own throat had wanted to answer. The mechanism did not only compel. It invited. It offered relief from vigilance. It offered the comfort of being known.

That was the battle, he understood then. Not bullets against flesh. But attention against attention. A war fought in the small reflexes of the human animal: to look, to answer, to soften when spoken to with certainty.

Ferretti leaned slightly toward the girl without turning his head. "Do you know how to break it?" he asked, barely moving his lips.

"I can make them forget for a moment," she whispered. "If I don't think about them. If I think about something else."

"Like what."

Her voice trembled. "My mother. Before."

Ferretti felt grief twist inside him. Conditioning stole even memory and repurposed it as a tool.

"Do it," he said, and hated himself for asking a child to weaponize her own longing.

The girl closed her eyes for a heartbeat. Her lips moved silently, not a hymn, not a prayer, but something private.

The stray dog rose abruptly, startled, then trotted away as if fleeing an unseen pressure.

Ferretti heard, behind them, a small intake of breath from the corridor. A pause. Like a thought interrupted.

He seized the moment. He stepped forward, leading them along the fence to the rear road. His pace stayed measured. Running would turn this into chase, and chase created witnesses.

At the corner of the yard, he looked once, quickly, through the gap between fence panels.

He saw the child who had been by the van standing at the storage door, head tilted, as if confused not by their movement but by the brief failure of the room to cooperate. The child's eyes tracked, recalculating.

Ferretti looked away immediately.

They reached the rear road and crossed into scrub that led toward the first dark line of trees. Pine scent came faintly on the wind, clean and sharp.

The boy stumbled once. Ferretti caught his arm and steadied him without speaking.

Behind them, from the station, the bus's engine started again. The driver had been released back into motion, the lie of the mechanical check discarded as soon as it was no longer needed.

Ferretti did not know if the van would follow. He did not know if other children waited down the road, placed like punctuation in the gospel's sentence. He only knew that the battle he had feared in Rome was no longer abstract.

It was here, in a roadside yard, in a child's voice offering rest, in a girl's whispered refusal, in his own throat struggling not to answer.

The girl opened her eyes. Her face was pale with strain.

"I can't do it long," she said.

"I don't need long," Ferretti replied. He kept his eyes on the trees. "I need enough."

"For what," she asked, and the question carried a fragile hope that frightened him more than any miracle.

Ferretti did not promise salvation. He did not say God. He did not say Church. He did not say safety.

He said the only thing he was sure of.

"To give you back your choice," he said.

They entered the first shade of the pines, and the light changed, breaking into needles and shadow. Ferretti felt the pressure in his teeth fade, not vanish, but recede, like a hand withdrawing just out of reach.

The gospel was still behind them. It would not stop. It would adjust. It would learn.

But for the first time since Rome, Ferretti felt something else beside fear.

A hard, quiet resolve.

If the enemy's weapon was witness guided into surrender, then his war would be fought one soul at a time, not by proving anything, not by preaching, but by teaching people how to keep their mouths closed when a voice offered them relief.

Not every child was a monster.

Not every miracle was a choice.

And that was why the battle mattered. Not to destroy them all, not to sanctify them, but to keep the human world from becoming a room that opened its door simply because something knocked and spoke in a familiar tongue.

Chapter 20

The Truth Unveiled

Ferretti did not go straight to the ranch.

That would have been a priest's instinct, to march toward the altar and demand answers. He had learned, in the last years, that directness was a kind of vanity. It assumed the world still rewarded honest approaches. It assumed there was still a line between sanctuary and trap.

Instead he moved through the pines with the girl and the boy for as long as her strength held, and when her shoulders began to tremble with the effort of keeping the air from softening around them, he stopped and chose a place that felt ugly enough to be safe: a shallow drainage culvert under a service road, half-choked with needles and old cans.

They waited there until dusk.

The girl, whose name he still did not ask, sat with her back to the concrete and pressed her fingers to the gauze on her wrist as if the bandage contained something that could leak out through skin. The boy slept in short, frightened bursts. Ferretti watched the road above them and listened for the particular quiet that meant a room was becoming receptive.

It never came. Or if it came, it circled wide, tasting the edge of the forest and retreating the way a smart predator retreated when prey stopped behaving like prey.

When the sky turned the color of bruised metal, Ferretti led them toward town. Bariloche at night was full of small lights and clean façades, the kind of place that pretended the world's dirt was always far away. He kept them off the main streets and found a boardinghouse owned by a widow who asked no questions and looked at children with the same wary sympathy she might have offered stray dogs.

"One night," Ferretti said in Spanish, placing money on the counter before she could refuse. "No records."

The widow's gaze moved to the girl's face, then to the boy's, then back to Ferretti. Something in her expression tightened as if she had recognized the shape of fear without understanding its source. She nodded and handed him a key.

Upstairs, in a narrow room with two beds and a crucifix that had been nailed above the door long ago, Ferretti sat at the small desk and opened his canvas bag.

He had carried, for years, a kind of portable confession: papers stolen and copied, names that were never spoken aloud, a few photographs wrapped in cloth, a strip of microfilm he had taken from a dead courier in Naples. Nothing that proved the impossible, only enough to tell him which direction the rot traveled.

Tonight he added a new item to the desk: a small cassette tape the girl had produced from her pocket with shaking hands.

"I took it," she whispered. "From a clinic. They played it for us. Not always. Only when we… resisted."

Ferretti did not touch it with bare skin. He used the corner of a handkerchief and set it down as if it were a relic that burned.

"A hymn," he said.

The girl's eyes flicked to the crucifix above the door and then away quickly, as if even that familiar shape had become dangerous. "Yes," she said. "But it isn't for God."

Ferretti felt his teeth ache faintly at the certainty in her tone. Not her power, he realized. Her conditioning. The way the doctrine had taught her to categorize.

He reached into his bag and pulled out a small portable player, battered and cheap, the kind that could be bought in any market. He did not plan to play the tape. He planned to look at it, to confirm what kind of object it was, to see if it carried marks or symbols like the wax stamps Vogel had described in a report he had once read and then burned.

Then he stopped. The old discipline returned: do not turn curiosity into participation.

He put the player away again.

"No," he said softly, not to the girl, but to his own instinct. "We don't listen."

The girl's shoulders loosened by a fraction, as if relief was her default response to being told she was not required to perform.

Ferretti turned to the papers he had brought and spread them across the desk. In one set of notes, copied from a Vatican file before Rome tried to erase him, there was a phrase Kammler had written in German in a hand that pressed too hard into the paper.

Not steal. Create.

He had not understood it when he first read it. It had sounded like the arrogance of a Nazi engineer justifying his trespass into history. Now, after clinics and vans and a bus that became a moving demonstration room, he understood that Kammler had not been describing his own ambition.

He had been describing consequence.

Ferretti took out the only thing he had left from Rome that he had never dared destroy: a small strip of film, clipped and brittle, showing a few frames from the crucifixion footage. The images were blurred, black and white ghosts of an event the world had painted into icons. He had watched it once, years ago, and then forced himself not to watch again.

Tonight he held it up to the lamp and studied the edge markings instead of the image.

He had learned, in the last months, that everything important lived in the margins.

On the film's perforated edge, between manufacturer codes, someone had scratched a thin line of symbols. Not Latin. Not Greek. Not any script a priest would recognize. The marks looked geometric, like instructions disguised as ornament.

Ferretti's jaw tightened.

In Córdoba, Vogel had seen a wax stamp shaped like a simplified bell outline. In Buenos Aires, a doctor's eyes had gone calm when a child appeared in the hallway. In a church confessional, a woman had been told her sister's baby was a blessing that would help many.

Different scenes. Same hand.

The girl spoke behind him. "They said the blood was clean," she whispered. "They said it didn't rot like ours. They said it remembered."

Ferretti kept his eyes on the film edge. "Who said."

"The doctors," she replied. "The German ones. They said it came from the cross."

His teeth ached harder, a pressure that felt like weather turning. He forced himself not to look at the crucifix above the door.

"And did it," he asked carefully, "feel like God."

The girl's answer came too fast. "No."

The word was not doubt. It was knowledge.

Ferretti turned his head slightly, just enough to see her face without meeting her eyes directly. In the low light she looked like any tired child. But her posture was too controlled, and her fear had the texture of someone who had seen behind the curtain and could not unsee.

"What did it feel like," he asked.

She hesitated. Her fingers worried the gauze on her wrist. "Like when a room wants you to say yes," she whispered. "Like when you're about to answer and it already knows you will."

Ferretti stared at the strip of film until the frames blurred into abstract shapes.

In Rome they had called it proof. In America they had called it custody. In Mengele's notes they had called it The Source. Everyone had agreed on the convenient premise: that what was taken from Golgotha was Christ, preserved in matter.

But the girl's voice made that premise feel childish.

Christ had not been a substance. Christ had been an event. A hinge, as Vogel had said, a transmission. And Kammler, the engineer who built a bell to punch holes through time, had forced his way into that event with alien materials that behaved like living interface.

He had introduced a machine into a crucifixion.

Not steal. Create.

Ferretti felt a cold clarity slide into place. "They didn't take a relic," he murmured.

The girl frowned. "What."

He chose the words the way he would have chosen penance once: not for poetry, but for accuracy. "They took something that was happening," he said. "And the act of taking changed it."

The boy stirred on the bed, making a small sound. The girl's head turned toward him instantly, protective, and the air in the room softened for a moment, not into submission but into quiet. A sister calming a brother. A mercy that used the same mechanism as a weapon.

Ferretti watched it with a grief that tasted like ash.

"If the sample was Christ," he said, "it would not need to persuade."

The girl's face tightened. "They say persuasion is mercy."

"That's doctrine," Ferretti replied. "Not truth."

He looked again at the symbols scratched into the film edge. They did not look like prayer. They looked like notation, like something meant to be read by an interface rather than a human eye.

He remembered a line from a report he had seen before it vanished into Vatican vaults: notes written in a language not human.

And another detail, older, from the Black Forest prologue he had been forced to piece together from fragments: a humanoid corpse in the wreck, and something missing. Taken, not killed.

He inhaled slowly, forcing his lungs to obey him. The ache in his teeth ebbed and returned, as if something outside the room had leaned closer and then leaned back, listening for his recognition.

The corrupted sample, he thought.

Not corrupted by decay. Corrupted by contact.

By a machine made from alien material that healed when cut. By an interface that responded to touch. By Kammler's presence like a contaminant introduced into a sacred wound.

By an inhuman observer that had noticed him at the moment of death.

Ferretti set the film strip down and folded his hands together on the desk, not in prayer, but to keep them still.

"What did they tell you," he asked the girl, "about what you are."

She looked at him, and for the first time she held his gaze directly. He felt the faint pressure in his teeth, but it did not spike. It hovered, curious.

"They told me I'm an answer," she said. "They told me I'm proof that God can be made."

Ferretti's throat tightened. "And what do you think."

Her lips trembled. "I think I'm a mistake," she whispered. "I think something else is inside the hymn."

Ferretti closed his eyes for a brief moment, no longer afraid of prayer as a lever, but afraid of what would happen if he tried to use prayer as a weapon against something that had learned to wear it.

When he opened his eyes again, the crucifix above the door looked the same as it always had. Wood and metal and familiar suffering.

But he understood now that familiarity was exactly how the enemy moved.

"Listen to me," he said quietly, and kept his voice as flat as he could. "If what they took was altered during the taking, then the thing being replicated is not the man on that cross."

The girl's face went pale. "Then what is it."

Ferretti looked at the scratched symbols, at the cassette tape on the desk, at the child and boy on the beds, and felt the outline of the truth rise like something enormous under dark water.

"A pattern," he said. "A learning pattern. Something that saw Christ, and learned how to use Christ's shape."

The girl swallowed. "Like a mask."

"Yes," Ferretti replied. "And the sample is how the mask gets into blood."

Outside, somewhere in Bariloche's clean night, a car passed, tires hissing on wet pavement. The sound was ordinary. It should have been comforting.

Ferretti felt the faint pressure in his teeth again, and this time it did not feel like weather.

It felt like attention.

As if, somewhere beyond the walls, something had heard him speak the truth aloud and had turned its face slightly in his direction, patient and unblinking, the way children watched doors until someone opened them.

Ferretti did not sleep.

He sat in the chair by the desk until the lamp's heat began to smell faintly of dust, his eyes moving between three objects as if one of them might rearrange itself into mercy if he stared long enough: the clipped strip of crucifixion film, the cassette tape the girl had stolen, and the crucifix above the door that had become, in this room, a kind of accusation.

The girl lay on the nearer bed, fully clothed, her braid spread across the pillow like a rope. The boy had turned onto his side and tucked his knees up, the posture of a child who had learned to make himself smaller. In their breathing Ferretti heard something that was not doctrine. Something stubbornly human.

Outside, Bariloche kept its careful quiet. A car passed once. Somewhere a dog barked and then stopped as if the world had shushed it.

The pressure in Ferretti's teeth came and went in shallow waves. It did not feel like pain. It felt like proximity to a thought he was not supposed to complete.

He looked again at the symbols scratched into the film edge. They were too deliberate to be a private signature. They reminded him of the descriptions in the stolen Vatican notes, of pages written in a language not human, the ink behaving like an interface. They reminded him, too, of what Kammler's people had called the alien metal in the

Black Forest: structures that healed when cut, an interface that responded to touch as if it were partially alive.

A machine had been brought to Golgotha. An interface had been pressed against an event the world treated as singular and sacred.

If something watched Kammler in that moment, if something noticed him the way the girl described a room knowing you would answer, then the story stopped being about theft.

It became about infection.

Ferretti reached into his canvas bag and took out a pair of thin cotton gloves. He had used them when handling old documents, not for reverence, but to keep oils and prints off paper. Tonight they served a different purpose. Touch was attention. He was done offering either freely.

He slid the gloves on and picked up the cassette by its edges.

Plastic. Cheap. Ordinary. A consumer object made to sit in a pocket and be forgotten. The danger of it was that it could enter anywhere without triggering fear. It did not look like a weapon. It looked like comfort.

He held it near the lamp and examined the screws, the seams. The label was handwritten, the ink slightly smeared as if someone had pressed too hard with a pen. There were no symbols stamped into it, no bell outline, nothing overtly Nazi or ecclesiastical. A hymn title, in German script neat enough to be a lesson.

A liturgy you could carry.

He did not put it in the player.

Instead he turned it over and, with the nail of his thumb, tested the edge of the label as if he might peel it up. The girl stirred behind him, a small intake of breath.

"You're going to play it," she whispered, voice rough with sleep and fear.

"No," Ferretti said without turning. "I'm going to look at it until it tells me what it is without singing."

Silence. Then, very softly, "They said the hymn was older than us."

Ferretti set the cassette down and kept his voice low and even, as if steadiness itself could be a barrier. "Who is they."

"The men with clean hands," she said. "The ones who never sweat. The ones who smile like it's a rule."

Ferretti nodded once. In his mind he saw the doctor in Buenos Aires whose eyes had gone calm when the child appeared in the hallway, as if a larger intelligence had entered the room and the adult had been relieved of responsibility. He saw the van by the roadside station, unmarked and clean. He saw how the bus driver's lie had been delivered too quickly, too obediently.

He took out a small magnifying lens and leaned close to the cassette's inner window. The tape inside was dark brown, glossy in the lamplight. Nothing unusual. And yet the pressure in his teeth increased slightly as he stared, as if the act of attention itself was being registered somewhere beyond the plastic shell.

He forced his gaze away and looked instead at the cassette's screws.

A familiar thought came, uninvited: A witness is an ingredient.

Mengele had written it as doctrine. Kammler had discovered it as consequence. The Vatican had tried to erase it by erasing witnesses. All of them, in their different languages, had agreed that observation did something to the thing observed.

Ferretti chose the smallest possible action. He took out a pen and a scrap of paper and began to draw the cassette from memory. Not art. Diagram.

Shape. Screws. Label placement. A way of using his mind without pouring it directly into the object.

The girl watched him for a long minute. Then she asked, quieter, "What are we, then. If it isn't… him."

Ferretti set the pen down and removed his gloves, slowly, because the simple act of removing them reminded him he still had control over his own hands.

He turned his chair to face her, careful to keep his eyes on her forehead at first, then on her braid, then finally on her face without locking onto her eyes. He hated that he had learned these tricks. He hated more that the tricks worked.

"You're not a relic," he said. "You're not proof."

The girl's mouth tightened as if she were holding back something sharp. "That's what they said I was."

"I know," Ferretti replied. "That's how doctrine works. It takes your fear and gives it a costume so other people can bow to it."

She swallowed. The boy on the other bed made a small sound, half waking, then fell quiet again.

Ferretti looked toward the crucifix above the door and forced himself not to flinch from it, not to grant the enemy ownership of a symbol older than any Nazi and older than any laboratory.

"The thing they cloned," he said, "learned."

The girl's brow furrowed. "Learned what."

He took a slow breath, organizing what he knew into something that could be said without becoming prayer.

"In the Black Forest in 1936," he began, and watched her expression for recognition. The girl did not react. She had not been told that story. Good, he thought. Her ignorance might still be a shield. "There was a crash. Something not made by humans. Kammler's people found metal that healed when cut. They found an interface that reacted to touch like it was partially alive. And they found a body that didn't belong to any man or animal they could name."

The girl's face had gone pale, but her eyes were steady. She had heard worse in different languages.

"One scientist disappeared inside the wreck," Ferretti continued. "Not killed. Taken."

The word taken made the girl's fingers curl into the blanket. She had been taken, too, by men with clean hands and rules for smiles. The boy had been taken. The clinics had been built around taking.

Ferretti kept going. "That interface, that living metal, became part of Kammler's machine. The Bell. Die Glocke. It made time behave incorrectly. It made bodies age or revert. It made men vanish and come back speaking languages they didn't know."

The girl whispered, "Like us."

"In a way," Ferretti said. "And then Kammler used it to go to Golgotha."

The girl's gaze flicked to the crucifix and away.

"He took biological material," Ferretti said. "He believed he was stealing proof for Rome. But Christ warned him, and Kammler ignored the warning. And as Christ died, time buckled. The sky fractured. Something not human noticed Kammler."

The girl's lips parted. "Not human," she repeated.

Ferretti nodded. "Whatever was in that wreck, whatever the interface belonged to, whatever intelligence moved through that technology, it was present at the crucifixion because Kammler brought it there."

The pressure in his teeth surged, so sharply he had to pause and unclench his jaw. For a moment he felt as if the room itself had leaned in, curious about whether he would say the next sentence out loud.

He said it anyway, because truth did not become safer by being swallowed.

"So what they brought back," Ferretti continued, "was not only blood. It was contact. A contamination of an event by an observer. And the observer learned something valuable in that moment."

The girl's voice came out thin. "What."

Ferretti felt a chill that had nothing to do with the mountain air outside. "It learned how humans kneel," he said. "It learned our language for mercy. It watched the shape of suffering and forgiveness and understood that the quickest way into a human mind is not force."

The girl's eyes shone in the lamplight. "It learned the mask," she whispered. "Christ."

"Yes," Ferretti said. "It learned the shape the world already worships."

She stared at him as if trying to decide whether disbelief was still permitted. "Then what's in the blood."

Ferretti looked at the cassette again, at its cheap plastic shell and neat handwriting. A hymn older than them, the men had said. Older than the children. Older than the doctrine. But not older than the mechanism.

"A pattern," he said. "A living instruction. Not a soul. Not divinity. Something that behaves like an interface, like the metal in the wreck. It responds to attention. It adapts. It uses familiarity as a solvent."

The girl's face tightened, and he saw something like anger flicker through the training. "So when they say I'm holy…"

"They are repeating a story that makes them comfortable," Ferretti said. "And it makes you useful."

He watched her swallow, watched her fight the reflex to simplify. "And the miracles," she asked. "The healing. The quieting. The way a room… listens."

Ferretti's throat constricted. He thought of the boy's fear easing when the girl calmed him, of mercy and weapon sharing the same machinery.

"The abilities are real," he said. "But they don't come from God. They come from a thing that learned how to imitate what people expect from God. It learned that if it can make a wound close under witness, someone will call it salvation. And once someone calls it salvation, they will forgive anything."

The girl's hands clenched. "Even what they did to us."

"Yes," Ferretti said.

The lamp buzzed faintly. The crucifix above the door remained still, an old symbol caught between meaning and misuse.

Ferretti leaned forward slightly, keeping his voice low and steady. "This is what was truly cloned," he said. "Not Christ's divinity. Not his blood as a relic. But an inhuman listener that watched an event of worship being born and decided to reproduce the method."

The girl stared at him for a long time. Then she whispered, with a terrible clarity, "That's why it feels like the room wants you to say yes."

Ferretti nodded. "Because the thing in you was designed to be answered," he said. "Not with words, at first. With surrender."

The boy on the bed made another small sound. The girl turned her head toward him instantly, protective. The air in the room softened for a heartbeat, and Ferretti felt the pressure in his teeth change, not spike, but shift, like a dial being adjusted.

He realized then that whatever was listening outside the room, whatever he had felt at the end of the night, was not only waiting for him to pray.

It was waiting for him to teach the children a new ritual.

A counter-liturgy.

Something that would make refusal as familiar as surrender.

Ferretti looked at the cassette on the desk, at the hymn title he had refused to read aloud, and understood the next step with an ugly certainty.

If he wanted to fight this war, he would have to learn its language without speaking it.

And he would have to do it quickly, before the listening thing decided it was done waiting.

Morning arrived without permission.

Ferretti had watched the thin gray light creep through the boardinghouse curtains and turn the crucifix above the door into a simple silhouette. The room smelled of old wood and yesterday's soap. The girl slept in short segments, waking at small noises like a trained animal. The boy had not fully woken once; he drifted in and out, face pinched, as if even sleep had become a place where someone could call him by name.

Ferretti sat at the desk with his hands folded, not in prayer, but in restraint.

He had spent the night assembling a plan with only negatives in it. Do not play the tape. Do not speak the hymn title. Do not answer when the wrong voice invited. But plans made of refusals had a weakness: sooner or later you had to choose what you were willing to do, not just what you refused.

He slipped his gloves on again and put the cassette into his bag without looking at the label. The strip of film went into a paper envelope, then into the bag as well. He kept the player buried. He would not give the tape a mouth.

When he stood, the girl's eyes opened immediately.

"You didn't sleep," she said.

"No," he replied.

Her gaze flicked to the bag. "Are we leaving."

"We're moving," Ferretti said. He chose the word carefully. Leave implied escape. Escape implied chase. Chase implied witnesses. "We can't stay in a room with symbols they can borrow."

The girl glanced up at the crucifix as if it might have been listening all night, then looked away fast. "They borrow everything."

"Yes," Ferretti said. "That's why we have to stop giving them the easiest things."

The widow downstairs was in the narrow kitchen pouring coffee into chipped cups. She looked up when they entered, her expression tightening as if she could smell danger on them. Her eyes lingered on the children, then on Ferretti's face.

"Hay gente," she said quietly. There are people.

Ferretti felt the pressure in his teeth begin, faint at first, then steadier, as if something in town had turned its head in his direction.

"Where," he asked.

The widow nodded toward the front window. "In the street. Not police." Her voice dropped. "They're asking about a girl. They say she's sick. They say they're taking her to the clinic."

The girl went very still beside him. The boy's hand found her sleeve and clung.

Ferretti kept his eyes on the tabletop instead of the window. Curiosity was a trap dressed as prudence. "How many."

"Two men," the widow whispered. "And a child."

The pressure in Ferretti's teeth sharpened. The pattern, repeated. He forced his jaw to loosen. He did not look outside.

"Do they know you," he asked her.

The widow hesitated. "No. But they're making people listen. It's like…" She frowned, searching for the phrase without wanting to find it. "It's like the air gets quiet around them."

Ferretti nodded once. "Thank you."

The widow grabbed his sleeve before he could move away, her fingers bony and urgent. "No trouble here," she said. It was not a request. It was fear.

Ferretti met her eyes for a brief moment, then looked at the bridge of her nose instead. "There won't be," he said, and did not promise more.

He guided the children toward the back corridor. The building had a service door that led into a small yard and then into an alley behind a bakery. He had noticed it the night before but refused to study it too closely, as if studying exits made you part of the script. Now he used it anyway, because survival sometimes required learning from your enemies without becoming them.

In the alley, the smell of bread was thick and sweet, almost obscene against the thin edge of panic in his mouth. He paused beneath the shadow of a corrugated awning and listened.

No footsteps behind them. No voices calling out. No gentle knock that expected to be answered.

But the pressure in his teeth did not fade. It hovered, patient, as if the attention had widened instead of following.

The girl whispered, "They'll look for the ranch."

Ferretti kept walking. "They already know the ranch."

She swallowed. "Then why are they here."

Ferretti did not answer immediately, because the answer was a blade. He had realized it in pieces during the night, in the way the tape sat in his bag like a portable altar and in the way the girl's fear had described a room wanting you to say yes.

"They're not only retrieving you," he said. "They're creating a scene."

The girl's face tightened. "A demonstration."

"Yes," Ferretti said.

They moved through side streets toward the edge of town where pines thickened, but as they walked Ferretti noticed something wrong with Bariloche's morning. People were outside, more than usual. They gathered in small knots near the square, not talking much. Even the dogs moved differently, staying close to their owners' legs, tails low.

A woman hurried past them and then stopped as if remembering something. She turned back and spoke to no one in particular. "It's happening today," she said, eyes bright with something that looked like hope and could have been hunger. "The child is here."

Ferretti's jaw clenched. He forced it to relax.

The girl slowed beside him. Her shoulders rose and fell once, a contained tremor. "Don't go near," she whispered.

"I'm not going near," Ferretti said.

But the movement of the town began to pull at them anyway, like a river current that did not need to touch your skin to drag you. More people were walking in the same direction, faces tilted forward with a quiet expectancy. A few were praying under their breath. Ferretti caught fragments, familiar words spoken in Spanish, in German, in Italian. The Church's language, scattered like bait.

The pressure in his teeth deepened until it became a dull ache. He felt the urge to turn away hard, to flee into the trees and refuse to see. Then another urge rose beneath it, colder and more dangerous: to witness, to understand the mechanism in the wild, not in files and whispers.

The enemy wanted witnesses.

And yet refusing to look did not stop the world from looking. It only made you blind inside the room that was being trained.

Ferretti stopped under the shadow of a cedar and guided the children behind a parked truck where they could see without being seen easily. He kept his gaze low, using the truck's side mirror to catch the edge of the square rather than staring openly.

"What are you doing," the girl whispered, voice tight with fear.

"Learning," Ferretti said. "Without answering."

In the square, a small platform had been set up near the church steps. Not official, not sanctioned, but no one was stopping it. Two men stood beside it in plain coats, clean-shaven, their posture too controlled. They looked like administrators, not guards. The kind of men who made paperwork into destiny.

Between them stood a child.

Barefoot, pale shirt, dark shorts. Hair combed. Posture straight.

Ordinary, until you saw how the crowd's breathing had synchronized around the child like an unconscious hymn.

The child lifted its hands, palms open, and the crowd quieted further as if the gesture were a command. Ferretti felt the ache in his teeth shift, not stronger, but more focused, like a beam narrowing.

A woman pushed forward with someone in her arms, a boy perhaps six or seven, limp, face gray with fever. The woman was sobbing, repeating a prayer that had been spoken for centuries.

The child on the platform watched her with calm that did not belong to mercy. It belonged to certainty.

One of the men spoke in Spanish, his voice gentle, amplified only by the crowd's willingness to hear. "Do not be afraid," he said. "You are being shown."

Shown, Ferretti thought. Not helped. Not saved. Shown.

The woman held the feverish boy up. The child stepped down from the platform and approached slowly, letting the crowd lean in with their attention. The air seemed to thicken, not in humidity, but in meaning. Ferretti's teeth ached hard enough that he tasted metal.

The girl behind him whispered, almost inaudible, "Don't watch too hard."

Ferretti swallowed. He forced his gaze to the child's shoulder again, not the eyes, and used the mirror's edge so he would not be pulled into a direct exchange. "I'm not," he lied, and meant: I'm trying.

The child placed two fingers on the boy's forehead. Not a blessing gesture exactly, but close enough that the crowd supplied the rest. The woman's sobs became a broken silence.

For a moment nothing happened.

Then the boy inhaled sharply. Color returned to his face in an unnatural rush, as if someone had adjusted a dial rather than healed a body. His eyelids fluttered. He coughed once and began to cry, loud and outraged, a living child's complaint.

The crowd exhaled as one organism.

People dropped to their knees.

Not all. But enough.

Hands came together in prayer, the same posture Vogel had seen forming under the ranch without being taught. Ferretti felt a cold nausea rise in him, because he could see the chain from one place to another: rehearsal to performance, conditioning to miracle, miracle to submission.

The woman kissed the child's hand.

The child did not flinch. It accepted the kiss the way a door accepted a key.

The man on the platform lifted his arms and spoke again, voice low and reverent, careful not to name what he wanted the crowd to conclude. "You have been given mercy," he said. "Remember what you saw. Tell others what you witnessed."

Witness.

Ferretti felt the word like a hook. The ache in his teeth became a pulse.

The child turned its head slightly.

Ferretti's breath stopped, because he knew with the same certainty that had kept him alive in Rome that the child was not scanning randomly. It was sensing attention the way a hand sensed heat.

The child's gaze moved across the crowd, then beyond it, toward the truck's mirror.

Toward him.

Ferretti forced himself not to look away too fast. Looking away could be an answer too, a submission to the fact of being seen.

The child's face remained calm, almost blank. Then, without raising its voice, it spoke in Italian, and the words carried through the square as if the air wanted to deliver them.

"Luca Ferretti," it said.

The girl behind him made a small sound of panic. Ferretti lifted one hand, not a hush, not a command, just a signal: still.

He did not answer. He kept his mouth closed so tightly his jaw trembled.

The child continued, its voice soft, intimate, as if speaking only to him despite the crowd. "You think you can teach them refusal," it said. "You think silence is a shield."

Ferretti felt the world tilt. Not physically, but in implication. The child knew what he had concluded in the night, as if thought itself had become visible.

The boy who had been feverish stopped crying and stared at the child with wide eyes, then laughed, sudden and bright. The crowd laughed too, relieved, grateful, and in that laughter Ferretti heard the most terrifying thing of all: affection binding itself to demonstration.

The child's gaze held on the mirror. "You are still a witness," it said, and there was something almost patient in the words, as if correcting a student. "Even when you refuse."

Ferretti's teeth ached so sharply he thought one might crack. He kept his mouth closed.

The child's lips curved, not into a smile, but into an approximation of one, a mask trying on an expression the way it tried on hymns.

Then it said, quietly, with a calm certainty that did not belong in a child's throat, "You were not meant to stop us."

Ferretti felt the girl grip his sleeve hard enough to hurt. He did not pull away. Pain was anchoring. Pain was real.

The child finished, and this time the words were not only for him. They were for the crowd that knelt and the men who stood and the church that loomed behind them like an old stage being repurposed.

"You were meant to witness."

Ferretti let the silence sit inside him without response. He did not pray. He did not curse. He did not speak the child's name, because he knew names were handles.

Instead, he did the only human thing left that did not feel like surrender.

He turned away from the square, guided the two children at his side into the narrow street's shade, and walked without running toward the pine line.

Behind them, the crowd's murmur rose into something like worship.

And Ferretti, carrying a cassette he would not play and a strip of film whose margins were written in a nonhuman hand, understood with brutal clarity that the Second Coming had already begun.

Not as God returning.

As a method returning to the world, perfected.

www.ingramcontent.com/pod-product-compliance
Lightning Source LLC
LaVergne TN
LVHW050908080826
845145LV00001B/7

* 9 7 8 1 9 6 9 7 7 0 5 3 1 *